TALLAMUN
A novel about a clash of
civilisations in a new world.

Te Norris

TALLAMUN
A novel about a clash of
civilisations in a new world.

FICTION4ALL

CHAPTER 1 - TAMBER

The horn of the hunters sang from the heights of Taskiluh Mountain to the east, blue peaks shadowed by thunderheads reflecting the fading sun.

Tamber White hair, son of Lantuk Twin Soul, waited beneath a shaking allo tree as leaves of yellow and bronze drifted down about his head.

He was three weeks into his naming hunt. The mountain foothills had proved good shelter from Yangmpabat parties, sent to search for him here and in the Yangti Woods that stretched back to the home villages of the Malai.

Damp air caressed his skin, moisture dripped from leaves like a soothing balm on his head.

He laid his head back against the wood, praying to Great Soul for guidance.

The spirit answered; the leaves of the allo hissed and a waft of bitter, yellow incense assaulted him.

He smiled tightly.

Favored of the gods.

The blessing, so Lantuk claimed, that was a curse.

The hissing stopped, the tree went still and the incense sent waves of wild happiness coursing through him and lit his muscles like a torch.

He heard his prey-beast bundling through the trees.

The Pugi male darted from cover five spans to his right. Tamber hefted his throwing spear, loosed it in one fluid motion and the blade sang true as it took the two-legged beast in the chest, knocking it to the ground.

As he made his way towards it, Tamber whispered a prayer of thanksgiving. The beast was struggling, pulling with hooked claws, disturbingly like fingers, against the sharp metal bedded in its puny chest. Tamber cast his shadow on the beast. Fur on the thing's head hackled and it growled in its incomprehensible tongue. Tamber raised his obsidian sword and swept the dim beast into oblivion, the blow cracking the skull, splashing brain over his doe-leather boots.

He bent and sawed through the gristle of the ears- proof for the Yangmpabat when they finally caught up with him that he was a man and deserving of the name.

That he had not skulked as they hunted him, but had hunted in his turn.

In his thirteenth year a man to be reckoned with.

Proud warrior of the Malai, as his ancestors had been.

***

Six sets of ears adorned the bandolier hung across his chest when the hounds driven by the Yangmpabat hunters finally caught scent of his trail. Two days earlier he had butchered a family of Pugi he stumbled upon in the trees. He had not deigned to take the ears of children or women for such trophies had no place on a warrior's baldric.

From the tree-lined valley below and to his west came the blast of onyx horns, sharp and shrill, as tradition demanded. The Yangmpabat announcing that they had found his trail. The sound sent a thrill of power through him.

***

Two tendays and three suns ago he had been driven from the village, cudgeled by men, stones cast at him by children and women.

His own father had hit him last, tears rolling down the gray kill marks adorning his face.

Tamber had smiled then, through the pain, and grabbed his father in a bear hug.

"I'll be back, Da." he said. "I'll make you proud."

Two tendays and more.

Even the legendary Tarnag had only lasted three tendays.

Tamber knew he could relax now. Let them catch up on him, take the final beating and let them drag him home in triumph.

A man at last.

That was not Tamber´s way. Tarnag's record had stood for five generations but it stood to be broken. Why not by him?

He quickened his pace a smile worming its way onto his face. Close to exhaustion as he was, he could still lead the Yangmpabat a merry chase.

Tarnag's spirit would have to watch out for its premier place in the world would soon be forgotten.

7

***

Night began to fall in a curdling glory of thick purple air.

Tamber climbed a knotty-barked ankha whose leaves were like little blades. He climbed easily; hand over hand, his body still limber despite the distance he had traveled.

The ankha soared above other trees and at the top he breathed deeply and scanned the forest below.

He saw them a league away, five hundred yards below down a steep, winding ravine.

The excited yapping of dogs and the howl of brutal meskini told him all he needed to know.

They had a fresh scent. They were hot on his trail.

Darkness would do nothing to stop them.

He weighed his options. The white river known as Seskinglincuhun, Burden's Fall, cut down the mountain towards the east. If he made it across, he could lose the dogs and the meskini. In the absence of scent, darkness would force the hunters to encamp, buying him precious time.

Howling from the east dragged his eyes outward. He scanned the area near the river.

His eyes caught a flash of darkening movement, a tight beam of evening light revealing shapes of men running at a crouch.

The hunters had anticipated that move, gotten ahead of him to the east. West lay steep canyons, impassable and dangerous. He grinned and looked

8

behind. That left only high mountain- a place lowlanders like him did their best to avoid.

The tree line ended half a league above, gave way to bare granite stunted with dwarf allo and spruce. Far above the rock gave way to snow and in the fading light the gleam of snow and ice was dark as fallen blood.

If they wanted him they would have to fetch him down from there.

His eyes traced the path of an eagle soaring in flight and his heart soared with it.

***

His lungs burnt and his head swam.

The air here was thin and bled daemons.

He forced leaden limbs ever forward. The sky above had grown fainter, false dawn approaching.

Through the long night, the sound of the hunters had grown ever louder.

The night had turned on his thirty-first day.

Tarnag's record had fallen. Tamber knew he should stop. His body screamed at him to lie down on the frozen snow and wait for the dogs to come- to take his beating as a man and return home in pride, to sit by fireside while the old women danced and sang Songs of Truth and the old men spitted meat by the fireside.

He shook his head, willing this weakness away.

They had to catch him first. He would not surrender.

An overhang of massive granite, shaped like the buried nose of a giant, slippery with ice, barred the way. It towered over him, blocking out light, making him queasy with vertigo. He edged left over a crumbling edge of rock, a sheer drop tugging at him, towards a crevice he had earlier spotted.

Chill wind whipped him, pulled at his hair. He leaned hard against the granite, its dampness welcome on his skin. The wind carried the excited barking of the dogs, closer now.

Always closer.

He had led them a merry dance, zigzagging back and forth across the face of the mountain, climbing ever higher.

His eye for land kept him out of trouble. An instinct told him where impasses would appear, and he found he could usually calculate a way around them.

Also, he had felt the hand of the Great Spirit, Atman Karra, breathing down his neck, the warm damp excitement of the beast spurring him on.

He pulled himself onto a ledge of frozen shale. The crevice ahead was too narrow for the slanted sunlight of late evening to penetrate. He stumbled forward, eyes momentarily blind, adjusting to the gloom. The shale beneath his feet tremored as if he was treading on something living. The stone walls seemed to shimmer like disturbed water. A faint wordless whisper, like nails on skin, wormed its way into his brain.

He spun on his heels in alarm.

Nobody there.

He shook his head, made his way fearfully deeper into the crevice, the whisper a chill wordless mantra. Something awaited him here. He could feel its unnatural mojo, like a giant cockroach crawling on his shoulder.

Further back a ceiling of rock stretched over the crevice making a massive roof. Left of center a worn funnel dripped ice water and the walls were covered in frozen lichen.

He ducked into the gloomy entrance to this sudden cave. His run had ended. More; he could not stifle a feeling that he had been driven here, like a badger run to ground by baying hounds.

A bellow of air blew against him, powerful enough to knock him from his feet. He scraped skin on sharp rock as he tumbled sideways, hitting his head against a bowl of granular limestone.

As his eyes blurred he saw her; body emanating light, long hair, naked breasts, body radiating heat like smoldering timber almost ready to burn, skin which looked, in places, rotten as a week old corpse. She leant close and planted a kiss on his cheek and smiled.

His arousal was painful and tight as she pulled him to her.

He screamed as consciousness left him, aware that she was taking him. Riding his soul.

***

Soaring on the wings of the falcon, above

11

seas of iron-green, he watched them come in long ships as large as the basking whales the Malai sometimes hunted.

On the ships stood men like beetles dressed in pale metal carapaces, a faint noxious aura about them. Frail they looked, these foreign warriors. The warriors of the Malai had nothing to fear from them, not individually, but they came in their thousands. Insects boiling in from the sea, floating on great wooden homes. Locusts or termites.

They brought death with them.

When their weapons spoke the Malai died and their whetted blades bit Malai flesh.

Ceaselessly. Ceaselessly.

The world fell apart.

Flesh burnt. Men were strapped to wood and died. Fevers swept children like a foul curse. Boils sprang up on their young bodies and dragged them screaming to Yimti's chill kingdom.

Blood and tears dripped from Malai eyes.

The callous earth drank the People dry as the gods mocked them for their weakness.

Like a plague the beetles kept coming, carriers of pestilence, bearers of death.

In his dream Tamber screamed and his scream was the voice of a bird protesting the future.

***

A dog barked- its wild, green-toothed fury

tearing Tamber from the oracle's dream.

Pain ripped through his arm.

He opened his eyes, his body already in motion; the hound's fetid breath in his face.

The large hound clamped its jaw on Tamber's right arm its thick-neck lowered, worrying him, trying to drag him from the crevasse like a stunned rabbit.

Pain like a hot blade tore through Tamber, making him sick, angry. He drew his skiri from the belt around his waist and stabbed at the hound. The blade sliced muscle and drove into the soft flesh of its neck. Tamber rammed the blade home, twisting and slicing to inflict pain. Yipping the beast fell away from him and lay flat on the ground whimpering.

Tamber levered himself to his feet, kicked the hound in the head and smashed its skull with his heel. He snarled and spat. The blood from the ragged wound on his forearm dripped to the frozen earth, wisps of steam rising as it fell.

"Tamber enough!" The voice was the deep bass of Tamber's father. "Take your beating as the man you have become and let me walk you home, son."

Tamber shook free of the rage that possessed him. He took deep breaths, sucking in his father's words.

Gods how he had missed his family, missed the company of people.

He blinked tears from his eyes.

He sheathed his skiri. The Yangmpabat, a dozen hunters and an equal number of slobbering

13

hounds, waited for him lining either side of the crevice.

As he passed each man raised the staff of his spear and brought it down on Tamber's back. They did so gently causing nothing but mild discomfort.

His father, the last in line, lashed out at Tamber's forehead, but pulled up so the wood barely grazed his skin. The old man's chest was swollen with pride and when he smiled the warmth in his eyes was like flame.

Father, look at me, Tamber blazed silently with his eyes. I have made you proud. I am a man and my Keni will be remembered for generations.

Neither man said a word. His father touched his cheek in gentle greeting.

"Come home with me, boy who is now a man. My Yemki. Come home. Your mother will be worried sick."

***

The village, walled by a palisade of stone, built atop a mossy earthen embankment, lay on the lee of a stony hill. Cresting the hill was the ziggurat that held the Gourd of Souls, and the chieftain's hall. Smoke rose in grey gouts from the flue holes in the roofs of low-eaved buildings which wound their way up the side of the hill.

The leader of the Yangmpabat pack blew his large yellow-boned aranyx horn, announcing their return. People lined up outside the village on a path that threaded through waving fields of flax

14

and corn. The dozen veteran warriors of the Yangmpabat shadowed their naked charges, those who survived the trial. Of the ten who had set out only eight had returned.

Two young men had been caught and killed in less than a tenday and their names consigned to oblivion. Their families would not paint their faces with the dark red ochre of mourning, nor would they mutilate their faces to show their displeasure with the gods.

They grief was to be suffered in silence for those men were gone as if they had never existed. They lived now as nameless slaves who roamed the great hall of Dasia Kerara, their souls but a pale shadow of the almost men they had once been.

Tamber's father strode beside him grim face betraying no sign of emotion but Tamber felt the older man's pride like a cloak covering them both.

Tamber puffed out his chest and swung his arms as he walked and, despite bone-deep weariness, his heart welled with a fierce wellspring of emotion.

The thin line of people lining the track moved aside as they strode by and fell into step behind, a thin and gentle song of welcoming rising from their throats.

One of the two striplings who had not returned was Tamber's oldest fried, Tengubkan. Tengubkan's father, a quarrier, stared with a blank face, shock-riveted, as he realized his son was no longer amongst the living.

The man might cry with his wives in the

stone hut he had built with the labor of his own hands. He might indulge in kai-wine or even walk the path of sacrifice. If he did, he would do so quietly. No public grief would be allowed him.

Tamber was moved by a brief impulse to reach out to the man, to whisper him words of comfort. He squashed the notion. Friend or not, Tengubkan had failed. He no longer existed. To grieve for him, or comfort his father, was to make a mockery of the process of Yemki.

This was the way of the Malai and it was this, the rigorous nature of their rituals that set them over all others.

The Yangmpabat procession reached the commons in front of the ziggurat. Three shamen and the chieftain stood in the center, surrounded by men of the elder rank.

Blank inscrutable eyes watched their approach.

The eldest shaman hopped forward to meet them, willow withes in his left hand. He spat in a circle, hopping one-legged and beat the drum in his other hand. Long greasy hair swung about his face. Bones, braided in his hair, clacked as he danced. His lined face was shadowed by the skull cap of the meskbear he wore.

He howled and beat the drums and the village held its breath.

When he had driven the evil spirits away he signed the mark of Great Soul and sat panting on the ground. The chieftain stepped forward. He clapped his hands. A Pugi male was dragged from a nearby stockade. The thing squealed words in its

16

unholy language as it was prodded forward on the sharp end of tintuk blades.

Its eyes were wide with fear. It started to blubber and its face melted as the tears fell.

Tamber swore. The beast's craven behavior was a bad omen.

The chief drew his sword as the Pugi was shoved to his knees. He swung the sword and the beast's head rolled, eyes and mouth still moving as his spirit left his body. The shaman watched with hooded eyes the roll of the head, sniffing the air and beating his drum in a spastic motion. Eyes and mouth ticked and Tamber could see the whites shining where his pupils should have been.

The shaman hopped carefully over the splatter of blood the Pugi's blood had left on dark stone.

He raised his hands to the sky and howled.

The people cheered. The omens were good enough.

The feast could begin and Tamber would receive his tintuk sword.

Tamber could not drag his eyes from the shaman's hooded face. The man's lips had twisted sourly and Tamber guess was he was being less than honest. Worms of fear wriggled in the pit of Tamber's stomach; worms with round white heads crawling amongst his intestines, growing and swelling, feeding on the courage of the future.

In his mind's eye he saw the oracle of the cave again, smelt her smell of sweet sweat and rot. He remembered the dream she had given him, a dream he did not understood and had almost

17

forgotten.

A dream of death.

The shaman was lying. This augury was a bad one and the shaman was hiding that fact.

To the north, over the enormity of the ocean, thunder rolled and clouds gathered dark and vicious.

Wind whispered with the stink of Great Soul's sulfur. Tamber knew this was the true omen. Thunderclouds shadowed the future and the wings of the world held nothing but fear for the Malai

The shaman glanced at him and smiled from behind a stump of rotted teeth.

We need to talk, young one. The voice in Tamber's head was a faint dry whisper. We need to talk.

The ceremony progressed. Tamber lowered his head as his father handed him his tintuk sword and the old men spoke of humility. When he raised his head again, his eyes shining with tears they spoke of tender nobility.

None could see the sore wound, the vacuum of the future, troubling his soul.

CHAPTER 2 - EDO

The wind was light and created roiling eddies on the surface of the dark mountain lake. Beyond the lake, emerald grass waved to the blue mountain, a lowering giant surrounding the valley bowl. Glaciers on the peaks gleamed blood-red as evening approached. Clouds drifting above were a damask curtain, lit from above by rays of silver and gold that spread a gentle light over the mountain scene.

Beautiful maybe, but Edo fucking hated it.

Mountain air was thin, cold as a nun's crotch. He preferred the rolling flatness of his homeland near Deira, capital of the young empire of Aonia. The horizon there was a maester's rule, straight and uncomplicated as the honest hearts of the yeomen who tilled those rich fields. In the folds of these hidden mountain valleys the Caedians had grown sneaky, treacherous and sly. Their minds were twisting goat-tracks layered with invisible ice.

Edo shook his head in disgust.

Local Caedian scouts were unreliable and nigh on useless. Slaves freed from Caedian rule were either grasping and greedy, or placid and witless. To date the only honest Caedians he had met had been tied to wooden racks.

The whole damned place was a disease and it was his job to eradicate the worst of its foulness.

He walked among his encamping men, checking with each deca. Work on the temporary defenses was well under way and the tents were in place. Food was sizzling at open fires. They still had an hour to sunset and by then the ring of defenses would be in place, his pickets set. The men would eat their food, grumbling, then take out their ivory dice as each was allocated his meager ration of watered wine.

When they woke they would break camp and begin a new day's patrol for Edo's orders were to scour this valley and the next before returning to their permanent camp at Kallingtorn.

Occasionally they stumbled on enemy spears, the ragged remains of the Caedian army turned outlaw, or feral hilka but most days were spent chasing the wind.

Edo knew his luck to be cursed. Born too late, see. The time of conquest was over. Lydia had fallen and the Caedians were spent.

Chasing the deposed Petriach of the fallen Caedian Empire, and other ragtag rebels and bandits, through the last stubborn vestiges of his realm was a mopping up action, lacking the excitement of a real campaign.

A man could not glory in such an undertaking. No glory meant no gelt. Without gelt or influence a man was nothing, especially in the army, and Edo had neither. Eso, bastard Eso, Edo's elder brother had both, but Edo would be hog-tied to a ravenous hilka before he'd go crawling in *that* direction.

Shaking his head, Edo strode towards the northern palisade where his men were emplacing a scorpion. Sounds of high-pitched whooping

20

drew his eyes to the east. Heeb, leader of the Scian outriders, spurred his sure-footed mare, a piebald of desert stock, up a steep incline to the plateau where the camp lay. Behind rode his four-man shaft, the hooves of their horses kicking shale, crimson cloaks whipping behind them.

A surge of excitement lit Edo.

His outriders had found something.

***

In Edo's tent Heeb threw his helmet on the trestle table and helped himself to wine. His dour face was smudged with sweat and dirt.

He smeared wine from his face with the back of his hand. "I think we've got the bastards at last. A full band of Caedian army deserters. Full bloods amongst them, judging from the armor." He pointed at a spot on the map they were poring over. "Found them encamped in a cave system below a waterfall. Here."

"Did they spot you?"

Heeb shook his head. "Virgins waiting to be plucked."

"How many are there?"

"Perhaps thirty. We scouted from atop this hill for a couple of hours. The cave system may be deeper than it looks."

"Defenses?"

"Rudimentary. Heaped stones and the like, made to appear natural. Looks to me like they don't want to attract attention. Little more to be seen from the surface."

21

Edo sighed. "I don't like it. We go in those caves and we go in blind. Can we flush them out?"

Heeb grunted. "The scorpion has range enough, we set up on the hill opposite." He drew a line with his hand on the map. "Douse the caves with tin fire and wait to see what we flush out."

"Any sign of horses?"

"None that I could see."

"What about hilka?"

"The jesse priest did his little dance number. Sensed nothing. If the Caedians are hiding a swarm they are well hidden. I reckon what we saw is what we get."

"Any sign of Kantos?"

"How many other bands of this size can there be in this region."

Kantos was a full-blood, a Caedian who had led a band of Caedian scouts working for the Aonians against his own people. Six months earlier he had turned on the garrison in Litone, slaughtering them. As wandering renegades, he and his men had plundered homesteads, both Aonian and Caedian, in the ring of five valleys surrounding Kallingtorn.

He was a magnet for renegades the length of the plateau: angry, buzzing flies drawn to shit. His men were an ever-spreading nuisance; the band had grown large enough to risk attacking Aonian patrols. A fatal error of judgement. If this was Kantos's band, then Edo's luck was in. Return with Kanto's head and they might even be furloughed in Hilda.

22

"Plunder?"

"Their armour was the real deal." Heeb shrugged. "Fullbloods equals rich pickings, and we know Kantos has been raiding. More than adequate, you'd hope."

Edo clapped Heeb on the shoulder, turned to his manservant. "Fetch the Entargiós from Deka Onyk and Lar. Heeb has found a nest of vermin and tomorrow we ride to eradicate it."

***

On the hill opposite the cave his gunners, the aspavil, laid a foundation of wooden planking over rough stone and mud. With long metal stakes they nailed the planking firmly to the earth, laid two scorpions set on metal runners onto the platform and, working as quietly as they could, bound the heavy weapon to the wooden platform. They estimated the recoil and allowed enough slack on the roller for the scorpion to move back and forth.

Edo sent out his runners, asking for a report from each deka. He waited impatiently as the light turned silver-gray.

The sun was peeping over the rim of mountain hazing the east by the time all the runners had reported back. His men were in place. It was time.

He gestured at the aspavil in charge of the first of the scorpions. The jesse priest said quick prayers to Miter and Fenor and cast a blood blessing on the artillery.

23

One of the three-man crew loaded the mouth of the wooden beast with Mil-fire in a wooden cask then bent with a second to turn the wooden-handled windless. The third used a crude metal sight finder to judge range. He called out a number to the other men. They left the handle of the windless as it stood and used a ratchet to adjust the heavy wooden muzzle of the weapon. The man holding the sight barked an order when he reckoned they had gone far enough. They released the metal catch, straining against the tension holding it in place, and the scorpion catunked then whiplashed backward.

The cask flew silently through the air and landed two spans to the right of the cave door. The cask exploded, spewing tin-fire to left and right.

A brace of scrubby bushes lit up like a bonfire. From within the cave came sounds of alarm. The second scorpion, already adjusted by its team, fired and the cask flew home into the dark maw of the cave. The explosion was followed by screams of agony. Men fled the cave, clothing on fire, unarmored.

They ran into a hail of crossbow bolts from the deka positioned behind a bluff of boulders to the right of the cave.

The agravil adjusted their firing positions and two scorpions catunked as the casks flew towards the second cave entrance. Caedian rebels swarmed out as the cask flew and exploded. Half a dozen caught the full force of the sticky fuel and were turned into living torches. Mil-fire burned until

24

everything combustible was used up and it burned with anger. Men fell to the ground screaming. Others were set on fire by their flailing comrades.

The handful of survivors caught in no-mans-land charged the second deka in their positions on the left behind a row of bent argul-trees They were met by a torrent of bolts. None made it to the trees.

Edo loved it when a plan came together. He ordered the scorpion to cease firing and beckoned to his warlock-meister and together the two men made their way down the slippery trail to the positions below.

The few remaining bandits stood huddled amongst flame-singed rocks near the entrance to the second cave. Edo barked an order at the warlock and the man sent his mekanus bird out to scout over their heads. It flapped back to them in a flurry of wooden wings.

Fat Harli, the Entargió in charge of this deka smiled grimly as the warlock collected the bird´s report- an unintelligible hiss and clack that sounded vaguely infernal to Edo's ears.

"The bird spotted seven men. The rest are dead or ash."

Edo nodded and ordered the Entargió to offer the bandits a chance to surrender. He gave them five minutes. It took them less than a minute to decide. They cast aside their weapons and walked out of the cave system with their hands over their heads.

Edo grunted with pleasure.

He had taken the bandits and their plunder

and lost none of his own men. Thus did he define success.

***

The prisoners were in a wooden pen, stripped naked. They had been flogged and the renegade leader had been disemboweled and decapitated. His mutilated body hung on a wooden cross near the entrance to the cave system.

His two deka had spent an hour fortifying the evening defenses. Food and a double ration of wine had been served to the men.

Edo was well pleased.

The bandits would be crucified in the morning. His standing orders gave him no choice in the manner of execution, though he would have preferred something cleaner and quicker. Crucifixion took too bloody long. Messy business.

The bastards deserved to die though. The jesse priest swore he heard the ghosts of butchered families moaning, chained to the men who butchered them; the spirits unable, in their grief, to gain release.

That brutal work done it would be time for him to return with the remainder of his prisoners to Kallingtorn. A minor triumph, but his alone.

Heeb pulled back the flap of the tent and peered in, wiping sweat from his mud-stained brow.

"I've tallied the plunder, sir. Thought you might be interested."

"Tell me."

26

Heeb shook his head. "We won't do as well as we thought. A dozen hirsh apiece for the men, double that for the officers. Your share should fetch a sixty."

Edo's jaw dropped. "A pox on the whore son spawn of Bloody Garge. These bastards have been raiding for so long. How many farmsteads have they turned over? A dozen or more. The gold alone from the column they hit should be worth more than that."

"You want me to put some pressure on them."

"Chop one up front of the others. Find out where they stashed the loot."

The Scian's smile made a jagged hole in his thin, weather-beaten face. The man's jaw was a lopsided lantern, his nose a tiny nub. Receding hairline and eyes dark as sin.

Edo felt a passing twang of pity for the hapless Caedians.

***

Edo was awake in an instant, his thin-bladed Jag dagger already in his hand.

"Just me boss," Heeb said out of the darkness. "Guards let me through."

Edo shook the knots of sleep out of his mind. "Hell of a way to wake a man up," he muttered as he laid his dagger on the trestle table near the bed.

Heeb chuckled. "For an ordinary man that might be so sir, but a Domin such as yerself

27

knows neither tiredness nor fear."

Edo groaned. "What is it?"

Heeb lit the wick of the everbright on the trestle table, pulled a flask of Caedian plumspirit from his pocket, took a deep swig and handed it to Edo.

The liquid burnt Edo's throat like flame and brought the night into sharp-hued focus.

"One of the prisoners, sir. He sang at the barest touch of a warm rod. His story may be worth a listen."

Edo drunk deep once more, handed back the flask and levered himself to his feet. The Scian was no fool. Whatever story was being spun would have substance.

"He knows where my gold is?"

The Scian shook his head side to side, a faint smile creaking his leather face.

"Something else, sir. Or nothing, but if it is something..." He did not finish but stared hard at Edo. His eyes gleamed with something dark and intense- a look Edo knew only too well.

Plunder lust.

"Bring me to him then. Let's see what the bastard has to offer."

***

The night was dark and chill. Forests of tall fir and spruce carpeted the nearby mountain, wisps of fog drifting amongst the trees. Somewhere a wolf howled.

They strode towards the wooden pen holding

the prisoners. An owl swooped past them, a blur of pale white silhouetted against an outcrop of graying rock.

In the distance they heard the faint hiss of an armored tugaspagó plodding through the mountains. With the tip of his index finger, Edo drew Miter's circle on his forehead, warding off the huge beast's evil. Mist rose from the nearby river and spread waist-high through the narrow valley and Edo knew that the souls of the dead, of those he had killed, wandered abroad with vengeance in their hearts.

Heeb seemed nervous too.

Nights like this, the darkness echoing with the fear of the fallen day's battle, did this to warriors. Heeb reached for his plum spirit, took a draught, handed it to Edo.

They skirted the pen, a stockade of poles beaten into earth tied together with hemp, and Edo barked an order at the guard standing easy at the gates, an auxix known as Sour on account of his warm personality.

Sour pulled open the first gate. It led into a small rectangular compound, little larger than a stable. A naked man sat back against the far wall, knees drawn up to his body, hands around his knees.

He had been tortured and the marks on his body told of his agony. At the sound of their approach the man opened a bruised eye. His body shook with palsy-like fear as they approached.

He pulled his knees even tighter and tried to edge away from them, as if the wood behind his back might open and shelter him.

"You have the privilege of the presence of our Domin, scum," Heeb barked. "Now, tell him what you told me before I pluck out your eyes."

The man shuddered, nursing a broken hand. Tears of pain beat a furrowed path down his face. He spat blood and bent over coughing.

"Talk to us."

The man shook his head.

Edo growled and Heeb grabbed the prisoner's hand and squeezed, putting pressure on the fractured fingers. The man screamed and Edo heard the worried whisper of fear from the larger compound, where the other prisoners were pretending to sleep.

"Not here!" The man breathed. He pointed towards the other prisoners. "For you only."

Edo shrugged. Whatever got the bastard to open his clam-like. "Out of here, Heeb."

He bent towards the prisoner. "If you are playing with us, you Caedian fuck I'll hang your balls from this barricade and feed your liver to the tugaspagó."

***

They dragged the man to a glade of twisted arank trees, his eyes showing white with shock. Heeb pulled off his helmet and filled it with frozen water from the nearby stream, allowed the man to drink, then sat him back against a tree.

Edo and Heeb took their places facing him.

"You have a story for me," Edo asked,

30

picking at the dirt in his nails with his dagger. The Caedian eyed the glinting blade and nodded.

"My name is Pora Ferie. Of Lydia. I am a quarter of the blood."

Edo waved his hand impatiently. He gave not a shit how much pure blood this Ferie believed he had. Caedians worshipped their ancestors in a strict caste system; as if the flow of blood in their veins tallied the worth of a man. Even now, after the downfall of their empire, they could not comprehend that blood counted for nothing beside greed, hunger and experience; a reality Edo had learned young and early in his own family. A lesson taught him most of all by his brother Eso

"I was a sailor. Worked my way up to captain of my own ship in the Lubneck fleet. In the northern wars we sailed out of Cumann. I was there when we blockaded Deira."

Edo growled.

"I was wounded and discharged. When I recovered I took sail as captain's second with a ship bound for the lands of the Chalguchik. Our Petriach and his advisor birds believed the Chalaguik had reserves of amna. Amna that the Birds of Paradise had figured out a way of using in war against you."

Amna. Raw natural magic that powered lights, mekanus toys and, of late, ever more powerful weapons. Edo knew that the new breed of scorpions, designed by captured Caedian engineers and warlock priests, were both smaller and more deadly, their range double that of the artillery the Aonians had traditionally used. But

31

amna was rare and expensive beyond gold, beyond firestone.

Edo felt his heart's pulse beat faster.

"You found a source of amna?"

Ferie ignored him. "A storm caught us up, tossed us about like a child's toy in a lake. I thought we were done for.

Five days the thing had us in its grip, five days driving us west into the jaws of Malyn of the Ocean. Gods help me I thought my last day had come and the Whirling Angel was come to take me home to the land across the Shield."

"Yet you made land?"

"Two weeks more it took us. We lost half our rowers of a bowel sickness that turned their stool to red water. What amna we had was used up and would not power the blades. The wind was silent. We ate the last of the food, had little water. Each morning the sun beat down on our heads and the ocean trembled with delight at our terror. Men grew delirious with fear and began spitting anger, killing one another. Then, late one afternoon, we spotted land. We hugged and kissed one another, and men lay with men as though with women, carried away by their delight." He made a sour face. Caedians were so stuffy. "We laid anchor that evening in a bay of turquoise water. The sand was golden. We landed a small boat and found a clear-water stream and large duck-like creatures swimming on a pond. They felt no fear of us. We trapped fifty of them in a hands-breath." His smile at the memory was radiant. "We had found that paradise the Laurel tells us about." Edo knew with a sudden thrill like a jolt of wheat-brandy that the man was telling the truth. Felt it deep in his bones. He could feel the fingers of his right hand trembling with something between fear and excitement.

"What paradise?"

"My people call it Yi'lain Di Talamoon."

Heeb had lived longer among the conquered Caedians. He had a Caedian whore in Kallingtorn. He knew something of their stories, their perverse gods.

"Jadi Eta'vit," is what the fucker means.

"Jadi Eta'vit," Edo snarled. "You are shitting me." The world of Eternal Youth, dripping with amna, gold and naked virgins. He wanted to laugh aloud, and beat Ferie into oblivion for wasting his time. This should have felt like a joke. A child's fairytale. Something eight-year-olds whisper with wide-eyed awe to their friends. Something sane adults disdained. And yet. Heeb was standing over Ferie and smiling. A crazed smile. Eyes gleaming. His face betraying no humor, no irony. This was not a joke to him: he wasn't just spinning the fucker along. Heeb, hard-headed, sociopathic Heeb, believed the Caedian's tale.

Crazy. Completely. This stinking bandit's life was forfeit. He would be crucified in the morning so of course he was spinning a web of lies, a net to stave off the future? Edo would have done the same in his place. But as Ferie had told his story a look of wistful hope had come over his face, as he traveled in memory back to that place and time.

This, though he had been tortured, fingers

33

fractured, one ear severed, his body wracked by pain? Edo raised his eyes to the stars, bright over the towering mountain.

He did not know how or why, but he knew that the man's story was the most profound truth.

Edo was not religious. He <u>was</u> superstitious like all soldiers but gods had never interested him. This was different. He felt something- the hand of fate and faith, faint whispers of the gods. He could feel their breath behind his back.

This was his destiny, the dream of his youth, offered to him now and once only.

He leaned forward. To the Caedian, in a gentler voice he said, "Go ahead, Pora Ferie of Caedia. Tell us of Tallamun. Tell us of paradise."

***

"We spent four tendays there. The second tenday we spent in the village of one of the chiefs. Gray-skinned. Big bastards. They paint their hair ochre and dress in wolfskin and fur. We slept with their women and ate their food. An inscrutable people but the men didn't seem to pay us much mind. Didn't much care. We grew stronger. Restless. One of our lads stole some amna in a golden amulet from the chief's hut and the chief had him disembowelled. That didn't go down well and the rest of us took up arms against the savages." He rubbed his mangled arm, shuddered. "We underestimated them. They fought well, drove us away. We took our ship further up the coast." He paused. Twas then we came on the mountain. Peak after peak, soaring and massive and green, far as we could see. It braced the sea, a sheer cliff down to the bay we had entered. We had a pater with us."

Edo held a hand up, looking to Heeb for clarification. "Pater?"

Heeb struggled for words, holding his hands wide. "Caedians worship at the Temple Laurel. Their pater are...jesse priests. Of a sort."

Edo shrugged and beckoned for the Caedian to continue. Our pater fell to his knees and started to pray. At first we thought he was demonstruck. Then we felt it too, emanating so that even the dimmest of us felt its touch.

That mountain was seamed with amna. Magic grew in its stones. I swear it hummed with blue flame from that power." He stared at Edo first and then at Heeb, struggling to convey to them the images and smells vibrant in his memory. "Never have I seen a place more beautiful. We dropped anchor. The captain tried to stop us pouring onto the small-boats but greed was a fever that had infected us all. The captain drew a weapon and killed the second mate. A midshipman and the first mate held the captain down and one by one we stabbed him. That way we was all in it together, see. The lads voted me as new captain on account of my previous experience. We took the small-boats ashore then broke up into mining parties. We dug for three days and found more amna in those three days than I have ever seen. Before or since."

Heeb spat. "So how come you ended up here,

scrounging for bludger with this scum?"

He gestured at the stockade to their rear where the Caedian bandits slept their last night on earth.

"We fought. Wild with our greed. Like animals. One by one we died and none would trust the other. Some lost their wits totally. Baying in the light of the small pale moon they get in that place."

Edo glanced at Heeb. The older man shrugged, said nothing but Edo knew he was equally transfixed.

Even in small doses amna had been known to make men do strange things.

"The tribes came after us then. Godless heathens, painted for war and wielding spears and black swords. Those of us who still retained a modicum of sense hightailed it out of there, onto the small boats. We left the others behind and most of our amna. We did not set sail immediately, though later I wished we had." His eyes glinted with tears. "The things the heathens did to those we left behind. All night long and into the next day. We set sail for home, sick of heart and mind. Not well enough, not strong enough; we barely made it. With shore in sight, most of us half-dead of hunger and fever, an Aonian warship attacked. Because they had made me captain my rations were better and I had remained stronger than the others. I threw myself overboard and was washed ashore. The ship went down with all hands. The tide brought me to a rocky beach, white waves crashing against gray rock. I was lucky to survive but survive I did. I walked for weeks. When I got to Lydia the city was encircled. Our ending had begun. Your people," he almost spat the words. "You took our city and made yourself our masters. Afterwards, I told no one where I had been and what I saw for who would have believed me."

"So why now tell us now," Heeb demanded.

Ferie glared. "You took three of my fingers, Scian. I am fond of the others."

"You are a fucking liar, Caedian."

"May the Laurel devour my soul if I do not speak true."

Heeb stared hard at the man, a long moment, tongue licking at his lips, his face a half-snarl. Like a hunter pondering a kill and its value. Was that hunger in his face? Greed?

"Come on, Heeb? You cannot believe this shit?"

Heeb turned to me, eyes moist with emotion.

"This one is a quarter full blood. You heard him. He has oathed the Laurel."

"So fucking what?"

"By his lights, he has damned his soul."

"To save his precious hide and remaining fingers. We'd both do the same.

Heeb shook his head. "Not him. One of his kind. Not that. He would rather die."

"Are you fucking serious?"

"For him to say that oath. He would rather sell his mother to us as a whore. His whole family for that matter. Ain't nothing stronger. It defines these fuckers. Trust me on this. I've lived with

37

these swine longer than you."

Ferie leaned forward, his eyes damp lights in the dark too, lit by that same feverish hope.

We are all mad, Edo thought. Mad as

"Spare me, Domin. Spare my life. I will take you to paradise."

Edo had to laugh at that. These fuckers. He pointed at the Caedian. "You and your band ambushed and killed fifteen Aonian soldiers. You burned murdered and raped through a large swathe of the New Aonian Territories. "

Territories settled by families from Aonia who had displaced the Caedian landlords were flashpoints of contention with the locals, both slaves and their former masters.

"The jesse priest can see the spirits of the dead hanging from all your necks, begging for their final release. Your death grants them that, nothing else. You want mercy? You shall have it and die quickly on my sword not on the cross. I have my orders. More I cannot do."

Ferie held his broken hands out. Sweat bathed his face. Edo turned from the man's fear, as from a disfigurement.

"I have a map."

Edo turned back, his heart thumping now.

"I had it made after I returned. I killed the cartographer after he finished my commission, slit his throat. It was my story, not his." Pora's smile was cruel and mad and for the first time Edo almost doubted him.

"Where is it?" Edo asked carefully.

Pora shook his head. "I hid it in Linden."

Edo growled. Linden, the free port across the Eastern Sea. A port whose independence was guaranteed by the Empire of Milesia and the only place where Caedians still lived free. Refugees had flocked there after the fall of Lydia and the Caedians now practically ruled the city. It was not a good place for Aonians.

And it was suitably far way to make the truth of his claim untestable. Edo needed time to think.

"Put him back." Edo said. Heeb pulled the Caedian to a standing position, started shoving him towards the stockade.

"Wait! I've changed my mind. Take the fucker's eyes." Edo barked.

Heeb drew his knife, kicked the Caedians feet away, straddled the fallen man and pressed the blade against the fold of skin beneath the left eye.

"Last chance, Caedian. Where is the map?"

Pora moved his head from side to side as the blade approached. "Linden! Its in Linden! For Temple's sake!"

Edo cocked his finger. Heeb rose to his feet and kicked the Caedian hard on the side of the head.

"Crawl to the stockade and ask that nice man to let you in, like a good fellow." Heeb said. "Me and the Domin need to discuss your fate."

They watched the Caedian crawl away, Edo's heart beating, an old fever working its insidious way through him.

Tallamun. The passion of his childhood. More now. Much more. A wealth of amna to be

39

had. A new chance. To prove himself. To make his name. To show his brother and the world what he was capable of.

Would he, for this dream of Tallamun, forsake duty? Kill?

And even if he believed Ferie, what of Heeb? He needed to know how the Scian felt before committing to any course of action.

"You believed him too? I see it in your eyes." Heeb's question is a sword thrust.

Too soon. He needed time to think. To clear his head of this nonsense, of the fever dream raging within him.

Christ he could see it. The pale green sea, waves crashing against rocks, the mountain towering above. And amna: a blue glow lighting up the sky like a haze in summer.

"We Should walk away. Bang him on the crossbraces tomorrow and never think on this again."

"Would you be able?"

"Able?"

"To forget. The chance that dropped in your lap like ripe fruit. One impossible chance in a lifetime. Spurned."

"No. Never. You?"

"No!"

Edo shook his head. "So, where does that leave us?"

Heeb sniggered, a sound both fearful and delirious. "No longer here. No part of this army. We cannot be."

"What would you have me do?" Edo asked

carefully, like a man testing hot water with his finger. "Our standing orders are clear. All bandits are to be killed. The Entargió is no friend of mine. If we let this one man live he will want to know why. The jesse priest. The other men. They will scratch at this like a scab. When they find out, the commandant finds out. Then you and me can say goodbye to Paradise. Best we can hope for is a pat on the shoulder and a note in some tit of an auditor's parchment. Found Paradise. Recommend for promotion in ten years." Edo spat on the ground

That was the kernel of the problem as Edo saw it- a problem he had at some level understood from the moment the Caedian uttered those magic words. If he let Ferie live, he would have to inform his superiors on the rationale for his decision, and once he did that they would take this knowledge from him and use it to enrich themselves, their own careers. In his minds eye he saw the blue mountain humming with amna, birds wheeling about overhead whilst a gentle wind blew and silver surfed washed up rocks.

He would allow nobody to take his dream from him.

"Spit it out, Domin. You already have a plan."

"If the Caedians were to stage an escape things would play out differently."

"We would never see hide nor hair of Ferie again."

Edo scratched his jaw.

"Not if one of us goes with him.

41

Heeb considered the implications of this. "He sure as shit ain't going to lead us to any map hung like washing on a piece of wood."

"Make it look like a breakout. Overpower Sour. Kill him if we have to. Free the other Caedians."

A path that led them both- Edo especially- into damnation. If they had to kill Sour he would be culpable in the death of a soldier under their command. Not the death of an innocent exactly, for none of them had remained innocent after years in this almost conquered land, but Sour was a family man with a young daughter at home, guilty of nothing more than carrying out his orders.

An unnatural crime, one to raise the wrath of gods, but, Edo would not be the one to wield the dagger. No blood would stain his hands. And if he played it right he could deflect all suspicion. That would be Heeb's burden. Edo was Domin. If he deserted the army would hunt him to the ends of the earth but Heeb was merely a Scian. An ally, little better than a mercenary, Expendable; the army anticipated treachery from such men. Edo would even be able to delay and misdirect the pursuit.

Heeb pursed thin lips, had worked it out already. "You get to spin the story when we are gone. Suggest he bribed me to turn my coat. Unfound plunder. That sounds reasonable enough. Then lead the posse away. I'll steal two mounts but I'll need money and supplies."

Tricky this. The quartermaster kept their

supplies under lock and key but Edo thought he could bluster his way to what was needed, even at the dead of night, without raising too much suspicion. And if not? What was one more death on a day full of death?

"There is a coulee behind this valley surrounded by trees. We passed it late afternoon today."

Heeb nodded. "I remember."

"I'll see you there before dawn."

They clasped hands and Edo looked the older man in the eye.

He saw pale, sickly-gray lust gleaming and was suddenly terrified of what that light meant, for he felt its pressure in his own eyes.

How far was he prepared to go?

***

Edo's heart beat like a warlock's gong.

Dawn was a thin border bleaching the inky darkness above the soaring mountain range.

Sweat poured down his back and puddled in his groin. He stank of fear.

He prayed he had not left it too late.

He hurried, stumbling through a patch of thorn, the needles tearing at his flesh.

He had waited, watching from a safe distance as Heeb stabbed the unsuspecting Sour then pulled open the door to the pen and led a dozen Caedians away from camp. Keeping to the shadows Edo had half-run towards the quartermaster's tent, the camp quiet, picket guards facing inward not out.

The quartermaster's tent stood near Edo's own tent, as army regulations stipulated.

As Edo pulled back the tent flap he knocked over a metal jar full of piss. The quartermaster woke, his voice sounding groggy and vaguely alarmed.

Edo spoke quietly.

"Elbario, its me." He pushed aside the tent flap.

"Sir?" Elbario was a middle-aged accountant-soldier whose only passion in life was the inventories he kept in thick parchment-bound books. His hair was tussled and he looked aslant at Edo, like a scholar at a loud child.

"Quartermaster I need an issue of rations and gelt. Enough for two men for two weeks." He paused scratching his chin. "Make it three weeks."

The quartermaster made as if to argue. Edo moved closer to him, using his size and bulk to good effect.

"Complain later to the Domin Lar if you must. For now do as I tell you."

Elbario made an O with his damp lips but nodded weakly. He bent for the trestle table near his bed and pulled out a set of keys. With furtive glances at Edo he strode towards the back of the long tent. He indicated packs of rations- bread and dried meat and cheese and gourds of water and of wine.

"You will take what you need, I trust Domin," he spoke in an uneasy voice. But perhaps I should I call for the company Entargió to help

44

you."

Edo shook his head, annoyed and impatient.

"Gelt, you little bastard. Where is the money?"

Edo knew at once he had made a mistake. His tone was all wrong, desperate and ragged. A man under stress with something to hide.

Very much not what the company quartermaster expected from his Domin.

With a furtive backward glance, the quartermaster betrayed a small metal casket at the back of the room.

Sweat made an estuary of Edo's forehead. His stomach roiled with snakes of fear. He had to get done with this, get out of here before he was heard or seen. Had to. If he didn't he was worse than dead!

He grabbed the key from Elbario's hand and strode to the chest. "Show it me you little fuck."

Elbario gabbled something, wringing his hands and stepped forward to block Edo's path.

Anger and fear flashed, red lights in Edo's head. In the turmoil of this place beyond thought he drew his dagger and stabbed Elbario twice; in the stomach and again in the neck. The quartermaster crumpled to the ground, moaning quietly, blood dripping from his wounds. Edo ran to the cask, fumbled with the lock, hands trembling as he tried each key in turn. Slick with sweat he dropped the set of keys to the ground, swearing.

Which of the dozen bloody keys had he already tried? He took deep breaths, forcing himself to be methodical. The lock holding the clasp gave way and Edo breathed a deep sigh of relief. He pulled the box open, grabbed a handful of silver hirsh and bronze stags and shoved them in his pockets then upended the box, tossing money around, wanting it to look as though the prisoners had ransacked the place.

He wasted more time tossing the quartermaster's store, running his dagger through sacks of grain, gently spilling caskets of wine and earthen jars of spiced pummle seeds, stepping gingerly around the quartermaster lying unmoving on the ground in a puddle of blood.

Trembling, with fear and nervous exhaustion, Edo made for the coulee where he had arranged to meet Heeb.

One of the mounts he was leading whinnied and he startled, his breath dissipating in the chill morning air.

"Heeb?"

The question went unanswered.

A branch crackled behind him and two men stepped out of tree shadow like bark made flesh.

They were in armor, carried naked swords and in their eyes was death. The soaring cross-plumes of their helms were unmistakable.

The two Entargió of the companies he led. Arak and Haldereso.

"Domin," Arak said. "We must arrest you. For murder." The man sounded regretful.

Soldiers stepped out from amongst the trees making a circle. Edo let go of the horse halter. For them to accuse him like this, openly without fear, there must be proof. A witness? Someone who saw him leave the quartermaster's tent? A servant perhaps or a guard? If so he would not be able to bluff his way out of this. A wave of black despair rushed through him and he fell to his knees. This could not be happening . Haldereso, the second Entargió stepped close to him, and lowered his sword till its tip bit Edo's neck.

"Traitorous bastard," the man hissed. "We'll see you spitted for this."

He raised his sword and brought the flat of the blade down on Edo's head.

Darkness fell like a southern night.

***

They strapped his arms to the wooden crossbar of a crucifix, lodging the frame at the base of his skull, so his arms were pulled wide behind his head. Haldereso jerked hard on the frame and pain flamed in the sockets of Edo's shoulders.

"A small foretaste you bastard!." He leant forward and spat in Edo's face.

Haldereso Después had joined the army as an enlisted man and crawled his way into the officer corp. He was a scarred veteran of Redburg and Whiteford but Edo had been promoted above him, on merit mostly, but rumor had it that Eso´s connection had secured the position. Under Edo's command Hal had been often surly, unable to disguise the bitterness souring his spleen. Edo understood to an extent- Hal was a competent and brave officer, cursed with a lack of imagination. To him the army was all and everything and even the importance of the gods paled beside the duty he owed it. Edo had no chance of bribing one such as him.

Edo was escorted by two burly legionnaires from C company and cast into a wooden box made of sides of dark oak affixed to one of the larger carts. They tied the crossbrace to a set of metal shackles so that he hung from the wood, neither sitting nor standing, the strain on his back and shoulders alleviated only when he knelt.

Gaps between the frames of heavy wood allowed Edo to see out. With a bellow of orders B company under Arak set out after Heeb and the fleeing Caedians, while C company, cart rattling behind them, threaded their way over narrow rocky paths on the way to Kallingtorn.

The men, their hearts lightened by their plunder, sang marching songs but Edo's heart was a dirge.

As the day grew older the heat in the pen sweltered. Light through the frame shone in his eyes bright and pitiless. Shadows crawled across the dark, pitted wood. Edo cried out for water.

A Plinix Lien from the Auirix platoon climbed on the cart pissed on him. Edo closed his eyes as the liquid fell on his head and the first tears of despair fell.

He had not risen far, a few baby steps compared to his brother, and now he had fallen.

Oh how he had fallen!

***

Three days without food and water.

Three grunts assigned to guard him rode the cart, made faces mocking him when he begged, delighting at his displeasure. A rare sport this, with an officer.

The Espargio when they came to check on him were no better. They shook their heads in tight circles and pursed cruel lips.

"The Trinuna will see what is to become of you, Domin. Until then you can starve for all I care," Hal gloated.

The high stonewalls of Kallingtorn hove into sight on the afternoon of the third day. The city nestled on the banks of the River Ke'el, farmland and villages outside its walls stretching leagues into the fertile hinterland. Mountains, purple and sere, surrounded the wide valley, swathed towards the south with pine and fir. Edo had hunted there-for wild boar and the huge-antlered gray stags local to Caedia. Those memories were amongst his happiest in this accursed land. He knew he would never hunt there again.

Fear hit him like an ague.

The Trinuna would judge him, and if he was found guilty he would be condemned.

He moaned and pulled at the rawhide binding his wrists to the wood.

He was only five and twenty. He was not ready to die.

***

They entered beneath the massive gates of the ancient city. Guards patrolled the roofs, scale armor gleaming in the yellow sunlight, spears glinting wickedly.

Edo raised his head as they passed into the shadow of the barbican. Flags flew from its roof, the blood-red banner of Aonia and the green sickle of Scia. A long row of blackened skulls had been hammered to the pitted stone with sharpened metal stakes. The heads of traitors, looters and thieves.

Edo lowered his eyes from their implacable stare.

Behind the barbican was a noisy market, dirty and loud, with hawkers selling rye that had been mixed with old wheat-berry. The vegetables and fruits in this lower market were rotten and blackening. Caedians, and some of the more impoverished Aonian settlers, buzzed around the stalls, arguing with the hawkers. Children ran in rags through the streets, some pausing to stare at the column of soldiers, eyes blank with hate and hunger.

Después barked an order and the men turned left down Laurel Avenue, towards the barracks, metal studs on the soles of their boots loud on cobbled streets.

The Avenue was the largest in Kallingtorn and had once led to a burg on the hill that occupied the center of the city. The fort had been partially demolished and extended and was now the headquarters of the Aonian army.

The burghers of Kallingtorn had held against the Aonian siege for six long months. When the breach in the massive walls was finally made Aonians and Scians poured through gap and a city of fifty thousand souls had died in the space of two nights. Hirperen Octi, Secuas Maximus of the coalition forces, allowed his army two days of looting and rapine. In the Grand Plaza he executed the leaders and priests of the city. He branded twenty thousand souls, mostly women and children, and sent them into slavery in Aonia and Scia. Aonian settlers and freed Caedian slaves had made their homes in the ruins but the city was but a dying shell of its former self.

An abject lesson in Aonian power- those who resisted would be put to the sword. The siege of Lydia, a much larger city with a larger garrison, had taken place two months later and had lasted less than a week.

Lydia had been spared the fate of Kallingtorn. Now, like a gargantuan beast in pain, the city moaned as the winds from the nearby mountains whipped its streets and its people grew pale and nervous as the city they loved sickened and died.

***

Once inside the walled barracks they dragged Edo out of the cart and threw him into a cell in an old cellar that had been divided into tiny rooms barely large enough to stand in. The room was lightless, cold and damp. A slop bucket was the only furniture and Edo sat in darkness as the heavy oaken door slammed shut.

Time passed slowly and, as the days passed, fear filled his mind with imaginary demons. Hunder and thirst drove him to the ground and a damp ague told hold of him. Finally, perhaps four days had passed, the door swung open and light from without dazzled his eyes. He struggled to his feet. A mailed glove slammed into his jaw and blew him back.

He spat blood and struggled to his knees. A boot made contact with the side of his cheek and pain exploded in his face.

He hugged the ground.

Guards pulled his hands behind his back and shackled him at the wrists and ankles with chains before dragging him to his feet and kicking him forward.

He was led to a round dark room, still in the cellar. The walls were stained and damp in the flickering light of braziers. Square oak caissons, marked with the symbols for mil-fire and scorpion bolts, were stacked against the far wall.

A dozen men ringed the room, all in full armor, wearing the jade cloaks of the Fifth. They wore full helmets; faceplates shut tight bearing the etchings of the faces of his accusers- stern Miptero First Soldier of the Dawn Gods and his Troubled Angels. The feathered plumes sweeping back from their helms were dyed crimson, and Edo knew that behind the hideous masks his accusers were officers. They had to be of course. He was entitled to meet a jury of his peers and the judgment they made would be final.

Unholy and inhuman those metal faces in the murky light. Cruel and merciless as all gods.

"Edo Obesta Colero Fuentas, you stand accused of treason and murder. How do you plead?"

Edo shook his head but said nothing.

One of the guards who had led him here pushed him hard and sent him sprawling to the ground.

"The quarter-master gave us your name. All of us heard it."

Edo turned to the man who spoke, mouth dropping. He recognized the voice.

The Entargió, Haldereso Después. Volunteered for this duty probably. A chance to settle old scores.

Edo's mind raced. Had he really left Elbario, the quartermaster, alive? The man had bled like a stuck pig but Edo had seen others survive such a loss of blood - for a time. The whey-faced bastard; blood gurgling from his mouth, crab-crawling from his tent, a hoarse midnight cry catching the attention of a passing guard. The alarm raised and a name whispered from dying lips. How could he have been so fucking careless. He should have finished the job properly. Slit the fucker's throat.

Mind whirring, a faint glimpse of hope, Edo struggled to his feet. The quartermaster was dead. Had to be. Blood loss would have killed him. The wounds. Edo had slit his innards. In the absence of a witness this jury would not dare put him to death.

"Then bring the quartermaster here and have him testify." He faced Hal.

"We took a deposition before he died. A dozen witnesses heard him call your name," Hal's smug voice rasped like a blade on Edo's soul as hope popped like a bubble.

A tall man stepped forward. The bronze pin holding his cloak in place was shaped like an entwined serpent. Másberia Damas, Secuas of the Fifth and leader of the army in Kallingtorn and the conqueror of Caedia.

"Quarter-master Elbario, dead. Legionnaire Gallin, known amongst his comrades as Sour, dead. Legionnaire Sinro assigned to Elbario's guard, dead. Three Aonians good and true. Dead. A dozen prisoners let loose to cause further havoc amongst our people and you think to play games with us, Domin." He stepped forward and slammed his fist into Edo's midriff. Edo bent forward, gagging for breath. Másberia drew his jag dagger and held it against Edo's throat. "It would give me all the pleasure in the world to nail you to a cross of wood." He pressed the blade hard against Edo's neck and growled. " By Miter's eyes I would see you see your soul torn asunder if I could." He grabbed Edo's ear and sawed through the flesh in one practiced stroke. Edo screamed. Másberia drew back and slammed his mailed fist into Edo's mouth, smashing three of his front teeth. Edo stumbled backward, fell, whimpering.

Másberia knelt beside Edo and opened his faceplate. In a quiet voice, so the others could not hear he said, "Your brother alone saves your traitorous hide. His influence rides far and, even here under the mask of gods, none of these men dare mute your existence." He shook his head. "So live, this is the judgment of the Tribuna. But it will not go easy for you."

He stood and turned his back on Edo.

"Brand his forehead then break all his limbs. Tie him to the horse. He stays a month. When you release him send him naked from here without food or succor. None here will ever speak his name again. From now on he will be known as Catem, as scum. This is the judgment of the Tribuna."

Tears rolled down Edo's face and he blubbered like a child as they brought him into the daylight of the courtyard where the massed throngs of the fifth were waiting for him to receive his punishment.

CHAPTER 3 - TAMBER

The shaman's name was Sesking'lincuhun, son of Uradier the Thief, but the tribe knew him as Sesk Wolftooth. Sesk lived alone by the seashore to the east of town, near the great flat bay where the salters gathered brine.

He lived alone in a dry cave, reached by climbing a palisade of boulders cast in a jumble by angry winter seas.

Tamber set off after sunrise. The day was dull and a chill wind blew. His head was dense with the remnants of the Kai-wine he had been drinking since their return, three days before. His stomach felt like bile. At the palisade wall surrounding the village he let out a whoop of joy and broke into a rapid trot. His head pounded like a merciless drum and sweat poured off him like a river. When he reached the ocean he tore off his clothes and ran into the great iron mother. He swam for a long time and when he emerged from the water the sun was peeking through the trees and his hangover had been blown away in the sheer joy and effort of his exertion. He picked his way along the cliffs towards the east. Water piled in great white crests against the rocks and stunted trees on the bare edge of the cliffs danced like maddened warriors on the eve before battle.

The cliffs gave way to the salt fields- deposits of brine the People collected in a sheltered bay whose head was shaped like a thin funnel. Except in the depths of winter, when the storm gods wrecked havoc on the coast, the tides were low and seawater percolated slowly into the great flat expanse.

Mushroom shaped mounds of red-tinged salt stretched to the distant horizon and the iron water glinted the color of blood. Tamber shivered. The tribe of salt makers were Malai, they paid tribute to the chief who ruled Tamber's tribe, but otherwise were a law unto themselves. They guarded their secrets with rabid ferociousness.

He made a ward with his left hand skirted the far side of the bay, away from the deposits of salt, keeping his eyes down so as not to awake anger amongst the distant figures of the silhouetted salters.

The shaman's cave was in a cliff on an exposed promontory. Reed covered marshes dotted the western edge of the island and a round hummock of gray granite rose like a massive spine rearing to meet the water.

Tamber climbed to the shaman's cave. Above albi kraaed and dived, their thin eerie voices the souls of the dead calling from the Otherworld.

In front of the cave was a wide, sandy ledge. The sand was dark and damp. Two human skulls decorated with seaweed and crimson albi feathers constituted a ward.

Tamber threw himself to the ground and sent a prayer to Yangti.

"What took you so long?" the shaman growled from deep within the cave.

Tamber stood. Brave as he was the thought of facing the shaman, of being made privy to hidden knowledge, turned his soul to sludge.

He was a warrior, not a prophet, a killer, not a seer. He did not belong in this place.

"Enter, pup, or are you afraid of old men?"

Tamber forced his feet forward, past the wards. He felt them like glowering heat on his back as he ducked into the chill cave.

The shaman sat cross-legged before a fire. Dark smoke issued from the fire- gouts of blackness which shimmered and danced. In front of the fire mounds of harrak insects were devouring the corpse of an eviscerated dog.

Against the far wall Tamber spotted Sesk's tools- skulls of animals, the tanned and flayed skins of a dozen Pugi, another half-dozen of Tang, the skull of a jar-nosewarrior from the Hills of Keruling still wearing his ceremonial headdress. Beside these were earthen jars. On a shelf of stone Tamber spotted herbs. He knew the names of the most common, the sort leeches and women used: kilwort, halsy, the purple flower of the lo. Most he did not recognize.

Draped over a wooden chair was the shaman's bear cloak and the mildewed skullcap he wore for official ceremonies.

The stench in the cave was of rotten eggs and fouled flesh and Tamber had to school himself not to gag.

Sesk the Shaman grinned at Tamber's discomfort and patted the woven mat of rushes on which he sat. His thin face was half-hidden by a dirty beard, streaked with white, his eyes were bulbous, the color of melting ice.

Tamber sat beside him and Sesk handed him a pointy leaf shaped like a lowland spear.

"Chew, boy. The spirits wish to inspect you. Then we talk."

Tamber placed the bitter leaf on his tongue and chewed slowly. The room swayed and his mouth and lips went numb.

"I had a vision."

Sesk nodded unhappily. "Tell me what you saw."

Tamber explained as best he could about the cave and the oracle. The vision she had granted him had faded fast and he remembered horror but not the details of what had happened. When

he was finished he turned to the Shaman who nodded, eyes white as his head swung from side to side in trance.

A smell of sulfur poured into the room and a chill deeper than winter invaded the cave.

"Why would the Oracle speak to a whelp like you?" Sesk's face had grown hard, a sheen of sweat bathed his forehead and his hair shone damp with sweat.

Tamber shook his head. "I want nothing to do with this." His head swam. The ants squirming on the dog's corpse had grown huge. With preternatural clarity he saw their feelers probing air and he knew they were coming for him next.

He made to rise. The Shaman's hand snapped out and locked around his neck. The man's eyes were red as the salt in the bay of brine and his face was that of a meskbear, snarling and vicious.

"Talk to me pup," he growled. "Tell me what

you saw."

Tamber shook his head, fear blanking his mind.

He would not remember. Could not.

The shaman had an iron grip on his neck. He leaned forward and pushed Tamber to ground, then straddled him. Tamber felt helpless, a new-born baby.

"Tell me you whelp!"

From close beside Tamber's ear came a rustling- a thin dry sound like the whispering of ghosts.

Tamber turned his head. The harrak were massive, blae creatures with long feelers and yellowed eyes. A horde of them. They crawled into his hair, onto the furs covering his body. Pincers bit deep into his flesh.

As they clambered onto his face he struggled, desperate to push them away but the shaman held him tight. Sesk, now more bear than man, loomed over him, mouth open in a fanged snarl.

Tamber closed his mouth tight as the harrak crawled into his nostrils, stabbed at his eyes. Pain swept through him and he screamed. In their hundreds they invaded his opened mouth and the pain was unconscionable as they ate their way into him.

Deep inside.

He yelled one last time then his mind fell way to nothing.

***

60

When he came around the shaman was dancing round the fire, hopping on one foot, a voiceless tune issuing from his throat.

Tamber sprang to his feet, skiri to hand, and sprang for Sesk.

The shaman pirouetted past the blade's swing, smiled his rotting smile, and stuck out a foot. Tamber flew head first into a ledge of stone.

"Hurts I hope you little whelp."

Tamber staggered to his feet.

The shaman held out a hand in the sign of peace. "I had to wake your memories, Tamber. You spoke to me of what the Oracle gave you. Sit and do nothing else stupid, for I may still have need of you and death does not need to be written for you this day."

***

"I dreamed of men dressed like beetles. They come from the west." Tamber said.

Sesk nodded. The day was late, the shadows in the cave solemn as evenfall approached. They had spent time praying to Great Blue Heaven, their souls drifting on the wings of smoke that wafted from the herbs Sesk had made them inhale.

"They came on great floating houses," he held his arms out wide. "They swarmed like harrak. They butchered our people. We fought but we died." His voice caught in his throat. "How can this be? Have the gods forsaken us?"

Sesk grunted. "The harrak are the omen of these men. I slaughtered the dog at dawn before you arrived." He gestured at the mute creatures remains. "Its innards were foul with rot. The harrak appeared as if from nowhere," he shuddered. "From nowhere, yet their shadows slanted from the west."

Weak light entered the lip of the cave as the sun settled beneath the distant waves.

"What should we do?"

"Mencunan and his revenants must hear our appeal. We must pray they will advise us."

A sudden chill stroked Tamber's back. "It is long since the Malai used the stones?"

Sesk's eyes reflected the firelight as the darkness gathered outside. "The future is at stake, Tamber. We need guidance and I fear we have not long."

***

The dozen warriors darkened their iron-gray faces with soot from the balefire.

Sesk handed them each a bone icon, and the dried husk of a harrak, as charms against evil sprits. They set off east, the moon a crescent like a grinning mouth, the stars gleaming in their multitude. Light disappeared as they entered amongst the trees and dark sprits hissed about them. Leaves rattled overhead though the night was windless.

Sesk mouthed charms and spat to drive the spirits away.

The Pugi village lay over a ridge of stone beneath the lowering peak of Black He Mountain, in a narrow valley through which the river Ja wound a gentle oxbow. The Pugi had camped for the summer on dry land above the willow-lined floodplain.

Tamber led his Yemki warriors towards the north. Fir swept down from the hills to within a spear's throw of the Pugi camp. The People ran through the darkened forest, silent as ghosts, leaping fissures and negotiating treacherous falls.

Tamber led them down a gulley through which a mountain stream gurgled over stone, then out from amongst the trees. The gulley was deep enough to hide them from the Pugi pickets if they crouched and moved slowly.

Less than fifty spans from the Pugi camp Tamber raised his right hand for them to stop. They waited in silence, listening to the sounds of the camp. Hounds barked but the pickets took no notice. Occasional shouts rent the night but the Pugi were mostly asleep in their huts made of woven willow withies. Tamber gestured at the pickets nearby then pointed at three of his men and gave the signal to attack. They rose at one from the gulley, silent as death. Tamber scrambled after them, up the loose shale onto a patch of damp and springy grass. The picket nearest to him turned in alarm, face wan in the moonlight. A spear shot through the night and took him in the chest. He crumpled backward. Tamber was upon him in a second. He ran his obsidian dagger across the man's throat then was up and running again. The three pickets posted to the north were already down and the Malai warriors roared their battle cries.

Hounds clambered, their barking urgent and fearful.

In the Pugi camp the beasts were stirring. Tamber let out a war cry and its shrill call was echoed by a dozen voices.

Three Pugi bulls, wielding short spears, ran at them out of the darkness. Tamber charged amongst them. He avoided the first spear lunge and stabbed the first warrior in the stomach then spun, sword whistling as it sliced. The head of the second Pugi fell, though the man's body stayed upright and stumbled on a few paces before crumbling to the ground. The last of the Pugi, an older male with concentric circles drawn about his eyes, snarled. Tamber lunged but the Pugi ducked backward, jabbering something inconsequential. Tamber roared his warcry.

The small man, fear in his eye, pulled away. Tamber feinted to the left then went right. He spun and backhanded the Pugi and the man fell, his body sliced in two from groin to chest.

Tamber spat on the ugly beast and bent down to take its ears.

Pugi were worse than animals. Pugi provided nothing, neither meat nor hide nor milk. Pugi stole food and ruined good forestland. They cut down tintuk trees and defiled sacred glades in their search for the shining baubles they found deep in the ground.

A spear slashed out of the night. The cold metal tip gouged Tamber's chest from left to right. Not a deep wound but painful nonetheless.

He bellowed his anger and ran amongst the Pugi and as he ran his sword slashed and cut and the Pugi fell. Male and female and children they fell and their cries were sown on barren ears.

***

They herded the survivors- a dozen females- towards the village. Tamber's wound stung and the taste of blood coppered his nostrils with the stench of death.

Two other Malai warriors had been wounded. None had been killed. Over two dozen Pugi had fallen to their weapons. The attack was an unqualified success and Sesk had slaughtered the last surviving male and painted his body with its blood. He did a one-legged dance over the body while braying a prayer to the horned god Taskiluh, the Old Man of War.

After the frenzy of death came the downtime- the time of fear and depression. Sesk wandered amongst the warriors as they walked home whispering words of comfort to them for they were heroes with nothing to fear from the wandering spirits of those they had killed.

Sesk had forbidden plunder- not that the Pugi had much to steal- for this was not an act of war but an act of in honor of the gods. This victory could not be besmirched by greed.

As they made their way back a thread like rawhide ran raw over Tamber's nerves. The Pugi, for all that they were vermin, had died well, defending their home and their young. They had fought…well.

He shook his head, angry at himself. He strode to the nearest Pugi captive, a middle-aged woman, and spat in her face.

These vermin deserved no pity.

He intended to give them none.

***

They arrived back at the village in time for the purple dawning.

They threw the tearful Pugi women into a pigpen and fed them pig slops. The children had fun watching the Pugi and the pigs compete for scraps of food.

The pigs, well fed and irate at the invasion of their privacy trampled one of the women and fed on her corpse. Sesk quickly put an end to the show, driving the children away with a show of mock anger.

"I need the beasts alive for their deaths," he said with his broken-toothed smile as the children squealed. Tamber and the warriors were feted in the hall and fermented kai-wine flowed like silver water.

As night fell they brought their captives to the edge of the cliff. Upakahun, the chieftain, in his tarnuk pelt, horned claws hanging from his shoulder, led the way. Elders and shaman followed dressed in the hides of the animals they had killed. They stopped in a circle near the idols of sacrifice- three man-sized stones of obsidian carved in the likeness of a family of three people.

The Pugi women were stripped naked and each bound by a wooden collar of precious tintuk. A gift for the Otherworld.

Sesk, dressed in his meskbear cloak and helmet, laid a sacrifice of corn and hops and dried fish beneath the stone idols and the tribe knelt and prayed to Mencunan. Sesk, aided by Tamber, tossed the screaming, struggling women, one by one, over the cliff edge. Albi from the cliff top caves flew high above, attracted by the sound of fear and prayers.

Two of the birds, wingspans larger than Tamber was long, landed in a flurry by the stones and waddled with precarious dignity towards the idols. They fed from the bowls of grain and fish then flapped away again, the air beating with the thunder of their wings.

The prayers continued till raw dawn spilt the darkness like a sore smile. Thunderclouds spread overhead and the day broke cold and damp. To the west lightning spilt the horizon, cords of light whipping towards the mute hump of bare rock that was Shark Island.

As the sun appeared, a haze of orange struggling to escape from behind the tyranny of the clouds, Sesk nodded to Tamber. They strode shoulder to shoulder towards the steam room. The People looked on- fishermen, salters, quarriers, sword-sculptors, chiefs and farmers.

Tamber cast a last look over his shoulder as he ducked beneath the lintel of the stone room. Sesk fed the fires and they sat side by side chewing on speargrass.

67

Tamber closed his eyes as the heat washed over him but try as he might no inspiration came. Mencunan and his Revenants remained silent.

The Albi cried outside and fate tolled the death of the Malai.

Tamber dreamed of a Pugi woman whose body was that of an Albi. Her face was a mask of terror and she flew above him, screeching.

She did not talk and no vision was granted him.

The butchery had been for nothing.

***

Sesk and Tamber met with the chieftain and the elders in the feasting hall of Yangwa, the ziggurat dedicated to great blue heaven.

They sat in a circle on the ground on a mat of rushes. In the center of the room a banked fire smoldered, the foul smoke it spat rising in lazy tendrils to the slanted flues in the roof of the large hall.

"Mencunan ignored you," Upakahun spoke.

Tamber bit back a snarl. Once Upakahun been great warrior, chosen by the elders to lead the tribe. Now he was an old man, skin slack and translucent, the fleshy face swollen by putrid liquid that darkened the flesh of his neck.

He was not long for the world and all of them knew it.

Sesk grimaced. "The god did not answer us."

Upakahun turned on Tamber. "This vision of yours, the one you say the oracle gave you, you

68

believe it was true."

Tamber nodded. "Aye, lord."

Upakahun pursed thick lips. "Men in armor like beetles, floating on houses on the sea. A peculiar vision. And none but you have had inkling of this. Not my household shaman." He gestured at the priests flanking him, two brothers who served in the temple. "Nor any other holy man." His smile was a leer. "Can we be sure you did not drink too much wine together."

Tamber's felt his face redden. His triumph in the Yemki hunt had made him a voiced man- one whose words would be given weight in the council. It had also made him enemies for many were envious that one so young could be given such a privilege.

The chieftain it seemed was one such- a waning star threatened by the brilliance of younger, brighter stars who standing ready to eclipse him.

"The vision was true," Sesk spat in the fire.

Keklah Keli, one of the twin shaman rubbed a hand through his beard, the hanging bones rattling. "Yet you did not share it. It was Tamber's alone"

Sesk hissed. "The chill of its wake sufficed, Keklah Keli. The harrak were an omen. Their evil weighed on me like a stone." He cast his fingers at the shaman. "Charlatans like you and your brother could know nothing of this." He made a gesture of contempt and turned away but Tamber saw the lethal looks the two shaman cast at Sesk.

Upakahun smiled slowly, the slow smile of

an ancient predator. "You sacrificed a dozen Pugi, yet Mencunan ignores you. Why would he do that?"

Sesk had no answer. The indifference of the gods, their peculiar silence, had been a great blow to him.

Sesk opened his arms, empty of an answer.

"Yet you feel you must pursue this thing."

"If Tamber is right then the future drips with our blood. We must act now."

The chieftain picked at his teeth. "Tamber is undoubtedly brave, but we do not choose warriors for their closeness to the heavens. Why is he favored of the gods?"

Sesk growled. "He is a vessel. Nothing more. He gains nothing by this. And that is why the oracle chose him."

Upakahun ran his fingers through thin, greasy hair. "The ceremony failed but still you worry at this thing. What is it you want from us, godspeaker?"

"We need Aburapadak."

Keklah Keli sniggered. "The hag speaks to no one."

"She will speak with me. She owes me a blood debt. That will be repaid."

Upakahun peered from hooded eyes first at Sesk, then at Tamber. Aburapadak was a seer who had once lived amongst them. One winter's day with snow blanketing the ground she had moved away, past the badlands where the Scelpi Tang had their villages. She lived now below the Eyrie on Mou Mout Mountain beneath the wings of the

70

falcon.

Though some thought her mad, most considered her to be one of the truest seers the villages had ever known.

If anyone could hope to understand Tamber's vision and what to do to act on it, she would.

With great officiousness Upakahun looked around the room; at the other elders, at the smoky ceiling, at the slave girls and housetrained Pugi who kept the fire warm and brought kai for their wooden cups.

Tamber sensed what the old goat was thinking. He smelled opportunity. He could be rid of Tamber and Sesk and live his quiet life again. The lands of the Scelpi Tang were dangerous, the people there no friend of the Malai. The steep slopes below the Eyrie were covered with allo and fir, dark even in summer.

Spirits walked there and the dead called from amongst the trees.

Tamber and Sesk might never return. But if they did...

Upakahun struggled to his feet. He blew air at the elders as he turned in a circle, facing each of them in turn.

"Tamber is our youngest champion. I would travel with him but my duties are here. He will have a pack of twelve and Yangnan will lead. Do any dissent to this?"

Yangnan was Upakahun's second, leader of his household guard, his sworn champion.

He glared at the elders as though daring them to speak, but most shrugged or stared back with

71

vacant eyes. Upakahun had given Sesk what he wanted, but made sure that if the expedition was a success glory would be reflected on him and his family.

What else was a leader to do?

***

They set off on a day in late summer afar Upakahun sacrificed a goat. Corn and rye waved yellow-golden in stone-ringed fields, tended by captured slaves.

Red-winged gree and screeching kao flew over fields left fallow, over waving fields of green pasture. White butterflies danced on the high grass and young lovers plucked crimson hearts and yellow-shades then soaked them in the blood and swore to keep love alive through the depths of winter.

In villages all along the coast the proud warriors of the Malai prepared for autumn raids. Tintuk spears and swords were oiled and the villages rang with the sounds of barking hounds and the eager voice of braves ready to kill.

Upakahun 's second, the grizzled Yangnan, a sable uran pelt thrown over his shoulders, led from the front as they left the village. He walked straight, head-high, his face impassive and age-darkened as tintuk. Tamber had been appointed his second. Sesk strode at Tamber's shoulder, dressed in his meskbear finery. With a mixture of ash and dung he had spiked his hair and the bones in his beard clanked as he walked. He looked both feral and powerful. Tang and Pugi slaves in the fields, tending the harvest and the herds, made warding signs, or spat to the left as he strode past. Their gods were not his, and they feared his power.

Yangnan led a party of twelve warriors, all fresh Yimti in their first year as warriors. None of these men had yet captured slaves or been given a grant of land. They had no reason to wait by homesteads until harvest was done. Unblooded, for them as for Tamber this was a chance to return decked in glory. They were eager as colts and they roared their warsongs as they marched. Half a dozen warhounds and a brace of carapaced meskini accompanied them, the hounds yapping about their ankles as they strode the narrow path that straddled the cliff-face north of the village. The ocean stretched to the horizon, white breakers raising huge white horses, driven by the wind and Yemlakken's breath.

For two days they made their way north along the coast and then turned inland where the massive forest of ancient pine spread back towards the distant brown mountains of the Mou Mout. They camped overnight on a sheltered shoulder of granite above the ancient forest. When darkness fell they set pickets, ate salt-dried meat and corncakes. A translucent fog shimmered the valley floor and swallowed the trees. Blue lights appeared over the fog, dancing wraiths the size of pinpoints. The warriors shivered as a cold wind from the west drove against them. Rain pattered on the leaves of their fern-roofed shelters.

Sesk performed a dance of warding, hopping on one leg and then the other, arms outstretched, fighting the sorcery in the forest.

When he finished he sat beside Tamber and bit into a chunk of jerky.

"Two day's amongst the trees then we reach the lands of the Tang."

Tamber shivered. The Tang were smaller than the Malai, descendants many said, of the first people. They were fierce and strong and unknowable. Their language and customs were strange and the People signed wards and spat for luck when the name was mentioned.

Tamber did both.

"The witch lives on the eyrie."

Sesk nodded. "In the all-ice, amongst the meskbear. But to get there we must pass the Tang and then Gorge of Skulls."

Yangnan cleared his throat and ducked under the ferns sheltering Tamber and Sesk. The rain pattered on the makeshift roof. Yangnan's sable fur glittered damply. Traces of the oak-cake he had eaten hung from his long, forked beard. He had shaved the right side of his head and dots of yellow tattoos there showed the kills he had made and the captives he had couped.

His eyes glowed crimson, from the light of the fire and Tamber guessed he had been at the kai-wine

He growled. "We set off when the fog clears. Shaman I want you to have cleared all the magic from that valley before we leave."

Sesk lowered his eyes, said nothing.

74

Yangnan made to leave. "War-captain," Tamber called him back.

"What?"

"Have you ever fought the Tang?"

Yangnan's face looked tired and old in the dim light. "Fought and killed them. And seen many a good man die to their tricky ways. Keep the men together boy. I'll lead from the front, you stay back. And warn your men to keep a close eye out for the forest was ever the friend to the Tang."

***

Overnight a gusting wind blew the rain clouds away and the day broke mild and bright. On their lip of rock above the trees Sesk sacrificed a fallow deer and performed his rites in its blood, as he screamed his defiance at the darkling forest and the tendrils of yellow fog still swirling about its branches like tongues of rot from the Otherworld. When Sesk was finished they scrambled down a rocky bluff covered by crooked hazel and entered the forest.

The dense undergrowth made the going tough. Yangnan led from the front, his frame that of a hungry mesk-bear angered to slaughter.

Tamber stayed at the rear, keeping their line tight and his men moving hard. A river, the Keni or Little Brother, wound through the forest and marked the border with the Tang lands but they would not reach it for at least another day.

When they forded the river they would travel only at night. Until then, Yangnan chose to march in daylight but he had stressed the need to avoid being detected for the Tang were more at home amongst the trees than the Malai ever would be.

Light dazzled, percolating through the leaves in tight yellow columns. Sounds were distorted as they edged past massive lichen-covered boles. When required, they cut their path through the deep undergrowth of bramble and fern.

Midday, the land rose on a spur of rock covered in stunted hazel hanging from precipitous rocks. The going was slow as they edged their way up a narrow deer track. On Yangnan's orders Tamber scouted ahead, keeping to the cover of tree and rock. He found a deserted campsite near a bend at the top of the plateau. Some time later he found human waste and droppings and a site where a party of hunters had grelloched a deer. The spoor scented old. The Tang hunters were long gone. As evening fell they reached a high, treeless plateau. Meskini called the warband to a halt near a narrow rill flowing through a through a vast canvas of peat like a glimmering snake winding through dark sand. A shoulder of limestone jutting from the moor nearby would give them shelter. Exposed on high land they dared not light a fire. The wind called like a demon over the empty land and the Malai sat in a huddle near the rocks and attempted to sleep.

**

They walked all next day and, as evening fell, paused beneath the shelter of wide-leafed oaks and thick thorn where yellowbells grew in fierce profusion. They adopted a fallen log, half rotten and infested with termites as a temporary palisade. From where they waited in silence they could hear the river as it tumbled over a noisy weir. Turquoise birds screeched from the canopy of the trees.

The ford was a third of a league away. They would wait till after the sun left the earth, dragged by Seiktematian Menian and his six hounds of night into Dasia Kerara's cruel realm of cold and ice.

Night under the cover of the trees was pitch. Wind whipped the leaves of the towering, ancient oak and whispered amongst the branches.

Malevolent whispers, thought Tamber. The beings of the forest, the spirits of the forest itself, they want us here as little as we want to be here.

This land is betrothed to the Pugi and the Tang.

He spat to his left to ward off evil. The bastards could have it. All he wanted was the witch.

The shushing current of the river was audible now. Yangnan gestured for them to move forward. They glided through the trees, swords and spears at the ready.

Tamber heard a sound. He stiffened, held his hand up. An owl flew out of the trees whooing and he breathed in relief.

The river was three hundreds spans across and, at this time of year, fordable at only one spot. Yangnan believed that the Tang would have

77

guards there. They found the path to the river, a man's length wide, spattered with dung of oxen and sheep, and skirted it keeping to the trees.

Voices carried in the forest and they heard the harsh voices of the Tang before they could see them.

Yangnan and ten others waited in cover of the trees while Tamber crept forward with the massive young warrior they called Small.

They skirted a thick patch of thorn and bramble and on their bellies eased towards the river.

Small hissed, leaping back, terror widening his eyes. Tamber sprang forward and wrapped his arms round the man, knocking him flat.

"Silence," he hissed.

Small's panicked eyes cleared, though fear-sweat oozed from him, the stench like a pig's midden. Small gestured ahead and to the left. Turning his head, Tamber found himself staring at a human skull planted on a stake two spans away.

The skull was decked with feathers and hung with flayed skin. Tamber could feel the dark malevolence of its emptied sockets like a sharp claw scraping at his soul.

His stomach knotted in fear. Sweat sprang up on his forehead. He wanted to flee, to run screaming through the forest, as Small had almost done.

He could not. He dared not. There was too much at stake. He breathed hard, steeling himself, spat at the skull.

Its grinning eyes bored through him and he

felt small as an ant in its presence.

He edged to one side, hoping to pass beyond the reach of the foul ward but almost stumbled on a second, the skull of a woman this time, whose grinning face sounded mocking laughter in his mind.

The Tang had built a wall of spirits. Skulls filled with the souls of the dead all along the bank, guarding the ford. Mere warriors dare not pass here. They needed Sesk.

Tamber spun around disoriented. Small was gone, fled back to the main party. Tamber shrugged. Who could blame him? He had grown up with Small and knew he could trust him in battle but with the noxious smell of sorcery souring his nostrils any man might run.

He was making his way back to Yangnan when Small whistled like a goojoo bird, one sharp shrill note warning Tamber to wait. Tamber ducked to his haunches, spear across his knees. Small had not run away. For a lumbering giant, with a reputation as a fighter not as a planner, he had responded quickly.

Quicker than I did, Tamber wryly acknowledged.

Small stepped into view, Sesk shadowing him. Small saw Tamber and grinned. Tamber smiled back and clasped his arm.

They had their shaman.

Back at the row of skulls Sesk kneaded a ball of mud, cut deep into the palm of his hand with a skiri. He dripped blood into his ball of mud and spat into it, kneading and chanting quietly all the

79

time. In a crouch he hopped forward on one leg imitating a crane, spitting curses at the demon in the skull.

Sesk was praying to Hanyeleh, Tamber knew, for Hanyeleh the falcon god was ruler over birds. She specialized in the removal of curses and once had fought the demons to a standstill on Mount Atinua

Tamber could feel the demon resist and a wave of fear and anger washed over Sesk like a stink. The demon would claw at Sesk's soul, pull at his hair, bite into his heart, chew on his liver.

Tamber and Small fell back a dozen paces, driven in terror from the demon's fury but Sesk kept going. When he reached the skull he spat a long volley of curses in words Tamber did not understand and broke the ball of mud in two. He jammed the mud into the eye sockets of the skull, fell to his knees, hair matted and sweat dripping from him.

The Skull's power was gone.

***

Tamber and Smell crept past the skull, eyeing it nervously.

Sesk had broken its sorcery but rather than crawl over it, Tamber pushed it out of his way, with the butt of his spear into a scramble of fern. They came out of the tree line onto the bank of the river. Willow grew close to the water and the damp soil was home to rushes and sedge.

The Tang were less than two hundred spans

80

away. Tamber could hear them talking.

"How many?" he mouthed at Small. Small, with better vantage on a hummock of mud, held up four fingers. Tamber signaled Small towards the right and advanced on his belly through the damp earth on the larger man's left. They stopped twenty spans from the Tang camp. A shelter of beech planks, open on one side, held a cover of plaited willow withes topped with fern within which a fire burned. Two Tang stood guard near a rough wooden palisade facing back into the forest. Two more stood near the fire. The men on guard wore graywolf skull helms. Long bear-pelts were wrapped around their shoulders and corselets of thick bark protected their chests.

In the darkness their voices rumbled and that sound was the sound of terror, for once these people had been a plague on the Malai till Yanat Lan had united the tribes and destroyed their power.

Still, Tamber was swept with an ancient, powerful revulsion.

The Tang were shorter than the Malai with powerful upper bodies and forearms. Tufts of dark hair pelted their chests and backs. Their foreheads were long and their skulls flat. Their eyes, deep-set and darkly gleaming, showed neither pity nor fear.

Like the Pugi they were little more than animals.

Tamber growled and sprang forward, his sword raised two-handed. He crossed the distance and swung at the first of the sitting Tang before

81

any reacted. Tamber swung hard and the first man's head flew from his shoulders, gushing blood.

The second pivoted with his spear. Tamber swung hard, from the hip, turning and bringing the impetuous of his charge to bear.

The blade sliced across the man's chest and he let out a pained whimper as he fell. Tamber stabbed him in the eye with the sharp point of his blade.

Small had taken down the first of the guards but the second man, a wide brute with staring eyes and wide snarling nostrils, had taken up a defensive stand and was parrying Small's blows with ease.

Tamber growled and padded silently behind the man. He brought his sword down hard and split the beast's skull.

As the warrior fell Tamber turned to the moon above, half-hidden behind a tenebrous curtain of cloud. He howled and beat his chest.

Small joined in and soon Yangnan and the other warriors of the Malai were amongst them.

Yangnan looked annoyed. His plan had called for secrecy but Tamber's blood was up.

He ignored the warleader's angry face and kept howling.

Since when did the Malai skulk in the lands of the enemy?

They had come to find passage but all who stood in their way would be killed.

***

Sixteen Tang warriors had been on their trail for two days. Against Yangnan's wishes Tamber had taken trophies. The boiled bones of Tang hands hung from a kirtle over the armor on his chest and rattled as he walked.

Their souls cried out, in terror in the darkness of death. Having lost their arms and their skulls and their eyes, their souls wandered; unable to fight their way to Great Blue Spirit. Tamber felt their power- the power of the uneasy dead- as an incense of desperation lending his sword arm power.

The Tang, those who tracked them, wanted the souls of their warriors back as Tamber had known they must. He had argued with Yangnan, a shouting match that went on hours. In the end Yangnan nodded reluctant agreement as Tamber outlined his plan. He took six men with him. Deliberately careless they allowed the Tang to find their spoor. The Tang thought they were the hunters but it was not so; they were the hunted and Tamber was leading them into a trap.

Tamber's band wound a weary path, gradually allowing the Tang to catch them up. Twice he had sliced open his forearm to drip spoor of blood. The Tang should think the men they following were hurting, tiring, wounded.

Easy prey.

In a defile ahead waited Yangnan.

When they heard the Tang yelling behind them, triumph ringing in those cruel voices, they took flight. The Tang ran nosily after them,

83

sensing an easy victory against a dispirited group of tired men.

At the far end of the defile they pulled up. Tamber unsheathed his sword from the baldric over his shoulder and planted it in the earth. He held his long spear business end forward and waited.

The Tang ran screaming at them, ochre painted faces distorted by battle anger. Tamber urged his men to hold.

As battle was joined Yangnan sprang the trap. Malai came screaming down the steep walls of the defile, meskini and hounds snarling and frothing, the men screaming ancient battle cries.

The tang stopped in terrible indecision twenty paces from Tamber. Their leader, a tall man with a livid scar on one cheek, bellowed at them, urging them on. Tamber stepped forward and cast his spear.

It was not a throwing spear, it was too heavy in the staff, but Tamber cast it two-handed, forcing it to spin as it flew. The distance was short enough to keep the blade angled roughly where Tamber had aimed it.

It pierced the leader's stomach and cut through him, exiting the far side. The Tang, seeing their leader fall and the hounds leaping amongst them like demons broke and ran. Tamber chased them down. They hid in the underbrush like frightened children or stood frozen, allowing themselves to be hacked to pieces as the Malai took their souls.

None escaped. None lived.

Tamber took the head of the last Tang, a bearded bear of a man who, alone, had fought to the end and had been chopped to pieces beneath a half-dozen blades.

Yangnan glanced at Tamber, pale eyes like melted ice. Tamber sensed what was coming and steeled himself for their final argument.

"Now we take their village."

Some of the men, Small amongst them, grunted in agreement.

Tamber smiled hard and shook his head. "I say no to that war-captain. We must make for the Eyrie."

"You brought this on us. We have killed the men. Now I want their women. I want their children. I am your war-captain and now you will do as you are told." Yangnan squared his shoulders and turned to face Tamber. There was death written in the glint of his eyes.

"This will not be."

Yangnan hefted his sword and banged it on the earth "No?" he challenged.

Tamber nodded. "You would defile yourself with the women of these beasts."

Meskini spat. "What a man lays with is his own business. Slaves are wealth, puppy and these beasts can learn to sow and wash."

"And who will carry the slaves into the badlands and up the Eyrie?"

Yangnan growled. "I am your war-captain!"

"Your wealth will bring death upon us."

Uncertainty invaded Yangnan's face and Tamber sensed the sea-change in opinion he had

85

hoped for. Men whispered amongst themselves. Their blood was high and they had won this skirmish but they knew what lay ahead of them. The going would be treacherous. The land they were entering was a stranger to the Malai and had been for three generations.

Booty would slow them down and the village would still be there when they returned. In his rashness Yangnan had boxed himself into a corner. If he relented Tamber had won and Yangnan's authority would drain away like snow in summer. Tamber would be the new war-leader.

Yangnan had one other choice and he took it. He lunged forward sword swinging at Tamber. Tamber parried, held back as the warcaptain attacked; fierce sweeping attacks, left to right and back again, the clash of blades sending shivers of strain down Tamber's arms and shoulder.

Tamber eased backward in a half-circle, willing himself to patience.

As Meskini attacked again, lunging forward, swinging from high over his left shoulder, Tamber parried and Meskini backhanded a careless blow at his head.

Tamber ducked and the blade whistled inches above the skull-helmet he wore leaving Yangnan's guard wide open. Tamber stabbed him in the chest ramming his blade home two handed. The blade exited through the back of the neck and Tamber, screaming now, lifted Yangnan from the ground and rammed the blade into the bole of the nearest lichen-covered hazel.

Impaled, Yangnan stared down at him, blood

bubbling from his lips, his body spastic as the pain seared him and his soul left his body.

Tamber sucked air into his lungs, teeth bared in a silent snarl as he waited in silence till the struggle with death was over.

Tamber planted one foot on the tree, grasped the sword and pulled. Yangnan's body slid to the ground. Tamber tugged off the man's pelt, threw it about his own shoulders. He cleaned his blade on Yangnan's tunic, bent and picked up his fallen blade and tossed it to Small who caught in on the fly.

"You are my second now."

The big man grinned and nodded.

"Warleader! Lead us to glory."

***

They skirted a ring of Tang villages, moving in silence though the primeval forest, not daring to light campfires. They caught and skinned rabbits, squirrels and small deer, ate the meat bloody and raw. Bands of Tang roamed the forest; birdcalls of the wawlan echoing through the trees, answered and re-answered as the Tang searched for spoor.

They kept to raised tracks, bad land, edging first north, then east, then north again, keeping out of reach of the vengeful warriors tracking them.

They came on a spirit house; a wooden structure topped with skulls and bones hung with macaw feathers.

Sesk danced for two hours, till the sweat rolled in rivers down his body. His eyes rolled

87

back in his head till the whites showed.

Still the way was not clear.

Whatever had set the curse in that place knew how to hate.

"They butchered a hundred Malai here, Sesk reported. "Skinned and ate them."

Tamber shuddered.

"Something lives here. A darkness I cannot understand." Sesk shook his head and the sorcerer's failure and uncertainty cast a pall of gloom over all of them.

What lay await for them where they were headed?

***

The Tang lands ended, the Eyrie still a dark bruise on the horizon; clouds tumbling across a violent sky, thunderheads in the west threatening rain, whipping bolts of lightning onto the long-suffering earth.

An albino hart with a mane of yellowing antlers fled diagonally across their path from left to right, and though Sesk made light of it they knew the direction of its passage as a bad omen.

The forest gave way to heathland- a wide purple plateau haunted by drifting mist. They set off across it with heavy hearts, aware of the purple mountains in the distance, lowering and empty like an old man's dreams of death.

Sesk took point now, for the threat from the Tang had vanished with the trees and in this place of strangeness, where the world they knew no longer existed, he would lead. They camped as night dropped behind twin distant peaks, as though swallowed by a huge mouth. As night fell cry rang out over the plateau, a dark winged cry like a demon crowing.

They sat silently around the campfires, the usual bravado and tomfoolery absent as they sat in silence and listened to the voice of the wind and pretended to be oblivious to the voice in the darkness whispering their names.

***

They awoke to a nerve-rattling scream, in that time before morning when light begins to open the clasps of night's rude hold, and air is thick and heavy with portent and meaning.

The scream echoed all about them for one long moment, faded away till silence reigned.

Sesk roused Tamber, and Tamber startled at the wide-eyed fear apparent in the older man's face.

A warrior by the name of Keklah Keli, Little Middle Friend, was missing. Where he had slept lay a white feather, dripping with a dark liquid whose texture seemed as blood.

Sesk knelt on the ground and sniffed around the feather carefully. He backed away hissing, spitting courses.

"What is it?"

Sesk shook his head, and pinched the bridge of his nose. "He is gone. The spirit of this place is a demon. Move on. Quickly!"

89

They gathered their packs and hurried off the plateau, souls being chased by truths they could neither comprehend nor see.

Tamber was the last to leave. He stared back at the yellow mist visible in dawn's first light and snarled. Demonic or not something had taken one of his men and Tamber felt no fear or horror.

He spat into the mist, the spittle landing near the feather dripping blood.

Tamber could not be sure but he thought his spit sizzled like fat on a griddle as it hit the ground. He turned and left, slowly, sick in his stomach.

Keklah Keli had been a good man. This was no place for a warrior to meet an end.

***

Tamber started up a narrow defile, the wind howling about him.

They had been in the mountains three days, climbing to the top of peaks and navigating through narrow gorges that divided them. Their supply of food, -dry bread and salted meat- was dwindling. They wasted time each day hunting pale, fleet deer.

At night mountain lions roared and winged harlik screeched. The warriors of the Malai huddled round the campfires like timid old women. Sesk had been broody and uncommunicative since Keklah Kel's death and Tamber sensed that the older man's reserve was a deep malaise. The shaman had learned to doubt;

he no longer believed in their quest and this timidity was sapping morale of all the men. He would have to do something and soon.

Tamber scrambled up a last slope of loose shale, breathing hard, sweat coating his hair and forehead beneath his bone helm.

From the top of the defile he looked east towards the Eyrie, a glistening ice-coated tower of rock like the fastness of a lunatic king. Birds circled it cawing. The sorcerer they sought lived up there.

Aburapadak the witch. Sesk said that she was wizened and ancient when he was young, and she had still lived amongst people, but age meant nothing for those with power. She had foretold doom on the Malai, a tale of outsiders from a far land, her tale not unlike Tamber's vision, and as mutterings grew against her she had slipped out of the village one gray-dawn and disappeared for good. Nobody went after her. In truth the tribe was glad to be rid of her but over the course of the next decade the tribe caught rumors from captured Tang, and learned she had made a new home in the fastness on the Eyrie. They were happy to leave her there, unmolested, this crazy witch, and year by year her reputation as a power grew till it was said the Tang cowered in fear when her name was invoked.

Sesk was sure she would be able to help them, for she had lived a lifetime in the Eyrie, a lifetime dedicated to finding a solution to the same problem that plagued them now.

So why was the fool of a sorcerer behaving

suddenly like a nut-shriveled old man.

Tamber could not understand it.

He half-ran and half-slid down the shale to the others. They had built a fire and were sitting around it in silence.

He plumped himself down near Sesk. "We start on the Eyrie tomorrow," he said.

Sesk glanced at Tamber, a weak smile on his face.

"What ails your spirit, sorcerer?"

"The spirits gather around us, humming like bees around a honey drink. Whatever it is that waits for us there amuses them?"

"Why should that worry us?"

Sesk turned his face to the east. "I fear the fury of the future, Tamber and or I would not be here. But what awaits for us there I fear almost as much. It may have been a mistake coming here."

Tamber shifted closer to the sorcerer, grabbed hold of his arm and squeezed.

Sesk gasped at the pain and Tamber squeezed harder, speaking quietly so none might hear. "Listen to me now and listen carefully. Fear is a disease. In future you will dance and spit and invoke your wards no matter what you think. Your confidence will be an inspiration. If I hear women's words like these from you again I will slit your throat and leave your body to the demons or the wolves." He squeezed even harder and sweat broke out on Sesk's face. "Are we clear, you and I?"

Sesk lowered his eyes.

"Say it!"

"I know no fear, war-captain," Sesk muttered from clenched teeth. "I know no fear."

**

On a glistening glacier, studded with rock the color of onyx, Sesk halted the war band.

"We can go no further, War-leader. The rest of this journey is yours alone."

Tamber argued halfheartedly but Sesk announced that the witch had visited him in her dream.

"This is what she wants, Tamber." Sesk insisted. "Only you may pass safely. The rest of us will be tormented by demons if we venture higher."

For a brief moment Tamber contemplated slitting Sesk's truth, but held off. He wasn't sure he believed the sorcerer and yet he had always known that the coming ordeal was for him.

The visions were his. The responsibility. The glory.

He left the others in the lee of an icy rock near a sheer drop that gave way to the valley of the Tang, half a kilometer below.

They had lost one of their number, Hillah on their last hard climb. Alerted by a moan, like pain or pleasure, Tamber had glanced down. Beneath him but further right was Hillah, eyes huge, umber as they locked on Tamber, a strange smile ghosting his face. Tamber understand somehow that the man's soul had been devoured. Demon possessed. Tamber watched as he let go of the rope then pushed himself off the rock face with his legs.

He cartwheeled as he fell down the side of the sheer cliff, slamming into overhangs of rock, his screams echoing for long minutes, like an unpleasant vapor.

"The demon consumed him. He was weak and the Eyrie needed a sacrifice. We will be safer for it, Sesk explained later.

The men had muttered complaints when they reached the relative safety of the peak and Tamber knew he was losing them. They had found nothing but death thus far, no wealth nor slaves and little glory, and the quest was far from over.

It would be easier alone.

A corkscrew pass between two steep cliffs of rock and ice led him higher. Wind howled and sleet drove the wind. Tamber pulled his cloak high so it covered his head and staggered onward. He came to a sheer wall of rock and ice, dropped the pack containing what little food he had, and pulled out his garnark; wooden sticks pierced with albi claws. He tossed the pack onto the baldric on his back and tied the claws to his boots. Gripping two of them, one in each hand, he started off up the mountain, knowing he must look like a beetle scurrying up a rock face from below.

The claws bit firmly into blue ice and rock. He pulled himself upward step by step. Within an hour his lungs were flame and his arms leaden. A wind howled about his ears and tugged at his clothes as if willing him to fall.

Within two hours he was numb in every part

of his body and only the force of his will kept him going forward.

He was less than half way there.

The wind howled and spoke to him in tongues.

Let yourself go, warrior. Fall and we will receive you.

He pictured a landscape of rolling fields and trees. In a hut in a glade in a forest caressed by rays of sun women waited for his embrace and a boar roasted on a spit. Hanging from the lintel of his house were the scalps and trophies he had taken and a dozen children ran about his feet.

The land all about him was his. The children were his.

Rich and powerful and loved he had everything a man needed.

He blinked awake, starting and almost fell.

He had stopped climbing and he was hanging by one hand only while the wind tore him from side to side with its sharp pincers.

He shrugged away his demon-induced trance and started forward again, aware that if he was to look down or up he would fall for he would see the distance he had traversed and the distance he had left and despair would swallow him like a curse.

***

He pulled himself over a lip of rock onto a narrow crevice that led to the peak and lay back, breathing hard. When a semblance of strength had returned he struggled to his feet. The air here was thin, chill as a northern winter, and the wind spoke in a screeching voice like an old harridan at a wedding.

He struggled up the last incline towards the peak. Black rocks peeked from gullies of snow. The stinging wind needled his eyes. Between flurries of snow he caught a glimpse of someone on the path. He drew his sword from its baldric with numb fingers and yelled a greeting into the teeth of the wind. The wind swallowed his words and the snow drove ever heavier as he waited, racked by indecision.

Was it a man or a demon waiting for him?

The weather made his mind up- he would freeze where he stood if he waited too long. He struggled forward

Through thick flurries the man came into view. He was tall, taller than Tamber by a head. In one hand was a drawn sword leaning on the ground. He was facing away from Tamber, head towards the peak. He stood motionless, free hand outstretched as if in greeting. Or warding.

Tamber hustled forward till he came level with the man.

Ice hung from the long moustache that hung to his chest and crested his bone helm. His skin was blue-black and the pelt of musk-bear he wore was frozen solid. His gibbous eyes stared sightlessly at something lost to sight forever. The look bespoke terror.

Tamber kneeled beside the dead man - if man he was for his teeth were long and sharp as those of a wolf -and prayed to the Great Blue Spirit for the spirit of this long dead warrior. He rose, fear invading him like raging water, straining at its dyke, and made for the peak.

A cairn of stones large as a house adorned the summit of the Eyrie, hung with frozen hides of human flesh. In front of the stone was a large round boulder inscribed with runes and behind it a dark opening. Tamber did not hesitate. He had come too far and was too sapped. If he stopped, allowed fear to master him, his courage would never return. He bulled past the warding stone and into the darkness of the damp cairn.

A long corridor opened before him and the dim light from white stone was enough for him to see by. The corridor was long and led deep into the rock.

He squared his shoulder and entered the den of the witch.

***

The corridor led to a narrow-ceilinged room, the air damp and cold, a chalky taste of stone settling on his tongue.

She was sitting on a stone chair, facing away from him.

Skulls ringed the room, some animal, some human, blank eyes staring at him in dim accusation. A hearth lay disused in the center of the room and the room was almost as chill as the wind-swept mountain. An old spear, the wood rotted and broken, its bronze leaf discolored had been stabbed head first into a massive slab of frozen granite.

All wrong! A terrible injustice here, its smell still lingering, like the smell of ancient cooking. Suffusing the walls.

Turning his stomach.

He approached warily, sword held like a ward before him in both hands. The witch was dead, had been dead for many long years, her body frozen and thawed and frozen again so that flesh had rotted and spoiled.

Her hair hung like a cloak down the stone chair to the ground and her nails were long as a blade.

He sat down near her stone chair, resisting the urge to hack her body to pieces in sheer frustration. The plan had been Sesk's, but it was on Tamber's behest they had come here, to the roof of the world. In the quest for what? A crazy old woman to interpret their vision. In the chill reality of failure the arrogance of the notion became apparent.

Desire had driven him here, hope and his damned arrogance. He saw that now. He understood all too well. When he came down from the mountain he would have nothing to show, nothing to report and his men would glower with distaste and spit bile behind his back.

Their murmurings of dissent growing louder till sooner or later one would challenge him, as he had challenged Yangnan.

He had failed. His dreams of glory lay shattered like melting ice at his feet.

A cavern of doubt opened in his soul. How has he had been tricked or fooled into thinking that this quest of his would grant an answer, would show them a way to defeat the beetle-men?

The cavern roared, became the mouth of a massive gran-whale opening to swallow him whole.

Tears rolled down his cheek.

The tribe would mock him and call him a fool and never again would the council seek his advice. The women would spit at him and the children cast stones, till they drove him from the camp.

That could not happen. There had to be something.

He had been so sure. Sesk had been sure. The long journey they had made could not have been so futile.

It started in his liver, a chill breath like the foreknowledge of rot and death. He felt it spread within him till it reached his heart, his mind.

Fear. Terror. An awareness of the shortness of human life, its grand futility.

He lay on the ground, had fallen, but could not remember how. Cold. So cold. The air heavy upon him. Footsteps sounded. The witch's corpse had arisen and moved close behind him. Its chill breath caressed his neck, like a hand old and dry, hungering for the warmth of flesh.

Old it was. Older than the mountains. Cruel it was. Crueler than the lion. Dark it was, dark as the Raven.

And equally callous.

Its talons were those of the raven and it fed on death.

It spoke.

"The brave warrior of the Malai ventures forth," it rasped, its tone mocking. Tamber Whitehair, son of Lantuk, grandson of Ki, hero of the new hour. I fear the witch you seek is dead and the time of revelation is not yet. Such a shame. Such a pity. A quest like none other led by a hero like none other. Tamber Whitehair. Hero indeed. Lacking remorse for even the memory of those he butchered."

An image flashed through his head- a Pugi woman they had sacrificed whose great brown eyes Tamber had spat in as he tossed her from the cliff face. In his ears a dull sobbing, the sound of a child pining for its mother. The broken body lying at the foot of the cliff, lapped by waves of white water. Washed up on a stand of shingle-glassy eyed and bloated- gulls and albi feed on it, cawing and fighting.

The birds steal the woman's soul, tear it to pieces, and shred it, blunt knives shredding bread.

He shook his head, started to his feet.

"Sit!"

He had no thought or will to disobey. He sat and the voice moved close to his ear, so he could feel its frozen breath on his shoulder and the stink that oozed from its mouth.

"When you leave here, take the spear. For now, stay a while. I have stories to tell."

Raven cackled and tan its talons along Tamber's back. "I have stories to tell."

100

***

Afterwards, for a longtime afterwards, he would remember nothing of what the raven spirit of the mountain had told him.

But in his dreams the words rang with horror and boiled his blood and brain.

He was not the same, the stories Raven told changed him profoundly. Raven stole from him much of what it coveted- warmth, vitality, love.

The terror and pain but also the sweet joy of impermanent flesh.

It left behind a shell, a message for the future, though he did not know that then.

As in a dream he made his way back down the Eyrie to where Sesk and the others waited. As he approached they stood waiting for him, as if waiting for a visitation from a chief.

He held up the spear in his hand, brandished it at them, and spoke words that he himself did not understand, shaking his head all the time.

In his delirium he heard them speak.

"He is addled."

"The demons have taken his mind."

Sesk spoke in the end. "No! The witch lived no longer. Raven has spoken through her to Tamber. He bears the mark on his soul."

He saw the terror on their faces. Raven, Yimti's messenger in the Middle World, the dark spirit that feeds on the soul of those who die. Raven, the scavenger, Raven the Prankster, Raven who once owned feathers of purple and amber that had made him beautiful, arrogant enough to challenge Hanyeleh for mastery of the skies. Hanyeleh defeated Raven, stole his cloak of color, forced upon him the color of the night, forced him to feed on the flesh of the dead.

Raven was a canker, a danger and the Malai both feared and reviled him.

"Kill him then," he heard one of his men say. "Kill before he turns his red eye upon us."

Tamber stood still, holding the spear, a vessel of the spirit, unable to act. He waited as they discussed his fate. He had no fear. He had no love.

He was the hollow man set to scare the birds.

Sesk walked to one of the warriors, one of those demanding Tamber's death vociferously. He walked with a smile in his face, a long stone blade in his left hand hidden flat against his leg. The red-faced warrior spat at Tamber, ignoring the sorcerer, his face twisted in fear-rage.

Sesk stopped in front of the man, his weapon hidden.

"He bears a message for us. Kill him and we lose that," Sesk said quietly.

The man growled. Fear had driven him past reason. He raised a spear and pulled back his throwing arm as he swiveled. Sesk leapt forward, driving his blade deep into the man's throat, and drove him to the ground.

The sorcerer rose, blood drenched. The choking warrior's blood steamed from snow and ice.

Sesk faced Tamber.

"Blood is spilled, demon. Feed now, tell us

what you want, then leave us in peace. "

Tamber cackled and spoke with a voice not his. "Blood the Tang," His mouth opened and closed of its own volition. "Feed me their corpses and I will tell you what you need to know."

***

Tall pine and fir stretched high above them, and the sound of their passage was muffled by the trees. A wispy fog drifted about the gray boles and light illuminated the gloom beneath sparser undergrowth, sporadically cutting through the forest in great shimmering bars.

Sesk led the way. Tamber was relegated to the rear of the column. The rotted spear he had brought back from the cave had replaced the tintuk sword in his baldric.

He believed he had left his tintuk sword in the cave but he could not be sure. His memories were dim and uncertain, his sense of himself fading like a dream.

When the other warriors had noticed he no longer carried his sword they had eyed him with contempt, mingled with pity.

In a place deep inside he could not fathom it himself.

As an omen it seemed to weigh heavy on them- he had, after all, been warleader. Their doubts had grown to a point where they were ready to scamper home- only Sesk's stubborn insistence combined with their fear of returning empty-handed drove them forward. The Raven in

Tamber's head laughed mockingly.

They entered Tang lands across a broad stream troubled by a roaring waterfall. The forest gave way to tangled masses of oak and birch and yellow lani They found a woodcutters track and followed it cautiously, sending out scouts with the meskini for this land was unfamiliar to them. As dusk fell, after the scouts had returned, Sesk called them to a halt.

The demon in Tamber spoke through Tamber. "One league ahead is a village. Attack it tonight. Death calls to the Tang and you must answer his call."

Sesk looked as if he might argue, and clouds of doubt darkened his eyes. The men stared at Tamber, their faces hard and unsmiling.

They knew -for better or worse- this was to be the culmination of what they had set out to do.

***

They crawled close to the Tang village on their hands on knees. The darkness was a heavy shawl and the silence made Tamber uneasy.

Sesk had spilt his forces, his plan to attack from east and west at once. Small was in charge of their small party and they had been crawling for hours along the damp floor of the forest, a light fog playing about them. By Tamber's reckoning they had to be in place, behind the village.

So why could he not hear the barking of dogs, or the muffled sounds of a village at night;

children crying, people copulating, chatting, laughing.

The silence was gelid.

He crawled forward beside Small on his hands and knees. Through the undergrowth he had a view of a half dozen mud huts, firewood heaped beside them.

The village was dark, absent all light. No fires burned, no lights shone.

"Where are they all?" Small said, the muttered words disappearing in the frigid silence, like a frightened gasp at the end of the world.

Terror like the memory of childhood horror reverberated in Tamber's soul. Ghouls and goblins and the keen of a midnight wind.

He shook the fear away and tried to think it through. What was Raven leading them into. Either, the Tang knew they were coming and had abandoned their homes or something had happened to them; neither thought was particularly cheering. If the Tang knew of the presence of Malai in the area they would have hardly have left without a fight, especially not against such a small band of warriors.

So the Tang might be lying in the darkness waiting for the Malai to attack, but if so why had they not set their trap carefully; lit fires, posted sentries made a pretense of occupation. That was what Tamber or any half-competent leader would have done.

This absence of sound made no sense unless the Tang were already dead.

A fresh chill of fear trembled through

Tamber.

Raven had sunk deep within him, but Tamber had a renewed sense that the demon was chortling happily.

He knows something we don't, Tamber realized. Something other than the Tang lies in wait for us here, something that we should not meet.

He sidled closer to Small, silently praying the giant would still listen to his advice, when he heard the loud bellow of a Malai warcry ordering an attack.

Sesk, the blind fool. Could he, of all people, not sense that something was wrong? The old man's senses must have been blunted by this chance of testing his wits against Raven. That or his desire not to be seen to fail.

Tamber hesitated for a second, as Small and the others piled forward screaming, but knew he had no choice. Where a warleader led the warrior was bound to follow and Sesk was warcaptain now, for the swordless, babbling Tamber was in disgrace.

Tamber stood, drew his skiri from his belt. His men were already on their feet, moving forward waving their long tintuk blades.

He sprinted after them, up a short grassy hill, past a boneworker's pit brimming with piles of bleached yellow bone, past a wooden stockade empty of livestock, and into the southern end of the deserted village.

They roared as they ran; shrill battle cries to frighten the spirits of their enemy.

The battle cries died quickly in their throats, caught like echoes of spirits heard at the Dawning of the Year, when the soft stomach of autumn was knifed by the chill blade of winter winds.

They pulled up near a darkened hut. The stench of death and rot and spilled blood was unmistakable; Tamber thought he could feel reverberations of pain in the air, tremors from the past, memories of fear.

Sesk and the other warriors had stopped outside a long wattle and daub hut, the chieftain's hut from the look of it, surrounded by a low wooden palisade.

Tamber yelled at stunned men to flee and sprinted to where Sesk stood, staring at whatever was within the palisade, like a man witnessing his own death in the haze of the future.

"Run, damn it!"

Sesk and the others ignored him, their eyes fixed to the contents of the palisade.

"Sesk! It's a trap!"

Sesk did not move and when Tamber turned his head to check on the men he had been leading he saw that they too were stunned and immobile like rabbits frightened by the fire-brands of hunters.

Tamber careened into the man standing beside Sesk staring at the palisade. The man grunted and moved out of the way but otherwise did not react.

Tamber peered over the top of the palisade. A mound of slaughtered corpses, all tossed together like faggots at the back of a woodcutters shop, lay heaped in front of the door.

Men, women and children butchered and cut to pieces.

On sharpened wooden stakes were a ring of skulls, half-eaten, grinning back at them. Tamber tried to pull back from their horrific gaze, but the power of the ring was too strong; voices cried out in fear, shrieked the terror of final pain. This had been no ordinary massacre. A strange fey magic had been worked here. He could feel himself falling under its spell- the will to run fleeing as he stood facing the skulls, a dim awareness crying from the back of his mind that by staying he was inviting death.

He didn't have long to wait

Out of the trees they came, silent as deer. The Malai warriors, feeling their approach like the warning of an approaching storm, turned to meet them, weapons not drawn or trailing low in their hands. They smelled of the earth from which they had come, from which they had clawed their way towards light, a dense bitter smell at once peaty and sickening.

A warband of thirty or more, led by a giant who stood a head taller than Tamber. Warriors, they carried obsidian swords, each the length of a man and inscribed with painted runes, they wore thick pelts of hide, of musk-bear and walray and jaguar. Some wore flayed animal pelts on their heads, faces barely visible behind gaping jaws. The rest wore bone helms, decorated with thick crimson feathers that made them seem taller, more fierce. They carried wooden shields bossed with a

108

strange, cool metal that reminded Tamber of starlight glinting on snow. The leader carried a totem pole on a lattice of wood on his back, decorated with brilliant feathers and the skulls of animals and men. They strode forward, unhurried and sure in their approach, in two even tows of fifteen.

They looked not unlike the Malai- tall and gray haired and broad of shoulder- but if they were Malai their insignia were of no tribe that Tamber had ever seen.

A chill emanated from them, blew before them like a winter wind. Their flesh was lined. Dry as the barkweed tents the inlanders built. Their hair was long, matted with dirt. As were their nails, long as the sharp knifes of the Moonpeople.

Tamber's intestines curdled as the men approached silently, slowly, with the stately grace of jaguars.

A voice inside him screamed. The dead walk.

A panicked childish voice, the voice of the boy who had lain alone in his father's hall and listened to a shrill wind howling outside, unable to sleep, aware of evil forms flitting through the air, of the dark spirits in the forest taunting, a boy who once had prayed those spirits would not come for him.

He knew. These things were revenants, their souls long since fled, though somehow life still imbued them and they had returned to share the space of the living. Come from a dark place, a place of silence and fear to claim Tamber's life

109

and his soul.

Their eyes held a deep blue chill, like pools in the depth of winter as the clouds roar and the light fails.

The fey spell from the ring of skulls broke suddenly, no longer needed. Small let out a blood thirty cry and ran at these newcomers, his tintuk sword flashing through the air.

One of the revenants stepped forward to meet him, parrying with his long stone sword. Small ducked under a lazy swing and sliced his blade across the revenant's chest, cutting through pelt and flesh as if through butter.

The revenant slipped to its knees, falling in slow motion.

Small turned his head and grinned at them, his typical gormless smile.

This will be easy, that grin said, for these men are slow, their weapons inferior and we are Malai and proud.

The revenant rose to his feet, in one smooth movement, and swung his sword over his shoulder and down. The stone keened as it sped through the air. Small had no time to react and the blade sliced through his skull and down into his chest, cutting him in half, as an ax splits a log,

He tumbled to the ground and the revenant grunted and said something in a strange, liquid language.

It smiled, drawing thin lips back over long teeth, and roared a bull-like warcry, a violent sound that caused Tamber's legs to liquefy.

Sesk tried to rally the others; he ran forward

dancing on one leg like a stork, weaving circles with his windbaiter staff, spitting curses at the newcomers.

One of the revenant warriors drew a blade, its handle amber, from the belt of his baldric and with a slow, unhurried wave of his hand cast it at Sesk. The blade spun through the air and took Sesk in the eye. The hilt of the blade, like a root, glowed bluely as Sesk continued to dance his intricate steps, apparently unaware of what had happened.

The warrior who had thrown the blade closed the distance to Sesk. With one hand he pushed the shaman to his knees then cupped the Sesk's chin as he withdrew the blade.

The shaman screamed and an aura swirled about the blade, something alive with fire like the essence of flame.

The warrior licked the blade with a tongue dark as a piece of dried jerky and Sesk screamed even louder, before collapsing in an empty heap on the ground like the husk of a corn left too long in the sun. The warrior bent over the corpse and severed the neck, and rose holding Sesk's head as a bloody trophy.

His hand, Tamber noted, was veined with blue like moldy bread.

The Malai edged away, terror in their eyes as the revenants closed about them, eyes glittering with detached amusement.

Tamber ran for his life, past the palisade, aiming for the forest on the far side of the village. He watched Malai warriors fall about him, and knew his time too had come.

Two of the revenants appeared in front of him, broad giants with weapons drawn. Tamber veered to avoid them and they did not move, did not come after him.

He reached the treeline and kept running, the forest floor littered with leaves crunching as he ran. Brambles whipped at his face, ripped his clothes, but he kept running, stumbling down steep levees, crossing streams. He fell and smashed a knee against an uneven jaw of granite leering from brown earth and humus. He forced himself to his feet, running, limping, running, till his lungs were fire and he knew his heart must explode.

Exhausted he fell against the knobby bole of holm oak, stilling his breathing, listening for pursuit.

There was none.

How could there be, you fool? a voice inside asked. You alone were meant to survive, you alone have been saved.

Raven cackled.

Though I fear you may soon realize you have no reason to be grateful for this bounty.

Raven's voice came from deep inside him, a voice heard thin and faint like the voice of a man fallen into a well.

Always remember, arrogant child, this was not done on your account. I own an interest in the warp of the future. I bind you now to remember what I told you in the cave, to hold that knowledge like a jewel. Remember, too, the secret of rebirth. The soil may give back its dead when asked nicely. You just have to know how. Remember and when the time comes you will know what to do with these.

The voice faded away. Raven rose from him on beating wings, the smell of dark and rotten meat overpowering as it left Tamber alone beneath the trees, in a land distant from his home. He had soiled himself in his flight, his hands shook like palsied leaves in an autumn wind and fear had penetrated and paralyzed every inch of him.

He wept, head in his hands, rocking backward and forward.

It wasn't meant to be like this, this shame, this defeat.

As a child he had dreamed of being Tamber the Hero, and in his childish play he had known with a deep certainty he was not destined to fail.

Now, here he lay, on the damp ground as wisps of fog grew about him, and fear trembled him, inside and out.

His dream of warrior glory tasted of ash in his mouth, a taste that sickened and depressed him.

And if Tamber the warrior was dead, who was he now? Who had he become? What future could there be for him?

This was not how it was meant to be.

***

He woke the next day- bone frozen, fear still a deep echo in his heart- and started to his feet.

113

The forest was silent, absent the sounds of birds and other animals, and laughter in the distance, mocked him.

His world had caved in. The membrane between the world of the dead and the living had crumbled; the laughter he heard was the voices of the dead, the men who had set out with him from the village, on the strength of his vision.

He heard Sesk, alternately laughing and crying. Yangnan. Small. Keklah Keli. The others. All dead.

Look at us now, they laughed. Food for carrion. See how the birds chew on our eyes and the wolves and the lions, the walray and the meskini tear our limbs apart.

See what you have wrought with us Tamber, son of Lantuk, hero of the Yangmpabat.

He ran through the forest, heedless of branches snapping at his face, heedless of the pain when he fell into gullies and tripped over the fallen boles of trees.

A pack of walray led by a yellow-eyed monster shadowed him, scavengers sensing he was alone. He ran at them, wielding a heavy branch he had found, screaming like a madman.

That night he found a place to shelter in the trunk of an old oak. Large branches rose from the bole, making a tent of leaves and leaving him a place to sit and rest. He had gathered berries in the day and stuffed them in his mouth, not tasting them as their juices trickled down his chin like blood.

When he slept the dead did not relent, they

114

chased his spirit, their thin bodies like gossamer their voices a constant din. He heard the voice of his grandmother, of the brothers he had lost as a child. He heard the clamor of Pugi, screaming at him in hate and fear.

Behind all was Raven, and behind Raven a cold white light whose presence he could feel but not hear, sense but not see.

When he awoke it was yellow dawn, the light thin and surreal. That morning he fished with his hands near the bend of a green river, his feet sinking to his ankles on the marshy bank as he climbed onto a weir and waited for the salmon to come. When he caught a fish he slammed it quickly on a rock to stop its wriggling then tore it apart with his hands and ate it raw.

His belly sated he ran again from the voices that trailed him, ran till his heart was beating fast as a drum and his breath was a hurricane in his mouth, and the voices were stilled for a brief moment.

He lay his head down and slept again.

He lived that way for half a year, the days passing in a blur of terror as the plaints of the dead grew ever louder, and they came ever closer to him, so he imagined he could smell their rot and feel their cold, blue hands caress him.

One morning he woke, winter a burgeoning shawl drawing down upon the land, and the ghosts were gone. A pair of galls screeched overhead and yalla birds were singing their plaintive winter tune. His beard hung to his chest, and his hair was matted with dirt and worse. His face in the freezing water of the river was barely recognizable even to himself- a hollowed version of the man he had been.

He washed his face in the water, smiling sadly at his reflection.

For better or worse it was time he went home.

***

A small group of children playing near parents collecting firewood spotted him first, shrieked. Alerted, the wood gatherers watched his approach with wary stillness. Some of the men bared their weapons, though he was clearly alone and, bar the puny spear he bore in his hand, unarmed.

They escorted him to the Great Hall to the sound of wailing aranyx horns. Keklah Keli the shaman and his brother, Tan, the silent one, stood shoulder to shoulder at the door. Tamber's father came rushing forward but stopped some distance away, staring aghast at the state of Tamber's dress.

Upakahun, the chief appeared from the Great Hall, his body even more bloated by the fouled water destroying his body. He stared balefully at Tamber.

"Where are the others boy?"

Tamber shook his head and glanced at his father. The old man turned away and Tamber knew what must happen next.

"And Aburapadak?"

"The witch was dead when we arrived."

116

"Yangnan?"

"Him, I killed..."

"What happened to the others?"

Tamber harbored no illusions. Upakahun hated him for his youth and arrogance and wanted him dead. Without evidence of wrongdoing or cowardice he would settle for gone. Tamber was still a tongued one and was due a trial of faith or blood but stories of dead men walking would be interpreted as lies and give Upakahun all the leverage he needed. Upakahun's shaman would scorn him and torture him till they told them what they wanted to hear, no matter how far from the truth. Stories of the living dead would serve no purpose but to visit shame on his family.

"The Tang jumped us," Tamber lied.

"When you killed Yangnan who assumed the role of leader?"

"I did."

"So you led them to their deaths, warleader."

Tamber tensed.

"And yet you still live. Did you run Tamber? Show the Tang your back like a woman? Did you lie down and beg for your life? Did you betray your men for your worthless existence?"

A large crowd had gathered around them in a circle. Tamber knew the faces of everyone in that tight round of humanity, as well as he knew his own. People he had known them all his life; uncles, aunts, friends, cousins.

The sister of his long-dead mother who had been like a mother to him.

His own father.

His three brothers.

One and all they stared at him with the eyes of strangers, faces swelling with anger, their bodies drunk on latent violence.

"Warleader. Where are your men?"

The crowd growled, a voice all but one, united in disgust.

"They died well. Honor their souls as heroes."

"Receiver of prophecies. All vanity..."

Upakahun spat at Tamber. Tamber lunged, fists clenched, but half a dozen braves rushed forward to hold him back before he reached the chief.

Upakahun pulled back behind his shaman, torn by a racking cough that went on for a long time.

When the coughing stopped he stepped closer to Tamber, face puce.

"Your vision was a lie, a deceit so you could have your own warband, so you could earn a name for yourself."

So I could take your place when the time came, Tamber thought sourly. That is what has got your back, up you old goat. And he was not wrong. The Tamber who left the village all those long months ago had thought like that, had seen a future for himself as chieftain of the tribe, had wallowed in pride and called it bravery.

Things had changed since then, he had experienced too much of suffering and death.

Tamber smiled and those who saw him smile growled, taking it as affirmation. A heady mix of

118

excitement, of rushing blood, an outpouring of sweat, rose from the crowd.

"You ran to save your own hide!"

"No!" Tamber stood his ground though the circle was closing in on him. "I stood with them but they died. I survived. Nothing more."

Upakahun laughed scornfully.

Angry now, Tamber pointed at Upakahun. "My prophecy is true old man. Raven has spoken. He will chew your gizzards if you butcher me."

Tamber saw the hesitation on the older man's face. To claim to be an oracle of the Raven was a grave boast, one that should be tested, but Upakahun's hatred was too great. Greater for once than his caution.

He waved his hand in dismissal "Let him run the gauntlet. If he survives let him crawl away from here and never show his face again. The one known as Tamber no longer exists."

A growl of affirmation from the crowd, with no dissenting voices, not even Tamber's father who had other sons to care for. The will of the tribe was clear.

They dragged him from the hall to the edge of the village. Two lines were made, villagers and slaves, the young and the old, wielding whatever weapon blunt weapons they saw fit, though some stretched the definition of what was allowed with mattocks of hardwood and clubs sided with blunt obsidian. They tried to take the spear from him, but he refused. "Kill me first," he spat back into their face. "I will use it against no one here today." He snarled. "Not at this time."

119

The men guarding him discussed the issue quietly then made Tamber swear an oath on the life of his father that he would not wield the spear against a member of the tribe.

When he was done they sounded the orynx.

Tamber started to walk, for he was not allowed to run. The villagers pummeled him, with fist and wood and stone. They cast stones at him and spat in his face.

He fell twice, both times to his knees, before reaching the half way mark.

He fell for the last time near the end of that tunnel of pain and hate and crawled the last ten spans, a long eternity of agony. His father stood at the end, a tintuk club with a balled knot of maple in its wooden jaw. As last in line, it was his choice whether Tamber lived or died. Tamber crawled to his sandaled feet and laid his head down, nestling the man's feet as he had done as a baby.

He sensed his father raise the club. Tamber waited for death, but his father let out a long agonized shriek and cast the weapon in the direction of the crowd.

He, for one, still believed in Tamber, though Tamber knew he could do more than grant this gift of life.

His father left, the crowds drifted away and Tamber drifted into unconsciousness, blackness taking him, though, even in the dark peace of his mind, his being was filled with the knowledge of pain.

When he woke it was dark and pain splintered him from head to foot. He crab-crawled from the village one painful inch at a time. When the sun rose, before unconsciousness took him again, he glanced over his shoulder. He had made less than two hundred spans.

When he woke again he was frozen, his hands blue, the pain like nothing he had ever experienced. A pack of hounds from the village stood looking at him with snarling curiosity. He growled and they moved away, but not far.

People passed him by, carrying water from the stream, trade goods for nearby villages. Children came and teased him, throwing stones till their elders drove them away.

Tamber did not exist and could neither be aided nor hindered.

He crawled for the next day, and the next, settling into a numbing pattern of pain and cold. On the third day he found he could stand. He stumbled forward for the best part of a day and towards evening came upon the slaughtered corpse of a jay. He beat away the scavengers who were scrambling for its meat, and on his knees he tore flesh from the scaled beast's body and fed. The tough, bloody meat hit his stomach like kai-wine and lent him strength to walk through the night till he came to Sesk's cave. He built a fire with wood gathered in the corner of the cave and made a tisane of willow bark and vervain from among Sesk's supplies. The pain ebbed and he lay back on bedding that still stank of the dead sorcerer and slept.

When he woke he grabbed his spear and forced weary, pained legs to the frothing sea. He speared two silver-tails and a kaily, gathered a sack full of mollusks, rekindled the embers of his fire and cooked one of the fish, after salting the rest of his food.

With his belly full, his pain dimmed by the tea, he laid his head back on the matting.

He had not been wrong; the world he knew was in danger. The beetle men would come. This at last he knew.

His trial of soul and body meant something.

Tamber would be the keeper of the flame, the one man who would keep the memory alive of what had been ordained. Sesk had died so he, Tamber, could take the old man's place.

An outcast who was the beacon of the future.

The spirits had given him the spear, and useless as that might seem now, it too had meaning. He would bide his time for the flame of truth burnt deep within him.

CHAPTER 4 - EDO

On a stone bench on the Hill of Sores, high above the harbor of Milese, capital of the Empire of Milesia, Edo watched the tide come in. Turquoise water stretched to a bright infinity as light glinted on gently rolling water and surf crept politely higher onto sandy beaches.

Across the breadth of the bay wind filled the sails of tall galleys and low-slung dhows. Edo counted a hundred ships already docked; the throng of accent and language from the cross-shaped quay a dinning babble. The smell of tar, salt, the rot of fish guts dumped in the sun, perfumed spices wrapped in cotton and laden on wooden pallets, filled his nose.

Ocean distance and ocean depths. Melancholy. So melancholy.

He drank deep of the earthenware jug he cradled in his hands. A passerby, a man in a long robe of russet leading his young son by the hand, stepped deep onto the cobbled street to avoid him.

Edo's perch, his temporary home since the whores he had guarded had kicked him out for being rowdy again, was a stone bench beneath a tall crowned acacia tree.

He was far from home and hearth and his soul was an empty void.

***

In Kallingtorn they had taken Edo to the vast

expanse of the courtyard, a dusty quadrangle of ochre-colored earth, dry at the time of year, so sand drifted, whirled, forming uneasy spirits in the gusts of winds blown down the mountain.

The massed ranks of the Longhorn fifth were drawn up, hard at attention, shields and spears to hand. They beat the spears as he appeared and howled abuse at him.

In front of the massive stone barracks they tied a wooden collar about his neck, bound him with chains to an upright pillar of thick and ancient oak, black with the spilled blood of a thousand floggings and executions. Másberia the Domin accepted responsibility for the job- for he had taken the bribe for Edo's commission and Edo had become his mistake to rectify. The Domin Lar smashed Edo's arms with large white stones then beat his legs with a blacksmith´s massive hammer pounding bones to pulp. When Edo fainted the warlocks laid hands on him and dragged him back to consciousness with nightmares worse than the reality he was being forced to endure. In a red fog of pain Edo opened his eyes in time to see Másberia raise the blood-spattered hammer over his head again.

He screamed as the hammer fell and, it seemed, in a place deep within him, he had never stopped screaming since.

Sweating Másberia had turned from Edo to the brand heating in a metal brazier. The Domin wiped the sweat from his eyes with his sleeve and pulled the red-hot brand from the fire coals. He stood over Edo and snarled as he rammed it forward.

Despite the currents of pain that had swept through him as his flesh seared and burnt it was the contempt in Másberia's look that caused Edo the most pain.

They left him in the stocks for two days then took him to the prison infirmary where he was kept on his own in a dark room. The warlocks tended him well, their magic accelerating his healing; they even showed him some small degree of kindness. Months later, the year having turned and the snow melted, he was healed well enough and two burly guards came to his room, marched him to the main gate. Stumbling on weakened muscles, naked but for a ragged cloak about his shoulders and a breechcloth about his loins, they cast Edo into the streets of the city. The barracks gate closed behind him with terrible finality.

He found a boarding room, made money working for a sutler and when he was strong enough took the first ship he found that would take him on as a deckhand.

In the years since passed he had avoided Aonia and Aonians, dared not even think of his brother. Shame was his all and everything. When he jumped ship in Milese that dark stain on his soul refused to whiten and the clouds hung over him like incense.

***

He woke with a start from cascaded nightmares.

Night fell in a mad rush of purple, pink and orange. Clouds in the almost cloudless sky turned golden, then crimson before the dark reached out like a stain to swallow them.

He stumbled to his feet, mouth parched, a cold chill infesting his empty gut.

He reached for his jug of wine but it was empty. The harbor was quiet now. Ships with sails furled bobbed uncertainly on a freshening sea breeze.

The pain and panic hit him with a force like a tornado.

He needed food. Most of all he needed wine. His tunic, gray and tattered, hung loose on his large frame. He searched its pockets for the iron nuggets called sphinx that passed for money in the trough of society he lived.

He had nothing.

Panic threatened to overwhelm him.

Pain thumped his skull as he staggered to his feet. Nearby was a fountain spraying water, topped by a stone statue of the goddess Ismai, in the form of a naked sea-nymph. Staggering towards it he submersed his head in the chill water and rose spluttering, shaking long hair from his eyes, catching a glimpse of himself, a faint image only in the darkening water. The face was that of a stranger; only the traitor's brand etched on his forehead let him know who he still was. Who he would always be.

He wiped the water from his eyes with the sleeve of his tunic and set of into this massive walled city of a million souls.

***

The wide, cobbled streets were tree-lined and laid out in grids, at the crossroads an ornate drinking fountain centering a plaza where inhabitants gathered like squawking pigeons. Windowless white-washed buildings fronted the streets. Odors of lavender and jasmine drifted through the city streets mixed with the smell of blood from the slaughterhouse and the smell of cooking meat from hundreds of road-side stands.

He made his long way east, past the Plaza of Souls and the camel racing stadium, to the La'mai Kalin, the embrasure of souls; a poor district where inns, cafes and cheap eateries lined the streets.

Beneath the mosaic dome of the Hal Ra Kalin- the house of the Middle Gods- he saw a stall selling shwar-chicken and dormice. Cheap food for poor families but still food that _he_ could not afford.

Lights from brasiers on stilts tended by slaves lent the street an orange glow and in its light Edo spotted that the stall owner, busy packing up his stall, had leftovers on a metal platter-chicken pieces and a sheaf of flat bread, probably stale.

Edo stood in front of the stall. When the man turned, noticing him, Edo lowered his head, gestured at the food and opened his hands to indicate his lack of gelt.

The owner, heavy set in a dirty linen robe rancid with grease, gestured at him to leave.

127

"For the love of Yanik," Edo pleaded, eyes cast down.

"Fuck off back to whatever foreign hole you crept from," the man replied.

The hole in Edo's stomach had become a cavern. His head beat and his hands shook. Before the stall owner could react he grabbed a handful of warm chicken and some bread and legged it. The man bellowed. Footsteps sounded. Edo glanced back.

The stall owner was chasing after him, in his right hand a wooden cudgel, his face red with fury.

Edo dashed it into a sidesteet, pushing aside a group of young men who glared at him as at a disturbed cockroach. He leapt a wooden cart filled with olives and ducked into the second side street to the left. The stall owner was dropping behind, his muffled cries carrying a note of tired desperation. Edo turned again, relying on the warren of the city to get him away, but ran into a long narrow alley blocked at one end. High walls surrounded him on all sides and the alley stank of hurried sex and excrement and rotten food.

He turned to flee but the stall owner shadowed the lighted entrance to the alley, smacking his cudgel against his off hand, grunting with happiness at this renewed sighting of his prey. The boys Edo had pushed aside had followed the stall owner, attracted to the prospect of violence like sharks to blood.

The stall owner hesitated as Edo turned to face them- Edo was a head taller and broader than any of them and his silver hair and yellow eyes marked him out as Aonian.

Aonians were bred to be warriors, the stall owner wasn't and the street kids just wanted some excitement to relieve the deadening monotony of their lives.

They hesitated.

Despite himself Edo cringed, lowered his head. The stall owner smelled fear and charged swinging his cudgel. Edo dropped to the ground, wrapped himself in a ball as the cudgel smashed into his back and the street kids starting lamming into him with their bare feet.

Pain seared through him, pain in waves like an ancient message from his nerves.

Pain he knew all too well. The memories scoured deep rose like bile in a drunkard's throat.

***

He awoke wracked by pain, waves of nausea dizzying him as he tried to sit up. He took stock. One eye was swollen and closed. His face was a welter of abrasions and his cheek was a thickening melon.

Blood tasted metallic in his mouth and his cloak and most of his clothes had been ripped from him.

The stall owner and the kids were gone, satisfied no doubt with their sport.

He sat against the cool wall and painfully brought his knees up to his chest.

He cried, sobs wracking from him. He had

fallen so far, so quickly that the world no longer made sense. His own fault, he knew. Greed and ancient dreams had brought him low but each time he thought he had reached the bottom of the pit he just kept falling.

A shadow, silhouetted by distant street-light, traced the entrance to the alley. Edo tensed as fear coursed in his blood anew.

If they had come back it could mean only one thing- they wanted everything he had to give. They wanted his life.

The strange thing was- Edo almost welcomed them. Their threat was like an offer, a gift of the quietness of death

The shadow moved forward, massive hands held palm down, a posture signifying a lack of threat.

"Let me help you, friend."

The voice held a gentle modulation that was almost childlike, though Edo could see from the bulk of the shoulders that this was no child.

Edo squirmed closer to the wall. If it wasn't the stall owner of the kids, come back to finish their bloody work, then who was it?

The shadow spoke again. "I mean you no harm. Yanik would not allow that."

Edo breathed a deep sigh of relief.

A monk of Yanik, the god of charity and hope, a god the Emperor was dedicated to above all others.

"I need medicine, food," Edo's spoke thickly his heart still hammering.

The monk moved close to Edo. He wore a

130

long cloak of simple linen hanging to just above his ankles and had his hair plaited in two long horns tied from the nape of his skull to the forehead. A series of tattoos, black points almost joined in semi-circles, spread from his eyes denoting the ripples of tears Yanik had shed when he sacrificed himself and his family for the old Emperor and the City of Garlin.

The man was a Eunuch- all Yanik's monks were- and his body was ridged and muscled fat. A livid scar sliced his face in two, making a ruin of his nose.

That scar he had not gotten as a priest.

A monk with a past.

"Come with me," the Priest's eyes were thin slits but with a gentle gleam that reminded Edo of moonlight in ponds of stagnant water.

"I don't think I can stand."

The monk leaned close to Edo, the sweet unguents he had used in his public bath like a delicate reminder of gentler days.

Edo could not remember the last time he had bathed.

"Lean on me, my friend. In the name of blessed Yanik I offer you sanctuary."

He touched Edo's shoulder and something in that touch, a coil of yellow energy that invaded his body and spread through it, dulled his pain.

On the monk's arm he staggered to his feet.

"You are one of Yanik's lost souls now, my son. Fear not for his mercy will keep you safe."

***

131

They walked for miles, Edo gasping from pain needing to rest more and more often, towards the vibrant heart of Milese, the unsleeping city. Loaded carts heaped with grain for the wall-side bakeries, and olives, lemons, oranges and figs for the markets convoyed along cobbled streets.

Dealers sold figurines of diamond and jet, blackwood harps from Incann, ivory horns from Jali and polished scales of the Iptong from Halla.

A million people clawing, a million voices clamoring, the stink of a million lives lived in cramped quarters.

It had overwhelmed Edo at first and then, despite the traitor's brand on his forehead, it had swallowed him whole. In its gut he was invisible.

No one knew him. None cared what he had done.

For that invisibility he would always be grateful.

Even now in the dead of night a sulfurous haze of smoke rose from the mil-fire workshops in the eastern precinct. They stumbled along the portico of a large public bath, a statue in front of its gates that of Yanik, gentle eyes raised heavenward. Around the god's head floated clouds of tart smoke from the ramshackle tenement nestled to the right of the baths; the familiar smell of gingis weed, the afflicted within lying on reed mats, sucking smoke into their lungs, soaring to the heavens on the wings of the gingis falcon.

Close to the center of town stood large

marble villas surrounded by tranquil parks, each with at least one artificial lake dedicated to one of the twenty gods, the lakes surrounded by the forbidden trees of the Emperor's aviaries on which meely birds sang day and night, their song the harmony of the inner city.

On a soaring column close to the wall of the largest walled villa stood a second, more massive statue of Yanik; on his knees in a simple gray cloak, bright green eyes awash with silver tears as he beseeched his brothers in heaven to save the emperor.

Edo paused to stare as they strode past, awed as always.

"Don't dawdle, man. You still have the smell of Aonia. The guards might take it in their fancy that you are a spy and boil you in sweetoil for the fun of it."

The monk sounded amused.

Edo took the man's proffered arm and they started forward again, slowly painfully.

"What do they call you, monk?" Edo asked, his voice hollow sounding, as from the bottom of a bucket.

"Balin, when they are being kind."

"Balin? That is no Milesian name."

"My dad was of Scia. I was born here."

Edo gestured at the man's ruined nose. "You strike me as an unlikely holy man. You did not earn that in any monastery."

"The paths we tred are the mystery of the gods. So it is said."

"Yanik, I presume?"

133

"Actually no. That was my mother. Clever old bat, she was." Balin smiled. "Save your breath and walk, Aonian. It is not far to the temple but I fear your strength fails."

***

The temple was in a walled compound east of the sprawling Emperor's palace. A tonsured monk signed a greeting prayer as he opened the gate and stood aside to let them enter. Beyond the walls was the garden of paradise. Beds of bluesimmon and white tear were islands amongst oceans of grass. Olive and cedar trees and purple shrub-like trees whose flowers smelled like lemon towered over the flowerbeds. A stream wound gently past the trees, the water moon-painted as it murmured through the grass. A fountain burbled on a plaza of marble in the center of the garden near the sprawl of buildings housing the monks.

A domed prayer hall, painted vibrant colors, and a long low building occupied most of the eastern quadrant of the walled compound.

"The Sanctuary. Where the indigent and we monks sleep. We have healers." Balin sounded worried. "Just a few more steps, Aonian. A few more."

Edo nodded and made to move forward. He toppled forward onto cool grass.

The darkness swam to meet him. He dived into it like a sweating man into water.

***

Consciousness returned in stages. A hand rubbed his forehead, the fingers cool and dry and gentle. He was reminded of his mother, of their bright house on a hill in Deira. Of the sea stretching blue into the bright infinity of the west.

He remembered how happy they had been, till the plague came and the riots began.

He missed her, more than anybody.

Her death still left an empty hole in his heart.

"Aonian, are you awake?"

The voice was a man's, yet soft and modulated.

Balin?

He blinked awake. He was lying on a low bed, topped by a thin cloth mattress. The room was a small cell. A lone window in the far wall let in butter-yellow light, outlining a thrush perched on the windowsill warbling a sweet and beautiful song.

Pain assaulted Edo from every part of his body.

He thought of alcohol and a shudder passed through him. He remembered...nightmares. Waking. Screaming for wine and gingis weed. Pulling himself from his bed. Arms, gentle but firm holding him down, feeding him a cloying mixture of herbs and honey that had made him want to throw up.

"How long?" he gasped.

"A week. You drifted in and out. When you woke the cravings took over so we laid hands on you...helped you rest."

"Am I a prisoner here?"

Balin laughed. "Yanik's offers sanctuary to those who need it and wish it. You are free to leave whenever you desire."

Edo lay back on the bed.

The swelling on his face had gone down. He ran his tongue along his teeth. Two rough gaps. Two teeth less to worry about. His ribs were still sore and when he moved bruises ached. All in all, he had come away lightly.

He levered himself to a sitting position.

Balin moved back to give him space. Nausea threatened to overwhelm Edo but he breathed deep, fighting it off.

It passed.

"Where are my clothes?'

"I burnt your rags. The brotherhood has funds, thanks to the Emperor's generosity. In the wooden casket at the foot of the bed are new clothes. Cheap but well made."

Edo nodded his thanks and swung his legs from the bed.

The only thought in his mind was alcohol. He could be in his favorite tavern in Lamai Kalin in an hour. He would work. They would feed him and he could help himself to the wine.

When he had enough money he might even risk a night on the wings of the gingis.

He pulled himself up on the bed. Balin was looking at him, eyebrows raised.

"Move aside, priest," Edo growled.

Balin smiled and edged towards the door.

"You will not keep me here against my will."

Balin smiled inscrutably. Edo got dressed. Balin waited and when Edo was ready he pushed open the door to the narrow cell.

Sanctuary was a dark wooden building with high ceilings, divided not into rooms in any linear fashion but full of nooks and crevices and tiny cell-like rooms. Voices drifted and echoed as if ghosts were holding prayer.

Edo sensed eyes upon them as Balin led the way towards the double doors in the distance.

Eyes full of pain and terror, eyes full of grief and crazed longing.

"The doomed are welcome here," Balin whispered. "We can help you."

"Keep your doom. Feed me wine," Edo barked.

He reached the doors, pulled open the left wing and stepped outside. Light hit him in a blue wash and as he blinked the sun-blindness away his soul soared. Fellfares in the tree sang a delicate song, an old monk with a gray tonsure knelt beside a bed of Old Matron, their purple leaves in bloom. With a trowel the man dug into damp earth and pulled a plant out by the roots.

He held it gently, almost reverently as he replanted it in a new spot nearby.

Two children, a boy and a girl were splashing in the water of the small stream. A young man and a young woman lay asleep in one another's arms on a bed of deep grass like a mattress as poppies swayed around them like the dreams of their young hearts. A group of men, some of them monks were standing, heads lowered in prayer

137

before a statue of Yanik.

Yanik- the god's gray eyes reminded Edo of the eyes of his father as he had once been. Before Mother's death and the madness that followed. Deep and inscrutable like a winter sky but with a boundless reservoir of love.

Edo fell to his knees awestruck.

The world was revealed to him anew, in all its simple, glorious wonder.

The weight of wine and gingis weed left his mind, the fat hissing monkey riding his shoulder taking its leave, for good he hoped. Balin laid a hand on Edo's shoulder.

"Welcome to Sanctuary, Edo. Praise be to Yanik, you are with us now."

***

Time passed. Days, blending into weeks, then months. Edo spent time in the garden with the monks, planting flowers and tending trees. They harvested the autumn fruit and had a celebration feast after a day of prayer and thanksgiving. Edo found that, in the midst of these quiet, honest men, a strange peace settled on him, a peace both deep and profound. He could sit for hours in the garden watching cloud shadows drift across the grass, pushing white butterflies ahead of them as he listened to the sounds of bird song and the slow murmur of water.

He and Balin became friends and spent their evenings together. Balin had been a soldier. Edo found that this gave them something in common-a bone deep awareness of violence that still haunted their dreams, something neither would ever escape.

"I was in a cadre of marines attached to the Emperor's Own," Balin confided in Edo on his second week in Sanctuary, one evening as they sat together by a roaring fire. "The previous Emperor, not this one. Our new man is a man of religion, not conquest."

"He can afford to be," Edo snorted. "He has a ring of high walls around his city and gracone cannons stuffed with mil-fire to protect him."

Balin shrugged and smiled. "They sent us north. The relics of the Lalik lived there among the Incann tribes of the north. We had learned of their intent; they planned on forming alliances with the demon shie, of renewing their attacks on our empire. We met their massed armies on the Plain of Lagros. Our backs were to a Yanik-cursed river and we had nowhere to run." He muttered something that might have been a quiet curse in Scian. "Our generals were fools."

"The one commonplace of all armies," Edo said, smiling without humor.

"They lured us into their trap then attacked. Thousands of them, two heads taller than the tallest man, each as broad as a cart. They stood upright, twin ridges like horns on their heads, mouths more muzzle than anything else. The long spears they carried were like lances. After the battle I tried one out. I could barely lift, never mind wield, it. As they came at us, our sappers threw wooden caskets of mil-fire. The caskets

139

exploded, burning hundreds of them but they still they came for us howling. I was in the wall of shields, terrified. And I was not alone. Men pissed themselves. Many ran. They smashed our lines in a moment and then began to slaughter us." His eyes misted with memory and its pain. "My brother, Arkil was my right shield. One of their bulls caught him a in a hug like a vice and wrung Arkil's head from his shoulders." Balin made a twisting motion with his hands, like someone twisting a chicken's neck. "They fed on our blood."

"Yet you won."

Balin barked a hard laugh. "The Emperor ordered the gracone cannon to flame the field. Summer on the steppes, see. Long grass, dry as tinder. Casks of mil-fire raining down. Exploding. It was carnage. The Emperor's Own were devastated. Half our army died, burnt to cinders or choked on black smoke mostly, but our numbers were greater than theirs by a factor of ten and so we won." He lowered his head. "They still sing ballads in the taverns. Call it a heroic victory." He sipped at a tisane of willow and vervain and leaned forward towards the fire in its hearth about which they were both sitting. "When the flames died away we rolled up their lines, slaughtered the few who still lived, and that summer we swept through the country massacring them all. Whole villages. Children. Women, Now only their ghosts haunt the steppes." He shook his head. "Two weeks after Lagros my company was in the north-country, a bleak wind-swept place. We stumbled

140

on a Lalik village and swept through it like mailed vengeance. My capak ordered me to slaughter an unarmed kid, a few years old." He shook his head. "I couldn't."

Edo glanced at his friend's face, curious. "Why the hell not? Why suffer vicious animals to live?"

"I saw a different truth, Edo. The Lalik are not like us, but they are not animal. Do animals build fires and sing to their young as they put them to sleep?" His voice cracked and Edo heard depths of agony there. "I saw them. Women playing with their children. The bulls laughing and singing, teasing the children as we waited in the darkness like wraiths from Dom's dark house. I saw old men whittling and young women sewing. The Lalik are different, yes. But animals? No!"

Edo placed a hand on his friend's shoulder. "What happened?"

"Capak tore the kid from my hands and smashed its head on the ground. Cap was a good man, all in all, and didn't want me court-martialed. The kid's mother attacked us with a mattock. I stood in her path to protect Cap. I was slow. She gave me this." He pointed at his ruined face. "My career in the army ended then." Balin sighed. "But I found Yanik in the sanatorium, brother Edo. I found my god and he has rescued me from the sins of my past."

That night when Edo slept he dreamt of Kallingtorn, a fevered dream of pain and honor and broken promises. Something shifted deep

141

inside him. He awoke after midnight sweat-drenched and stood naked at an open window as a gentle wind ran its breath over his skin. The garden's perfume-lavender, sweet lilac and honeysuckle- filled his nostrils as he took deep breaths. The moon was a sliver like a whore's painted nail.

The dreams had granted him release. He would accept his fate. He had made mistakes, had paid for them, now it was time to move on. He did not sleep for the remainder of that night and when Balin came to collect him he was still standing at the window, a smile on his face.

"Yanik has touched you, friend Edo?" Balin asked.

Edo said nothing for a long time.

"Perhaps the healing has begun," he answered finally. He turned to Balin, away from the window, suddenly aware that he was ravenous. "I think I wish to know more about your god, brother."

Balin's smile was a bright beacon.

"Breakfast is served in the common room. You eat and I'll talk."

Edo made a face, Balin laughed and they walked together out of the room into the light of a new day.

***

Edo listened and learned.

Yanik was a simple man, born five hundred years earlier into the family of a blacksmith in the

142

eastern district of the city.

A comet fell the night he was born and a silver one-horn was spied by a lookout at the balefire on Mount Arl. As an adult Yanik became a preacher, and in time his oratory made him the most famous holy man in the city. When the host of Incann began their long push south, led by Illan Karnak known as Bloodhand and accompanied by a herd of Lalik wardslaves and Shie Butchers, panic swept the city. The number of the enemy was myriad and Karnack's cruelty legendary. Tens of thousands fled taking with them only what they could carry, others begged the Emperor to negotiate with the Incann. Rioters ravaged the poor districts and the myriad holy places were filled with frightened men, women and children.

The world was ending and the hordes of darkness had arrived.

The Emperor seemed equally paralyzed. He waited in the city in his palace, behind the bulwark of his guards, doing nothing to stem the relentless tide of the Igrann as they sacked and looted all along the coast and then entered the wide intervening desert of the Dead Sands. On the day the city spotted the dust of the hordes of Igrann- a swirling brown cloud driven into the sky by the hoofs of a million stamping horses and padded feet of ten thousand Lalik as they crossed the desert- the bulk of the Emperor's southern forces had still not arrived from their distant posting. Soon the city learned that Incann outriders had entered the Pass of Mahl, less than a day's ride away. The circumvallation of the city had begun.

It was only a matter of time before the city died.

On this, the empire's darkest day, Yanik braved the guards at the entrance to the palace demanding a short audience. The Emperor, desperate, aware of Yanik's reputation as a wise and holy man, granted the request. Yanik met the emperor in his throne room and berated him in front of his shocked council.

He scolded him for his lack of faith in the gods, for his cowardly refusal to meet the Incann army head on, for his failure to spit in Bloodhand's face.

The Emperor shushed the outraged council and let Yanik speak.

"Send me forth," Yanik said. "Alone, I will delay the enemy host and allow you to be reinforced. I will give you a week. On the eight day, in the still time before dawn, you must issue from the city with every man you can muster. The battle will be fierce but you will prevail."

The Emperor cried then in great relief, for despair was taken from him and he knelt before Yanik as before a god, for an emperor would kneel to no ordinary man.

"Rise," Yanik said "for till I meet my brothers in the Great Above, I am only flesh."

From trembling lips the Emperor promised Yanik he would grant him what his heart desired. Anything he wanted. Yanik puzzled this a moment.

"For me I would have nothing. From you I

would have the following. Treat the poor as you would your brother or sister. Treat the stranger as your friend, when he is no threat. Let none in your empire hunger. Be a father to your people but suffer not the way of the tyrant. Do this and earn the love of the gods. This is my sole request of you."

Yanik left that morning, riding alone from the eastern gate on a dun donkey, to the sounds of wailing from his supporters.

He disappeared into the Pass and the city waited.

The Incann did not appear, neither that day nor the next. The Emperor later learned that Incann outriders took Yanik prisoner. Clearly a holy man, and thus one of knowledge who might have information about defenses in the city, he was taken before Bloodhand. Whatever he said caused Bloodhand to fly into a rage. The Incann leader ordered Yanik flayed alive.

Yanik, it was later reported smiled, and kissed the ground at Incan's feet. "I do this he had said, not because you are a lord, for in truth you are but a brutal tyrant, I do this because you are a man and death will claim you on this day in one week."

That night, as Yanik suffered his cruel torture, Bloodhand took ill with fever. His army stopped in its tracks, anxious for their lord, riven by disunity in his absence, disturbed by the prophecy.

Scoured, flayed and disemboweled Yanik died the second day crying out to his brothers in

145

heaven.

With Bloodhand ill, the Incann waited six long days, the main body of their army a sprawling column stretching back into the badlands. Men died of hunger. Men died of thirst. None dared move. The order was clear. As long as Bloodhand was ill they were to hold their ground. He did not recover in time.

The Emperor of Milese, his army, swollen finally by the armies of the south and by two hundred thousand militia, poured through the pass and into the desert at dawn on the seventh day. The fighting was long and hard but at dusk the Incann broke and were slaughtered or driven into the desert where they perished in the hollow light and blazing heat of a summer sun.

The Emperor entered Bloodhand's tent, a massive construction of linen and cotton. Bloodhand lay delirious in bed and when the emperor emerged, holding Bloodhand's severed head, the long dark hair matted in blood, a trembling cry shuddered through the victorious army.

"Who gave us this victory?" the Emperor called as he tossed the head aside.

"Yanik," they answered. "Brother Yanik, the holy man who faced an army before ascending to his brother gods."

They interred the flayed remains of the holy man who had become a god in a mausoleum in the palace.

"They corpse still bleeds today," Balin confided to Edo. "and will continue to bleed, as he

146

wrote in his testament, till injustice is banished from the world."

Fed by such stories and lifted by the goodness and generosity of this simple community, Edo began to sleep like a baby and wake with a spring in his step. More than once he considered taking vows, joining the brotherhood, for the story if Yanik was inspiring and Edo observed the genuine good the monks did helping the poor and hungry in the city.

That was before he found the library and the ghosts of his troubled past renewed their haunting.

***

Edo strode the sleeping corridors of Sanctuary, alone and stiff in his anger.

He was angry because he had fought with Balin, a rare occurrence.

"Do not take your vows, Edo. You are not for here." Balin's gentle eyes looked pained as he said the words. "Violence still bleeds through your skin and your heart is full of raw desire."

"If I commit to my vows I will honor them."

Balin smiled sadly and shook his head. "You are not for here."

Edo had stormed from the room, Balin calling after him. Edo ignored his friend's entreaties to return and for an hour or more he strode dim corridors, ill-lit by candles in high sconces. He judged he was in the farthest reaches of the north-west corner when he came to the door, closed and barred.

No other room in Sanctuary was ever locked; many had no doors at all. Community, the monks preached, meant reaching out, not hiding within.

He ran his hand along the door's dark wood, its belly girded by straps of bronze, puzzled and intrigued. He sensed secrets here. Secrets whose voice called to him like a whore's temptation; a whore whose heart was sere and whose voice beautiful as a ice in sun. The place was locked for a reason, its position away from the living, working and praying areas of sanctuary was telling. He did not understand why, but he knew that behind this door was something meant for him; a hand of fate guiding him.

Like a dark stain on an otherwise beautiful carpet. He shook his head, forcing himself to ignore the temptress call, turned about and returned to a sleeping Balin.

He did not press Balin anymore about his vows, he knew Balin had been right, but for the next few days the room's presence, its dark mystery, gnawed at him till he could resist no longer.

"What lies behind the locked door?"

Balin glanced at his friend, eyes troubled, at what he had caught in the tone of Edo's voice. "In some of us resides a thirst for knowledge. The dark behind the doors feeds that thirst and occasionally a brother may forget the path of alms so we keep the contents locked. Let us talk no more of this."

Balin strode away, forcing Edo to hurry after him. Later that night as they prepared for sleep

Edo asked, "You said a thirst for knowledge is dangerous but your religion allows scholars?"

Balin nodded unhappily. "Yanik does not forbid it."

"What do they have to study?"

"The archives of the old Emperor, the contents of his library bequeathed to us. Behind the door we have the archives of the ancient kings of Milese and Cardinia. We have copies of most of the works of the ancients. Philosophers, poets and those who study the natural world. We have the works of inventors. Of naturalist and explorers."

"You have maps."

A beat pounded in Edo's chest like a desert drum. With it came hunger and thirst, appetites familiar and vaguely sickening.

Balin shook his head. "There is a section of cartography and the journeys of the elders. What of it?"

Edo shrugged. "Before I came to Milesia I was on the cusp of a great discovery. A new land far away. At the time it caused me no small amount of grief."

"Yet you chase this phantom still?" Balin asked perched forward, eyes searching Edo's own eyes.

"When I was a child I made a vow in Feror's temple that I would find this place in <u>his</u> name." He was aware of Balin staring at him strangely, at the passion in his own voice, of the ta-tump of his heart like a galloping colt

"Feror. Your god of wind and chaos. A hard

149

taskmaster I hear."

The old rush of blood excitement took hold of Edo. Feror had guided him here, he was certain. The library would hold something of the information he sought. He leaned forward and grabbed Balin by the wrist.

"I need access to the library."

Balin pulled away, got to his feet, brushing his cassock uneasily.

"A curse haunts those books. The room is uncanny and thus locked from sight. Many who enter its halls are swallowed. We call them the Buried Ones. The thirst for knowledge takes them out of sight of the glory of god. I do not wish that for you, Edo."

"Balin, this is not something I control. I think ...I was brought here for this very purpose."

Balin looked doubtful.

"Please!"

Balin shrugged. "If that is what you wish brother, come with me."

The lock was rusty and monumental. Balin took a long bronze key from his pocket and slipped it into the lock. It gave with click that sounded old and shrill. Balin pushed the heavy door open. The room within was deep, windowless and dark. Balin lit a tallow wick on an alcove to the left of the door. An opening, a half circle on the far wall, gave onto a set of stairs that led into the cellars below.

"Please don't do this Edo."

Edo could feel the pull of whatever was below like a undercurrent of tide. "I have no choice, Balin."

He moved forward, expecting Balin to accompany him, but the monk grabbed his arm, stopping him.

Balin gestured at a key on a metal spike, identical to the one Balin carried, hanging near the door.

"This opens the door if you wish to emerge. I'll inform the Princips to have one made for you alone."

Distracted, Edo patted Balin's shoulder, wishing him farewell, then turned and bent low beneath the entrance. He felt his way blindly down a winding circular staircase, the air dry and musty. He emerged into a long, rectangular low-ceilinged room, lit poorly by torches. A thin. pale-faced monk at the entrance glared balefully at him but said nothing.

The room, a subterranean cellar, stretched the length of sanctuary. Shelves held books, old manuscripts and dusty maps. Edo walked the length of the aisle, like a dream-struck lover. He could smell age and dust and the hidden mysteries of the words and pictures on the pages of the books he passed.

Tallamun was here, someplace, and he would find it.

***

Like a rat beneath the floorboards of a palace, he scurried about in the dim light of that cellar, day after day. The slug-faced monks who worked

151

there largely ignored him. Some seemed to never leave the cavernous room. They slept amongst their books and ate food brought to them from above, cold meals they chewed without tasting before returning to their manuscripts as soon as they could.

They were no less obsessed then he was, though for the sake of his health and sanity, Edo forced himself to return to the cell he shared with Balin at nightfall. Most nights Balin waited for him, a pot of tisane brewing on the small hearth, face blankly unhappy.

"A monk who worked in that library was the man who discovered mil-fire. By the name of Lapalit." Balin muttered one night. "He had read an account of inextinguishable fire from a thousand years ago, in the lands of the Mrmaks. He tracked down the source documents, spent years deciphering the language of the original and another dozen years working on the formula. Finally he presented his findings to the emperor, Kilium theThird. When the emperor discovered that mil-fire worked, when he understood its full potential, he ordered all of Lapalit's originals destroyed along with every work in the Mrmak language we possessed. He wanted no one but his closest advisors to know the secret. Lapalit was locked in a room in the palace. He was blinded, had his ears and his fingers cut off, and his tongue removed."

Balin sipped his drink.

"A salutatory warning," Edo laughed. "Unlikely to be my fate, however."

"Sometimes knowledge we harvest bears dangerous fruit, brother Edo"

Edo smiled, hushed his friend and hid his annoyance.

No parable would persuade him to change course.

***

Edo pored through books in old Milese, a language he barely comprehended. He read books in Aonian and Scian and skimmed works whose language he did not understand. When he could he press-ganged other monks for translations.

The year turned and turned again before he found what he was looking for, and when he did he sat back against a dusty podium, books pooled all about him, his skin pale and covered in fine dust unaware he cried, tears of joy and relief, his tears streaking the dust like streams.

***

The book was old, from a time before the empire of Milese, from a time before Bloodfire rained from the heavens, before even the ascendancy of the Caedians,

A time when men had fought the indigenous Shie, struggling for a place on the great eastern continent of Tallamun. Driven by despair, a group of northern priests, followers of a long forgotten god, had set out on a pilgrimage; west in a boat little better than a large coracle, thinking to

153

intercede with the gods in their palaces on the peaks of Kayspine.

They were blown off course, becalmed in fog that was thick as a cloud, driven hard on high waves that cast their wood and hide boat about like a child's toy.

Exhausted, half-dead of thirst and starvation, they put ashore on what they first thought was an island, a land thickly carpeted by trees thick of ochre and gray bark, taller than any the priests had ever seen.

Even from a distance they sensed the amna.

They prayed to their god, sacrificed one of their number in sheer gratitude, and set off inland where they were attacked by a tribe of men-beasts painted in woad and ochre. All but four were butchered, managed to stagger back to the glinting bay where they had beached their boat.

It took them the best part of a day to get their boat to water, grunting and heaving, sweat pouring down their faces as they cast fearful glances at the tree line. Their hoisted their mainsail and set off home, best they could. Two died on the way struck by a pulsing, bloody flux and a third fell ill and survived only two days after landfall. The lone survivor returned to his home, the islands northwest of Incann. He lived long enough to relate his tale to one of his brothers in a monastery. Long enough to draw a map.

Beware, he warned in his epilogue, for the land he discovered was no paradise but a devil's playground. All those who venture there do so at

154

peril of their lives and their souls.

His name was Warold Lanok, priest of the god Kili, and his tale was written in the year of the Great Peril three hundred years after Moonfire's Ascendancy.

It took Edo some time to work out the dates according to the Milesian calendar.

One thousand four hundred years, he reckoned, certainly well over over a thousand years had passed since Warold Lanok had lived and died. Edo weighted the slim manuscript his hand.

He held it to his chest and laid is head down on the bench where he had been reading and slept like the dead.

***

Three men strode across the planked gangway and onto the deck of the trading galley "Vixganix" on the morning of its departure from the busy eastern dock in the city of Deira, capital of the empire of Aonia and Scia. The boatswain knew at once that these were no ordinary passengers. They had the feel of men whose lives had been lived in the clasp of violence. Gala, the captain welcomed them with nervous enthusiasm, then hustled them quickly out of sight.

The passage across the Bearing Strait and straight up the coast took three weeks. The three men kept to themselves, staying below decks in their aft quarters during the day. They could be found walking the ship on quiet nights, whispering quietly to themselves, ignoring the crew.

The crew grumbled, as a matter of course, but a stern warning from the captain and his promise of an extra share of the loot when they reached Deira kept their mouths shut.

At nightfall as the ship passed the boom at the edge of Milese harbor it was hailed by one of the warships of the Emperors Custom's Office. The three men hid in the second, deeper, hold, between the salted fish and barrels of wine as the captain- in routine fashion- bribed the officers and led them on a cursory inspection.

When the captain gave the all clear the boatswain went to alert the men. They rose stinking, slimy with salted fish, faces grim and unsmiling.

The crew set about unloading the ship for their schedule was tight as the three men slipped down the ramp into the darkness of that foreign city, weapons hidden under long cloaks, dressed like tribesmen of the eastern Milese empire, shawls of black and amber wrapped around their heads.

Their employer had given them directions and their tall leader knew Milese well- one of two reasons why he had been chosen in the first instance. They slipped through the night, unchallenged and ignored by the multitudes still walking the streets.

When they came to the gate that led into the monastery the leader rapped hard on the oak door. The monk who pulled open the gate peered at them with a look of faint distaste. They told the man who they wanted, but he shook his head and told them to come back in the morning, for the brothers were all asleep and could not be disturbed.

Without waiting for the monk to finish they barged through the door, and quickly and quietly subdued him. They were under orders not to kill unless strictly required, so one of their number bound and gagged the unconscious man, stashed his body out of sight and took his place; a subterfuge that would not withstand close scrutiny but would buy them the time they needed.

With unerring accuracy they found the cell in the main building of the man they sought. A priest was asleep on the second of two stone benches and woke as they entered. He looked around, blinking in fear and confusion but this was not the man they had been instructed to find. They threatened the priest with a knife but he refused to tell them what they needed to know.

They bled him till for the information they needed. It took time- time they could ill afford, so when they were finished the leader slit the man's throat and they left him there in a puddle of his own blood.

Regrettable, of course, but the bastard had put them to a lot of trouble.

They took the key the monk had given them, slipped in shadow past cells where sleeping monks lay.

The cellar was a long library, a half-dozen monks pottering about. Engrossed in their work

157

none looked up from what they were doing at the strangers who wandered past .They found the man they sought in a dark alcove at the far end of the room, asleep. They grabbed him, silenced him and poured a dark liquid from a glass vial into his mouth. Milk of vervain and poppy, enough to sedate him and make him easy to manage, though not enough to make him sleep.

They held him as he struggled, a scarf wrapped round his mouth to muffle his cries. When he was sedated they pushed him ahead of them across the room, up the stairs. They made the gate without incident and set off into the city, quickly now for they had no way of knowing when the monk at the gate would raise the alarm.

They reached the ship as dawn was breaking and the captain ushered them into the hold. They fed their guest more of the milk of the poppy, enough to knock him out, for the last thing they needed a custom's guard made curious by muffled cries.

They laid back, exhausted, their mission fulfilled.

All in all, despite the death of that one monk, their mission had been a success, the leader thought, as he laid his head down on a rough, hempen stacked with trade goods bound for Deira.

At least the fish were gone, sold now, though their stink remained like greasy cloud. In their stead were casks of Milese wine, bails of fine cotton and a pallet of amber wands of the type used by warlocks in their dark ceremonies.

The ship pulled up anchor, deck hands

shouted as the longboats heaved their oars and the mainsail was raised.

The ship swayed on the sea and before it had left the protection of the harbor the four men in the hold were fast asleep, specks of Balin's dried blood still on the killer's hands.

***

Edo gasped awake, sunlight bright in his eyes. He was disoriented, had no recollection of where he was, how he had come to be here.

Three men sat opposite him, eyeing him with a detached curiosity, like farmers eyeing sick cattle on a farm. He did know he was on a ship; light from a hatchway above swayed on the faces of the three men as the ship rose on the sea's gentle swell, and the tang of salt was sharp in his nose.

One of the men smiled faintly as he awoke, and reached over and handed him a flask of water.

"Remember me, Domin?"

Edo squinted, dredging the flat planes of the familiar face and voice up from the sinkhole of his past. Truth hit him like a punch in the guts.

"Heeb?"

"Relax, Edo. You are safe now. Back amongst your own."

"How..."

Heeb waved a hand. "Save it for later, Edo."

"Why the fuck am I here, Heeb?"

Heeb shrugged. "Your brother sent me to get you."

"You what?" His voice rose, a harsh whine.

Heeb continued, blithely unaware of Edo's growing rage.

"His commission. A good job we made of it, too, if I say so myself. Minimal casualties. One stubborn bloody priest."

The rage suddenly swelled, like a fire fed a diet of pure oxygen. Edo could hardly speak

"Who. Did. You. Kill?"

"Asleep in the room we was told was yours. "Heeb made a line across his face with the edge of his hand. "Big man. Big scar here."

Edo sprang forward. His shoulder took Heeb in the abdomen and Heeb blew air out like a beached whale as he fell back. Edo scrambled on top of the Scian and grabbed the man's hair hard and twisted with one hand, while beating him with a clenched fist with the other hand.

Edo felt the gristle of the nose explode. He scraped his knuckles on teeth.

It took all of the other men to pull Edo free and pin him to the ground.

Heeb rose to his feet and kicked Edo twice in the abdomen. Pain flashed like harsh splinters but Edo didn't care.

The rage in his soul was a tornado.

They had killed Balin.

The two men flanking Edo held him down, as Edo bucked and struggled. Heeb held Edo by the chin and fed him liquid from the small vial in his hand. The liquid tasted chalky with a hint of rotten sweetness. Edo swallowed and the men continued to hold him till a wave of black tiredness swept him.

His limbs were numb, his eyes closed

"What the fuck was that all about? He was supposed to be happy to se you." Edo heard one of the men ask Heeb.

Heeb said nothing but growled and lashed out at Edo again. "Should have left the fucking ungrateful bastard where he was. Tie him up. He ain't getting free till we make landfall."

When next Edo woke it was dark and his mouth was dry and thick as jerky. The ship was bucking on a wild sea. He tried to move but his hands were tied behind him and his feet bound to something ahead. He tried to roll onto his side and dry retched as waves of nausea swept over him.

Balin's death had been added to his ledger. His best and only friend, the only honorable man he had known, was dead because of who Edo was and the things he had done. Edo didn't understand fully, not yet, but Heeb was here again, an apparition of the past, and Edo did not believe that to be coincidence. Balin's death was like one more sacrifice; the blood price of Tallamun demanded by Feror.

The place was a curse; his curse, and he was helpless as a baby in its grasp.

He breathed deeply trying to clear the nausea, closed his eyes and prayed to Yanik for his lost friend, all the time trying to avoid thinking of what the future might now bring-

If Heeb had been speaking the truth he would soon come face to face with his brother's scorn and that was not something he needed to dwell

161

hard upon.

***

They took Edo from the ship, bound in chains and led him into the city of Deira; a port city built on a steep hill facing a wide, calm bay of turquoise water, sun-burnished breakers gleaming silver as they pounded the rocky promontory to the east. The harbor listed under its weight of docked ships. Bare-chested wharf hands unloaded cattle, sheep, olives, figs, silks, carved deep-wood furniture, pelts from Incann and the lands of the north, jade and amber and dyed cottons.

Anything and everything the wealthiest citizens of a newly wealthy empire thought they might need.

Edo had come home.

Large white-washed buildings, island tenements, crowded over the narrow streets, each apartment block home to a hundred small flats and a hundred large families. Stalls beneath the loggias sold fast food and local necessities. The slumming rich lounged on sedans carried by Caedian slaves. Furloughed soldiers in small, taut bands wandered the streets, pushing through the crowds with callous arrogance, in search of action or trouble.

Heeb had gone ahead, leaving the men who had waylaid Edo in Milese, as escort. Edo knew their type, Scian mercenaries, army retired, working now as the private enforcer of one of the richer citizens.

162

In this instance Edo's brother.

His brother! What in all that was foul did Eso want?

Gulls flew over the rooftops, casting their shadow on the flagged streets. Horses neighed as they pulled carts laden with oak barrels of wine. The sounds and smells were the well-spring of his youth, and familiar to him as his own stink.

Deira! The place where he had spent a restless, embittered youth, the place he had run from hard and fast as he could, and which still called to him now, despite everything, saying I am your home. In green parks older men sat pored over the pieces of the Karneo, moving them with utmost concentration. In the cloth market hawkers sold reams of deep-died silk from Chambray or ivory-handled fans from Jilla. The poor, having nothing else, sold themselves. In the Zirkus Market, two leagues square, matrons wandered amongst stalls selling and buying rotting fruit, sheep offal, bags of the hardy desert wheat brought in shiploads from Scia, all sold for a nominal price so nobody went hungry.

Fortune tellers, herbalists and soothsayers did a roaring business from gaudily covered stalls on the fringes of the market and bellowing touts sold tickets to the chariot races at the stadium.

The guards led Edo northeast, towards the council buildings and the twin temple of Atyrel and

Funir; massive and gleaming, twin colonnaded buildings on a soaring plateau that dominated the city. On the slopes below the

163

temples were the council buildings, the gleaming marble of the law courts, and spread around these like a rash, the villas of the wealthy.

His brothers villa amongst them, and that was where they were headed.

Edo spat on the ground and, not for the first time in his life, hoped his brother would freeze in Mael Din's frozen wastes, deep beneath the earth.

***

The two guards ushered him into the pampered grounds of his brother's walled villa, the sprawling roof of the main building gleaming, tiles the color of rust.

A fountain in the shape of a marwhale blew water into the air and drooping willows ringed an artificial pond on whose water emerald lilies floated.

Guards in burnished scale armor pushed open the main door of the villa. A liveried manservant at the end of the gloomy vestibule let them into the bright atrium, decorated with images of the gods. Edo noted Funir in full battle armor wielding his carrion sword, the zephyr of wind that was Feror blowing thunderhead clouds across an azure sky, Shalon the Hag in her rags in the forlorn city of Dammerang, Caent the stag peering from the depths of the ur-forests and the virgin Liena, naked and forlorn, kneeling by the Pool of the West, her wounded tears watering all living things.

The floor was Stiren Marble from the

Northlands above Caedia, of cream streaked with black. A rectangular pool in the center of the room was a home to tiny golden fish.

There was no sign of Eso, though manservant's flitted across the room, bearing trays of food and jugs of wine. Edo surmised they were preparing an important meal.

A gaggle of middle-aged men bearing the medallion of the council lounged on sofas along one wall; officials of the court, come to politic or make law.

Edo's escorts halted before the tablinum, his brother's study at the end of the atrium. The latticed doors were closed fast but Edo could hear voices from inside and understood the timbre of his brother's voice, a drawl that was at once commanding and oddly captivating.

Edo's brother, Eso-Agoa, had made his first fortune as a lawyer and, though he was now a councilor of the first rank, that rhetorical training was unmistakable, though the words were muted by the walls.

The door opened, Heeb leaned out and ushered them into the room.

Eso-Agoa, sat at a long sofa. Behind him was a long table littered with manuscripts. He held a glass of honey wine, tiny in his meaty hand.

He stared at Edo, eyes liquid with emotion, and barked an order at the two guards.

The men bent to remove the chains, freeing Edo from his burden, turned on their heels and left. Heeb stayed, taking a perch on a chair covered with horsehair.

Eso pressed a glass into Edo's hands and waited, silent, his lips moist.

"Heeb told me what happened. I am sorry for your friend, Edo. It was not my intention..."

Edo scowled, saying nothing, ignoring the wine.

His brother looked older than he remembered, had put on weight and had more gray in his hair, but- and this was typical- age suited him. It added gravitas to his already considerable size and sat well with his resonating voice.

"You look well, Eso."

Eso smiled sadly. "I wish I could say the same for you, little brother."

Little brother! The bastard still dared call him that.

"Has Heeb told you? The trial is set for next week."

"Trial?" Edo shook his head. "I have already been tried. It wasn't much to my liking."

Eso made a face. "I brought you here for vengeance, Edo. That bastard Damas has been a thorn in my side for years. When you fell into his hands..." Eso's voice trailed away and his face purpled. "What he did to you... I swear by Garge's bloody sword he will pay."

Damas -Másberia Damas, the man who had smashed Edo's limbs with his own hands, who had cast Edo out of the army like an angel sent from the grace of Atyrel. For Edo but another monor figure of his dreadful past.

"Damas did his duty, Eso. He followed the law."

166

Eso scowled and walked to his desk. He cast about for a moment and pulled out a letter, smeared with blood.

"He sent me this, Edo. It is a copy of your discharge papers and holds an account of your trial and punishment. "He brandished the paper in front of Edo. "He dipped it in your wounds. That is not the law. He wanted to wound me."

Ed o shrugged. "He is your enemy and taunts you, not me. What he did to me had its own justification. I can live with that."

Eso grimaced and turned away. He clasped his hands behind his back and said in a too quiet voice, "He will walk free if you do not testify."

Edo smiled to himself, light suddenly dawning. This was not about family or vengeance. This was politics, pure and naked and deadly. Aonian style. Eso was fighting a duel with Damas, a duel that was to be conducted in the courts, a duel that by Aonian law could have but one end- slavery or banishment for the plaintiff or the defendant.

Eso was famous for the theatricality of his trials and Edo knew his brother well enough to second-guess his intentions. Edo would be presented at some critical juncture, a surprise witness, used to undermine Damas's credibility.

Tainted testimony of course, for Edo would have to lie, but that was the kind of law Eso liked best. Testimony bought and paid for could be relied on, manipulated.

That explained the secrecy, the need to send hired men to find him, the need to smuggle Edo into the house bound in chains like a common criminal.

Since their father died fishing for marwhale Eso had been a father to Edo; a hard, unrelenting figure, critical and unloving.

Edo owed him nothing, and Balin's death was as much Eso's responsibility as Heeb's. Balin- the only true friend Edo ever had, friend and mentor.

Eso could go hang.

"Your affairs are none of my business, Eso. I made that clear when I joined the army. I want nothing to do with you, the council or your dirty machinations. Take your chances against Damas next week and I wish you well. Truly. But I will not aid you."

"He told me you'd say that." Heeb had helped himself to wine and was sitting looking at the two brothers with an amused grin.

Edo stared at the Scian with vast distaste; the man was a reminder of the unsavory deeds of his past. He said a quick prayer to Yanik, an invocation for peace at troubled times.

"I refuse to testify against a man who did his duty as he saw it."

Heeb shrugged. "Edo the righteous. How unusual? Strange how banishment changes a man." He rose to his feet then. "I guess I'd better be going then." He glanced sharply at Eso.

Eso smiled grimly and nodded.

"Collect your money. Kill the Caedian for all I care. I have no further interest in your scheme."

***

168

The Caedian!

Edo wanted to sink into a deep hole and keep sinking. As always in his dealings with his brother he felt ineffectual, like the child he had once been, Eso bellowing at him to do better as he whipped him for his childish misdemeanors.

Eso would never leave things to chance, would always have leverage, as sure as the sun rises and the waves fall.

"Where is he?" Edo asked Heeb.

"In the city. Safely stored. Him and that book you had in the library when we found you."

Edo breathed deeply. They had Pora Ferie, the Caedian who had renewed Edo's interest in Tallamun, the man on whose word he had committed murder. Somehow Heeb and the Caedian had evaded capture and made their way back to Deira. It made sense. Lacking the funds to mount an expedition of his own, Heeb would have contacted Eso; a logical thing to do given Edo's involvement in the affair. Eso had spotted his opportunity, had tracked Edo down and set the rescue plan in motion.

Only Balin was dead.

Edo could not forgive that, not now, not ever.

Still the thought of what he could do, the map combined with Ferie's memories, caused a surge of excitement to swell through him. Tallamun was closer than ever, the shimmering hallucination of his youth glittering once more, within reach, so real he could touch it. A chance for a new beginning, a place where he could escape the weight of his family's history.

He turned to Eso. "What do you want from me?"

Eso smiled, a slick smile, charming in a viperish sort of way.

"Testify against Damas and I will fund your trip. Break that bastard and you will finally see this Tallamun of your dreams, little brother."

Edo glanced around, at the trappings of wealth and power his brother had accreted, like a shellfish accretes a pearl; the rosewood table from Incann, the brightly painted busts of the gods and of Eso himself, the gold inlay in the mosaic on the wall.

Eso was poison, his deals velvet gloves hiding poisoned needles, but he held all the cards here; he had the Caedian, the book and the money to finance the expedition.

"I will want three galways, a brace of amna cannon, weapons for three dozen mercenaries, food for a winter, tools, livestock and ten harns worth of trading goods; gold, bracelets, iron. I will want a contract in writing signed in front of a testee and the penalty for reneging is your left hand and his death." Edo pointed at Heeb.

Heeb narrowed his eyes, evidently surprised. He opened his mouth as if to say something. Edo cut him off.

"You killed my fried, you fuck and I'll see you hang for that some day."

Heeb blanched and again made as if to protest but the look on Edo's face stopped him.

Eso's smile was greasy and insincere. "'I'll

170

have the papers drawn up, and a goat each slaughtered in the temples of Malyn and Feror, in honor of our agreement." He laid a hand on Edo's shoulder. "Lunch should be ready. You and I need to catch up." He guided Edo to the door. "We have so much to talk about."

Edo shook his head and let himself be led.

He cares nothing for me, he schooled himself, and the only principle driving him is his ambition. We will talk, yes, but the talk will soon turn to the trial and somehow, by the end of this meal, our strategy will be plotted and the lies I need to tell will be sown like weeds in a field. He shrugged. It did not matter. Tallamun was closer than ever, he could feel it, like one of the sirens said to inhabit the Incann Straits, in the distance of time and future and place calling him, calling him, whispering promises to him. A siren whose voice promised much, both pleasure and danger,

and as he thought of it his brain spun dizzily and his mind lightened.

This was the meaning of his life.

Even Heeb's furious stare burning his back did nothing to dissuade him of that.

CHAPTER 5 - TAMBER

Tamber survived in the cave- one could not call it living- a prisoner of own mind as much as an outcast. He fished, when he remembered he was hungry, often as not eating the fish raw. The villagers ignored him. When by chance he wandered near the village they made warding signs with their hands, and children ran away screeching with fear.

His wounds healed, but badly. His right leg trailed stiffly, so he limped and when the weather was cold his bones ached. His left hand recovered, so he could grasp things but never fully close his fingers.

His days as a warrior had ended.

His hair grew long and turned from gray to yellow. His teeth decayed, and in a huge amount of pain, he made a tisane and pulled them out with tongs of wood.

One day he woke to find the body of his father, discarded on the rocks beneath the cave.

One of the old man's legs had withered, an ancient wound Tamber guessed, but one younger than his banishment. The man looked emaciated and Tamber guessed he had had not been able to fend for himself and had died of starvation.

Then his corpse had been brought here.

Tamber struggled with the concept, unused as he was to thinking of others. What had happened to his brothers? How had they allowed this to happen? Only one explanation was possible. His brothers were dead, killed in a raid or in an ambush. His father had died of starvation, his mother too unless her family had taken her back.

Uncles, aunts, cousins. His sister. They had all failed to help and Tamber knew why.

His disgrace had fallen like a cold shadow on them all and his father had borne the weight. Tamber had seen such events before, as a child. His brothers would have been driven to succeed where he had failed. They would have taken risks, volunteered for raids no sane warrior would choose to volunteer for. His sister. She had been married to a cousin of the chief. She would not have wanted to help for fear of impugning her own children with the taint of Tamber's betrayal. He sat down on the beach, cradled his father's chill head on his lap. He moaned in pain and anguish. He had helped destroy his family. He was no longer a Malai and more than ever he was truly alone.

A dark, bitter cloud infested his soul.

He buried his father in soft sand on the lower beach and when he slept his dreams were filled with the voices of the dead calling to him. Occasionally, Raven appeared in blood-tinged nightmares, the spirit's voice full of mocking laughter.

Tamber waited, through the changing seasons, watched waves break against the rocks, spreading white spume, beneath the edge of his cliff.

One dark day in winter, storm clouds like dark souls pounding the seashore, the harrak came

173

back, gleaming blae shells swarming over the ledge of the cave, pincers clicking with a noise like the scratching of a blade on bone, into the gloom of the cave. Tamber tried to scramble to his feet, but the harrak were faster than he was, and quickly swarmed up his legs. He beat at them, stamped them to the ground, futilely, for they came in myriads like trees in the forest or stars in the sky. The pincers burnt into his flesh and myriad pins of pain wept through him. They covered his chest, a million tiny creatures weighing him down. He roared in pain as the first of them entered his mouth, the pain a fierce and ugly burn. He choked, screamed. They invaded his nostrils, cutting off his air. He flailed wildly. He made it to his knees, flailing wildly, killing hundreds of them. They dug into his eyes, blinding him, the pain now a roar like the roar of the waves dying at the onslaught of the land. He fell forward, they crawled into him, through every orifice they could find. His mind closed down and a fierce coldness took hold of him.

***

He woke in the place between.

Sheer rock rose above him on three sides, the rock grayish granite flecked with pink. Flurries of snow caught in his long beard. The air felt somehow young, rarely breathed and pure as mountain springs.

Sparse trees- clinging to the ledge of the cliffs, gathered in the narrow valley around a

174

winding river of grey water-were like no trees he knew; small with frond-like branches, widely dispersed, quite unlike the rich growth of the forests of his home.

To the east was a flood plain, water and marsh in places covered with masses of pea-green algae. A pale, sharp light glinted from the hard water and hurt his eyes.

A jah trembled through the plain, fully five times the size of a man, its gray body armored and its snout oozing fangs like the heads of Malai spears. Above were yalang but larger than those he knew, soaring on the thermals above the rock and ice their loud calls sending tremors of primeval fear through him.

He stood in the center of the valley, near a pool around which a small herd of horned arank were drinking, the amber soil churned by their hooves. Cresson colored leaves, like plates floated on the water and dark red insects, the size of a clenched fist, buzzed around the nodding heads of the arank.

"Tamber Whitehair son of Lantuk , welcome." The mocking voice from behind him was flat sibilant, framed with strange syllables like the accents of the Malai settled along the Jronaeny River to the far south.

He turned to face the owner of the voice and started.

Raven stood shoulder to shoulder with another.

For this meeting Raven had assumed the body of a man- broader and larger than Tamber so

175

Tamber had to crane his head to see the gods bird-like face, its yellow eyes glinting and hinting at hidden depths, of things hunted screaming, then torn apart by powerful beaks. The smell of deathly carrion made Tamber blanch. The companion was small, hunch-backed and thin, his skin a livid pink, his eyes small and darting.

"What are you?" Tamber heard himself ask the smaller of the two.

The little man chuckled and spoke in a voice too deep and dark for its body. "I am Kali of the forests. The night spirit. Moondark's brother. You may not know me, Malai. Your people have forgotten the sap of the trees."

Tamber stared at him and felt eels of unease wriggle in his stomach. True, the Malai did not worship the spirits amongst the trees anymore, nor did they sacrifice to appease them, but they had not forgotten their power completely; for once the Malai had come through forests on the long migration, the memory of which the shaman still sung. The Malai remembered; spirits quivering through the trees on fogs of yellow sulfur, voices chill as vapor, voices that could invade a man's soul and tear it apart.

Small beings, pale as thin ice, seen flitting through the darkness, dark red blades in their hands, people, sometimes whole families, disappeared come morning leaving nothing but traces of fear and the smell of blood.

Tamber made a warding sign in the shape of stag and mouthed a curse.

The spirit that called itself Kali chuckled.

176

"Ridding yourself of me will not be so easy, Tamber."

Tamber backed away. "What do you wish of me?"

Kali turned to Raven and something passed between them that he could not follow. "The bird and I have signed a pact, a pact we hope will save your people and mine." The revenant bowed slightly, its mockery deep. "We are your guides, holy man."

The eels in Tamber's stomach bit deep on his innards. Holy man? Raven and Kali together? The bird and the tree. The killer of the skies and the open fields, the killer of the deep forests. They were offering themselves to him.

Not offering. Demanding.

His ears roared as a wind blew across the primeval plain, he fell to his knees, onto chill damp soil, wrapped his arms about his body, mouth and eyes closed tight, hands over his ears, unwilling to accommodate these bastard things. They came close to him, rubbing his hair clucking, speaking quietly in words he did not understand. He felt their excitement as a mug of heat building around him and still he resisted.

He tore at their hands like a young child trying to beat away its elders.

Malai shaman spent hours in the sweathouses, imbibing smoke, or fasted and wandered the mountains looking for visitations from just such spirits as these. When the shaman found such spirits, like as not wild and unarmed having forgotten their origin, these spirits gave them

177

powers; to foresee the future, to kill with a touch, to curse the souls of others.

But Kali and the Raven were no simple spirits, they were ascendants, the gods who ruled the spirits beneath the Maker in Great Blue Heaven.

To possess such a bounty was to possess nothing; he knew from bitter experience that it was to be possessed. Spirits as powerful as this would drive a man's own soul from his body and leave him lost and isolated wandering and lost, far from hearth and home, fodder for the shaman and their wiles.

Tamber's resistance suddenly dissolved in a pale wash. For his people he was already dead, a scrap of nothing worth less than the animals they husbanded in the stone-walled fields near the village.

He had nothing. Nobody.

He shared neither hearth nor heart with another Malai.

Kali and Raven would, if nothing else, be company, welcome or not.

Tamber felt the cold fingers of the spirits dissolve, turn to threads of air and enter him with a great sigh of pleasure- enjoying the feel and splendor of his flesh.

Kali whispered in his ears.

We are yours now, Tamber. And you belong to us. Watch what must be done. Do not resist or we will break you on the wheel of ages and tie you to the Hounds of the Chariot.

"Show me," he whispered.

178

The beetle men come. You do not have much time. We need you to nurture one for us. One whose memory will be instrumental in raising the tribes against the outsiders.

"Who?"

Tamber saw a face flash before his eyes, and still he could not comprehend for the face they showed him- was not human.

He shook his head.

Yes! they cried together, voices sibilant and hard. *Yes! This is what we dream of the future. Find him. Save him! Learn from him!*

He opened his eyes again. He was alone, kneeling on the damp soil of an ancient world. A herd of Arank plodded slowly by, less than a dozen spans from him, their massive heads nodding, blithely unconcerned with his presence.

The animals here do not sense me. The realization struck with a weight like a falling hammer. Here he was the revenant, the wandering ghost.

He did not belong. Wherever he went.

Time to be going, Tamber. Take us back. The voice in his head was Kali's. He closed his eyes and sputtered awake in the cave.

It was dark night, a faint moonlight glinting on the pale rock of the cave. A fierce eastern wind whipped the sea outside and it broke below the cave with a sound like black thunder. He was aware of them, the spirits within him, a pressure behind his eyes. He lit a fire and danced around it, weaving wild circles close to the heat.

In the flames he saw it, the juvenile half-beast

179

fleeing through the forest.

Still he resisted.

<u>Go. Now.</u> Kali ordered, the voice faint now that they had returned, little more than a nagging hint like a conscience.

He sighed, reached for the spear and made his way through the cave.

The sea spumed about him and the wind howled as he made his way around the rock face and into the forest behind.

180

CHAPTER 6 - EDO

Dom Másberia Damas, Secuas of the Caedian Fifth, showed up at the forum on the hill in his plain tunic and purple robes, a crown of Ivy perched on his head above a riotous mane of hair that flapped in the wind like a bellowed challenge. Damas had laid the once great empire of Caedia low and his victories had extended Aonian borders to the wild clans of the far north.

He arrived beneath the soaring statues of the five founders onto the marbled expanse in front of the law court with a Deka of armed soldiers, a full company, their kalit leading the way, galpipe to his mouth, the cream-colored horn screeching. The gathered crowds muttered with disgust and hissed as the men of the Fifth passed by. Soldiers, and civilians, were forbidden to bear arms or armor within the precincts of the city. Only the Council Guards were allowed carry weapons larger than a dirk and their positions were elective, thus easily controlled.

Since the Confusion and the fall of the Despot in his Citadel, and the Rise of the Council and the Rule of Five, it was understood deep in the heart of each citizen of Deira, that to allow an army to march the streets of the city was tantamount to allowing the Rule to fall, was to allow dictatorship to return.

What these brave citizens untied with their valor, let no man knit together. No more despots, no more armies, no more shall we shed our own blood.

The words of Enmacente the Liberator when he emerged from the smoking ruin of the Citadel,

the Despots lank, purpled hair dangling from his hand.

From this day forth, we rule ourselves. No soldiers will walk the streets of our new Republic.

In Edo's experience life was rarely that neat. For a thousand years the Republic had survived, even thrived, on the strength of its volunteer army, an army born of the gutters and alleyways and dark, fir swept hills of the land. For a thousand years these volunteer soldiers, merchants, chefs, blacksmiths and farmers, had cut a red runnel through the hearts of their jealous neighbors, and in so doing had carved out an incidental empire.

The protracted war against Caedia had changed all that.

Men were required to campaign for years at a time, and in their absence farms and businesses went to seed and families drifted into destitution. So the professional armies had been instituted, two generations earlier, armies of veterans paid by the state, given plunder by their leaders, men with allegiance first and foremost to the corp, secondly to their general.

Only distantly to the Republic itself.

The balance of power had changed.

When Damas walked to the Law court, past the thousands of spectators who had shown up for the scheduled hearing, he was thumbing his nose at the Council, spitting in the face of history.

With a bright flash of understanding Edo understood, as Damas and his men hove into view, what Eso stood to gain if he succeeded in humiliating this overbearing general; if he brought Damas low, then a place at the head of the council when the next Pole was taken must surely be his.

Damas took his seat opposite Eso in the Skyroom, the vast open space surrounded by columns of ribbed green marble, like a massive stone forest.

The crowds of spectators, swelled tenfold by rumor of what Damas had done, pushed closer and closer to the court, their seething energy causing the assembled judges, witnesses and lawyers to fidget nervously. The Council guards struggled to control the crowds; stones were thrown at the soldiers of the Fifth who assumed a defensive formation.

This further enraged the crowd and it took a massed charge of the guards, wielding the staves of their spears like clubs, to avert a riot.

Eso smiled and turned to Edo. "Damas miscalculated marching his men here. He thought he was well loved, and let's face it, he was. I fear he has just squandered his goodwill."

Edo stared at Eso's smug face. "You manipulated this, didn't you. Planted the idea, made him believe the crowds would welcome him at the head of his men as a conquering hero?"

Eso shrugged. "Maybe so. Maybe not." He smiled. Maybe you are finally learning little brother."

Eso slapped Edo on the shoulder, got to his

feet and walked to the center of the Skyroom where he took his place, in front of a pedestal facing Damas. Damas the warrior stared daggers at Eso, the man who had accused him- the greatest servant of the Republic- of treason.

The politician facing the warrior.

Both men stripped out of their clothing and stood naked facing one another, one man's body lean and scarred the other marked only by the ravages of too-comfortable living.

Each knew that only one would have his clothes returned. The loser would be sold into slavery at the flesh markets on the eastern suburbs of the city before nightfall.

On stone pedestals, dotted through the crowds, were Speakers, men who would repeat word for word the statements of judges, defender and plaintive.

Eso had confided to Edo that, of the three dozen Speakers, over twenty had been bribed to twist the emphasis of words in Eso's favor, for the crowd had its own primal power in this vast assembly and it was not unusual for looting to break out at unpopular verdicts, for judges to be torn apart in their villas at the hands of irate mobs.

The five judges took their assigned places-the five pedestals of judgment set perpendicular to and facing both men- features hidden beneath animal masks carved of wood- the Jaguar of Garge, the Eagle of Feror, the Marwhale of Malyn, the Stag of Caent, the Raven Oalon.

Five gods inhabiting the bodies of five mortals for the space of a morning, to bear

184

witness to the proceedings, to sanction the disposal of the guilty. Yet: the four men and one woman behind the masks might be gods today but tomorrow they would be politicians once again, and within the year they would be poled.

Even gods could heed the anger in the voice of the people.

Damas took the stand, and blustered on for two hours about his victories, his service to the Commonweal, his love of the people.

Wandering, narcotic ramblings. Damas was no rhetorician, and his words lacked fire. He denied all wrongdoing, proclaimed his loyalty to the empire and denied that he had ever conspired to undermine it.

Edo's mind drifted until Eso took the stand.

His opening blast was that of a master, accusing Damas of planning covertly to overthrow the Council and have himself proclaimed despot. When he was finished, after five minutes, the crowd was seething fire again.

They settled into the humdrum round of witnesses.

Edo played his part; when he took the stand he claimed that he had been brought down by Damas in part to discredit Eso, in part because he had learnt of the dastardly plot to overthrow the Council. Damas had his supporters, dozens of them, mostly army or ex-army, and many testified but they all suffered from the same lack of credibility- if Damas was plotting the overthrow of the council how could the council trust any of these professional soldiers.

185

The sun was setting, the sky a brilliance of orange and gold, the water streaked with reflected flame, when the Council returned after a brief period of reflection.

Damas was found guilty of treason.

At a signal from Feror's Eagle a brace of amna cannon were turned on Damas's deka. Five deka of guards who had been drafted in during the course of the day, trained crossbows on them.

"Order them to lay down their weapons, or have them slaughtered," Damas was told. Scowling Damas nodded at his Entargió and the men laid their weapons aside.

The Eagle ordered the men arrested and crucified along the length of the Marwhale Way, a stern warning to other traitors. Edo noted, with a dark amusement, that his old second, Halderso Después, was the Deka leader.

So he gets his heart's desire a command of his own, and look what that gets him; Edo knew that should have been salutary, a warning, but he was not a man to believe in signs and circumstance. The fates and the gods decided what happened to a man, they rode the slipstream of his mortal path for their own amusement.

Edo was sworn to Feror and had to trust in the gods whimsy to protect him.

In any case, the entire Fifth was to be disbanded its soldiers spread amongst the punishment legions in the north.

Damas, hunched like a wounded dog, a specter of the proud man who had arrived early that morning, was dragged naked from the Law

186

court, three guards at his side. Edo later learnt that the Secuas never made it to the slave market, he was set upon by an irate mob as his guards melted away, and was torn limb from limb. The torso and limbs were hung from the branches of an old oak less than half a league from where his men were being crucified.

Afterwards, the dark settled, the city calmer, Edo wandered towards the quays, to the small fondaco, the inn and merchant's warehouse his father had once owned.

He sat outside, on a low stone bench, facing away from the house towards the shimmering, moon-flecked water of the way.

Tallamun was his.

Three men had died for it and Damas was ruined, in part, on account if it.

The ledger of debit was growing- he knew he would need to seek balance for Balin and the others.

He knelt on the cold stone flags of the paved entrance to his father's old fondaco and prayed, not to Feror this time, but to Yanik the Merciful for forgiveness.

***

Edo was born in the fondaco.

He retained dim memories of his mother; a warm body pressed tightly against him, the smell of sweet perfume and a gentle hand stroking his feverish brow.

His father ran the fondaco, an inn and an

187

enclosed warehouse space for foreign merchants near Butcher's Quay. The traders, after disembarking, stored their goods in the warehouse, lived in rooms in the inn. These men, for Edo remembered no women amongst them, came from Incann, Northlands, Caedia, Milesia, Scian, Harnoi. They spoke Aonian with halting tongues, their musk strange; smells of searing heat and bitter cold. During the day they stood behind stalls in the warehouse as Aonian merchants sampled their goods, at night they sat at battered tables in the common room drinking and eating, the room a confused babble of foreign tongues.

Edo remembered his dad walking amongst them, slapping shoulders, slipping with indecent ease from one language to another, laughing, happy.

Eso, eleven years Edo's elder, would take his place behind the counter, serving wine, processing orders for food.

Good times those, before it all fell apart.

Their mother died when Edo was just five, her body a raging fever, red pustules swelling beneath her skin.

Thousands died that year and Deira wailed as the bodies of the ravaged were cast on huge pyres beneath the lowering temple of Mal Din, the Crippled God, the fearsome mien of his eternal brother Garge the Dark scowling from a ruby-red column of Milesian marble at the entrance to the temple.

It changed then, the life Edo had known. His father mad with grief took to the wine he once served his customers. He neglected his business and took to marwhale fishing, rowing out in the early mornings, coming back at night to an open bottle, shutting himself in his room, nursing his grief like a mid-wife a baby, while Eso, all of fifteen years of age, was left to manage business.

Old enough to help, Edo served those strange men, and listened to their talk and from their breathless whispers, he learned of Tallamun; the fabled land of eternal youth, where fruit grew like leaves on trees and age could not touch a man.

Where a man could touch the spirits and talk to them.

In his childish imagination he knew his mother would be there waiting for him, her spirit arms opening to welcome him.

Wrapped in grief- the death of his mother, the withdrawal of his father, the sulky violence of his brother-the notion became a beacon that kept something alive within him. Goggle-eyed he hovered near the tables as hard-faced men regaled one another with tales of their adventures, and rumors of that distant continent.

At night he dreamed of it, of sandy beaches and turquoise waters alive with sleek-backed dolphins, of a land matted with untamed forests laden with fruit and the magic of amna.

When he woke it seemed to him that Tallamun was more real than the drudgery that his life had become, chained to the inn.

Despite Eso's amused mockery, Edo never doubted. Much of what he had learned of Tallamun was a lie, this he knew, but he was certain the place itself existed.

As sure as he himself existed.

Eso's aim, even then, was set higher. He argued with their father, fraught arguments that lasted hours; he wanted to be a lawyer. Eso cajoled, begged, screamed, pleaded but the older man was set so deep in the slick groove of his mourning that no argument sufficed.

With the thick stave of his innkeeper's sigil their father beat Eso till he was blue, year after year. Occasionally he beat Edo too, till one day Eso stood up to him, grabbing father's forearm tightly, his eyes hard and cold and brooking no discussion. Father disappeared on a bender for a week after that and when he returned, stinking of wine and filthy from head to foot, he announced he intended to sell the fondaco and buy a yalak farm in an inland valley. He told them to get used to the idea, for they would be coming with him; if they didn't he would sell them as chattel in the slave markets, as was his right as head of the family. The next morning he set off in his rowboat as usual, and never returned. The empty boat drifted to shore a day later but the body was never found.

Eso grieved for a while, held the weeping Edo in his arms, promised him all would be well. For reasons of his own, Eso went ahead with his father's plan, sold the fondaco to a rival, bought himself an education in the Scribus, and, after ten years of study and hard work and sacrifice in which the brothers shared a two-roomed apartment in one of the living blocks above a

190

brothel, graduated a testae and rhetorician; a lawyer whose fame rapidly spread and whose wealth accumulated with obscene ease.

Edo rose from his sitting position, his legs aching with stiffness, his head numb. Prayer had cleared up nothing. The deaths remained, a stink on his conscience. Tallamun remained, a distant dream, a memory of his youth.

Tarnished now.

Edo turned from the fondaco. Music, sweet and cerebral drifted from the Temple of Liena, dogs barked somewhere close by. The moon was up, an enormous ball of molten metal backed by pin-bright stars.

Edo had no choice. He was promised to one god and in thrall to another. Tallamun was his destiny and he dared not shirk it.

He set off up the hills of Deira oblivious to the sounds of the city at night, his eyes towards the future.

CHAPTER 7 - GEHSI

The warriors came at night, silent as deer for all that they were bulky, eating up the leagues from their distant homes, dark forms flitting through the darkness. The silent warhounds they had brought with them surprised the guards at the edge of the village, ripping out throats with frightening ease, slobbering over the corpses as their masters patted their heads. Their shaman priests carried poles of flame, their warriors long oblong shields and the massive wooden swords they wielded like twigs. Gehsi's father, his two older brothers and two uncles stood against them outside their reed hut, stone-tipped spears shaky in their hands.

One massive warrior, wearing an antler-skull helm sliced Gehsi's father in two, stabbed eldest-brother in the stomach. Gehsi ran at the Malai, brandishing a club but mother and grandmam grabbed him and pushed him into the hut with the other children and the sisters.

He lay under a blanket listening to the sound of slaughter outside. His mother died blocking the doorway, screaming and praying for mercy.

The warriors knew none

They grabbed the younger women, shoving and kicking them outside, and hacked at the remaining women and children.

Gehsi tried to hide, kneeling behind a basket of grain but a gray-skinned warrior, chest tattooed with blood-red spots kicked at the basket, slashed down at him with his sword.

Gehsi toppled to the ground, bleeding from a shallow wound the length of his chest. When the warriors left they barred the door and for a long moment the darkness was absolute, the silence terrifying. Gehsi lay amongst his slaughtered siblings, the smell of blood a dank cloud, and stifled his screams though his fear was overwhelming.

When the warriors set fire to the roof of the hut he crawled towards the back, away from the doorway. Smoke billowed, choking, as he tore at the weave of withes. Sparks of fire fell about his ears and tears of pain rolled down his face. He lost two nails on his right hand before the withes gave way. He pushed and shoved splintered withies aside, making a gap to sneak through. Carefully he poked his head through the gap, eyes streaming from the smoke, stifling a cough from his choking lungs. He took stock, heart thumping; the village was aflame and Malai warriors were herding their captives- young women and older girls- in a column towards the east. He glared at those Malai, branding their images on his mind's eye; hard, inhuman faces, eyes glinting as they exulted in death and victory, hideous weapons, pale skin.

Brief images, flickering like fire burning a wall, searing his soul.

He swore to Agni that some day vengeance would be his.

If he lived. And just now things did not look all that good. He crawled towards the nearest

193

unfired hut, belly low, keeping his head down, gaining some protection from the high stalks of the jingu crops. Beside the nearest hut was the body of a man Gehsi recognized, Shuangceng the healer. Shuangceng had died fighting, his skull had been spilt open and blood matted his gray hair. His sword, a wooden blade sided with stone shards, lay to one side and Gehsi picked it up. He hefted it in his hand, feeling its weight. Gehsi had not yet come of age, his naming day lay a year ahead, but he was tall for a Pugi and strong for his age and had trained hard and long with his brothers.

The weapon felt good in his hands. He crawled past the hut, and hid behind Shuang's vegetable garden. A scatter of Malai were sweeping the village, searching for plunder or for any of the villagers who had fortuitously escaped their blades. Gehsi could hear their voices loud and cruel and victorious, like the barking of wolves after the hunt, coming closer.

For a long moment he stayed where he was, frozen to the spot, sweat dripping from his face, his heart beating like a sparrow.

He had no choice.

Between the garden and the hut was an open space, beyond were dense thickets of Alo and beyond these a series of interlocking gulches he knew well .

If he could reach the trees he had a chance for the Malai did not know this land as he did and he would run rings around them in the darkness.

He sprang to his feet and sprinted for the

194

trees, head down, willing himself to be like Tuigouzu the deer, fleet of foot and invisible to his enemies.

A shout rang out behind him. He glanced over his shoulder; two Malai warriors had spotted his escape, and were loping after them.

He put his head down and ran.

The Malai were larger but slower and he made the trees well ahead of them. He slipped off to the left, pounding along a thin trail. The darkness was profound but this was his land and he knew it like he knew the face of his kin. He pulled up after three hundred paces at to the edge of a brambled levee, lowered himself to the ground and found the gap between the brambles he knew would be there.

Voices sounded behind him, the loud voices of the Malai, still undaunted, still following him.

He snaked through the brambles, pulled himself out of their clasp and edged down the side of the levee, sure he had thrown the pursuing warriors.

He waited at the bottom of the drop, controlling his panting. He heard the footsteps of the Malai pounding past above, then fading away into the silence of the night.

But Yall the crow, the misfortunate one, was dogging his steps that night. Geshsi waited till he was sure the Malai were gone then started off to the east, to the nests of the people deep in the forest, but despite the care with which he stepped, he trod on a rotten branch and the sound of the branch echoed through the night like a curse. The

Malai yelled, closer than he would have believed; they must have been waiting for him to reveal himself. He heard them slashing through the bramble trying to reach him.

As the sounds came closer a strange paralysis overtook him, one born not of fear but of anger and a deep reluctance.

He still had time, he could run, throw the off his pursuers, for he had more than one escape route and he had tracked and fought with his brothers on this land since he was born.

That knowledge, in the end, was what stopped him.

This <u>was</u> his home.

His brothers, his sisters, his mother and father; lay dead, their flesh fouling or scorched by fire. To run now would feel like betrayal.

The Malai would come to know the heat of Pugi anger.

He cast around, searching for a plan, for there was no way a half-grown Pugi could take on two fully grown Malai face to face.But he knew the ground and they didn't, his eyesight in the gloom was better than theirs and he could climber faster and harder than they ever could, as was his people's want when they culled Agni's bounty from the treetops. His people were of the forest not of the plains or the seashore. When the Malai fought they planted feet firmly on the ground and hacked at one another till one stood victorious. The lore of his people was clear on this and their strengths he would use against them.

He tucked his sword into a belt and

scrambled towards the stream, the same wide brook that ran through the village.

He splashed into its chill water and scrambled about, searching, as the Malai sounded ever closer. He hefted two large stones, almost too heavy for him to carry and ran to the copse of nearby weaver trees nearby. He called out as he ran, fearful cries of a frightened prey. The Malai quickened their pace, smelling an end to the hunt, blundering carelessly towards him.

He ran a dozen paces past a tree, then made his way carefully back on the same tracks. At the tree he leapt high, placed the stones on a ledge between the lowest braches and the knobbled bole, then called one last time.

Pain from the wound on his chest seared as he pulled himself up onto the wooden ledge. He found a perch, half hidden by branches, so he had a full view of where the deer path led from the stream.

The Malai approached, more cautiously now that the sounds of his escape had stilled. He could hear them, talking to each other, the clicking sound the made when they spoke like the sound of locusts swarming fields of corn.

He waited.

The first Malai came into view, stopped below him. He hefted the first stone, balancing his weight against the tree.

Gods damn it, where was the other one?

Footsteps sounded behind the tree, hidden from his field of vision and the second Malai said something to his partner.

The Malai he could see started to move.

Far from ideal. Better to have both of them in view but if he didn't act he knew they would find him.

With a loud grunt he threw the stone with all his might; it caught the Malai on the head, smacked into his bone helmet and cracked it like a nut. The Malai dropped to his knees, pitched slowly till his forehead touched the ground. The second rushed around the tree, shouting, waving his sword, gesticulating.

Gehsi waited and when the second Malai bent over the first cast his stone.

This time his aim was off. The stone slammed into the Malai's shoulder.

Without hesitating Gehsi leapt from the tree, aware of blood slicking his chest and stomach, the pain neutralized by his battle rage. He landed on the man's back, held on with one hand and with the other rammed the wooden hilt of his sword against the warrior's head, near his unprotected ear. Again and again, till the bucking, screaming giant fell to his knees with a sobbing grunt.

Gehsi flipped backward, a quick summersault and landed on his feet. The Malai was already staggering upright again, sword half raised.

Gehsi slashed at man's weapon hand and the blade sliced to the bone, the sword dropping from the bastard's hand. Gehsi closed the gap, avoided a clumsy lunge, sliced at the man's unprotected legs.

The sword cut deep into flesh and bone, almost severing the left leg, and the Malai

198

whimpered as the leg gave way.

Gehsi leapt to one side, and when the man toppled he dashed behind him and finished him with a strike to the back of the neck.

The first Malai, still unconscious on the forest floor, went the way of the first.

Gehsi backed up to the cold bark of the tree, sweating, bleeding, in terrible pain.

He roared, and the sound of his voice sent a bunch of ala birds into flight. He roared again and it seemed to him like the forest answered him in all his pain and rage and desperation.

CHAPTER 8 - EDO

They met in the forecastle, Heeb and Edo and Pora Ferie- the Caedian who first charted this course for Edo with his stories of Tallamun- and Alik Jar, the leader of the their Deka of mercenaries, a Scian with a darkly hooded face and eyes blank as coal, who Edo knew to be fine tactical leader of men, though prone to rage and sudden violence.

Ferie still showed scars of his capture, a lived pink half-circle from eye to chin like a madman's grin, a mangled hand never fully healed. He wore a black calfskin glove on his left hand, to hide the missing finger. He was dressed in the Aonian fashion, but his blond hair and pale eyes gave away his origin.

He was taller than Edo by a head and the look in his eyes, a faint contempt, made Edo want to smash his face into pulp.

Not Ferie's fault. Years of warfare had left Edo with a hatred of all things Caedian, and Ferie just happened to be a too-typical specimen of his people.

"Sit," Edo ordered.

The Caedian sat, almost primly, squeezing his knees together like a virgin, the faint tick on his cheek the only indication of the emotion raging within him.

"I am sorry for what happened to you, Domin." The Caedian spoke hesitantly, a faint tremble hitched to his voice. "You suffered too, I believe."

Edo held a hand up, palm forward, ordering him to shut him up.

"When last we spoke you told me you were a ship's captain."

Ferie nodded, swallowed his adam's apple. "Ten years in the navy."

"You know how to sail these things."

Ferie smiled uncertainly. "They are more similar to the warships of our fleet than are your warships. Yes I can sail it for you."

"Good. He turned to Heeb. The Caedian sails the ship, reporting only to me and you. Give him two men, men you trust. They will enforce his will should the crew resist. Is this clear?"

Heeb nodded, his face a dark scowl.

Edo turned back to the Caedian. "There is room here." He indicated the bunks on the walls of the narrow room. "You sleep with us, to keep you safe. Many of the men you are working with on this expedition have lost brothers to your people and their bastard hilka. Be wary when you deal with them. When you are not on duty I want you here transcribing your memories of your last expedition. I want a map of all you remember." He took the Milesian book from the table. "Use this to jog your memories."

He turned to Alik. "Take the Caedian and introduce him to the men. Impress on them his importance to this mission. Dismissed."

The three men made to go.

"Heeb! Stay with me a moment."

Alik and Ferie left, the door closed behind

them.

"We have differences." Edo turned to the room's lone storage area, a narrow dresser with a hinged top. He lifted the top and pulled out a bottle of Lentrian red and pulled out the cork with his teeth.

He poured the liquid in two alabaster mugs and handed one to Heeb.

"Put them behind us?" He raised an eyebrow.

Heeb stared at him hard. "Religious and forgiving. Not the Edo I knew."

Edo shrugged. "People change."

Heeb sniffed the wine, smiled. "We have a job to do. I am sorry about what happened to your friend. Unfortunate circumstances. Not what we intended."

Edo shrugged. "The past is done. To the future. To Tallamun."

Heeb echoed the sentiment and drank, finishing the drink in one liquid swallow. He held out a hand and Edo shook it.

"Will that be all, Domin?" Heeb asked, with evident relief.

Edo smiled. "For now, Heeb. Tell the men I'll be out in a minute."

Heeb saluted, turned on his heels and left.

Edo waited for the door to close then spat on the ground. Heeb was right. People did not change, not really. The influences of those around them and their circumstances could force changes upon them. But fundamental change...

He shrugged. Heeb served a purpose, an important one as Edo's Second, a role with which they were both familiar.

As such Eso's demand that Edo take Heeb with them explicable. But Edo knew, if they returned to Aonia, that Heeb's life would end in a back alley, his throat slit.

Vengeance demanded it.

Yanik might not approve and Balin's restless spirit certainly would not, but that was the least Edo could do for the one friend he had ever had, who gave without wanting, who had shown him glimpses of other, better lives.

He knelt on the ground, the sour taste of the wine and his forked words still on his tongue, and prayed to the god of forgiveness.

For forgiveness.

For being the man that he was.

For not being the man Balin had shown him he might become.

CHAPTER 9 - GEHSI

Gehsi backtracked, planning to stay in the allo forest and make his way west, deeper into the forest. There were tracks, old as any deer path; the ancient roads of his people, tracks the Malai knew nothing about. They would lead him to safety.

Before dawn he found a perch in the lap of an old allo tree. When he woke it was bright, and a brace of red-ribs burst into flight as he stirred. He knew at once he was in trouble for voices echoed all about him; the rest of the Malai warband in pursuit of their brothers' killer or killers.

The Malai were clumsy in the forest, blundering through the undergrowth with all the grace of demented walray, but he could tell from the excitement in their voices that they had found his spoor.

He dared not lead the bastards to the cluster of nests in the depths of the forest on Blue Mountain where his father had been born- to do so risked the lives of countless Pugi. He knew a path that led towards the coast, away from the nests, away from safety.

He would track back, leading them to the coast and try to throw them off. If he succeeded he could always double back and head for the nests. If he failed -at least he could take comfort in knowing he taken two of them with him, in the knowledge that the bulk of his people still lived in isolated safety.

He leapt from the tree, landing on padded

feet. Through the trees he saw the, the distant, sun-blasted silhouettes of three Malai warriors, carrying their heavy swords, bone helms on their heads and lizard hides draped over their shoulders.

They did not spot him, continued west. He waited till they were out of sight then turned northeast. From here the deer track was hidden behind a culvert of dense weaver trees at the rear of a scree of limestone.

He ran through the forest, controlling his breathing, careful not to make noise on the dry underbrush.

The plateau of bare limestone was dotted with flowers and deep craters, a sere and dangerous landscape, exposed on all sides and difficult to cross.

He girded himself for flight and sprinted from the treeline, leaping from rock to rock, over deep crevices. The end of the plateau gave way to a grassy knoll and, higher, a dense forest of old-growth yantze. He got to his knees and crawled beneath the dense overhang of branches and fallen trunks.

Within was a long winding path, like a tunnel, dark and cool after the heat of the day. He took stock, sucking air into his lungs.

He thought he had lost the Malai, at least for now, but he would continue north and east, towards the coast. Tomorrow he could double back, and make his way to the nest.

He was about to set off again when he heard the yowling of hounds and the loud excited voices of the Malai.

They had tracked them to the plateau and were less than a league away.

He gathered his strength about him, acutely aware in an instant of the throb of his wounds and the leaden weight of his limbs.

As the first of the hounds reached the treeline, yowling and barking like maddened spirits, he set off at a fast run, praying for guidance and delivery from Tuigouzu, the antlered god of fleet-footed deer.

***

The chase lasted three days.

Gehsi snatched berries from trees for sustenance as his strength ebbed and the wound on his chest took on infection. At nights, when he grabbed rest, fever swam within him and his body was racked with chills.

Still he kept going, pulling away from the blundering Malai and time after time, having crossed streams or having climbed the soaring face of yet another rock formation, he was sure he must have lost them.

After three days he had no strength left. He had heard neither dogs nor Malai for half a day, and knew that he could go no further. If they caught up with him again he was finished.

He found a sheltered spot near a weir, water splashing ten spans below. Yellow mamai fruit grew on the bushes ringing the stream. He lay his head on the ground and slept, the fever churning through him, mixing with the dinning sounds of the small waterfall.

When he woke the sun was in his eyes, blinding him. He tried to stand, but his legs gave way after a few paces and he slumped to his knees. He heard a clicking sound from behind him and turned.

Two ang stood staring at him, fangs bared. They were less than half his size, young males he judged and they would not usually have attacked a Pugi, but their amber eyes glinted with hunger and a dim awareness of his distress.

They opened their mouths, clicking as they flew from their perch, landing near him. They raised their scaly necks, the air from their wide wings wafting a dense musk smell towards him. In his long flight he had lost the obsidian sword, dropped it while crossing above a deep ravine, and was forced to scrabble now for a clutch of nearby rocks. He hefted a large one and cast it at the first of the ang. The stone flew with no great strength and the ang hopped aside, still eying Gehsi quizzically, as if puzzling how weak Gehsi really was.

It turned towards its companion and squawked. The companion lowered its head, beat its wings, rose into the air and dove at Gehsi. Gehsi raised his hands and long claws raked his arm. The second circled him, flew onto his back and stabbed him with the sharp spear-like tusks, protrusions rising from its beak. Gehsi arched his back as the pain seared through him and flapped about with his fists, futilely trying to knock the beast away. The first of the two animals bit deep into his wrists, rows of sharp-toothed teeth jabbing into the flesh beneath his skin as the second stabbed him again.

Blood flowed freely, down his back, along his arm.

He almost gave up for had no energy to resist anymore.

Almost, but he had not survived this long to die at the hands of these filthy carrion.

Rage took hold of him, red and pure, stemming from deep in his spleen. He howled and reached with his free hand for the beast gnawing at his wrist.

He grabbed its neck and smashed the bony head on a nearby lump of moss-coated granite. He smashed again and felt the beast's grip loosen. He cast the body from him and turned on the companion, still straddling his back, lapping at his blood.

The ang flapped its heavy veined wings, shrieking in vague alarm. Full grown it was unable to fly far and landed on the lowest branch of the nearest alo, just out of Gehsi's reach.

Geshi´s blood dripped from its beak and it opened its mouth and ran a long red tongue around the blood, making a sucking sound.

Then it pulled back its neck, raised itself to its full height and screeched.

Birds flapped into the air, through the canopy of leaves, startled by the call.

Answering screeches sounded through the forest. The ang seemed to be calling for reinforcements, informing its kind of a wounded creature close to death, ready for the killing.

Gehsi slumped back against the bole of the nearest tree.

He could not reach the ang and he didn't think it would attack him, but when others came it would rediscover its courage.

He had only to wait.

Death was hot on his heels.

He had only to wait.

CHAPTER 10 - EDO

The galway were trading ships; triple-masted, thick in the beam, shaped like a nut sawed-off at the stern and of the type used to cross the choppy unpredictable waters of the Bearing and the Sea of Incann.

Short, sturdy, durable; the nautical equivalent of dray horses. The Aonian navy used the single-masted rhaemis; powered by rows of lifeless nauts, murderers and thieves whose souls had been possessed by a single warlock who captained the ship. The rhaemis were sleek, fast ships but prohibitively expensive and fared better in the calm waters of the Middle Sea and the coast up to Sartra. Edo was pleased. The galway suited the purposes of their expedition far better. He renamed them, as was customary when taking possession of new ships; the Abril, the Adas and the Vorco, for the three spirits of the western, northern and eastern winds.

He sacrificed a goat in honor of each spirit and painted the hulls with blood, tying the carcass of the butchered animals to the yardarm of the bowspirit, where it would watch over them once the gulls plucked it clean.

Eso had kept his word, and Eso spent a week by the docks, gulls flying high circles above them, the sun egg-yellow warm, the sea like a blur of promise glittering with light.

Edo bellowed orders as the ships were laden with everything he had asked for, and more.

Cattle and horses were tied to the masts in giant slings. In calm weather the slings would be lowered to the ground but when the weather set in the slings could be lifted and the animals kept from breaking their legs or doing themselves damage.

The day before they were due to depart they spotted a family of jaywale in the distance, the massive creatures spitting water in great funnels.

A good omen, they all agreed.

The crew Eso hired were ex-navy, and to bolster them were a deka of tough hard-bitten men, veterans of the north, both Aonian and Scian, who had not settled back to civilian life but craved adventure. Danger. The promise of the far world, the land of Dreams that was Tallamun, worked on them like an itch they could not reach. They talked amongst themselves of wealth beyond imagining, of the villas they would buy and the women they would bed.

Edo saw it differently; these men were addicts to the pulse of their own excitement. They would never settle, never come to a place of rest.

Violence was their only passion, that and the hunger for excitement.

He knew he would have to assert his authority over them from the beginning. If he failed in that then they would take against them in a flash.

Eso had insisted Heeb accompany the expedition, against Edo's wishes. Edo still bristled at the sight of the Scian; but Edo knew him for a brutal and experienced Span Deka, one who knew

211

how to motivate men. If they could forget their personal differences, for a time, they would make a good team, as they done once before.

Eso threw a grand banquet on the night before they left. He invited the Council of Five and the Priests of the various temples. The other guests were from the senate or testees from the law courts. A few select generals, many who were bitter enemies for they had supported Damas, were also in attendance. Eso wanted to build bridges, and this extravagant expedition was, he said in his speech, a symbol of their unity and the unity of the Republic, its will to grow and expand.

Slaves, their hair shorn, served food and wine to the groups assembled in the perfumed gardens of Eso's villa. Musicians played and the women of the temple sang.

Eso, with two priests of Malyn, wearing wreaths of seaweed and chains of mollusks draped across their shoulders, sacrificed a dun bull; an impressive beast with wide flaring nostrils and long horns that must have cost a small fortune. The beast's blood steamed in the night air as it spilled onto the flagstones. The priests pulled out its innards and proclaimed the omens good. Edo was forced to sit at the high table with the Council of Five, his rehabilitation after the trial complete, his name exonerated of any wrongdoing in Caedia. Wrongdoing that had been laid to rest with Damas. The brand on his forehead was another story- a pale scar that would never disappear.

The meal finished he drifted to the edges of

212

the gathering, sipping watered Aonian wine and, having made small talk with more people he could hope to remember, bade Eso goodnight.

When he woke it was light and bars of sunlight spilled into his room from behind the shutters. He got dressed; a long tunic of white, the crimson patch on the shoulder denoting his position as captain, woolen hose, leather armor, a plumed helm, faced with the snout of a wolf.

In languorous procession they made their way to the ships; Eso, the priests, Ferie, the mercenary leader Alixx Jar, Heeb, revelers from the night before who had stayed in the guesthouse overnight.

Edo boarded the ship, then turned back to Deira, one hand on the wooden rail. Eso was looking at him, eyes moist.

"Little brother, take care of yourself," he ordered.

Edo nodded, waved as they pulled anchor and set off. He glanced back, once only. Eso was still there, on the docks, surrounded by people. His hand was raised, whether in benediction or farewell, Edo could not say.

A lump in Edo's throat told him all he needed to know. His brother, who loved him in his twisted way, had done all he could for him, had cleared his name and set him back on track.

Now it was up to him-he had to find Tallamun. More- he had to make the journey worthwhile by proving its economic worth.

He spared a last glance at Deira and his brother then turned his back on his home and turned to face the turquoise sea that surrounded him like a dream.

**

They sailed for a week with a gusting southwesterly. The ships glided over the sea, like impatient dolphin straining at the masts. The two square mainsails and the lateen towards the stern filled with wind, like joyous bellies replete with a fine meal. The good weather and the fast time they were making kept spirits high.

The storm hit them like a sucker punch.

It appeared on the distant horizon before daybreak. Heeb woke Edo from a light slumber. He scrambled onto deck. Ferie stood there already near the helmsman, sniffing the air, body tensed and leaning forward from the hips.

The light was purple, pre-dawning but even Edo, a relatively inexperienced sailor for a Deiran, knew they were in trouble.

Heaped thunderheads swirled high to the west, swelling with every passing second, and thunder boomed and echoed, like the sound of distant waves beating a phantom shore. Lightening flashed and the clouds billowed forward, faster than Edo would have thought possible.

The gusting, water laden-wind that had sprung up, tried to steal the words from his mouth as he spoke to Ferie. "Can we skip past it?"

He thought at first that the Caedian had not heard him, but the Caedian swiveled on the balls of his feet and faced him after a long pause, an ironic smile playing on his lip. Condescending bastard sees me as a land lubber, but I guess that is his prerogative. He is the expert, our man of the hour.

"Skip past? My guess is no. Best to baton down everything we can and run before the wind. When it catches we furl the mainsails and pray. I'll signal the other ships. Prepare yourself, captain. Pray to whatever gods you know, for our little world may soon end."

***

Waves tossed the ship about like a child's toy. A wind whipped shrilly, moaning and screeching, a harridan's call, and Edo imagined strange creatures, long and thin and dark flitting above him in the violent air, teeth bared and claws whipping towards them, dismal mouths calling the ships to their death.

The galway slipped into wave troughs, falling forward, a lurching sensation building in the pit of his stomach as the prow dipped, fell forward, the bowspirit slamming into water. Then a long moment, breath held as the ship struggled to right itself. When it did, the prow rose from the sea in a flurry of water, surged forward over the tops of waves higher than the tallest buildings in Deira sliding on that great liquid back till it dropped.

Again and again.

They watched the yard arm of the bowspirit crack and heard a stifled scream as three of the

215

deckhands- men he had ordered to attend to the slings of their small herd of cows - were swept overboard. The ships timbers groaned and cracked, as if dissatisfied with the world, but held.

Held.

He had tied himself to a wooden strut back from the helm and watched as the Caedian, Heeb and the helmsman fought the rudder.

Eventually the Caedian threw up his hands in disgust and bound a rope of hemp to the helm, tying it fast as he could.

Nothing more they could do.

They retreated behind the forecastle, beckoning at Edo to follow. He shook his head, a mountain of water breaking over him, taking the breath from his lungs.

When the water receded he dug deep breaths of salted air and coughed up the bile he had swallowed.

He faced the waves, tied to the wooden railing, facing the wind, facing the harpies and their shrill cries.

His mind was with the ship, urging it on, feeling it crack beneath him, as nails came loose and timbers warped.

With the force of his mind he willed it to hold.

Again and again water assaulted him.

He spat it out, spat in its eye.

Their journey was destiny.

Feror and Malwyn were with them, and the fey spirits of the storm could do their worst.

"This ship will not sink," he yelled into the

216

teeth of the rain. "It. Will. Not. Sink."

He screamed the words again and again.

The ship will not sink.

217

CHAPTER 11 - GEHSI

The ang slowly gathered, squawking and hissing. Back against the bole of a tree he watched them through waves of pain and fever, a pile of rocks nestled in his lap. He counted a dozen and still they were drumming and cawing, as if debating whether to attack now or let him die first.

He had wrapped gallas grass around his wrist but the wound on his back was deep, oozing blood and too far back for him to staunch.

He felt himself slipping through the veils of the world, a dull haze filming his eyes. Only pain kept him focused, but even that faded with time as chill heat, part fever part loss of blood, took hold.

He closed his eyes for a moment.

Startled awake.

One ang, larger by a head than the others, was scampering towards him, less than four spans away. He cast a stone and the stone caught it square on its domed head between the protuberant eyes. It took a step back, flapping its wings, shrieking.

Three others moved forward on his right and he thought he heard others behind him, over his left shoulder.

He cast a stone, then a second. The first hit its target, slamming into the outstretched neck of one of the approaching ang. It crumpled to the ground, twitching. Clearly incapacitated as it let out a thin, hissing wail. The second stone missed completely but his missiles served to hold the beasts in check. Squawking came from behind him, loud and excited.

He craned his head. Could see nothing.

When he turned back a pack of eight had built a semi-circle in front of him, a dozen spans away. He had three stones left, two large and round and one flat with a cylindrical snout, that he intended to use as a hand weapon. He cast the throwing stones, his aim erratic, the ang far enough away to easily skip out of reach. He struggled shakily to his feet, brandished the remaining stone at them and yelled in final defiance. They came at a flapping run towards him, sharp beaks open, long tongues licking forward, amber eyes glinting with the prospect of food.

He caught the first beast a sharp hard blow that killed it outright, bone crushing beneath the blow. The dead ang's momentum knocked him back and a second ang, claws flashing landed on his chest.

He fell to the ground, rolling, lashing out.

Too many of them. All over. Getting in each others way but still he was bitten, stabbed, clawed. He lost the stone as wounds opened all over his body. He curled in a ball as best he could, all awareness draining from him, bar spikes of pain, the beating of stiff wings and the rotten smell of wild breath cackling near his face.

***

A fierce roar sounded through the trees like

219

an elemental cry of nature, a roar that, even in Geshi´s weakened state, rang of fear and anger and death at night; this was the voice of the real enemy, the cry of a murderous Malai.

Gehsi was lying, still curled in a ball, face smeared in the damp mud. The attack seemed to lessen in intensity and Gehsi took the opportunity to raise himself on his hands and sidle away from the carrion. The ang were facing away, guarding him now, hissing and scowling at the intruder at their feast trying to steal their spoils. Geshi turned away, crawling as hard as he could. He heard a loud thump and then warm blood sprayed his neck. He closed his eyes, kept crawling. When he judged the distance far enough he turned on his back, too weak to even think about standing. His face and hands were a ragged mass of flesh, his body, had fared little better; blood poured from him like from a salters wooden sieve.

He opened his eyes. Three of the ang lay nearby, one cut in half, the others decapitated. The survivors shrieked in outrage from the branches of nearby trees. A Malai warrior stood over him, long teeth glinting, hair matted in greasy braids. The man had the body of one who was in his prime but his hair was matted with dirt and his face lined with seams of age.

The Malai spat at the ground near Gehsi's face, raised a spear in two hands.

Sunlight glinted off the copper of the spear and a thrill of disbelief and awe ran through Gehsi.

That spear. It couldn't be. After all this time.

220

It dove towards his head, till with an almost imperceptible flick of the wrist, the Malai turned it aside so it embedded itself in the earth a hand's span from Gehsi's ear.

The Malai roared, spit flecking from his pale lips and Gehsi waited still as a rabbit trapped in light.

Something strange was happening here; he did not think this Malai was not one of those who had been chasing him, and despite this show of anger, this bastard intended Gehsi no harm.

How Gehsi knew this he could not say- though he realized now that the spirits of his ancestors had been with him, guiding him to this place. The presence of the spear was confirmation of that.

Gehsi lay back, head falling through soft grass to the damp earth beneath. A butterfly, white with a black diamond marking, flew across his sight, and he took it as a vision from Agni as blood leaked from his body and the darkness descended with a rush like flooding water.

CHAPTER 12 - TAMBER

The Pugi, little more than a child on the cusp of adulthood, lay sprawled beneath Tamber. He had wanted so much to strike the thing dead, run it through with the spear.

He had not killed in a long time, had not hunted.

The old hunger was still there.

The beast-man, for male it was, was bleeding from a thousand wounds, small and large. His face was a mask of blood, the flesh scored in places to white bone. The Pugi had lost most of the deerskin hide that covered its body and when Tamber knelt beside it, he saw that there were deep wounds, front and back and an older, scabbed wound on the chest and stomach that oozed pus.

He touched the Pugi's head with one hand. The things breathing was shallow, its brow fevered and hot.

<u>Take him. With you.</u> Insistent, these voices in his head. He eyed the stave of the spear, still tempted. Butcher this one Pugi child, and he could free himself of Kali and Raven.

The idea, at one level, was appealing but what purpose would it serve?

If he wandered south, towards the dense ring of Malai villages near the Moahr Cliffs or north to the Delta tribes, or beyond towards the lands of Frozen Ones the best he could hope for was to be taken on as a hired hand working a meager patch of land. At worst they would catch him, torture him, eat his liver and dance around his corpse, filled with the strength he had bestowed on them.

For that was what the Malai did when they captured warriors of tribes not their own.

His own people, in the twelve towns and villages of Irgal Bay, would stone him if he came too close.

He laughed bitterly.

The only company he had were the lunatic voices of the beings that inhabited his head, and a Pugi pet.

He bent down, cast the boy carelessly over his shoulder, shocked by how little he weighed, then set off for his lonely cave.

***

Back at the cave he laid the beast on a bed of hides. He stripped it of its hides and washed and dressed the wounds with a poultice of spider web, vervain and willow bark powder.

He wrapped the wounds in scraps of old but clean mil-cloth, the last he had. He held its head high and forced it to swallow a tisane of herbs, the Pugi spluttering and coughing.

When it was asleep he walked back into the forest with one of the large stone axes he used for cutting firewood. He cut withies from the nearest copse of allo, working all morning till his body was soaked in sweat. He carried the withies back to the ledge before the cave, handful by handful, then started to work on them, twisting and bending the green wood. It took him three days, days he spent either working on the wood or taking care of the comatose Pugi.

The voices in his head were mercifully silent, had left him alone with his new companion.

What did men do with animals? Penned them of course.

The wooden cage he constructed was large enough to hold the Pugi lying down and almost large enough for the beast to stand, strong too for alo wood was nigh on unbreakable.

When he was finished he threw fresh hides into the cage, lifted the Pugi in two arms, then laid him flat on his back within.

The door was a simple flap that he could lift. He bound it tight with catgut and wrapped one end round a stone beaker.

If the bastard woke and tried to get out Tamber would know about it.

When it was finished it was dark, moonless.

His fire was embers. He stoked it, then laid down beside its warmth, falling asleep to the sound of crackling fire and the beat of the breakers outside, strangely comfort by the simple presence of another living thing sharing hi sleeping space.

He slept long and hard, and the day was a long yellow arm well before he woke.

CHAPTER 13 - GESHI

Sharp stabbing tremors of pain and vivid thirst brought him back to hazy consciousness. He opened a gummy eye, throat dry as beef jerky.

The Malai was sitting across from him, squat-legged behind a fire; broad, ugly face scowling.

Gehsi reached out and touched the wooden cage surrounding him.

Penned like a fowl.

He tried to sit, struggled forward on threading weaves of pain and nausea.

He had been cleaned, his wounds dressed. As Gehsi had surmised the Malai had no designs to harm him. At least not right away. Perhaps wanted to break him and use as a slave, or worse. Having noticed Gehsi stirring, the Malai held out a wooden bowl filled with steaming liquid and passed it through the door of the cage. Gehsi drank deep, ignoring the scalding heat, aware of hunger ravening his stomach. When he was finished he handed back the bowl and nodded thanks.

The Malai showed his teeth in what might have been a smile and gestured at the fire. Gehsi tried to crawl out, but his strength failed him and the Malai rose smoothly to his feet and lifted Gehsi to a place near the fire. Gehsi- gagging at the man's loathsome, alien stink- lay on his side, the warmth from the drink narcotic, pain-relieving as the Malai spoke words Gehsi did not understand, talking to beings Gehsi could not see but whose presence he could feel like a dim ache of a nascent headache.

Gehsi could not decide whether to laugh or cry. He had saved by the enemy and the enemy, it seemed, was some sort of crazy holy man, isolated from his own kind like the <u>flightless</u> among the Pugi who spent their lives in the canopies of the trees and adrift on the high mountains far from the Verman and the Temples of Night.

Gehsi cast a sly glance at the spear, resting against the wall on the far side of the cave. Markings were etched on its side, a concentric ball and within them the figure of three male warriors and an armed female of the warrior caste, arms raised to the sky.

No Pugi could ever have mistaken it for anything but what it was.

He did not know how it had come here, not did not really care, but he harbored no doubt.

The spear had been blessed by the Eyeless Holy Men of Tuolizei Tuozheiang, the warriors in the circle were worshipping Tusuonao, god of the dead, and the spear was called Qiazhua, Raiser of the Dead. Forged in the great nests of the past, it was prophesied that when it was returned to the Pugi the ancestors would arise and drive from the land those vermin who held the Pugi in contempt and captivity, who slaughtered them at will.

Gehsi, despite the pain, felt the swell of excitement in his breast. Fate and the spirits of the ancestors had brought him here. He would survive, and when he was strong enough he would kill the Malai and make his way back to his people, a hero.

The Malai, still talking to himself and chanting, began to dance round the fire.

Gehsi felt his eyes grow heavy, his body demanding rest, and he drifted into sleep to the sound of a harsh language which for him was synonymous with butchery and oppression. A strange lullaby indeed.

CHAPTER 14 - EDO

Sometime after dawn the storm passed, sudden as it had appeared, the mountainous waves becoming mere hills, the shrill wind fading away to a distant echo.

Edo, cold and frozen, fumbled at the knots binding him to the railing and took stock. He reckoned they had lost half their cattle, torn from their slings and swept overboard. Already sailors climbing out of their quarters beneath the fo'castle, were seeing to the masts, checking the rigging, carrying buckets from the bilge. He hurried to the main deck and scrambled down. Six men, striped to the waist, were operating the bilge pumps. Others carried buckets to the stairwell and a chain of men waiting above.

Ferie and Heeb had gotten below, before him, and stood staring at the piled mound of their supplies, in hemp sacks and wooden barrels.

Edo stopped to their right, hands behind his back, hiding his nervousness. "How bad is it?"

Heeb turned towards him fingering the stubble on his chin; bleary-eyed, pale-skinned and soaked from head to foot, but then there was not one of them but looked like a drowned rat.

"Half the grain gone. As much of the amna powder rendered useless. Jerky and wine should be okay. Half the cattle and five horses lost."

A disaster, Edo knew. He had hoped to be self reliant when they arrived, had planned on milk from the cattle and using the horses as both dray horses and as mounts for his scouts. The flour, rationed and doled out appropriately would have been enough to see them through a winter. No longer. He had to hope the other ships were not so badly hit.

"How did the men fare?"

Six sailors missing, presumed swept overboard. Two of the mercenaries. Nobody seems to know what happened to them." Heeb shrugged. "Old scores settled perhaps, not that we'll ever know."

"Your report, Captain Ferie?"

The Caedian turned. The scar on his face glowed pinkly, a strange contrast to the pallor of his skin and the lines beneath his eyes.

"Nothing good. We were blown off course and there is no telling where we are exactly. Plus we have lost sight of the other ships."

"What is your dead reckoning?"

"The lobe put us two hundred leagues west of Deira the night before the storm hit. The storm blew us south, then southwest. We were doing no less than eight knots and straining at the seams for a day. So, add another fifty leagues." He shrugged. "It's a big sea and our target, what I saw of it, was a large island. Don't worry. I'll find it. My worry is the other ships."

"Are the signals lit?"

"Of course."

If they are out there we'll find them." Edo said with more confidence that he felt, for they were up a large and violent creek without a paddle- a leaky hull to boot- if they didn't?

229

***

The harsh signal, a rancid blue, from the rod of glowing amna on the crow's nest could be seen, Ferie reckoned, for a dozen leagues in either direction, for the storm was a distant memory; a gentle swell filled the sails and the Abril moved before the wind like a colt.

The sky was blue, the swell of the sea turquoise glistening with white. A family of dolphins, their sleek bodies the color of black pearl, tracked them; swimming playfully nearby for a dozen leagues.

Faint wispy clouds, high to the west, barely marred the spotless azure.

The two master carpenters Edo had insisted on having aboard each vessel were busy hammering and fixing, but the bilges were empty as they would ever be and the ship, battered as it was, had been deemed seaworthy by Ferie.

Demensidos the warlock wandered amongst the numerous wounded- two sailors hit by flying spars, a mercenary who had fractured his leg in a mysterious fall, the cook who been thrown against a bulkhead, presumably by the force of waves and not the anger of displeased customers-feeding them herbal concoctions, laying hands on them and dancing as gouts of foul scented incense wafted about their heads.

Minor injuries were numerous and to be expected but, with the exception of the cabin boy whose ribs had been staved in, by a falling barrel

230

of salted pork, Edo was expecting them all to recover.

In the sharp light before noon the Vorco hove into sight, sails glinting silver. Edo found himself cheering with the rest of the crew, heart full of joy. Ferie waved his floppy hat and grinned at Edo. Edo grinned back.

The Vorco hove into view and its captain signaled his report. They too had caught the full brunt of the storm's fury and had suffered, though their losses overall, both men and supplies, were a tad less than the Abril. Of the Adas there was still no sign.

Night fell and day broke, a second beautiful day, like atonement for the violence of the storm, and Edo knew the Adas was gone.

All hands lost.

They waited another day, circling about, cutting patterned grids through the water, before they gave up.

As night fell, the sky a ball of molten orange, the sea red as death, the warlocks intoned the Prayer for the Fallen and Edo cast a symbolic wreath, brought from Deira, of knotted ivy into the sea.

The crew stood in silence as it floated away. When it had disappeared from sight they turned about their business, guiding the ship through yet another night, on the way to the fabled land.

***

Edo sat in his cabin, poring over Ferie's

sketchy map- drafted from memory, using the beautifully drawn map in the book from Yanik's Sanctuary as a mnemonic aid.

The best I can do, Ferie had sworn, though Edo had registered doubt in the Caedian's voice. How could there not be?

A decade had passed-more-since Ferie had made the voyage and he had not set out searching for Tallamun, but been blown off course, ending there by chance. Still; Edo had seen the Caedian work, every spare moment of his free time, beads of sweat on his forehead and a look of fierce concentration on his face as he added detail to the sum of their extant knowledge. Gods knew the man had tried, but then he had to. They had come too far to turn back. If Ferie failed they were all dead men and the cavernous ocean would swallow them as a giant a gnat.

Edo coughed into his hand, a rasping hard cough that tore at his throat. His tongue was dry with thirst and the salt sweat of his body stank.

He stretched, working out knots in his back and glanced at the amna clock. He was due on deck. He forced himself to his feet, heart pounding with vague apprehension; his mood alternated between periods of depression and sour aggression; he was not alone. Boiling under the sun the ship was ferment, like juice in a sealed barrel cooking in the sun, threatening explosion.

Their ration of fresh water had dwindled- a week ago when Ferie had conducted his last inventory they had less than a quarter left of what they had started with on the Abril and on the

232

Vorco five barrels of water had been soiled by salt during the night of the storm, a fact not realized till they broke open those casks. At the sight of that precious, useless resource Edo had to school himself not to cry or lash out in blind anger.

During the day the sun was a golden press, hot as coal, stamping its blistering fingers on their necks; nights belonged to a sultry temptress, her promise and goad replete with vengeance and violence. Day or night, the wind had died down to a gasp that barely wrinkled the sail and left them becalmed in this torrid zone of death.

Edo pressed the flat of his palm against his forehead, worrying at the knot of pain spasming in the hollow behind his eye.

He stood, eyes dilating, a wave of blackness threatening to knock him to his feet. Like many of the others he had been stricken by a strange wasting fever, a fever that kept him constantly thirsty but unable to hold down food.

He took deep breaths, waited for the weakness to pass and made for the door, passing the bunks where a sleeping Heeb lay snoring.

Heeb, Ferie and Edo worked four-hour shifts, the three of them, struggling through days like exhausted automatons but Edo had found, as the days drifted by, sleep evading him, exhaustion weighing him down, worry like a damp blanket fending off tiredness.

He pulled open the wooden door from his cabin, blinked as the sun flashed in his eyes. The sound of water lapping on the starboard bow mixed with ugly laughter.

Laughter that stopped and faded away to nothing as he appeared, leaving a hollow threat in its wake.

Five sailors, men whose names he barely knew but whose faces he recognized. Troublemakers all. He glared at them as he made his way at double time up the wooden steps to where Ferie manned the helm.

"What was that all about?" Edo asked.

Ferie shook his head, saying nothing, his mien troubled.

"Did they say anything to you?"

Ferie blinked.

"Feror's balls, man. They don't need to love you. They <u>do</u> need to obey you. Get some kip. I'll take over."

Ferie stared at him hard, as if debating saying something. He clamped his mouth closed, nodded from the waist in the formal Caedian way, turned his back and left.

Edo almost called him back but then thought better of it.

He would always wonder afterwards. If he had intervened then could he have stopped what happened?

***

Two weeks passed.

Between the two ships they had water left for a week, rationed at a cup a day.

Food for longer, of course, but what good would that do?

234

The men had spread tarpaulins, hoping to catch rain that never came. Two mercenaries drank their fill of salt water and unsated, attacked the guards near the casks in their craving.

The mercenaries were cut down, their bodies cast without ceremony overboard, the trail of blood attracting white dorsal-finned sharks.

The sun tortured all of them, beat them with its brazier glow and sucked their innards.

The men had gone beyond anger, into a state of listless apathy and the ship threatened to come apart as routine maintenance and base discipline failed.

Edo yelled when he was able to muster enough energy and threatened to have men flogged but in truth he was struck with the same malaise and his threats rang hollow, even to himself.

They would die here if the wind refused to blow. They all knew it and helplessness had paralyzed them.

Demensidos the warlock and Cocto the priest of Malwyn spent their nights in prayer and dance.

To no avail.

The days passed in that blind haze of heat, they had five days of water left and earlier that week one of the two bosuns was found lying face down in the bilge, no obvious marks of violence on his body.

Edo suspected the worst, for the man was a notorious bully and champion of sycophants. Edo had the men lined up on deck and questioned them, but in the absence of witnesses or evidence there was nothing he could do. He warned Heeb to arm the mercenaries and have his own weapons always to hand, but Alix Jar leader of the mercenaries, had turned sour and uncooperative and Edo was no longer certain he could trust the Scian.

No longer could certain he trust himself.

The longer this went on the more he felt like screaming at the brazen sky. Only the responsibility of command kept him in check.

Edo was on deck, the sun rapidly setting in a blaze of orange and pink, a faint impression of a full moon already high in the sky.

For all that it was dusk, the heat was unbearable. Edo sat back against the helm, closed his eyes. He must have dozed, a shout of fear startling him awake.

Heeb and Ferie, wearing armor and wielding long swords, came storming out of the forecastle. Above the crows nest drifted balls of molten fire, a slow swirling dance, a sound like air whistled through clenched teeth.

Edo estimated they were little larger than a cow's head, pinkly orange they swept across the sky in goose-like formation, at a height about twice the length of the mast.

As they passed over the ship, drifting away into the gloaming, Edo breathed a sigh of relief and was about to turn to Ferie when they swarmed back.

Faster than any living thing he had had ever seen they made for the mast; something, a sense of cohesion perhaps, made him think they were sentient.

Devils? Spirits of the gods? An inkling, faint as dust on a moth's wing, impregnated itself on his mind.

One of the two lookouts on the crows nest fell to his knees, screaming prayer to the gods as molten fire sped towards him. The second sailor was dashing for the rigging- skipping along the yardarm ignoring the jackstay, balanced like a rope walker-balls of flame silhouetted against his back. Edo beat the air with his fist, screaming incoherently, urging the man on with every tendon in his body. As the sailor swung over the yardarm one foot snagged in a lose rope dangling from the footrope. He own momentum threw him off balance, tossing him sideways. His fingers clutched air as he hung over emptiness for one awful moment, a fly suspended in aspic. Edo lowered his eyes.

The sailor toppled to the deck head smashing into it with head and shoulders. He lay still, unmoving, a broken doll.

The balls of fire reached the crow's nest, ringed the remaining lookout, swooping and diving like birds of prey.

They engulfed him. Fireballs dissolved on touch, became thin flaming lines that entered through his mouth, nostrils, burnt passages through his eyeballs. Flame licked from him. He shuddered as if in the grip of a strange fever then got to his feet, long hair flaming and burning, skin blackening.

He smiled, looking down at them from eye

sockets black and red like smoldering coals, eyes that no longer existed.

But could see.

He grinned and in that grin Edo saw ageless cruelty. The lookout held his hand out as if in farewell, stepped onto the edge of the bowl that was the crow's nest and thrust himself forward then out. He slammed feet first into the turquoise water, disappeared beneath the gently pulsating waves in a muted splash.

For a long moment a deathly silence reigned and then flame sprang from the water, hissing, shooting into the air.

It coalesced again into tight ball-like knots, drifting high and away from the ship. Edo did not breath again till it was out of sight.

When it was sure it was gone he ordered two men up to the crow's nest for tendrils of flame flickered there. They went, reluctantly, each carrying a bucket of water to damp the fire.

Ferie came and stood beside him.

"What do you make of that?"

Edo shrugged. "Ask Endemios what he thinks? I'll be in my quarters."

Edo sat on the bed, gasping, the thirst like a grasping plague, his lips cracked his vision uncertain.

Ferie cracked the door open and bundled inside. "The warlock's all at sea."

Edo forced a smile. "Him and me both. Is it not legally impossible for a warlock to have no opinion."

"Oh, he has an opinion. Lacking insight or

value, granted, but it qualifies as an opinion. Fire, he says, inflamed by spirits. Where, why or how he cannot say." Ferie's smile was a half-grimace.

Edo knotting his fevered brow. "He as terrified as the rest of us."

"Shitting his trousers."

Edo rose, ignoring the faintness that came over as he stood. "I think I know what they are."

He rubbed the pain from his head, walked to the table opened the stoppered jar and poured a hand's width into his bone cup.

"Edo?" Ferie asked querulously.

The Scian's face was lined with exhaustion, pale in places, in others lobster boiled by heat. Sweat poured in runnels down his face and slicked his beard.

"We have crossed a boundary. Some meridian point. The new world lies close by. The fire flames are harbingers."

Ferie sat down near him on the bed, pulling at his long hose.

"Harbingers?"

"Guardians of Tallamun...seeking sacrifice...their toll the cost of entry." He paused, gesturing. "Fire opposes water. These things can exist only near land. Like seabirds." He rubbed gritty eyes. "The wind will return now. If the sacrifice appeased them...otherwise I imagine they will return and claim more of us all till they are satisfied." He reached out and grabbed Ferie's arm. "We have done it, Caedian. Tallamun lies nearby." He gestured to the west aware Ferie was eyeing him strangely.

239

"A strange conceit, Domin. You truly believe this?"

Edo shrugged.

"I would pray but I don't know whether to hope you are wrong or right."

***

The witching hour, a bone pale moon in the sky, silver glistering off lapping water. Edo stood on deck, taking his turn at the helm, Heeb standing quietly near him. Edo had told the Scian his thoughts about the origin of the fire spirits but Heeb, face gaunt and eyes dull, had seemed unimpressed.

Ferie took sightings with his astrolabe, checked his charts and the map. The chances were good, he said, that Edo was right. Now the three of them waited, in bated silence, for the first sign of wind.

Edo knew, with the certainty of faith that land lay somewhere to the west, out of sight but within easy reach. A day's voyage, perhaps two.

If the spirits were satisfied with their sacrifice and wind lifted their sails, releasing them from their indenture like custom's officer releasing new arrivals.

A hubbub of noise, angry voices, from the deck near the forecastle caused him to turn, bells of alarm ringing in his head. A dozen of the crew had gathered on the main deck. They carried billhooks, axes, and wooden clubs.

Their leader was a tough Deiran, by the name

240

of Deva Dispasos; broad shouldered and flat-nosed with small, bitter eyes, Edo had singled him out as a troublemaker right from the start.

He led the dozen, his eyes ablaze and his lips thin with anger. The mob took the steps to the upper deck at a fast run. Edo stepped forward to shield Ferie and reached for his sword silently cursing the fact that the heat he had neglected to wear armor. The heat had gotten the better of his good judgment.

"Domin, move aside." Dispasos barked.

"Be about your business, sailor!"

A rush of blood-fear roared in Edo's ears, sour sweat pricked through his skin, as his body prepared itself for imminent violence.

An old feeling, one he had not experienced for a long time.

Too long.

His body sang as his palate dried and the drug of violence worked through him.

Dispasos spat sideways, sneered. "Give us the Caedian and we are gone."

"Heat twists all our minds, sailor. Leave now and we will forget this ever happened." He took two steps closer to Dispasos baring his teeth.

The men nearest Dispaso pulled back, a mere step or two but enough to convince Edo that their commitment as mutineers was not what Dispasos might have hoped. Dispasos glanced around, face darkening, took a step closer to Edo and that seemed to give the others renewed backbone.

"Domin, we hold nothing against you." He pointed behind Edo. "It is that bastard Caedian we want. He brought us here. Those fire demons wot destroyed Janu came from him. Fucker."

He bulled forward but Edo stood his ground and Dispasos gave ground.

Ferie?

Of course. Deep hatreds of blood and history. The old enemy; a safe, mindless target. Easy to lash out at the Caedian in the absence of anything- or anyone- else to blame.

"I'll say it one last time, sailor. Return to your posts and I will forget this ever happened."

"With all due respect Domin, not till we have the Caedian." Dispasos growled the words, his thick lips pulling back over yellow teeth, dull eyes gleaming with a dark excitement; indication of how far he was gone down the path of rage; a heady mix of sweat, fear and anger like a cloud of incense wafting from his thick body.

A man who would not budge, fixed in hate, reveling in this new role as leader, eager to make the role permanent.

Edo raised his voice, speaking beyond Dispasos to the others. "Listen carefully, you men. The fire spirits were a sign. We will have wind in our sails before daylight. I expect to make land within two days. Tallamun will be ours. Riches and fame for the taking. We will need you all then, every man jack of you. But I swear that if you are still standing here in two minutes I will hang you from the yardarm and have you flogged to the bone. Then I will feed you piece by piece to the sharks. Do. You. Hear. Me."

He kept his gaze glued on Dispasos, those

beady eyes ringed with red glinting in the moonlight and so sensed, rather than saw, men in the mob disappearing into the night.

Dispasos tensed, sensing it too. Knowing he had to do something to keep his nascent mutiny alive. He raised his billhook over his head and pivoting his body swung at Edo. Edo ducked inside the arc of the billhooks range, lashed out at the large sailor, a clumsy stroke that took the sailor on the cheekbone, cutting through flesh and into bone, slicing him from ear to chin.

Blood spattered Edo's face,

Dispasos howled and lashed out wildly. Edo swayed to one side, the viciously curved blade catching him on the shoulder, a glancing blow that cut through his tunic and gashed along his shoulder blade,

The pain was fierce but nothing to the damage he had done to Dispasos.

Edo stepped inside, too close to swing, reversed the sword. The hilt was of horn, capped with metal that sharpened to a ball-like nub. He rammed it into Dispasos's left eye. The eye turned to jelly, exploding under the blow. The sailor fell away, to his knees, dropping his weapon, hands on his face, moaning.

The would-be mutineers had largely dispersed. Two sailors, to dumb or slow to take the hint, had waited too long. They were kneeling on the ground.

Over them stood Alik Jar and six of his mercenaries fully dress; bowl-like helms, dressed in full plate.

Convenient, Edo thought. They appear now, having left me to deal with this.

He glanced over his shoulder at Heeb and Heeb looked away, face reddening. He too had not intervened.

Perhaps it had all happened so fast? Perhaps Alik Jar could not have gotten here sooner? Perhaps Heeb had been too shocked to react? Edo didn't believe any of that for a second. Heeb and Alik Jar had chosen to wait; to let things play out. Had they known Dispasos's plan? Edo knew it was possible. Heeb had always been good at gathering intelligence. Edo would have to be careful. With the possible exception of Ferie he had no allies on these ships.

Anger swept him like flame through like tinder. He grabbed a handful of Dispasos's hair, pulled the sniveling man backward.

"Fucking traitor," he hissed and spat. He was tempted to run his blade along the man's bare throat but had a sudden, vivid inspiration. He laughed happily, collecting strange looks from the men around him.

The wind had not risen. The fire spirits had not returned. Not enough blood had been spilled to gain the ships entrance to Tallamun. Fair enough. Dispasos and the other two had given Edo all the pretext he needed. If the spirits wanted blood he would give them all they needed.

***

On Edo's orders, in front of an assembly of

sailors and mercenaries from both ships, Demensidos the warlock strung the three mutineers from the yardarm of the mainsail. He strung them by their wrists, so their arms would bear the full weight of their bodies.

Heeb had protested.

"Kill Dispasos if you wish but lock the other two in chains. You cannot afford for the men to turn against you."

Edo shook his head, smiling. He would not kill the men, would not need to.

Tallamun needed sacrifice. Edo had not come all this distance to fail so close to shore. Sacrifice it would have.

"You have my orders, Entargio. I expect them carried out. Now!"

Heeb took his rod twelve thin rods of willow banded together and to the beat of the drums flogged the men.

A hundred lashes, two hundred, till blood ran from their backs and they had slumped to dim unconsciousness.

When they were finished Edo had the men cut down and lifted overboard, naked, into one of the rowboats. He ordered the boats cast off and the bloodied tunics of the men hung from one each of the ship's masts. The mutineers were less than a third of a league away when the fire spirits returned. They swarmed the boat, the men screamed as skin blackened and blood erupted gaseous from skin like steam from a kettle.

It took a long time for the three men to die, for the screams to abate, for the boat to sink but as the gunwale sank a gust of wind sprang up.

Edo held his breath as the slack sails billowed and then bellied.

"Man the rigging," Ferie barked.

A ragged cheer went up from the crew as the ship turned towards the west, as the sails unfurled fully and the ship plowed through the ocean.

Edo, for his part, left Heeb and Ferie on deck and went to his tiny cabin lay on his bunk and slept without dreaming till well after dawn.

CHAPTER 15 - TAMBER

The Pugi was a tough little bastard; Tamber had to give him that.

There was hardly a hands-span of his body untouched by some wound or other.

As Tamber cleaned and washed the wounds, applying poultices to the more serious, talking to the Pugi quietly- as to a hound you wanted to keep quiet- the Pugi bit its lip. Tears in his eyes. It did not cry out, never whimpered, never pulled away.

Tough little bastard, for something hardly better than an animal.

Except it…he could speak.

Two months after arriving, in a hesitant tongue, the Pugi thanked Tamber in the Malai language. His accent was terrible, of course and the words almost comical in their slow, hesitant drawl.

But he could talk.

That night Tamber conversed with Raven and Kali.

"He is an animal," Tamber insisted. "He is not like us."

Kali, being Kali, laughed cynically. "Then why do you question us?"

Raven joined in the laughter. "Ask yourself this, sorcerer. If the Pugi are animals then why do your people worry this issue so much?"

Tamber scowled and snarled at them, and banished them from his mind, but he dreamt that night of Pugi he had slaughtered in their villages. He saw them with a new light, talking to one another in words whose meaning he did not understand but whose tone was plain; things he understood from his own people; love, joy, sadness, anger.

The Pugi were men, he began to understand- a different nation, perhaps a different race-but men for all that. That were owed a dignity the Malai had long denied them. For the People lied to themselves and the lies enabled them to do things they would not otherwise do- use the Pugi for food, set Pugi males in pits against one another, use them as chattel, feed their corpses to the pigs.

He awoke in a cold sweat, his blood chilled and a damp, grey wind blowing outside, shaking the hides covering the entrance to the cave.

He got to his feet, chest bare keeping his eyes averted from the sleeping Pugi, and pulled back the hides. He stood on the ledge of black-gray rock staring down at the roaring sea, waves smashing against the headland to the east.

Clouds, alternately gray and white, drilled by but when the sun came out the day oozed warmth and the sun changed color from gray to gray-blue.

Not the shadow play of spirit magic- the magic of the shaman- but the powerful magic of the earth; shape and substance changed into something new. Eternally and without pause.

He reentered the cave. The Pugi was still asleep in his cage. Tamber looked at him and jerked back, shocked as if lightening-struck.

The face was the face of a sleeping boy, young and like all juveniles without tusks, his skin darker and yet more animate than the pale gray of the Malai.

Earth magic. The power of substance and change.

For Tamber was staring not at an animal but a man.

He sat down on the furs opposite the cage and cried, grief welling within him; grief for the dead, grief too for the ignorant living amongst his people.

When the tears faded, and the grief eased leaving a hollow emptiness that felt healthier he stoked the fire, boiled the albi eggs the Pugi had found in a nest high on the cliffs.

The Pugi awoke to the smell of food.

Tamber threw the eggs in a bowl and handed them to him.

In Malai he said in a solemn voice, "I am sorry. For everything. Forgive us, boy."

He was never sure that Gehsi understood, but later that day he broke the cage of wooden withies apart and stacked it for firewood at the side of the cave.

Gehsi stared at him with dim apprehension when he saw what was happening but Tamber smiled over his shoulder, a look he hoped was reassuring.

When he was finished he boiled a tisane of vervaine and for them both and patted the rug near where he sat.

Gehsi sat close to him, face a little wary.

Tamber smiled again and then they talked. In Pugi and Malai, learning from one another as the day faded and the earth changed all about them.

CHAPTER 16 - EDO

"Land ahoy!"

Edo ran the length of the poopdeck, pushed his way towards the starboard rail. With nervous fingers he clenched the rail tightly. He could see nothing. Not yet. Fuck! Come on, Feror you old bastard. Now or never!

He waited, breath stopped in his throat, a prickling against the balls of his eyes.

A thick murky fog shielded the water, like a lowering spirit. He could feel it out there, the fabled land tugging at his soul.

Birds flew over the ship, squawking, gray gull-like creatures larger than dogs, red-brown eye rings lending them a fierce, predatory look .

The first mate was calling depth but the bay was a good one, deep and without hidden treachery. The cry went up again from the crow's nest as the fog swirled, shifted, dissolved like a curtain parting above pale-blue water.

A wide bay, cliffs to the north where the restless sea broke itself in gouts of white water. One long sandbar like an accusing finger pointing from the south and, directly across from the prow, perhaps a quarter of a league away, a long flat beach, the water rolling slowly up its course with the gentle caress of a lover .Behind the beach was a hump of land, covered with grass and red and yellow flowers. Further back trees, tall and straight with dirty-gray boles, stretched towards the sky. The scent of leaves and grass, a warm piney smell drifted towards him. Tallamun.

Edo inhaled deeply and let out a long sigh, a faint tinge of disappointment spoiling the moment. He had expected something more pristine, less real.

He shook his head. Foolish. Reality could never compete with the world of dreams.

What mattered was what they had achieved-for the glory of Aonia and their own glory they had found this uncharted land.

Edo had believed. He had refused to be deflected from his path and now he had succeeded.

A brace of birds, their plumage a brilliant turquoise, rose over a reed-covered expanse of mudflats and skated across the water, their song a clear, pellucid tune.

They headed across the bay, in front of the ships.

A cheer went up, and men starved of sensation waving hats and helmets, emissaries of one world waving to the gorgeous emissaries of a second.

The birds, banked flew so close that Edo felt like he could reach and touch them, hold them in his hand; small and tender and precious.

The shouting grew, a wild crescendo of delight as the song caressed them.

A mercenary fired an amna-powered crossbow, the retort loud. The bolt flew straight, took the first of the two birds in the body, almost severing it in two.

The bird fell from the sky, bloodied and

broken, like a falling stone, head over heels.

The cheering died away as the bird, weighted down by its plumage sank into the waters.

The man who had fired was smiling happily, his mates congratulating him on the trueness of his aim. He turned and caught Edo's sharp glance and, blanching, turned away.

"Fucking idiot," Heeb muttered. "You want me to talk to him."

Edo shook his head. "Enough blood has been spilled getting us here, Entargio. Let it be."

Edo turned back, caught a last glimpse of the lone bird disappearing on the eastern horizon. He needed neither priest nor warlock to tell him that this was an inauspicious omen.

He shrugged. It was what it was.

A new beginning in a world fresh as morning dew, a world full of promise and hope.

A world already tainted by the death and greed you carry with you, a small voice inside him whispered. In his mind's eye he saw Balin's small, knowing smile.

Neither time nor distance changes a man, Edo. No matter how far you run you will not escape yourself.

No, brother Balin. Wait and see. Here I can be reborn. I will build the New Kingdom on these promised shores.

Balin shook his head, smiling sadly as blood oozed from his neck and his skin darkened.

His laugh was cynical and cold and Edo trembled.

You will never build any thing Edo, but that

which is tainted with death.

***

Edo scrambled from the long boat into the knee-deep water. He strode from the shallows, brightly colored fish small as a finger darting about his boots, and took his first steps on the golden sand of Tallamun.

The fog had almost evaporated and the day was bright, the sun already a warm and gentle prickle on his bare flesh.

The twelve men of his guard followed him up the beach, armed and wary.

Dark brown shells littered the sand and crabs scuttled away at their approach.

Edo did not pause to examine them. He walked up the gentle hump of earth, through grass that reached up to his waist.

He stopped short of the tree line and turned to Heeb grinning from ear to ear.

"We'll build it here."

"Really? And what exactly is it?"

"A stockade. We have pasture for the cows and there is fresh water close by. I sense it."

A dark cloud crossed the Scian's face.

"What's bitten your ass, Entargio?"

"A stockade, cows seems...permanent."

"So fucking what?"

"Amna, Domin. We came here for wealth. I am not a bastard farmer."

"And just how much further do you think we will we get without water? Without food?"

Heeb said nothing, but his silence was telling.

"We are staying put. We need to rest. We will explore the land around this bay first. Rebuild our stocks of food and water. Let the wounded heal. When the time is right we'll set off again in search of our mountain of amna. Got that!"

Heeb's eyes deflated.

"Unload the ships and set pickets near the trees. Begin by building an embankment there." Edo drew a square in the air. Get men working on felling timber and have the carpenters ready. I'll take six mercenaries and explore the interior. Look for game." He clapped Heeb on the shoulder. "There is fresh water here. I can feel it."

"Is that all sir?" Edo nodded and Heeb turned on his heels.

"Entargio"

Heeb turned towards him.

"This is but a beginning."

Heeb glanced back but the look in his eye was skeptical as he contemplated the mountain of work that lay before them.

CHAPTER 17 - GEHSI

"I go there," Gehsi pointed at the sea, mimicked casting a rod.

Tamber growled. "Try not to come back with any more garlfish. Last ones almost poisoned me." The Malai spat in the fire.

Gehsi smiled despite himself for the Malai, despite his dour demeanor, had a generous heart.

Over the course of a year he had nursed Gehsi back to health, had sewn wounds shut and applied foul smelling poultices, had helped train him with sword and spear as he regained his strength.

Gehsi had learned a lot about warfare, for Tamber had shown him that the Malai relied not only on their brute strength but an almost unholy bind to their weapon, a connection so strong that for the best of them their weapons, the swords they called tintuk, became an extension of body and will.

An extension of their keni.

Strength and speed, a lethal combination.

Something to tell the elders about when he returned to the nest.

Gehsi climbed down the rocks towards the roaring sea. Spring was late and though the days were lengthening a fierce chill crackled the air. Heaped thunderclouds, towering and black, loomed over the water to the east, promising further storms, and the sea reflected the leaden light of the sky.

Gehsi was young, his brain still sharp, and he

had quickly learned the Malai tongue. Tamber, for his part, had learned to speak Pugi but with a dreadful accent that made Gehsi smile softly.

Gehsi had once asked Tamber why he no longer carried a tintuk sword, but Tamber had glanced away, a hollow look shadowing his eyes, and refused to say more.

The old man- for Gehsi no longer thought of Tamber as one of the butchers who had taken his family from him, who had slaughtered his village and a dozen of the new settlements in the space of half as many years- was alone, lonely, but his loneliness seemed not to have embittered him.

Far from it. In the silent struggle Tamber conducted with the voices in his head he had been tempered; a wounded jaguar, dangerous, waiting for yet unseen prey. Wise, too, for a barbarous Malai. Gehsi had learned much, was eager to learn more. In a strange manner Gehsi did not dare examine closely, Tamber had become a surrogate father, filling the void in Gehsi's soul; where despair and grief and once reigned tender shoots of hope now grew.

Still, Gehsi would have to return the spear to his own people for it was their sacred property. A day would come when he had learned all he could and he would have to return to the nests.

He angled down a slippery ledge of rock, crusted with cockles and hanging seaweed. High waves in the narrow channel to his right, churned and boomed. He made his way towards the relative shelter of a strip of sand beneath an overhang of rock and struggled into the chill

257

water, the salt stinging his legs. He bent his legs against the force of the sea and strode into its bosom till it lapped about his waist. He hefted his fishing rod. The long white line of knotted gut, weighted down by an obsidian horn and topped by a sharp, cruel hook, flashed through the air and landed in the water.

Tamber had encouraged Gehsi to fish. The powerful waves, he had said, would make Gehsi strong and Gehsi found in the water a time to think and dream. As his mind drifted the morning grazed past.

He had caught two tinfish and a blue-yark and was considering returning to the cave when a roar startled him. Gehsi glanced around to see Tamber scrambling down the ledge of rock from the cave. In his right hand was the spear Qiazhua.

A shape rose from the water three spans to Gehsi's right.

Gehsi caught a glimpse of bared fangs, veiled eyes covered in a thin film of translucent green like scum on a pond.

It shot towards him, upper body glinting; fins long and webbed, but boned like fingers.

"I wiiilll guttt you. Taaake you to the coooold depths."

Pale webbed hands reaching for him.

He froze in the face of its strangeness.

Qiazhua the spear whistled past Gehsi's ear and embedded itself in the beast's bony chest.

Gehsi felt a sudden squall of fear, for the fate of the spear as much as for his own skin.

He slipped sideways, avoiding a threshing

hand, grabbed the shaft of the spear. Two-handed he pulled it towards him, wrenching it from the apparition's chest. It slid back into the leaden waters and disappeared, leaving nothing but a faint eddy that rapidly disappeared in the churn of waves.

Spear in hand Gehsi stumbled towards the spot where Tamber stood on pale sand, hair whipping in the wind. Tamber reached out and pulled Gehsi out of the water.

"What in all that is holy was that?" Gehsi asked, panting.

"We call them halrik." Tamber made a face. "Foul creatures. Born of Yemlakken's rage, of a curse he put on the Men of Old. The Tinan. Once human, now it hunts fishermen, salters, the gatherers of seaweed and sometimes the dog-men of the Milka stones. The souls of those the halrik catch are spirited away to great torment in Yimti's chill kingdom. A lonely place. Barren of hearth flames."

A shadow crossed Tamber's face. Gehsi understood; Tamber himself was an outcast, abandoned and lonely as any captured soul in Yimti's Kingdom.

Gehsi shook his head. In the nests people were punished, sometimes they forfeited their lives or their freedom, but they were never banished. He could not imagine a worse fate.

Tamber laid a hand on Gehsi's shoulder. "Come, little man. Let's cook these fish you caught, and get you dry."

He lifted the three fish in his broad hand, a

259

hand that reminded Gehsi of the shovels the farmers in the forest nests used to dislodge roots, and strode ahead.

Gehsi followed behind, his mind churning with the aftermath of fear and a swelling fondness for this strange Malai who kept saving his life, who was willing to teach him and care for him and wished for nothing in return but companionship.

*****

Tamber told Gehsi of the gods of his people.

Of the great halls of Dasia Kerara where the souls of warriors went when they died, there to be waited on by the pale souls of the disgraced and the despised. He told him of Yengti, of the chill kingdom of ice and snow, ruled by ice and death where lost souls went. Of Tolukah, the horned god of the trees, whose boon to the people was the Tintuk tree, who had sacrificed his own child for the sake of weapons of wood, but whose favor the Malai had lost in the wars with the Greenmen; of Taskiluh the Old Man of War who had given the people Kai-wine and the gift of eternal life when they fell in battle;of Yangti the god of wind and air; of Haneyleh the falcon god of winged creatures; of Tengubkan, god of the jah and the lizard men.

He told him of Great soul and the power of keni, of the reputation that could make or break men or women.

He told him of Mencunan, patron of revenant

spirits, and of the spirits he talked to in his dreams, Raven and Kali. He told him of his visions, of the tribe of beetle men on massive houses who would sail across the ocean and take their land from them.

Locusts dressed in armor.

Men with the souls of cripples, eyes greedy and cruelty, for whom honor was nothing, life nothing. A commodity to be bought and sold.

Tamber had had a long time to think and the words trickled from him slowly, night after night as Gehsi, hands clasped on his chin, listened with large eyes.

Gehsi, the silent Pugi, soaking in the stories of his enemies.

One night Gehsi cleared his throat and told Tamber of the nests, his voice hesitant as he spoke. He described the red boles of trees whose tops soared high as cliffs, of the villages nesting in these trees, the great stone buildings one layer built on another as the generations passed, the vines from which hung the fruit they call solga whose flesh was like the taste of heaven, of the houses built of timber and wood perching high on the thick canopy of alo, of the ladders strung between trees, trails from house to house from village to village.

"How many of you are there?" Tamber asked mystified.

"More than the sand on the beach," Gehsi answered his face somber and pale.

Tamber shook his head and went silent.

There had never been many Malai. They bred

261

slowly. Wars between the tribes, had thinned their numbers. If what Gehsi said was true then the future lay with the Pugi.

He felt sadness but no great surprise.

Gehsi told him, of the spear Tamber owned, the spear they called the Raiser of the Dead, the spear that would awake an army of the ancestors on a day when the nests were challenged.

Tamber's mind worked frantically.

He remembered the dead who had walked in that Tang village many years before,

A mystery.

Who were those dead warriors and how had they come to be?

Tamber sensed that the answer to this mystery was a deep well, full of power, ancient beyond measure.

A secret at the heart of things if only he could decode its meaning.

Gehsi grabbed Tamber by the arm, a bright grin lighting his face.

"Come back with me, Father.'

Gehsi had taken to calling Tamber father; at first in gentle mockery at the age gap between them, for Gehsi joked that Tamber looked old enough to be his distant ancestor, but of late a fondness had imbued the gentle mockery.

A further sign of the bond developing between them.

Tamber raised his eyebrows.

"Come to the nest. My people know the lore of the spear better than I."

Tamber shook his head. "I am Malai. They

will butcher me and hang me from a tree."

"No, father. You walk with me and I will stand guarantor of your behavior. None may touch you as long as this remains so."

Tamber stared at him for a long moment.

"You will have a tribe again, Father. People around you. I will take care of you in your impending dotage."

Tamber lashed out playfully at the boy's head. Gehsi ducked and reached for Tamber's elbow. Tamber found himself nodding, smiling, his eyes misting over.

The thought was like a bright impossible dream.

Tamber shrugged.

"I would be honored, Gehsi, my son. Honored."

And he found he meant it too.

263

CHAPTER 18 - TAMBER

Tamber was fishing on the rocks when the arrack came again, hard shells glistening, their passage presaged by a faint crackling noise.

He cursed under his breath, lay down, resigned to this third death, of the rebirth that would inevitably follow.

The beetles burnt as they entered him and seared a chasm like a tunnel through his chest.

Each tiny bite cored his soul until the darkness descended. When it passed he was regurgitated back to consciousness.

He opened his eyes, dizzy and faint, on a mountain; a valley laid out beneath him its green forest like the pelt of a wild creature.

A brace of ang swooped over his head and he heard a jah roaring, hunting somewhere close by. He shivered as a frozen wind bit his face and numbed his lips.

The wind's voice was a howl equal to the voice of the jah, equally ferocious, tumbling flakes of snow, blinding Tamber in its white, vicious haze.

To his right was an outcrop of rose-colored granite. He took shelter behind it and found Kali and Raven waiting for him there, tapping their feet in studied impatience.

"They are come," Raven said with a long tongued smile.

Kali stared at Tamber with hard eyes and licked its lips. In its hand it held the raw and bleeding leg of some mountain creature. Showing teeth like a jah's mouth the god bit deep and tore flesh and gristle from the bone.

"They are come," it repeated, spraying a fine spittle of blood in Tamber's face.

"So soon?"

Raven laughed.

Kali laughed.

"The beetle-men have paid the blood price of entry. They are but few. For now. You will be tested by them. Tested by your own kind."

Tamber raised an eyebrow. "What is it you really want of me?"

"You must persuade your own nation to forge an alliance with the Tang and the Pugi.."

Tamber chortled, genuinely amused. "You expect me to ask my people to make an alliance with animals."

"You know better than that, Tamber Whitehair. You know what the Pugi are. What Gehsi is."

"I have no voice, Raven. Haven't you noticed?" He wiped his hands. "I do not exist."

A hiss sounded from behind him and Tamber turned, dread contracting his groin.

A dark shadow stood behind him raised fingers pointed like accusation, the nails long and dark, the fingers rotting, eyes inky, and oozing smoke.

"I am Garge of the mountains." The god laughed, a whispery sound like dead leaves rustling. "I believe you fucked my sister."

The oracle, the female spirit in the mountain

who had ridden him and granted him his first vision during the trial of the yangmpabat.

Cursed him. Set him on this dark and lonely path.

She too had been a spirit of the mountain, dark in her heart like the deepest gulley or cave, a being of damp misery.

"When they learn of these newcomers the best of your people will remember you were first to warn them. Some will approach you. They will ask for your advice. They will listen. They will know you as Nonei." Garge said. "Many will not listen. Those who do not hear your words will die and their deaths will sow the seeds of the future."

Tamber shook his head. "I will do as I can but I fear..."

Garge's eyes glittered and veins of blood ran through them.

"You are right to fear, Whitehair. For doom approaches."

With a sudden insight, that hit like a bolt of summer lightning from a lone cloud in an azure sky, Tamber realized why these gods were helping him.

They knew fear, in as much as creatures like these could know fear; fear of the invaders and their foreign gods, gods who would usurp the place of these ascendants and render their existence empty.

Till they became as meaningless fables.

Stories to frighten children.

They were all in this together, the gods and the people who worshipped these gods.

266

The thought both frightened and amused Tamber.

"I will do as I can but I am but one man."

Garge skipped on one foot and opened a toothless mouth, the tongue flicking out, damp and slimy as the meat of an oyster.

"You are no longer simply a man, Tamber Whitehair. The arrack have claimed you three times and you have survived. Three souls are at your bidding. We will teach you much, things you need to destroy, things you will need to build alliances."

Kali spoke. "Your education begins here."

The gods sat cross-legged on the icy ground, oblivious to the howling wind and Raven gestured for Tamber to sit with them. They held their hands out in front of them and he felt himself swell and change as the world dissolved beneath his feet, flashed by in a sharp, inconsequential blur. He saw mountains rise and fall, rivers swell and grow and ice-like mountains taming the land. Ice that melted as the rivers returned and trees took hold in once stony ground.

He saw creatures, empires, grow and die.

Men growing, melting, molting.

He lived myriad lives. Once he was a bird flying high above a copper desert, once an ant on the face of a wooden palisade, once a wolf eating the flesh of a butchered Jal child.

He lived a hundred lives. A thousand.

He killed and he was killed and the blood beat in his ears and the voices of the gods followed him in his long migration.

267

Teaching him. Talking to him.

The lore of the ancients, the secrets of his ancestors.

Until he started awake, stiff from lying on the rocks, Gehsi standing over him, a look of concern on the younger man's face.

Gehsi held out a hand to pull him to his feet, a flicker of concern and something darker in his eyes.

"What is it, little brother?"

"I saw what happened from the cave. Those creatures..."

"The arrack," Tamber said quietly.

"I saw them burst out of your forehead. Yet you still live."

"Live. Yes? I live."

Gehsi came close to Tamber, sniffing his scent- a common practice among the Pugi when meeting someone again after a long time.

"What is it little brother?"

"You are changed, father. Your scent is different. Older?"

Weak as a foal, his mind still racing, Tamber grabbed the little man by the shoulder.

"I have lived a long time with death, Gehsi. As long a time as it takes a stone to dissolve." He shook his head as the memories of that other place faded like an interrupted dream. "I have brought back hope, I think. For your people and mine. Hope, Gehsi. And terror. The beetle men are here."

CHAPTER 19 - EDO

The stockade was ready in a week, a heaped embankment of earth with a dry moat to the front, topped off by a palisade twice the height of a man.

They built one large communal hall using the malleable wood of the local trees and its hard, sticky bark; a place to sleep and eat. They built pens for the animals- the milking cows, pigs, fowl and the half-dozen horses that had survived. The weather was warm, warmer than home, and they spent most of the time stripped to the waist outdoors, reveling in the simple fact of being on dry land again.

Edo wandered most, spending every day traipsing through the forest, fully armored mercenaries to hand.

The land was rich, bountiful. They caught wild pig and lizard-like creatures with little difficulty and the turquoise colored birds proved to be a great delicacy when spitted.

On the fifth day they stumbled on tracts of a wild cereal, larger than wheat and paler than barely, which Edo ordered harvested and stored. It made a passable porridge and poor bread but it was nutritious.

Edo took time to consult with Ferie. The Caedian reckoned they had been blown south of their original target. His best guess was that it would take another three weeks, give or take, sailing north along the coast. Unless this was just another island and the shoreline did not continue

269

unbroken. Unless they had not yet reached Tallamun. Unless...

Edo made sure his uncertainties were broadcast loud and clear to the men, for most of them had their fill of ships, at least for a season or so.

Edo was not worried. He was certain in his heart; they had reached Tallamun and, though he sensed impatience amongst the men, for amna and the wealth they had been promised, he did not share it.

Unlike them, he had no pressing reasons to return and he had never imagined Tallamun as a pot of gold to be quickly plucked and discarded.

The place was vast, huge and inviting.

A place to escape the morbid, corrupt reality that was Deira. A place to live and grow, to make your own and die in.

A place where a group of like-minded people could live simple, gentle lives dedicated to the gods, or to one god in particular, owning allegiance to no one, threatened by no one.

He named the stockade and the slowly growing sweep of buildings around it Balintown and secretly imagined a new life here; a simple and good life, a life lived in peace like that of the monks in the temple in Milese.

He kept his thoughts for himself and directed the search for amna, one small part of him hoping that they would find none.

For this land without greed was as close to paradise, he knew now, as he would ever come.

***

The natives appeared out of the tree line at dawn on the fourth day.

Edo summoned Heeb and the two men stood on the narrow, wooden walkway that served as a battlement for their palisade.

They counted six braves.

Large men- the smallest head and shoulders above the tallest Aonian- wielding long wooden swords the length of stabbing spears. Their hair ranged from blond-white to a red wheat and their strange gray-black skin was the color of basalt. From the side of their mouths rose curved teeth, vaguely like tusks, which gave them a wild, porcine look.

Deadly boar, Edo thought, muscled and defensive. We have to be careful with these people.

A cry went up through the stockade, and soon most of the crew and mercenaries had downed their tools and were on the walkway staring at the pig-men, muttering quietly to themselves, their nervousness palpable.

One of the pig-men raised a massive, curved horn to his lips and blew. The sound rang through the trees, out across the water, sending flights of birds into the air.

Edo shivered, for the sound brought to mind forests and wild animals, animals he did not know, pounding through undergrowth where no light reached, followed by men of singular purpose whose eyes were pitiless and dull. Ahead

271

their prey waited; slipping quietly through shaded trees, teeth bared, ready to tear and bite.

Tallamun it seemed owned a dark side.

A spooked mercenary brought a loaded crossbow to bear but this time Heeb and Edo were ready.

Heeb stomped across the walkway to the mercenary, knocked the crossbow aside and slammed his fist into the man's nose, knocking him back.

"We do nothing," Heeb roared. "Nothing till we take their measure. Do you hear me?"

When Heeb returned, having paused to kick the shaken mercenary a few more times to emphasize his point, Edo clapped him on the shoulder.

"So what now?" Heeb asked through clenched teeth.

Edo grinned. "We offer to trade and we stay behind these walls, till we know more. Who knows? If we play our cards right they may bring the amna to us and we gather it with fattening arms." He grinned wildly and clambered down the flimsy ladder. Halfway down he threw himself off and hit the hard-packed red earth at a run.

In one of the storerooms were the boxes of trinkets he had brought with them- an idea he got from Ferie. The natives Ferie had lived with on his first journey had set great store in golden seashells of a certain shape; small, thin and oblong. These they traded with other tribes up and down the coast; for food and weapons and tools, for feathers and stone, but mostly for other shells.

The shells, Ferie had learned, were both decoration and currency. Like a rich Aonian's golden arm rings or the excess that was a noble's explosive display of amna on Republic Day.

Edo had laughed in incredulous delight at Ferie's story for he recognized the shellfish Ferie was describing from his days in the fondaco.

In Aonia the shellfish were called willie-wickles and could be bought for half a hirsh at a dozen wooden stands near the sea. Salted and ladled with butter and garlic they were cheap and nutritious and Edo's father had sold them at one stage; the perfect snack for drink-quickened men.

Edo reached the storeroom, broke open the lid of the first casket.

In Aonia, in the weeks before they had cast off, he had bought willie-wickles by the cask full, the stand owners sniggering at the price he was willing to pay. He had ordered the meat scraped from the shells, and the shells pierced and hung on a chain of thin catgut.

Now, he grabbed a handful and ran to the stockade gate, gesturing at the guards to let him through.

He stood facing the pig-men, the land sloping slightly to the tree line perhaps eight hundred spans away.

He jumped up and down, yelling, waving the necklaces. He saw one point at him and grinned in what he hoped he was a friendly unthreatening manner.

Feeling alone and vulnerable, the dark eyes of the pig men boring, through him he walked halfway to the tree line and placed the winkle necklaces on a protruding rock of pink granite.

An offering to twisted gods.

He turned about, facing the fort, back exposed, the hair on the nape of his neck rising, sweat pricking his buttocks and strode back to the stockade, nonchalantly, fighting the fierce urge to run.

When he reached the open gate he turned about. The pig men were gone, the necklaces still in place.

"What happened to them?" he asked the guard.

"Fucked if I know," the guard, a thickset Kallin mercenary with a large red nose, muttered. "Disappeared they did. Like magic it were." he shook his head.

Edo growled in disgust at the fear in the man's eyes and ran back to the walkway.

"I kept my eyes on them all the time. Shortly after you turned back they melted away." Heeb's voice trailed off. "Like smoke over water. More like ghosts than men."

Edo shook his head. "Gimmicks, Heeb. Meant to frighten us. We'd do the same." He turned to face the Scian. "In Caedia we faced a screaming charge of undead hilka, you and I. Why the fuck are you so spooked?"

"Something...about this land...." Heeb shuddered, eyes focused over Edo's shoulder. "We are not welcome here. Even the warlock whispers of revenants who appear in his dreams. Of blood magics that pull at him like ghastly fingers."

"A primitive land. A couple of bloody natives and already you are shitting your breeches, Heeb."

"The men mutter. They want to return to Deira. This land haunts them."

"You are my Second. Do your duty and clap them in irons if they mutter. Even if it is in their fucking sleep." He pushed past Heeb. "We have work to do." He winked at Heeb and gestured to the tree line. "They will be back."

That night a thick silence, edged with fear hung over the stockade.

Edo doubled the guard and took first watch himself.

He rose at dawn and made his way to the battlements. Heeb and Ferie had beaten him to it. The necklaces were gone and in their place was a stone sword, taller than any Aonian could comfortably wield.

"Seems your offering was accepted," Ferie smiled grimly.

Edo ordered the sword brought to him. He picked it up and examined it; a crude if vicious thing. A useless curio, but that was unimportant. What was important was that the pig men had responded to his offering.

"Load the amna cannon, Ferie. Heeb, have every man with a decent crossbow stand ready. I think we can expect to see our new friends again sometime soon. We may well need to impress on them the advantages of trade."

Heeb crossed his arms, staring grimly at the nearest trees. "And teach them the risks of easy plunder, no doubt."

***

The natives did not return that day. Nor the next day. Nor the day after that.

Three hard, sleepless nights as tempers flared and the shadows danced with the movement of their eyes till they imagined a thousand screaming pig-men standing outside the palisade waiting to tear them apart.

Tense and expectant, scanning the skyline and waiting with sweaty fingers wrapped round their weapons.

In the copper wreathed dawn of the fourth day the pig men came in force, appearing from amongst the trees like shadows, like fog.

It took Edo half a minute to register their presence. They wore hides of dark gray and black, of wolf and mesk bear, over heavy, quilted jackets.

On their heads were helms of bone and wood. They wielded massive spears of wood and swords of a strange red wood, curved and vicious looking, and oval shields faced with leather decorated with crimson symbols like hands of blood.

They drew up in rough lines of ten, five deep. Edo counted fifty warriors and another half a dozen leaders, priests of some sort who inhabited pelts of bear or wolf or the skin of a strange lizard-like creature at least as tall as a man.

They wore the skulls as helms and stared

276

through the jaws of these creatures, barking and moaning as they danced in circles in front of the line of troops.

A warning shout came from the far side of the palisade and he turned to where the mercenaries on the stockade wall facing the ocean were pointing.

Half a dozen canoes were powering towards the lightly manned ships. The canoes were massive hollowed trunks of some dark-wooded tree, powered by oars, each holding about twenty warriors.

"How long before they reach the ships."

Ferie squinted at the canoes.

"Five minutes. Maybe a little more!"

Edo had not known if the men pig-men had ship-building technology but he had not been prepared to take a chance. Heeb and twelve mercenaries were manning the ships.

"Should I signal to Heeb to use his cannon."

"This is a small test, Ferie. A jab. To see what we are made of. If they push us too far we'll jab back but we don't want all out war." He turned to the plinix lar of the first gun squad. "Send a signal to the ships. Order them to fire with all they have if the boats come within boarding range. They are to hold fire for now. Make sure they understand that. Then have your team ready their scorpion. Load it with mil-fire. Fire a warning across the bow of that first boat. The second shot goes only on my orders. If we are forced the fire twice the second shot will send that first canoe to Mal Din's deeps. Is that clear?"

The Plinix-lar barked orders at his men jabbed the cube of amna in the receptor near the muzzle and primed the shot.

Edo covered his ear. The loud retort was accompanied by a scream as the amna was torn apart, its nature sundered with a scream, and the shell flew towards the first of the native ships. It burst aft of the canoes lighting the day with an orange flame like a vicious flower.

Edo could see the men on the second and third canoes pulling frantically to avoid the flame spreading across the sea like a poisonous mushroom. The men on the first canoe rowed harder, still intent on the ship.

Edo waited, giving them a chance to turn, a chance they did not take.

They were almost in boarding range and Edo could see arrows being strung, spears and grappling hooks of stone held ready.

The plinix lar turned towards him.

"Do you have the range?" Edo asked.

The gunner gave him a sideways grin. "Say the word."

"Do it!"

The long thin barrel length of the scorpions tail leapt forward and amna screamed. The shell broke over the canoe and fire clothed the warriors in frozen flame that burnt in water and singed flesh like snow in January.

Warriors leapt screaming into the water but the mil fire, like a parasite kept them company as they sunk beneath the swell of the seas, hands waving.

They drowned or they burned. The canoe was a ball of fire, black gouts of flame spitting into the leaden sky.

The remaining canoes beat time away from the galways towards the east, fast as they could.

A roar went up from his men and Edo felt the atmosphere of nervous fear, terror even, that had slowly built over the men dissipate in the heat of the milfire.

They had scored an easy victory. Their fear of these pig men and their strange magics had proved unfounded.

When Edo turned around the line of warriors and shaman by the tree line had disappeared.

Ferie glanced at Edo. "Don't reckon we made any friends today."

"I disagree. I think they were testing our strength. We have demonstrated we are not weak and since we have things they want, things they easily cannot take from us, they may trade now."

Alix Jar, the mercenary came striding towards them, his eyes dull and angry. "Snakes like that should be butchered not coddled. If they are weak then we can take from them what we want." He hawked a glob of phlegm over the palisade like a missile, and Edo could not help the shiver that trembled down his back like an omen.

***

Edo's eyes were grit and cinders. He could barely remember the last time he had slept more than a few hours at a stretch.

It had been a week, and the waiting had stretched them all to breaking. Tempers frayed, fights among the men had become common as muck.

The morning rose, light and fragrant, starlings darting about the palisade and the massive red-plumed seabirds squawking and diving over a glistening sea. Edo was finishing his breakfast, listening to a drawled complaint from one of the junior officers when the cry went up from the wall.

"The bastards are returning!"

He pushed the officer aside and ran for the nearest steps, calling Ferie to him. He flew up the steps two at a time.

Hundreds of warriors had filed out of the tree line. They drew up in ragged lines, bodies swaying as they sang a discordant, throbbing tune that set Edo's teeth on edge.

The chiefs wore headdresses of lizard skin, silver and tan pelts draped over their bodies. In their hands were long, knotted staves topped with round balls.

"Tintuk wood they call it," Ferie explained. "Hard as steel, yet in the hands of their craftsmen malleable as softwood."

"Can you speak their language?"

"They seem not dissimilar to the tribes I lived with." He hesitated. "Perhaps so."

"Make sure of it. Everything depends on you."

A group of tribesmen dressed in the skins of jaguars sounded long horns and beat long flat drums. The sound sent shivers through Edo.

Three dozen men dressed in flayed human skins, the skins complete so that hands and feet flapped as they moved, moved forward from the host of warriors. They moved like beasts; crouching, sniffing the air, shrieking.

Live eyes glittered behind the masks of the dead.

The sight was both threatening and vaguely comical.

"Shaman," Ferie muttered. "More warlock than priest, though they perform the offices of both. Second in power only to the chiefs."

Edo's stomach churned.

The shaman gathered in a loose line, perhaps two hundred spans in front of the lines of warriors, chanting and shouting, making obscene gestures with hands and hips. On the palisades men muttered and cursed, dark knots of superstition in their souls twisting at the sight of the living dead.

Edo knew intimately the power of blood magic; had experienced its foul use in the Deserts of Arroy, and it terrified him.

Heeb stomped up beside them, face red, beard half groomed, eyes still bleary, the top clasp on his uniform still undone.

Edo saluted him, keeping one eye on the shaman. A path opened through the knot of warriors and three men were prodded at spear point towards them.

Hands bound behind their backs, these men were shorter, stockier than the pig men, their skin

281

a light amber.

The shaman drew curved obsidian knifes out of their costumes of skin and swooped on the three men, beating them to the ground, stabbing as they sang their discordant song. When the men were butchered they rose, chunks of flesh in their hands, blood dripping in the yellow sun.

They bellowed and screamed in ecstatic frenzy and chewed on the flesh of their victims.

"They seem unbowed," Ferie said dryly. "I fear they seek another lesson in manners."

"Simple enough. We'll put the fear of the god into their shaman. The warriors will wilt when they see those madmen run."

Heeb looked unconvinced. "I hope so," he muttered. "There are a lot of the buggers."

Edo squared his shoulders determined not to let fear spill from him, to give heed to the voices in his head screaming.

So many of them. So few of us.

"Have the mounts readied. Ferie, come with me. Get yourself into full armor. Its time to go and meet our hosts."

***

Eight snorting war mounts- all that had survived the crossing- a cross between the desert horses of Scia and the mountain strength of the horses of Aonia. Fearless beasts, mostly bay or chestnut sorrel, they had been instrumental in winning the war against Caedia. Their ability to stand up to the massed assault of armies of revenant hilka had allowed the Osdom of the Western Army to press home the numerical superiority of his heavy infantry and archers.

The men, even the infantry, worshipped the beasts and loved them for their fearlessness, even looked on them as harbingers of luck.

Edo understood their importance.

Luck and confidence in their own abilities were all they owned in this vast new world.

The horses had been fitted with cotton barding, thick enough to soften blows from maces or clubs. Over the barding was a sheet of chain mail studded with polished copper scale so it gleamed like fire. On the horse's heads were chamfron of studded metal with shaped and flared, copper crinets guarding the necks.

They waited, snorting and stamping, breath pluming like smoke- Edo thought they looked like fierce dragons or tugaspagó, the armored beasts that appeared from swamp mud in the dread of night and terrorized whole towns in the northern highlands of Aonia.

Edo had given command of the palisade walls to Heeb. Ferie would ride on his right as interpreter, should such be needed.

The other six were ex-cavalry, part of Alik Jars mercenary contingent, all dressed in full mail armor, and covered with glistening scale. Two of the riders held lances with banners- the falcon of the Fuentas Clan and the reed, cross and bear motif on a jade backdrop that was the banner of the Republic.

A dozen foot soldiers carrying amna-powered

crossbows stood in line behind the horses, shuffling feet and muttered prayers betraying their nerves.

Edo mounted, pulled closed the visor of his helm closed and barked an order at the guards. Two men lifted the heavy wooden cross brace and tugged open the gate.

The visor narrowed his vision; focus for what had to be done. Still Edo felt his stomach twist as he caught sight of the massed line of warriors waving their weapons on the hill beyond the gate.

They looked unnatural, barely human, as unreal as the bright plumages- turquoise, jade, saffron, cerise, of the local forest birds.

As the gates banged open, the horns of the natives whined a deathly, discordant melody, and the drums beat a harsh tattoo.

Edo's breath was warm in the full helm, the beating of his heart a faint echo in his ear, sweat making a delta of his back.

He signed a prayer ward.

"Forward at a slow walk. Keep silent and stay together." he ordered.

He dug his spurs into the horses flank and made for the gate. Outside the palisade they drew up line abreast and started off at a slow walk.

The crossbowmen fired one volley of crossbows, deliberately wide of the mark, the retort ringing through the valley like thunder.

Edo ordered the horses into a canter and then a slow gallop and the horses responded with an easy gait, glad to be free at last and in the open, doing what they had been bred to do.

A fierce joy, transmitted itself through his mount, coursed through Edo's thighs into his buttocks and chest. His mind soared with joy, finally free of the incremental worry and the stress of command, of waiting.

In violent action was release.

Forgetfulness.

He grinned and roared his warcry, lowered the cavalry lance and leaned over his mount aiming at a small knot of shaman to his right. The native priests had stopped their obscene dance. Had turned to watch the on riding horses racing towards them up the shallow hill of sea-grass and hard-packed earth, as white jallies flew circles high above.

The shaman froze, figures in a frieze.

Dumbstruck as Edo had hoped.

What must it be for them? Snorting, gleaming creatures from nightmare pounding towards them, thunder sparking from hooves, fogged breath snorting from nostrils, the sun gleaming like blood on armored sides.

Bearing men like armored beetles, sharp glinting blades. Wicked. Strange. Terrifying.

A cluster of chiefs had gathered on a grassy knoll. Edo saw one wave his hand as he backed up the slope, pointing at a group of nearby archers.

A volley of stone-tipped arrows whistled through the air. Edo was hit, the stone blade clanking off his metal armor, spent and useless.

The chief was surrounded now by others, shouting and red-faced.

Angry at him, Edo guessed for prompting the

285

wrath of these strange armored men,

Unable to comprehend how their weapons had not worked, wondering frantically what magic was at play here.

They would look to the shaman now; for support, for enlightenment.

Edo had hoped it would come to this.

The line of horses was three hundred cubits from the shaman, who still stood blank-eyed, staring from their bloodied masks of flayed skin.

Run, you bastards!

First one, then the rest of them, broke, stumbling, backwards up the hill to where their warriors and chiefs waited, tearing at the skin masks covering their face, hitching up flayed skin like skirts so as to run better.

Edo laughed aloud and reined in his mount, the others following suit.

The shaman were in disarray, tails between their legs, humiliated. The warriors and their chiefs would know that the power of their entire nation had been undermined.

"The gods favor us, you heathen bastards," Edo bellowed aloud for the benefit of his men.

Edo pulled up the visor on his helm and turned so the others could see the grin on his face.

"See how they run, lads. Tails between their legs. Worse than women. Their arrows do not harm us. So do you fear these fucking savages?"

They roared their answer.

Edo watched the shaman disappear into the ranks of the warriors, and saw the chiefs on the knoll gesturing.

He knew he had done all he needed to do.

They fear us and so they respect us. Now comes the time of trade.

***

"I am Ambakan of the Shanlak River Tribe. This is Tingan of the Red Three Band Tribe and Unyabuhiof the Pale Reed Valley Tribe." He indicated two other chiefs with crimson headdresses. A dozen lower chiefs and twice as many shaman had squashed into the open-sided pavilion Edo had ordered built.

The chiefs spared Edo, Ferie and their guard of mercenaries carrying cross bows but a cursory, disinterested glance. Their eyes were on the heaped pile of shell necklaces Edo had laid out on a woven reed carpet, eyes bulging like deep jars full to overflowing with moldy water. Greed was the terrible universal.

Ferie translated and the chief waited till he finished speaking.

It was their third meeting. The first two had been strained, formal, hesitant and held in the open, involving one or two of the chiefs and a shaman or two dancing slowly about them, sniffing the air as if for suspected subterfuge.

Ferie had at first struggled with the language.

"The words are the same, he complained, but the sounds are different." But it was close enough to what he remembered, close enough for him to cobble together understanding.

That was all Edo needed.

"Do you speak for these people, Ambakan?"

Ambakan nodded as Ferie translated. The chief spoke in a deep bass. "I am the Jah of the Jungle, the Eagle of the seas, the Lion of the prairie. All who see me tremble and bow their heads. The Pugi and the Tang sing dirges to my prowess."

"What the hell does that mean?" Edo asked Ferie quietly.

Ferie chuckled. "You asked me to translate."

"Only so I could understand."

"I guess it means he is the top dog."

"All right, then." Edo smiled at Ambakan and held his arms out wide. "He likes the look of our shells. Tell him we have more where they came from. As the stars in the sky or the sand on this beach. Add some more color. He seems to favor bombast." Edo waited patiently as Ferie translated then indicated the shell necklaces. "Tell him all that I have gathered here is his and his alone. A gift from me to him."

As Ferie finished a ripple of excitement swept through the crowd of assembled natives.

"Tell him we need food, water."

Ferie translated and waited as Ambakan launched into a long and effusive tirade. "We come here not as enemies but to trade. We come in peace."

Ambakan made it plain he didn't much care where they had come from or why. His lack of curiosity was singular, matched only by the extent of his greed.

The discussions continued.

For two days. Three. The chiefs were adept at making long-winded speeches, signifying nothing. "Just like the politicians at home," Edo muttered to Ferie after a particularly pointless exercise in oratory.

When Edo had Ferie explain to the chieftains his desire for amna, for stone of the ground, he could sense the amusement rippling through the chiefs.

"They think we are half crazy." Ferie muttered. "Amna is nothing to them but a soft stone with no value for building, useless for casting weapons."

"It works both ways. Let them know we value this substance but not how much. Let them know we are serious in this but not how serious. Keep them guessing."

At the end of three days the chiefs slaughtered half a dozen hapless slaves, and to Edo's great dismay began to cook the corpses in s stone-lined pit they dug into the hillside above the palisade.

"Tell them I need the terms now. I may puke if I have to stay for the rest of this," he barked at Ferie.

Ambakan with great reluctance and a tinge of anger hinting at a burgeoning stock of bitterness signed the treaty, scrawling a mark beside his name as the shaman danced and sang his praises.

Edo and his men were free to use the land around the palisade fort for the distance of a league. The chiefs granted them this land in perpetuity, for as long as the grass grows and the fish slip from the rivers, as long as the Jah hunt and the albi sing the songs of the ancestors. Empty formulae that meant nothing but Edo knew that, as long as he had shells to trade with, the terms of the agreement would be kept.

Edo returned to the palisade, the smell of roasting flesh in his nostrils, sick in his soul though he could not quite tell why.

He had come such a long way to his brave new world. Was this all it had to offer him? There had to be more...

CHAPTER 20 - EDO

Winter sat deep, a firm heavy grip tight about them like a closed fist. Snow spat out of heaped gray clouds, sporadic blizzards knitted a dense weave of glinting snow around the palisade. The massive trees, the natives called them alo, were dressed in winter finery, snow bounding their tops, necklaces of hoar ice hanging from their branches. Dense white fogs that tasted of salt and sea haunted them, morning and evening, the air damp and sticky in the thick bowels of that heavy soup.

Edo had ordered a trading post built, and a small shantytown had grown up around it outside the palisades. The dark earth between the houses was treacherous, mud and ice where it wasn't completely frozen, the mud deep enough in places to suck away a man's boot.

The houses were long, rectangular, in the native style, the walls made from woven alo withies, the roofs thatched with bark.

Ferie and Alik Jar had set up in the trading post, two hundred spans from the fort, with a deka of his marines. The post was surrounded by a sturdy wooden walls, and Edo had embrasures built into the walls of the building so that it could be easily defended. From fort and trading post they had a field of fire across the width of the beach.

Protection against attacks which had never come.

Ambakan kept his word.

Slaves from the tribes of the amber skinned people were brought to them. Heeb and Edo collected over a hundred and had a pen made to house them. A dozen of the choicest, mostly women, were set up in one house in the shantytown, whores for those, native, soldier or sailor, willing to pay.

The tribes of the pig people, Edo learned they called themselves Malai, brought them amna, food, water, venison, corn cakes and lizard meat.

In the warmth of the trading post a fire burned in an open hearth, the smell of freshly cut wood was like a pure incense, they haggled and traded, the supplies of shellfish necklaces slowly diminishing.

Steadily Edo grew wealthy, almost beyond imagination. They all did. The thought brought him no joy. The whole business was so dreary, so mundane. Had they really come so far to do so little?

This was not what he had pined after in the depths of his dreams for so long.

Not this.

He was living, another man's dreams, fulfilling another man's desire. This dream, dreary with the toll of ledger and weighing scales, of goods bought and sold, people bartered for magic dust, was Eso's dream. Heeb and Ferie and Alix Jar all shared it. It was the Aonian way and their eyes became oily with greed when they imagined the chests of amna stored away, the golden orbed hirsh, they would receive as their share of the booty when Edo and his brother had taken their cut.

Edo would to Aonia return a wealthy man but what value was wealth without purpose.

He sighed.

All through the long winter a slow, initially vague, plan fermented in his head; bitter at first when it lost its tartness it became a golden sparkling wine that left him intoxicated.

He wanted nothing of Eso's mercantile, grubbing world. He did not want Tallamun mined, logged and despoiled, used up for the wealth and privilege of a favored few.

Used by men like Eso whose pores sweated money, by men like Heeb who carried out the whims of their masters, without pause or conscience. That was not what Edo wanted for this new land.

This was his land, the land of his dreams.

Tallamunn deserved better.

From the moment he had laid eyes on Tallamnn he had been in love, a love deeper and more profound than he had ever felt for another human, with the possible exception of Balin. Everything about this place touched him to the quick, stirred his soul to wonder; the harsh shrieks of red albi diving from the cliffs, copper sunsets in the forest, boles casting purple shadows whose texture seemed more substantial than granite, the hissing cry of the yalla flitting through the trees- harsh cries full of sadness and bitter loss- even the stars gleaming above; brighter and more numerous than he remembered from Aonia; the early moon, an impossible orange, as it rose over the sea's distant horizon.

He came to realize his presence in this land was no accident and as the nature of his purpose came clear to him it was like a fog lifted from his eyes.

Balin his one true friend, the one man who had wanted nothing from him, had died on Edo's account. The wound still festered. But before he died Balin had shown Edo the path to Yanik's grace and thus his death was not in vain. Edo had seen, had felt it; the glimmer of possibility of a different kind of world, a world re-imagined. A world where men were equal and perfect in the light of their own one god. It would be a world without favorites, a world without greed, led by men of vision and hope, where men and women lived to be the best their natures were capable of.

Yanik's world. The world of that god of innocence and love.

Yanik had brought him here, not Feror. Had sent Balin to show him the truth. Edo would return to Aonia and with his share of their wealth he would fit out a ship, two if he could, and sail to Milesia.

In Milesia he would tell them of this new land, this place of wonder.

He would bring Monks, settlers, all who would listen to him. They would settle here, become a part of this world. Tied to it like the trees, like the natives who hunted the dark forests.

Tallamun would be home for a new nation of pure men. Edo had no illusions. He knew what he was; a brutal soldier in a brutal time but others, men like Balin, had a chance for a better world and Edo would be the arm that cleared the path for them to their paradise.

CHAPTER 21 - GEHSI

The Malai warriors appeared at noon, distant dots on wind-swept sandbar, bearing weapons and in full wardress.

Tamber had known to expect them.

Since the arrack he knew many things, things that scared Gehsi; the older man's eyes held a jaded, fierce look, as though he had seen too much of life and death, found both wanting.

"We could run. Make for the forest."

Tamber simply shook his head. "They are not alone, Gehsi. A second party stalks us from the east. A third from the cliffs."

Quietly accepting this- Tamber understood how Malai warbands operated-Gehsi grabbed the spear of his people and squatted in front of the shaman, watching the figures approach over a denuded landscape of stone, of reed march and mudflats. Malai warriors. Blood in their minds, no doubt, the stink of death exhilarating their nostrils. He fought to control his rage, torn by the choice that faced him. He could run now, leave Tamber to his fate; bring the spear back to his own people. He would be feted, worthy of a plaited headdress and the boon of a crimson flower from the temple.

He had evaded Malai war bands before, he could do it again for Tamber had trained him to be strong, fit, fleet of foot but his chance of escape was narrowing with every moment he hesitated. He sighed.

He could not leave. His fading memories of the nest, of his parents and his family, were nothing to the debt he owed this solitary Malai.

Gehsi would not abandon his stepfather.

The warriors arrived at the tumble of rocks beneath the cave.

"We call you Nonei," the lead warrior bellowed at Tamber, casting Gehsi a scornful look. "Lord Upakahun would speak with you."

Tamber laughed, incredulously. "That old bastard still lives then?"

"Upakahun son of Upakahun would speak with you, Nonei."

"So tell him to get off his arse and come and visit me." Tamber growled and touched the poison-tooth of the alkj' jah, that hung on a necklace of knotted gut, round his neck.

They had hunted the beast yesterday, tracked it to a valley in the foothills of the Taskiluh Mountains, Gehsi wearing armor of wood and padded cotton, a defense against the poison for which the beast was infamous

They had trapped it, back to an impenetrable thicket of coarse, needled arg and it had dived at them spitting poison, its eyes a frantic glare as it soared past them on feeble leather wings.

Diving Tamber had caught it, two handed, wrestled it to the ground. Avoiding the snarling fangs he had leaned over the writhing animal and bit deep into its neck, wrestling with his teeth at the sacs of poison ridging its neck.

Blood on his lips, the poison staining his mouth Tamber had fallen to the ground, writhing.

Gehsi stabbed the broken beast with his spear, disgust crinkling his face, then knelt beside Tamber. Poison coursed through the Malai; his face was puce, the veins on his forehead and neck became marbled purple as foam burbled from his mouth.

As Tamber had instructed Gehsi built a fire, skinned and gutted the jah and waited.

Darkness fell and stars had sprinkled the moonless sky before Tamber opened his eyes again, moaning. Gehsi helped him to his feet and Tamber, weak as a foal and disoriented, leaned on Gehsi as they returned to their camp. In silence they ate the beast and when they were ready Gehsi kicked out the fire, gathered their weapons. Tamber leaning on Gehsi they slowly returned to their cave by the sea.

Tamber had not explained and Gehsi had not asked. But he <u>did</u> understand that the hunt had been connected to this visit of the Malai war band, for Tamber had foretold their coming, and had warned Gehsi to be ready.

The warriors climbed towards the cave and when they reached the broad ridge directly below the cave they fanned out in a half circle, showing no sign of fear or respect.

The lead warrior, the one who had addressed Tamber, now pointed at Gehsi.

"I become hungry. We will butcher the Pugi for meat before we return." Then to Tamber he said, in a cold voice. "Nonei, you may walk with us or we will carry you on broken legs. The choice is yours but Upakahun would speak with

298

you and you will come with us today."

"What do they call you, you bastard son of a bleating bitch?"

The warrior raised his head high, beat his chest and roared. "I am Malalauh son of Tebkan, Proud warrior of the Malai, my keni is larger than the alo tree. The Tang quiver at the sound of my name and Pugi shudder and shit themselves when they smell my stink on the evening wind." The warrior spat at Tamber. "Who are you Nonei, to ask me such a question?"

"Take another step Malalauh and you will die. I will trap your keni, devour it as sweet corn and spit the husk into a fire into Yimti's hall.

A smile of contempt erupted on Malalauh's face.

He gestured at the large, heavy-set warrior to his left and said, "My stomach rumbles. I could eat a live jah. Kill the Pugi and get a campfire started. When we've eaten we'll take the sorcerer home."

The man strode towards Gehsi swinging his sword, the striations in its side keening as it cut air.

Gehsi ducked the blow, rolled forward and was behind and on his feet before the large warrior could react.

He jabbed his spear against the back of the man's knee and the blade sliced cut through bone and cartilage.

The warrior tumbled forward on his face, breath slamming from his body. Gehsi leapt on his back and stabbed him through the neck.

The other warriors rushed forward but Tamber stood in their way, blocking them, right hand outstretched, fingers splayed.

"Stop now or die."

Gehsi twisted the spear drawing it from muscle and hard gristle of the felled body. When he turned Tamber's face had changed, his skin taken on a hard, sheen like the leathern skin of a alkj' jah. His eyes were ink and ice, pools of stagnant water in winter at day's end.

His face, its gray pallor, like deaths bridesmaid.

Malalauh shot forward, roaring, sword swinging two-handed, the blow aimed at Tamber's lower body.

Tamber stepped forward inside the arc of the swing, a blur that Gehsi could barely follow. The sword swung harmlessly wide and Malalauh stumbled forward, off balance as his arms crashed into Tamber's right shoulder.

Tamber held out his hand, his fingers splayed and hissed.

The wind keened. Waves thundered against rocks, spuming the air. A raven flew over their heads, kraaing.

Malalauh fell to his knees, his face swelling, clutching his throat.

Tamber stepped back, pulling the tintuk sword out of Malalauh's unresisting grasp as the smitten warrior's face turned purple, his tongue flopping like an air-drowning fish. His death was slow, painful and the other Malai did nothing to intervene.

Tamber owned the poison of the jah. The jah had become a part of him in some way Gehsi could not hope to understand..

"Father?" Gehsi called, aware of buds of fear in his soul

Tamber turned towards him and the snarl on his face vanished and his eyes let in a milky light, almost gentle.

"You did well little one."

He put his arm on Gehsi's shoulder.

"This is Gehsi." Tamber turned to address the remaining Malai. "He is a Pugi and you are to consider him my son."

The warriors stared him wide-eyed and bemused as if the world had turned on its head.

"Any who try to harm him will die as this garbage died." He gestured at Malalauh. "Inform your chief that if he would see me he must come himself, alone, bearing the fitting tribute of one who seeks answers. Those are my terms." He paused. They did not move.

"Go now!" His bellowed voice was the roar of the storm, the trembling of the earth. The warriors backed away, pausing only to collect Malalauh's corpse, though their eyes gleamed with something like panic.

Tamber turned his back on them and made his way to the cave, guiding Gehsi by the arm.

Inside he sat, cross-legged on the ground, slapped his thigh and burst out laughing.

"Upakahun will come now, Gehsi my boy. Wait and see if he doesn't."

Gehsi smiled back but his heart was troubled

301

and anxious.

The gods that spoke in Tamber's mind were eating away at his mind, devouring his soul and their knowledge had made Tamber into someone, something, both better or worse than he had once been.

Fear for Tamber ruled Gehsi's soul.

***

Upakahun was a young man, clear-eyed, fresh-faced with bright, sharp teeth. He wore his hair long and self-inflicted scars- signs of his ritual status, blizzarded his arms.

He had dressed in his finest cotton robes and wore the skin of a green jah across his shoulder. In his hair were crimson albi feathers and in his right hand was a tintuk club with a round ball, etched with wards, as befitted his status as leader of his tribe.

He entered the dimness of the cave, bent over, blinking.

In his right arm was a stoppered bowl. He lowered his head in silence handed it to Tamber, who sniffed delightedly at the liquid within.

Kai-wine.

Tamber gestured for the chief to sit opposite him, across the fire.

"What do I call you, seer of the ages?" Upakahun asked when he was sitting cross-legged. His voice was low, well modulated and respectful.

From Tamber's stories Gehsi knew about

Upakahun the elder- an old man fallen so in love with power that he was ready to crush dissent, to stifle talent, so as to protect his own position.

But a son was not always subject to sins of his father. Perhaps Upakahun son of Upakahun was a leader worthy of the name.

"The men you sent called me Nonei, so Nonei is who I now am." Tamber said.

Upakahun shifted uneasily. "Your prowess was hidden from us, Nonei. For the disrespect my men showed, I am sorry."

"Your father banished me. Stole my name."

"I am not my father." Upakahun opened his arms wide. "He spent the last years of his life hunted by fear. He neglected much, made many mistakes. I would that he had died younger when his fame was greater and his fear had not yet weakened him."

"He destroyed those who challenged his will. He weakened the tribe."

Upakahun nodded. "You make fair judgment."

"So can we expect the same from you?"

Upakahun grimaced, ran his hand through his hair. "I am a great warrior. I survived the Yangmpabat for three tendays and then five more. The memories of the great feats of Tarnag and Tamber are no more. In the year of Gray One Stag I led an alliance of our people against the Blue River tang. We destroyed three villages and returned with twice a hundred slaves. Now the Tang pay us tribute. The chiefs of the Ima, the Warapat and the Pehatkan Angkada bend their eyes in my presence and call me lord."

"I am happy for you, Upakahun Keni, son of Upakahun the Snake, and if your boast is finished be gone from my sight." Tamber spat at the dirt just in front of Upakahun's feet.

Upakahun's face knotted with anger. "You misunderstand me."

Tamber smiled. "So you did not come here to bore me to death with a recitation of your keni?"

"I have been a great warrior. That is no vain boast." Upakahun's eyes drifted towards his sandaled feet, almost shyly. A strange sight on such a fierce some young man. "I would be a great chief."

Tamber snorted. "And so you would have the banished advise you. How does your war council feel about this?"

"Most do not approve."

Tamber leaned forward, a vaguely predatory move, and his eyes assumed the texture of hard steel." Then why are you here?"

"You foresaw the arrival of these newcomers." he spoke in a quiet voice. "I need to know…"

Tamber stared at Upakahun with hard, appraising eyes and Gehsi knew that Uphakahun had answered well, showing both with humility and sense.

"Where are they now, the ones who wear strange armor?"

"They built a camp in the lands of the Delta people. Those lands have been bequeathed to them for eternity."

The Tribes of the Delta, a branch of the Malai lived two tendays march away, towards north.

Tamber sniffed. "I smelt their presence on last moon's full wind. Their stink is rancid. Their presence intolerable. To grant them land...folly."

"They ride blood-red jah and have weapons that echo thunder." Upakahun looked uneasy.

Tamber shook his head vigorously. "Powerful weapons and control of dark magicks we do not understand. But they are men. Men die."

The cloud on Upakahun's face lifted and he smiled. A bright smile, somehow naive with all the optimism of successful youth.

"Tell me what you know," Tamber said.

Upakahun shrugged. "They came in early summer. The chiefs of the Delta called a host together but the shaman ran shamefully when the beetlemen appeared on the field of battle. Afterwards the chiefs met with their leader."

"They have names?"

"I have heard it said but I cannot pronounce it."

"Tell me of them."

"They are sheeted in armor, like beetles. Arrows do not penetrate beneath this material."

Tamber's raised an eyebrow. "So having failed to destroy them the chiefs trade now with them?"

"For food, for cowrie shells and others. Silver and gray shells never seen before. Valuable for their rarity."

"In exchange for what?"

"Food, hides. Slaves. Stones."

"Stones?"

"The gray stones of the Takan Oranamantuk Cliffs."

"Stone?" Tamber repeated, pushing the word through tight lips.

"They value it. They pay for it. To the tribes of the Delta it is nothing so they trade and snigger when backs are turned."

Tamber rubbed his chin. "This is not a sentimental race. They did not come here to collect trinkets. These stones, they are important. Upakahun, we must not condescend merely because we do not understand. "He stopped, reached to the side and fed some withies to the ebbing fire. He glanced at Gehsi and Gehsi saw from the look how deep Tamber's excitement ran; Upakahun had the potential to become the leader Tamber had been waiting for. A chief who would listen and act wisely.

But Tamber was too cagy to let Upakahun know what he was thinking.

"I still do not know why you came to me, Upakahun of the Telukamat, Destroyer of the lesser Tribes, Son of Upakahun, Grandson of Megmat the Fierce. What is it you wish of me?"

Using Upakahun's title for the first time- a mark of respect and a signal that Tamber was willing to help.

"Three of the Tribes of the Delta have signed a pact of peace and trade with the strangers."

"Hah!"

"They call themselves Confederacy of the Three Nations. They wish the Telukamat to join with them."

Tamber shifted on his seat. He unstoppered the bowl of wine and Gehsi fetched three stone mugs. "I take it you have summoned a council of the tribes."

"I sent the messengers at the turn of the moon. The leaders of the Lower Five Villages are here. The chiefs and warriors of the Lagen Marsh People and the Angka are expected tomorrow or the next day."

"What worries you Upakahun? Why come to me? Can a trade pact harm your people?"

The young man said nothing for a long time, his eyes distant as he gathered his thoughts. "Many on the council favor signing. Others remember old slights of the Delta People. They nurture bad blood and oppose this confederacy. The decision point is a knife's edge."

"And where would you lead your people? To war or trade."

"I have not spoken, Nonei, for I fear speaking is pointless. Half the old men talk of ancient raids and display their scars. The other half sweat greed like congealed fish oil. They would be wealthy" He blinked. "To me all words rings hollow."

"Because of the Newcomers?"

Upakahun nodded.

"Men still speak of things as they were," Tamber said. "They do not understand that the world has shifted on its axis. Do you wish to understand?"

Upakahun's face betrayed strain as though truth were a distant blur, a deer seen shifting

307

through shadow in a darkening forest. "Help me, Nonei."

"The beetle men turn old certainties on their heads. The old men of your council will have trouble with this."

"Speak at the great council. Persuade them. Persuade me."

Tamber stood stiffly, groaning. He walked to the mouth of the cave and stood staring at the pounding waves, hands behind his back.

When he turned light from without was a pale nimbus that gave him a ghastly, leached appearance.

"We will come." he glanced at Gehsi, a question in the quizzical rise of his eyebrows, and Gehsi nodded agreement in turn.

Upakahun turned to Gehsi, and smiled. The smile reached the man's eyes and Gehsi smiled guardedly back.

"Introduce me then to this strange son of yours, Nonei." He paused, chuckled. "Though I fear I fail to see much of you in him."

CHAPTER 22 - EDO

Heeb burst into Edo's office, face flushed with worry. "Alix Jar and his scouting party are long overdue."

Edo was busy tallying the week's receipts adding notes to his master ledger and captain's log. He scowled and fixed his attention on the Scian.

"Jar left at dawn. Took a patrol to the foothills of the Pengan."

"Pale Reed Tribe territory."

Heeb nodded.

"Who approved this?"

"An exploratory patrol, Edo. No need to bother you with it. Six crossbows and two Tang scouts. Three riders for extra muscle."

Edo glanced at his amna clock, the ethereal dials crawling along Dieran marble. Outside the window, light was fading, the trees darkening, a pink glow damping the west.

"So why aren't they back?" Edo rose, stretched, and scratched his chin.

"Jar may be a hothead, but he is experienced enough."

Edo thought he heard strain in Heeb's voice, protesting an accusation Edo had not even raised. The truce with the tribes was holding though their supply of shells to barter with was almost finished and the chiefs no longer delivered amna in the qualities they once had.

Alik jar had argued that the natives were

holding back, betraying a confidence and the terms of the truce. Winter had done that to them; driving them inward, into the worst of themselves. Unpredictable at the best if time of times, Jar had become like a untamed beast penned too long in a cage, eager for escape. Eager for blood.

Edo prayed Heeb was right that the mercenary had done nothing stupid.

He walked outside, Heeb at his side. Beneath a roofed but open-walled hut on the west wall the carpenters were working; double shifts that often went late into the night. Hammers knocked and saws rasped, fixings spars, planking and other parts of the ship that had been rotted by weather and storm.

The ships were being refitted, caulked and trimmed so they would be ready to sail when the weather turned for the better.

Sailors and native bearers were busy carted thick sacks of provisions- food and water and other necessities- into the long hall at the center of the fort.

A month, at most two and they would be ready to return.

Edo wanted no trouble, not now.

Knew, in his secret heart, that it was inevitable. The tribes were restless, his men were worse. The friction between them had been pushing them apart for so long that, like opposed boulders of stone, when the rocks rolled back into contact sparks were inevitable.

Edo cursed.

"We cannot risk another patrol so close to

nightfall."

Heeb looked around, sniffed the air. Troubled.

"Fair enough. First light then, if they do not return."

"Perhaps."

"What would you suggest otherwise?"

Edo shrugged. "I have a bad feeling about this, Heeb. Double the guard. I'll talk to the carpenters. We need to take precautions."

***

A horn blew.

Edo started awake from a dense and chill dream. He levered himself out of bed, still dressed in his uniform.

Outside, the men of the watch had lit the signal fires on the braziers above the gates and the mercenaries, risen from their beds were scrambling for the walls.

Edo heard Heeb's bellowed command and the men of the night watch pulled open the gates. Alik Jar and two of his men scrambled inside, blood on their uniforms, heads hung low with exhaustion.

No horses. No crossbows. One carried a bloodied halberd, and Jar had held on to his sword.

Edo's heart sunk and sweat prickled his forehead.

The dim premonition of doom growing.

"Escort them to the warlocks in the infirmary," Edo ordered a Plinik Lien who stood

311

to one side.

Alik Jar avoided Edo's gaze, stumbled past like a disheveled ghost.

The gates were closed quickly and a dark tension fell over the night as men strained down the sights of their crossbows and the scorpions were primed.

"See anything?" he bellowed up at Heeb.

"No pursuit beyond the tree line. Nothing!"

"Full watch through the night. No one sleeps till we find out what happened. Heeb you come with me. Jar has some explaining to do."

***

Jar lay on a trestle bed in the long infirmary hall, at the back of the great storeroom, his face a dull gray, his eyes lucid, darting nervously to the sides as Edo approached. The two remaining mercenaries lay on beds further down the hall, one moaning, pain twisting his sweat soaked body, the other staring at nothing, his face still blank with shock.

Demensidos the warlock was attending the wounds in the mercenaries shoulder and face.

Arrow wounds. Club wounds.

When the warlock had finished, Edo pulled him to one side.

"Will they live?"

The warlock smiled darkly. "Amna cures all and asks little. They will live. The wounds are largely superficial but Ageara one will lose a hand."

Demensidos made to move past Edo to the distressed mercenary. Edo put a hand on his shoulder, holding him in place, staring hard at the hooded face, made gloomy with tattooed runes and the man's natural predisposition to despondency.

"If this is what I think it the natives will demand vengeance. We may need some help. Can I count on you?"

The warlock turned towards Edo and the smell from his unwashed body caused Edo to gag. He held up his left hand, the fingers missing, the palm and the back of the hand blue and amber, the designs spider-like, intricate, impossible to follow with the naked eye.

Chillness emanated from him. It was always thus with warlocks; their knowledge soured them, churned their innards like mud daub, made stony monsters of their souls.

Edo was glad the man was on their side.

The warlock turned his palm face up and the spider-like designs extended along the stumps where his fingers once were, building ghost fingers from the interstices of flesh and magic.

The ghost fingers snapped, and a dense heavy energy rolled through the room. The warlock smiled.

"A plague on their souls. Fear not Domin, I am cooking you up a victory. I will need three more days."

The man chuckled, showing teeth long and yellow, like the teeth of an ancient scavenger. Edo's heart beat faster, fear a nagging specter behind his back.

The gifts of warlocks were never free, and the price sometimes incalculable.

The warlock made his way past Edo to the wounded mercenary, whose screams suddenly tore through the hall. Edo stared at the warlock's back, stomach souring, aware that Tallamun was slipping away from him, that a watershed had been reached and the tide had swung against them.

***

Edo pulled over a chair place it next to Jar's bed and straddled it.

"What happened?"

"We reached the Pengan at midday. Rested there. Ate. Two leagues on, we came to a river, deep and green, banks marshy and lined with drooping willow. We followed it, looking for a ford, hoping to make a preliminary exploration of the far bank. We followed it perhaps three leagues through deep forest, sun hidden from us. A scream sounded from amongst he trees. A creature came lumbering towards us." Jar shook his head, eyes focused on the ceiling, remembering. "Huge it was. High as two men. Moved on four legs like a lizard but with feelers like claws. A great gaping jaw. Red lips and mouth."

"It attacked you."

"Jar nodded." We fired on it. Wounded, it blundered away. We could hear it screaming as it

314

moved. A lonesome sound that. Fierce yet lonesome." He rubbed his chin. "We followed the river, found a ford that we could wade across. Beneath the trees there was no sound, no birds. An eerie place. Still we pressed on."

"Your orders were to explore but return before nightfall. Why did you continue?"

"A feeling. Nothing more. I knew we would find something."

"Something?" Heeb asked greedily, risking a glance at Edo.

Jar nodded. "I'll come to that. It was getting late, we were thinking on turning about when we came on a large village. We could see down on it from a knoll of trees to the west. A Malai village but with lots of those little slaves wandering about, carting stuff on their backs.

"Carting what?"

Jar stared at both of them in turn.

"Amna. A hundred bearers each carrying perhaps a hundredweight of amna, and that was only what we could see."

Heeb whistled and Edo felt again the water of the future lapping at their heals, building slowly but inevitably to a torrent that threatened to destroy them.

"You returned then as you should have, to report this to us?"

Jar shook his head vigorously.

"No! Entargió, I thought I should find the source. We skirted the village, along the edge of a mountain lake. The going was slow, the land flat marsh, the reeds not tall enough to hide us. We

315

left the horses in cover, moved low, jumping at each lonely cry of a marsh bird. The place felt accursed."

Edo waved him on, impatient now.

"The source was a mine leading to a cave scaffolded with wood, at the top of a long winding trail. We watched from the shoulder of the nearest hill. Bearers carried the amna down the trail. A long trail of them like ants."

"A mine?"

"An amna mine." Jar's eyes sparkled.

"Go on!"

"We turned about. The sun was getting ready to sink, the light already giving up the ghost. We made it back across the river to the trees..."

Jar hesitated and a sheen of sweat suddenly coated his lips, small thin pearls glimmering in the light of the braziers on the wall.

"They came out of the trees, surprised us. We were walking the horses. The forest was dark, almost night dark. We lost three men in the first attack and the horses spooked. After that we ran."

He held his hands up.

"They lost interest after a league or so. We trudged through the dark. Then we were here."

Edo nodded, rose to his feet, gestured at Heeb to follow him.

Heeb threw him a surprised glance but followed. They pushed through the door and Edo took deep breaths; the air fresh, still chill, but with a hint of spring.

A gentle green taste.

"His story stinks."

316

Heeb raised an eyebrow.

"I believed him"

"Fuck that, Heeb, I want to know what really happened. Question Ageara. Take him someplace quiet. Use whatever force necessary. He is no longer of use to us, anyhow."

Heeb opened his mouth, as if to protest, eyes glimmering with anger.

"Do it now, Entargió or I will you feed your liver to the Jah."

Heeb made a sour face, saluted, turned on his heels.

Edo watched him go, biting his nails, that dim premonition growing.

A month, Yanik, I need at least a month before the ships are ready.

Do not let fate conspire against us.

***

Edo spoke with the master carpenters, in tones of great urgency, promising them a further detail from the ship crews to speed the work.

The two men laid down their hammers wiped the hair out of their brows. The air in the yard of their workshop smelled tart, of sweet wood, freshly cut. Fine wooden dust tamped the air, catching in Edo's lungs. Slowly they shook their heads, scowling at on another, at him.

They would not budge.

Five weeks. A month tops. The ships would be ready then, not before.

Edo growled, disgusted but hardly surprised,

317

and stomped off towards the palisade.

Half a dozen mercenaries stood guard around the wall, all awake, their spirits high as they joked and laughed. He called to them, they saluted snappily enough.

Over the glimmering sea floated wispy red clouds, strange and darting. The moon stood full, a painful silver, and stars decked the sky.

Trees on the distant hills loomed, inky black against the deeper darkness, fog roiling within, thin fingers reaching out to him.

Walray clucked and screeched and occasionally Jah bellowed sadly. Lonely devils inhabiting the darkness.

"He lied."

Edo started; lost in thought he had not heard Heeb's approach.

"Jar initiated the attack."

Heeb nodded. "They found the village and the mine as he said. He got greedy; thought a surprise attack would drive away the Malai. Get in. Grab what you can. Get out. You know the drill."

Edo stubbed the ground with his toe. "What was the stupid fuck thinking?"

"He wasn't, Domin. He had a hard on for the amna and he followed his dick. They all did, so Ageara says. Put it to a vote."

"Damn their eyes!"

"Once in the village they got trapped in an alley-space between a ziggurat and the main hall. Malai warriors on the roof." He snorted. "Get this; the cunning bastards used amna to stone them,

318

knock them off the horses. It was too narrow to charge. The crossbows got one volley in. Then it was all over. It was pure luck Jar and the other two got away."

Edo turned, saw a walray flitting over trees in the distance, heard the lapping of the waves on the seashore; saw the dark bulk of the ships swaying on the sea."

"What do you want me to do with them?"

Edo let out a frustrated groan. "Dock the bastard's pay. Reprimand him. Leave it at that. I've a feeling we will need every warm body fighting on our side before this is over."

***

Ambakan appeared the next day, his face a dark and livid scowl, flanked by three blood-coated shaman. Twelve warriors accompanied him, large men wielding massive swords of hardened tintuk, swords that gleamed like dark bronze and hung from baldrics over their shoulders.

The chief strode through the open gates, swinging his arms, looking neither right or left, the shaman scampering ahead of him yowling, arms flailing, dancing on one foot.

The crane dance of Hanyeleh

A dance of mockery. A dance of power. A dance of anger.

Edo had set out two chairs facing one another across the muddy courtyard, eighty spans apart.

He gestured for Ambakan to sit then lowered

himself into the hard wooden chair, clasping his hands in his lap, his hands trembling faintly. Ferie took his position to one shoulder, Heeb to the other.

Ambakan barked something in his tongue, the inflected syllables like pounding hail.

"He says our men attacked a village near the Pengan. Killed twenty, five women and three children included. Says, additionally, we killed five of their herd."

"Herd?"

"The small amber ones. The Pugi slaves."

Edo placed a hand on Ferie's arm. "Tell him we acknowledge our responsibility for this, that we will take care of the men, punish them. We will pay a blood price in shell necklaces for each man, woman and child."

Ferie repeated this. Ambakan's face grew darker and his eyes flashed fury. Edo squirmed in his seat, found his hand edging towards the dirk he carried in his belt. The shaman clicked and muttered and cast their hands towards him, like starving men tearing at food.

They danced. They spat. They pulled at their hair.

Ambakan finally shot some words at Edo, face twisted with anger.

"I take it that didn't go down too well."

Ferie shrugged. "As far as I can figure you insulted them by offering blood money for their dead. Equates them to the amber ones. "

"The slaves?"

Ferie nodded.

"Damn. That's no good."

"No."

Edo struggled to remain calm, though his stomach churned. He forced himself to look at Ambakan and smile disarmingly, ignoring the temptation to glance at the windows of the nearest building. He tensed, made a fist of his hand to stop it trembling. He could smell the stink of his own fear, sour in his nostrils. Ambakan, it seemed, would demand vengeance and Edo could not, would not, deliver Jar and the two others to the Malai chief. For all that Jar and his men had transgressed they were citizens of the republic. Their right to a fair hearing was inviolate. They deserved better than the farce that passed amongst the Malai as justice. The cannibalism in particular, Edo found revolting. But that was not all. Not by a long shot. Jar's defeat- silly bastard running back here with his tail between his legs- meant they had <u>all</u> lost face and <u>that</u> gave the Malai an inkling of how weak they truly were. If Edo delivered Jar and the other two to Ambakan without a fight Edo would come across as soft. Pussywhipped, Edo's Papa would have said. Do that, and I might as well lie down here and let the barbarian cut my throat right here, right now, for he will know his own strength and our weakness.

Edo had hoped that Ambakan could be bought, that greed would take precedence over pride.

A futile hope.

So be it. If war was inevitable it was better to strike first, a hard disabling blow than to tarry.

He raised his left hand, still balled in a fist above his head. The horn blew.

The guards on the palisades lowered loaded crossbows. A knot of crossbowmen filed from behind the storehouse.

In the main barracks men appeared at the window, crossbows at the ready.

He lowered his head. The screech of amna was deafening, the retort of explosions but a dim echo in its wake.

A combus landed amongst the knot of Malai guards to Ambakan's right, exploded. Blood gushed and limbs flew. From the roofs, from the slit windows in the barrack's building bolts flew.

Ambakan shot up from his seat drew his sword and charged at Edo. Ferie handed Edo the sword hidden behind his seat and Edo stepped forward. The Malai was tall, strong, quick. Pounding towards him like some enormous wild animal. Proud and fearless.

Edo knew he would have no chance in a head to head.

He signaled at the nearest crossbowmen, ten paces to his rear and a bolt shot out, smashed into the Malai's kneecap. Still Ambakan came, dragging one leg, screaming defiance, waving his weapon, shadowed by a brace of guards and the remaining shaman. Fifty paces or less, the guards slowing to keep pace with their chief.

Edo turned to the crossbowmen.

"Kill them all but the chief. Take his other knee. Lets see how fast he moves then."

He turned and walked away, sick in his

322

stomach as the bolts flew through the protesting air and Tallamun shrieked with the sounds of war.

**

Edo started awake.

An owl hooted, a jah screaming mournfully. His pounding heart banished sleep like morning dew. Fear had become his second skin, like a wet blanket, dark and stuffy that lay heavy upon him through the length of the day, pounding into his nights.

In his dreams pale wraiths flitted through dead trees at the edge of sight and ogres, wearing the face of his brother their eyes full of blood, chased after him. Hands with darkened nails rose through the earth, wrapped his ankle, pulled him through the earth; breath deserted his lungs, his mouth filled with coarse, rank mud. As he suffocated the screams of the dead trembled through him, a vibrating cord, and the tension rising to a point where he snapped awake.

He rose, dressed called for Ferie and grabbed a tisane made of local herbs as he made his way to the prison infirmary where the Malai chief had been imprisoned.

Ambakan knees had been blown to shreds and a stray bolt in his shoulder showed signs of infection. But he lived, and Edo intended to keep him alive. For now. The chief swore and spat when he saw Edo.

"He says the ancestors will eat your liver. That the shaman will stalk you in the darkness and devour your soul." Ferie translated.

"The living men under his command haunt me more than any ghost, Pora. Bring him to the palisade wall. Display our prize. The bastards need to know he still lives, that we will keep him alive till they attack."

Ferie signed a ward of blessing.

Edo snorted. "What?"

"I hope his brothers love him more that they do ambition, for if not..."

The Malai warriors had gathered overnight and were like flicking locusts, faintly glimpsed amongst the shadow of the trees. Edo could field a mere handful against them.

When they attacked it would be a massacre.

They hauled Ambakan outside, the Malai blinking as the sun invaded his eyes. They tied him to the base of the flagpole, visible to those distant warriors. A shout went up at the sight of him, and drums started to beat, a ragged hypnotic sound further denting Edo's confidence.

The faces of his men, sailors and mercenaries both, on the wall told a similar story. Morale was low and nerves ragged, Ambakan the single bargaining chip that might see them through.

***

Footsteps sounded outside his office door. Ferie pushed the door open, his face flushed with excitement.

"The warlock wants you in the infirmary. The owl is keeping his cards close to his chest but I think he's cracked it."

Edo sprang to his feet, bulled past the Caedian, half-walking, half-running, sword flapping in its scabbard.

Demensidos stood by the main door of the infirmary, face a pallid blur beneath the shadow of the lintel.

"Is it ready?" Edo asked breathlessly

The warlock's humorless yellow grin made Edo's heart sing.

"Follow me, Domin."

The warlock led the way to his inner sanctum; a combination living space and healing room hidden from the main ward by a heavy wooden door made of rough planking.

The warlock made his way to a stoppered wooden jug, smiled sourly over his shoulder at Edo. "You sure that is what you want."

Edo nodded.

"A thimbleful to drink for each man. Some may feel poorly for a day or so. Nauseous. The Malai have no natural resistance. Their deaths are assured."

Edo nodded. "Have your medics distribute the potion. I will take mine last."

He turned on his heels to leave, the brightness of hope leavening his heart for the first time in days.

The warlock cleared his throat. Edo stopped, turned his head towards the man. The warlock's face was inscrutable and shadow magick danced about his eyes.

"Once this starts, Entargió, the deaths will be

indiscriminate. Women. Children. Tang and Pugi as much as Malai."

Edo turned back to him. "This land rests in our hands like an unpolished jewel. The beasts who inhabit it have done nothing to deserve its bounty. Exterminate them and we can build anew."

He walked away.

"As good an excuse as any, I suppose." The warlock shouted after him, and the man's dark laugh chased him into the pale light of a dull day, the wind blowing clear and salt-laden from the sea and thick clouds, dark with impending rain, moving in slow procession overhead.

Edo faced the east, the damp air like a balm on his skin, blowing away the fear lodged in his gut, the anger that the warlock's scorn had kindled his anger. The warlock was a poison, as were all scrambling and visionless men. Men like Eso. Heeb. The vast majority of his countrymen.

He was not doing this on their account. His oaths were sealed.

He would survive these savages, and nothing on earth would stop him returning with a fleet of settlers.

Yanik's kingdom on earth would be secured.

***

The Malai came with a flag of parlay on the fourth day.

Edo watched them come, the warlock at his side.

326

"Final chance, Entargió. Do you wish to go ahead with this?" Demensidos's eyes flickered with dark amusement.

"I have no wish to die here, Demensidos. Do you?"

The warlock shrugged. "I do this at your behest. The price to be paid is yours, Entargió. Not mine."

Edo watched a shaman approach, followed by a posse of chiefs wielding wooden swords. Tall men, they carried themselves upright. Their warriors bore wooden swords, wore panther helms.

Tall and impressively martial, they looked like men of honor, like worthy enemies, reminding Edo of the Warriors of the Free Tribes who had for a time fought at their side against the Caedians. Yet this was an illusion. Edo had witnessed how they treated the other tribes, the other nations of this land. The Tang and the Pugi were either chattel or beasts of burden.

Sacrificed as food for the gods, cannibalized to fill the bellies of this belligerent people.

He had fought Caedians, brought mayhem to their cities and their children for their singular sins; the sealing of revenant souls in living bodies.

What these tribal butchers did with their prisoners was no less an abdication of humanity.

He turned to the warlock and in a clipped voice said, "They treat other nations like animals. The Great Lord Yanik is clear on this. Treat with those you meet as they treat you. What do you think those bastards will do with us if we fall into

327

their clutches?"

The Warlock shrugged. "I, for one, will not live to see that."

Edo glared at the man. In his experience Warlocks resorted to such inscrutable answers only when doubt, an alien concept for them most of the time, began to bite hard at their heels.

"I lead here. I assume full responsibility."

The Warlock bowed. "The vial is yours. When the chance arises open it and splatter a few drops on one or more of them."

"How much time do we need to buy in these negotiations?"

"Hold them off for a day. Tomorrow at dawn they will be a spent force. Within three days their world will be at an end"

The warlock smiled, blackened teeth in his red mouth, like rot in living flesh. Edo shuddered and strode away, aware of dim eyes burning holes in his back.

They met on the swathe of green, halfway between the palisade wall and the tree line.

Tingan of the Red-Three-Band Tribe led the delegation. Ferie, as always translated. They talked for three hours, the demands of the Malai plain beneath the usual hyperbole- release Upakahun, deliver the men responsible for the original massacre and a number of men equal to the Malai who had died when Upakahun was captured.

Do this and they would consider honor satisfied.

"Tell them if they attack us many will die,"

Edo barked after being forced to listen to Tingan for almost a quarter of an hour. "Tell him that if we are attacked we will destroy our remaining store of shells." He smiled and shrugged, smiling sweetly at the sour-faced Tingan. "For what value are shells to us when our trading partners are so hostile."

Tingan, for all his and his people's greed would not budge.

A blood price had to be repaid and the price, steep and hard, was not negotiable.

A knot of red pain ran down Edo's back, a dense sharp pain stabbed both sides of his forehead. He rubbed his eyes, moaned showing them his fear for the first time, knowing the danger of this tactic; for seeing his fear they would surely sense weakness as a predator smells blood.

"Tell them," he barked at Ferie. "We agree to their terms but I need one night. Time to sell their terms to my men, time to draw lots for those who we deliver to their mercy."

Tingan growled his answer.

"They want Upakahun now."

Edo shook his head. "Gods damnation, Caedian. For the sake of your own life persuade them. Tomorrow or there is no deal."

Tingan crossed his arms as Ferie waxed lyrical, stumbling over unfamiliar words, a circle of sweat evident under the arms of his tunic, his back bathed in sweat. Ferie looked like a desperate man; a perfect performance in the circumstances. Tingan, his amber eyes lifeless in a pallid face, the tusks twisting his lips nodded at Edo and stood. He would grant them the boon of this one night.

Edo held out the vial, pulled up the stopper.

"Tell him," he said with a forced smile. "We too have our traditions. We need to bless this agreement with sacred oil. Tell him I must anoint him. Tell him, in our culture it gives him power over us. Make him believe it Ferie. For the sake of your hide, make him believe it."

Tingan listened, face slightly averted, eyes never leaving Edo's face.

He said nothing when Edo finished. A cold, heavy silence fell. Then he held out his hand and beckoned Edo forward.

Edo came close to the man; smelling grease and smoke fires and an unpleasant musk. He held out the vial two-handed. Its gaping mouth-usually so innocent- brought to mind the mouth of a hungry arg, one of Mal Dinn's twisted children, come to swallow whole the world. Edo chanted the words of a bawdy prayer-song, about the salacious exploits of Miptero the Hero-god.

A drinking song, part desperate prayer, one which all soldiers knew.

It was all he could think of, and it sounded officious enough given that the Malai could not understand a word he was singing.

He swung his hand forward and out and drops from the vial splattered Tingan, the nearest shaman and two of the guards. The liquid was clear, slightly perfumed, oily but not unpleasant.

Tingan scowled, turned his back.

He turned around once, ten paces away and pointed at Edo's chest then barked something.

"He says he will back two hours after dawn tomorrow. We are to have Upakahun here waiting with the men we will deliver to justice. If we do not," Ferie's adam's apple bobbed. "He says-"

"What?"

"He will drink your soul."

A cold hand ran down Edo's back and he shivered lightly.

Tingan saw the reaction and showed his teeth, but there was neither humor nor pity in the smile.

We have shown them the extent of our weakness, Edo thought. Shown them our fear. They know they own us. If the warlock is wrong we are all dead men for Tingan's words mean nothing. He is a viper. He rules a nest of vipers. Whatever we give them will not be enough. They will have only one goal now- our total destruction.

He spat sideways, and turned on his heels.

So be it.

Tomorrow's dawn and the warlock's potion would decide everything.

***

The massive wooden gates of the fort swung shut and Edo breathed a deep sigh, noticed for the first time the uncontrollable trembling of his hand. Jar and Heeb and even Demensidos clustered close about him, faces drawn and fretful. They cast a volley of questions at him. The mercenaries were dressed in full armor and even the sailors armed and armored, wielding long pikes, crossbows and thin-edged swords.

"Heeb, make up a roster for tonight. Make sure no one sleeps without armor and weapons to hand. If the potions fails we can expect them at dawn tomorrow but they may come earlier."

He turned his back on them and made for his quarters where he tried to get some work done. He could not concentrate. At nightfall he lay down, still fully dressed, on his bunk bed but could not sleep. He rose and went outside, paced the fort through that long night like a crazed ghost searching for a trace of peace. Dawn was a faint whisper on the horizon when he called reveille and took his place on the wall. He inspected the scorpion, those fitted with amna and those powered by torsion, making sure they were all ready. Heeb followed him like a lapdog, his face grimy beneath an unkempt beard.

Once proud citizens of Aonia the men on the wall with him looked more like ragged refugees but, and this was all that counted, their armor was free of rust and the amna pure and dry.

They were professional and if the Malai came in force they would give accounting of themselves before they died.

The purple dawning bled thin light, the eastern horizon a churn of boiled crimson, faded pink and deep, almost black, purple.

It was like the first dawning of creation.

The knot in Edo's stomach was large as a turnip, and the nauseous bile in his stomach was an acid spring.

The waiting hung hard on him.

When there was still no sign of Tingan or his host by midday he made up his mind

"Saddle the remaining horses, Heeb. Let's go and see what had become of them."

***

Edo guided the horses through lichen-covered boles of Yangtze fir.

Sun dappled the needled ground and the contrast between light and dark was blinding. A faint hint of salt from the sea mixed with the sharp tang of the trees. The sound of surf on breakers was audible even here.

They rode line abreast, close enough to see one another. Edo's orders. He wanted them to stay compact, be able to break off contact at the first hint of danger. Even if the warlock's magic had worked they had no way of knowing the state of the enemy's morale and fitness, its willingness to fight. They were horsemen in a wooded area, alone and vulnerable.

One of the Tang hunters, a man who hunted jah for a living, one of a dozen or so who had set up a stall outside the palisade where he sold the purplish skins, was their guide. Short and muscular like all his kind, he moved easily ahead of the horses, the wide head shifting from side to side on a thick-neck that blended like a short pillar into muscular shoulders.

The Tang could run for hours without breaking sweat, Edo had learned. They had proved to be invaluable as scouts and Edo had arranged with their leader for the remaining vials of antidote to be distributed amongst their tribes. He needed all the allies he could find.

With large, bulbous noses and wide, hair-lined nostrils, their sense of smell was keener that of any Aonian.

Any Malai, for that matter, as far as Edo could tell.

The Tang scout held up his hand, beckoned Edo forward.

The man spoke slow, halting Aonian, his accent thick as treacle.

"I smell death ahead."

He pointed west, sniffing the air to underline his point. "Something bad." He scratched his head. "Sick blood. A smell bad."

"Lead us to the bastards. Slow and careful like."

The Tang nodded, nose puckering, then loped east.

They came to a wide space, recently cleared of trees, stumps still weeping. Three Malai lay on the ground unmoving as blue-black flies the size of cherries swarmed their bodies.

Edo eased himself from his saddle, loaded his crossbow and held it ahead of him as he approached the bodies.

The flies landed on him in great pulsing masses as he approached. He swatted them away, and knelt on the ground near the Malai.

All dead. One of the men lay face up, mouth opened, tongue hanging out. The face was a mass of reddish-black pustules. Where the pustules had broken they were cone-shaped lumps, like the craters of exploded volcanoes, a thumbs-width high. Similar craters ran the length of the man's arm in one long sickle-shaped line. Blood had seeped from beneath his cotton tunic, from the armpits and the crotch and oozed black scabs from broken pustules.

The face was twisted, like a nightmare mosaic, barely recognizable as human.

Edo got to his feet, breathing deeply, struggling not to spill his guts in front of his men.

"Well?" Ferie, said as he approached. Ferie's mount was a dappled Scian stallion, whose snorting breath billowed clouds of fire as it pawed the ground.

Edo smiled weakly. "Dead all right. As doornails. Died badly, too."

"Them or us. That's the way it is."

Edo snorted air, trying to cleanse himself of the stench of death. "Gods, let it be so."

He pulled himself into the saddle.

"Let's see where the rest of them are hiding."

***

The forest's silence lay heavy on them and shafts of slanted sunlight lent the deeper forest a cathedral-like feel, like the temple of Miter on Dennra's Hill in Deira seen in early dawn with the sun shining through yellow glass. Edo was starting, just about, to relax when a Malai warrior charged from a thicket of trees and ran straight for

335

them screaming. Edo, surprised, was caught scrambling for the hilt of his sword, the man almost upon him, his balls contracting to wizened prunes.

Till he looked again.

"Miter's rancid eyes!" he yelled, spurring his mount out of the way.

The roan stallion spurted forward, ears flat, a shiver, like disgust, running the length of its withers. Edo sniggered a little hysterically. The horse's senses were better than his.

The Malai running past was unarmed. Blood streamed from his eyes, making a red-black mask of his face. His pustules were smaller than those of the dead warriors they had found. Still unbroken they were tipped with white knobs like hills of curdled milk.

As the man sped past screaming Edo granted Ferie a wry smile. They had been scared witless by a dead man walking. Well, running actually. The Caedian shrugged, fitted a bolt on his crossbow and fired. The bolt took the man between the shoulder blades and he toppled forward twitching.

Edo watched in dark fascination as the man died. He imagined he saw dark wings beating the body, curved yellow fingers, shaped like claw,s scraping flesh. Shalon's talons.

The Hag, source of the dark blood magic the warlock's used. For the first time the enormity of what he had done struck him- he had indebted himself to the Hag, sold her the souls of these dead Malai, made a pact of his own whose terms he did not, could not, know. The thought that she owned him made him almost physically sick.

No! Yanik will protect me. I am his man, his instrument. I will be the author of his people's future. I have nothing to fear from the Old Hag.

The Malai war camp lay less than four hundred spans away- neat circles of wooden shelters made of entwined withies and the greasy, waterproof bark of the ki'all. Edo dismounted and climbed a nearby knoll, in a wide space, empty of trees where he had a better view.

The bodies of the Malai littered the ground. The living wandered amongst them like frightened sheep who had lost their way. Many were naked. None were armed. All were covered in plague rash.

Edo spotted some women, some children amongst them. He turned to Ferie.

"How many do you reckon?"

"Three, four hundred dead. Another hundred infected but still moving." He said something in Caedian that sounded like a curse. Or a fervent prayer. "So many!"

"But not all."

Ferie nodded. "We counted three times as many. Warriors alone. So where are they?"

"Dead in the shelters. Scattered like those we met in the woods. Returned to their villages."

"Or marching towards the fort?"

Edo nodded, the possibility appalling but real. He gestured at the Tang scout. The man shot towards them, up the knoll, at double time.

"Circle the camp. Look for spoor of the

missing warriors. Tell us what you read. I need to know if any got behind us, making for our fort."

The Tang nodded, cold eyes innocent of any emotion Edo could read and loped towards the west and a knot of ancient Yangtze. Edo schooled himself to be patient.

The scout returned in less than an hour and made directly for Edo.

"What can you tell us, Kikia? Are they marching against us?"

The Tang shook his head. "No smell not spoor behind. They go west. Villages there." He pointed. "And there. Small groups. No army. Broken I think."

Edo smiled in relief and clapped the man on a shoulder.

To Ferie he said. "Mount up. Weapons loaded and ready. "He barked a harsh laugh as he surveyed the raggle-taggle men of his tiny command. "Gentlemen, our time is come. It seems we have a nation to conquer."

***

Edo yelled his old warcry of the Longhorn fifth as they burst from the trees, six-armored men on snorting, armored horses and one lone scout; the battle a foregone conclusion.

At the southern edge of the camp they fired three volleys of amna charged crossbows and waited as fire swept the buildings. Then they cantered into the camp where they cut through scattered warriors, men already bleeding from

338

myriad wounds, some already blind.

Sabers slashed through bone, muscle. Blood gouted from severed arms and mangled faces. After the first slow sweep Edo pulled up, ordered the men to him. They dismounted and in a staggered line wielding swords and axes, they picked their way through the camp, slicing and chopping.

Again and again, the work hard, so Edo's muscles burnt with tension, fending off the hands of distraught men, closing his ears to those distressed voices, till the mail mittens on his hands and the greaves on his arms were slick with blood.

Edo found Tingan the chief, blind and helpless, lying on his side in one of the shelters. The Malai was still alive and staggered to his knees when he heard Edo enter.

Blood dripped from Tingan's eyes and he held his hands out as Edo approached. The look on his face, a confused mask of terror, left Edo unmoved. He swung his sword, a powerful overhead swing that sliced both arms off above the elbow. Tingan fell back and Edo straddled him.

Tingan would have done all this and more to him, to his men. Edo searched his soul, for a gesture, something to say that would ease the Malai past death's gate.

He found nothing; an empty pit devoid of pity.

Two-handed he swung at Tingan's neck, cutting through bone and muscle. The severed

339

head he carried from the tent into the spring air. He lifted the visor on his helm, tore it off his head. Killing was hard work and sweat coated his aching body.

A few stragglers remained- two of his men were standing over a gaggle of supine Malai warriors, blades falling as they chopped and Edo spotted Kikia the Tang whooping as he chased down a fleeing male, little older than a child- otherwise the bloody work was done.

Edo plonked his rear on a rough wooden stool near the entrance to Tingan's tent as Ferie strode towards him.

Ferie balled his hand into a fist and shouted something in Caedian.

Edo responded with a tired grin. They had done it, destroyed the Malai. They were safe.

Now all they had to do was ready the ships and return.

As heroes. Wealthy men. Explorers and conquerors.

So why did he feel so empty?

***

The next day Edo led a column to what the Tang informed was the Malai capital, Twin Brothers Leaping, a large town on the bend of a river with three large ziggurats each at least thirty meters tall. He took Ambakan with him, so the chief could see for himself what his rashness, his unbending desire for vengeance, had wrought.

The Malai were a spent force: that much was

340

clear from the moment Edo pulled up at the edge of the village and the elders moved to greet them, on their knees, groveling.

Begging for food, for water. For healers.

Edo brushed the entreaties aside and spurred his way into the villages, his hand on the hilt of his sword.

Just in case.

Survivors gave way before him, hesitant and afraid. Bowed by the plague's destruction. Some fell to their knees as if praying to him.

The great god on a beast of iron; the creatures that had brought them low.

The villages were like the Scorched Plain of Ici, after the Great Waste. A time Aonians still remembered as the Troubles. Reufeti Mairea, the Fourth Protector, known as Small Mairea , had fought a civil war against the rebellious cities of Migacial and Atat. After breaching their walls he laid the cities waste in an orgy of destruction. Edo had seen representations of that time in faded mosaics in the great hall of Mal Din's Temple in Deira. Those representations of suffering were the closest thing to the destruction he had brought upon the Malai that he had ever seen.

Near the stone houses of the Malai men, women and children lay in heaps, their rotting, blood-spattered bodies, swarming with flies. The plague had not been fussy and had claimed the lives of Pugi slave and Malai master alike. The few survivors wandered amongst the dead like ghosts, pale-faced and hungry.

Their inability to understand the magnitude of

341

destruction had sucked the will from them, made them barely capable of feeding themselves, let alone beginning the hard work of burying their dead.

Edo held a perfumed cloth over his face to defeat the stink, but the heavy smell of rot was like an oily slick.

He dug his spurs into his mount and rose from that place of the damned as quickly as he could, his men in formation behind him.

The Malai were finished. He knew he should feel bad; even the warlock seemed to expect him to feel some guilt, if not outright grief. In truth in the stillness of his deep heart he exulted, for his was no ordinary mission.

He had brought the Kingdom of Yanik, that great and glorious city of his mind, one step closer.

He had brought the haughty to their knees.

When the darkness fell, in the stillness of the small wooden room where he slept alone, he smiled and the smile launched him into dreams.

Victory was his.

***

The plump shipwright devilled his jowls with his right hand, balancing on his toe like an exotic dancer as he ran his left hand along the spar. To Edo it looked perfect but the carpenter walked around it again, eyeing the wood with vague disdain as if it might rise up and bite him.

Finally he turned to Edo.

342

"It'll have to do."

"What does that mean, you slime-licked bastard."

The five weeks he had given the carpenters were done and gone. Edo's patience was at an end.

The man used his fingers to count. "If we are lucky this will suffice as a spar for the spirit-sail. The caulking is almost done. Rotten boards refitted" He shook his head, tutting. "We could have done with another week."

"Count yourself lucky that your head is till attached to your body." Edo waved his hand in the direction of the tree line. "The longer we tarry here the more likely it is the Malai will recover their balls. We load provisions and make ready at daybreak tomorrow. Work through the night. If my ships are not ready I will feed you to the first sharks we meet. Am I clear?"

The carpenter spat into a dry dust of sawdust unsettled beneath his foot and smiled without humor. "Aye. But tis a long journey, Sir. We used unseasoned wood to repair what was rotted, and unseasoned wood is liable to warp. I cannot guarantee it will hold."

"Damn it, man. Get us afloat. We will deal with problems as they arise."

The shipwright shrugged, threw a glance at his companion, a thin ferret of a man, standing next to a barrel, a hammer in his one hand a long, bent nail in the other."

"Entargió, understand the risk you take. The ships may float but they are not seaworthy.

Caulking is not complete. Nails and jointing is loose. We have fixed this as best we can but we have neither proper men not material. In Deira theses two beauties." He indicated the ships. "They would be held in dry-dock for a month or more then fully caulked before they went anywhere near deep water again."

Edo snarled.

"Will our situation improve if we stay another week?"

The shipwrights exchanged glances, and the thicker set of the two blew air from pursed lips. "Without refitting them ashore. Not more that spit's flight."

"Then we leave, damnit. If we are not ready by tomorrow I will nail you two to a brace of planks and leave you to the tender mercies of our jolly savages."

He turned on his heel and stomped away, trying to subdue a smile.

In two days they would be away.

CHAPTER 23 - TAMBER

Tamber and Gehsi marched through the Malai village, swollen with warriors from the other tribes of the nation of the Southern Telukamat. People turned to stare after them, eyes baleful.

Upakahun had offered to escort them himself, with a band of his own sword warriors, the men of his blood, but Tamber had declined.

The People must know he came of his own accord.

"The men with blue paint dressed in saffron hides are of the Kehan, the men with the blackened teeth, their hair dyed white are the Yangpi Dinuma. Those with shaved heads painted amber are from the Kehan Yangdeh, the others are the Seilah and the Angka."

"And yet they are all your nation?"

Tamber nodded. "Together with the three tribes of the Moss Delta. Since the time of the First Fathers when we conquered them. We are one nation. One blood. The other tribes are as vermin. So it is. So is has always been."

Gehsi shook his head, lips tight with dismay. "All Pugi, no matter their tribe, are as one. We are born in different nests but that does not dilute the bonds of blood. We do not fight one another, nor visit envy on our neighbors, without dire reason. I fear a strange curse works on your people to divide them so."

Tamber glanced hard at Gehsi. "The nations

of the Malai have always considered it a warrior's strength. The spark that strengthens raw wood."

"And you believe that?"

Tamber made a face. "In the face of the threat these newcomers pose we are weak as foals. Prey for new predators." he shook his head. "Yet, I fear my people will not see it so."

"Force their hand, Tamber." Gehsi urged vehemently. "In unity lies defense. My people will need yours. Divided we are all vulnerable."

They approached the ziggurat, surrounded now by a milling crowd of warriors, excited children and stern faced mothers. Tamber saw faces he recognized, people he had known as brother, cousin, friend, their faces lined and older now. Faces both dark and hard as they took in their approach.

A Pugi in the center of a Malai village did not walk with his head held high, a weapon naked in the baldric over his shoulder. The banished were not expected to return, even under the pretext of a new name.

What Upakahun was attempting threatened to turn the world on its head.

People made way for them, but without grace. A sense of threat hung on the air like the smell from a rotting corpse, maggots moving within desperate to burst out.

An old woman, mouth pulled back in a vicious grin, spat at Tamber, then at Gehsi.

The spittle splashed Gehsi's face, warm and fetid. A flare of anger sparked in Tamber's eyes and Gehsi saw the older man check, swallow hard, sucking the anger deep within.

Fuel for what Gehsi guessed must come.

They walked on.

"That woman..." Tamber offered, his face a knot of flickering emotion.

"What of her?"

"She was once a neighbor to my father. She aided my mother in the childbirth that killed her; she practically reared me herself, with her own large brood."

Gehsi shook his head, keenly aware that isolation was still a source of pain for Tamber.

A brace of swaggering bucks, made brave by kai-wine, approached Gehsi, murder in their eyes.

"Since when do herd-slaves walk amongst us wielding weapons." The larger of the two pressed his face into Gehsi's, his teeth showing, the knots of muscle in bare arms like knotted fiber as he raised his arm to strike.

Tamber closed on the first of the men, fast as a snake. He held up his hand, palm forward, and said in a distant voice that sent a chill through the crowd "The magic of the Jah speaks from these fingers. This Pugi is called Gehsi." He paused. "He is my son. Lay a hand on him you will die with the poison of the Jah coursing through your veins and in the afterlife there will be no succor for I will torment your spirit till your keni begs for a place in Yimti's chill kingdom." He levered his head back on his neck, opened his mouth and let out a blood-curdling shriek, a shriek that turned Gehsi's liver to dark ice.

"Noooooo! The air is fire. Chill is the wind.

Noooooooooo! It burns. It burns."

The voice of the dead warrior Malalauh speaking to them from beyond the grave, words desperate in their cruelty, their dereliction of hope..

Gehsi's heart tripped in its cage, and he imagined himself a sparrow caught in the hand of something large and old and brutal.

The two warriors pulled away from Gehsi, terror etched on their faces, and disappeared into the body of the crowd. The crowd itself ebbed, pulling away from Gehsi and Tamber, fear displacing their inclination to violence.

Tamber's eyes were dull charcoal moving from side to side and the too-supple way his neck twisted as he rolled made Gehsi nauseous.

For it was the way a Jah moved, its long tongue darting from its sharpened teeth, as it loomed triumphant over its prey,

Gehsi understood that the Jah they had killed lived somehow in Tamber. Tamber had become Jah.

He didn't think he would ever understand more.

Upakahun rushed from the courtyard of the Ziggurat, his personal guard surrounding him, his long hair flapping as he covered the ground towards them.

He put an arm around Tamber and then pulled Gehsi close to him.

"Those men will be punished."

Tamber shook his head. "No! When the time comes you will need all the men you can muster.

The memory of what I harbor will haunt their dreams for a long time to come. That will be punishment enough."

**

Upakahun marched through the long dark hall, past hanging furs and wooden dividers that lent the large room a maze-like quality. Chiefs and Shaman sat around small fires drinking ferment-korn and kai-wine, talking in hushed, anxious tones.

They passed the raised alcove in the center, the circle where the chiefs and head shaman would sit when the council of elders met. It had been strewn with fresh rushes, perfumed with flower petals. Precious tintuk wood for the center fire lay heaped near the hearth.

"The chiefs of the Lagan Marsh arrived last night. The tribes are finally assembled."

"So your council can begin?"

"After the sacrifices at tomorrow's dawn."

Upakahun led them towards a framed wooden door set in the far wall, the private quarters he shared with his most trusted shaman. Two guards stood before the door, faces dark and impassive and as Upakahun approached they moved aside.

A shaman in a meskbear cloak had taken a place in the shadows to the right the door. Human finger bones hung from the man's gray hair and they clicked, the sound of locusts in sunset fields, as he stepped forward to block their path. A lined old face, rheumy eyes glistening with malicious

349

intelligence.

"Keklah Keli?" Upakahun's voice betrayed a practiced vexation. 'I have no further time for your complaints."

A name Gehsi knew from Tamber's stories. Keklah Keli had been Upakahun the Elder's chief shaman, no friend to Tamber.

"To bring the outcast here is a mistake. One you will regret."

"Do not threaten me, old man. In this place I will judge what is fitting."

"Your sunder a thousand generations of tradition. Your father's spirit spits curses at you."

Upakahun stepped close to the shaman, his face puce.

"I pay my ancestors the homage owed them. They want for nothing."

"The outcast is filth."

"You are a greedy worm, shaman. Your advice ruined my father. It will not be the ruination of me. Leave now before I take my toes to your arse. You will have a chance to say your piece tomorrow."

Gehsi turned at the sound of approaching footsteps. This new man- from the quality of shells he wore around his neck, and the deep crimson of his Jah-skin headdress, a chieftain - took up station beside Keklah Keli. Taller than Upakahun, broader than Tamber; fat larded the muscles of his chest and arms. Thick lips forced themselves into a pinched smile.

"The gods curse me today. First the cur and now the master," Upakahun muttered, his words directed at Tamber were barely audible to Gehsi.

"My new shaman deserves your respect, Upakahun. He served your father faithfully for three decades."

Upakahun turned to Tamber. "Nonei, this is Tabaduh, chief of the Three Lagan Marsh Clans. More than any other, he gives ear to this worm of a shaman. Together they oppose your presence here."

Tabaduh pointed at Tamber. "You father would never have countenanced this. Men of voice should not have to listen to it."

"Fear blinded my father. That and the advice of fools." Upakahun shot a daggered glance at Keklah Keli.

Tabaduh frowned. "We both know that a majority already speak for an alliance with the tribes of the Delta. Put your weight behind us, Upakahun, and we will carry the doubters." He gestured at Tamber. "The warnings of the banished are not worth spit in the wind.

"I am of no fixed mind, Brother. I will listen before I decide. I suggest you do the same. Now I must show my guests to their quarters."

Upakahun pushed past the chief and his shaman.

"We will finish this tomorrow," Keklah Keli whispered to Tamber as they hurried past and Gehsi saw the glow of hatred in the old man's eyes.

Tamber shot out his right hand and Keklah Keli stepped back as if stung as the tips of Tamber's fingers grazed his chin.

The smile on Tamber's face gave Gehsi heart, though a dense uneasiness filled his soul. He did not think he would be at ease again till they left the Malai village far behind them.

***

In Upakahun's private rooms they sat around the fire on woven rugs, bright crimson and orange in the style of the Kehan. Upakahun lit an usher's wand of elder tintuk and waved the smoldering wood around the room, trailing smoke behind him as he chanted the song of Keganya Sega Walualu, a prayer of welcome from the whirling spirits of the dirt.

Urging them to sit, he served Kai-wine in stone bowls decorated with jade and sapphire shells bowing to one each one in turn, honoring them as guests.

He sat cross-legged.

"Tabaduh and his lapdog are vociferous in their condemnation of you. After you killed Malalauh, they wanted me to send a host against you."

"Malalauh came to my house with violence in his heart and showed me the respect due an animal."

Upakahun nodded. "The men of Malalauh's party were divided on this issue. You are an outcast, but even so it was agreed that Malalauh showed you a fatal lack of respect. Still, you need you to be wary. Anger and fear fuels the emotions of the People. None will acknowledge but all are afraid. The newcomers..."

"Toss the natural order on its head. Throw doubt on the superiority of Malai strength. I know. I have lived with this knowledge a long time."

Upakahun frowned. "The elders have granted you permission to speak but you may not attend as a voiced one. You will appear as my guest at the end of proceedings before the decision is reached. Choose your words carefully Tamber. For if you fail I fear Tabaduh will have his way and we will bind ourselves in trade, for better or worse, to the northern tribes and the wealth the newcomers offer."

***

It would have been unseemly, partisan even, if Upakahun had given them a bed space in the hall. Tamber understood this and did not question when Upakahun stood and gestured for them to follow. Upakahun led them to a large longhouse in the middle of the village, surrounded by a low stonewall. A vegetable garden tended by two old Pugi women occupied the eastern part of the enclosure and a group of rickety outhouses dotted the western wall.

A middle-aged Malai stood in the doorway, her back ramrod, eyes focused on the far distance, gray hair hanging loosely at her side.

Tamber's sister.

Upakahun spoke. "We seek shelter for weary travelers, Yar. I hear tell you still have space in your hall."

Yar turned without a word and closed the slatted wooden door behind her. Gehsi could feel the emotion in Tamber, gravid and damp like the prelude to a hurricane.

No other house would have them. Upakahun's own longhouse was reserved for the various chief's and their families. In the end Upakahun apologized, shrugged and led them to an outhouse at the edge of the village. Upakahun ordered it lined with fresh rushes and had food and drink brought to them. Despite everything it still stank of cowshit.

The ceremony began at dawn. Tamber and Geshhi stood together, distanced from the crowd, on a grass-covered knoll above the commons. A dozen Pugi were butchered. Their meat would be roasted through the long day.

Gehsi turned from the sight, an intense rage raging in his heart.

"This will change, Gehsi." Tamber laid a hand on his shoulder. "I swear it."

Gehsi shrugged at the hand and walked away, needing to be alone. At the edge of the cliff he stood, the salt wind in his hair, breakers pounding on the rocks as albi squawked and flew circles below thudding gray clouds. The force of the wind, the din of the ocean channeled his anger; the hot flame of rage became a cold hard anger like a diamond forged under great pressure. Tamber came to him and led him in silence to the outhouse.

The summons from the Council of Elders for

Tamber came after sunset.

Tamber had spent the day, squatting on the ground, eyes closed, lost in contemplation.

The young shaman who came to summon them, waited outside while Gehsi shook Tamber out of his trance. Tamber blinked his way back to consciousness, stared at Gehsi, uncomprehendingly, the whites of his eyes glinting with yellow fear.

"Do not desert me!"

The roar came from deep within him, a place of violent gusts and desert sands.

Gehsi laid a hand on his shoulder and Tamber looked around, like a beaten old man, eyes lifeless and impotent.

The sight turned Gehsi's legs to milk and water.

"I will be by your side, Stepfather."

The said nothing more as Tamber washed, dressed and left the outhouse. The young shaman walked ahead of them saying nothing, as though afraid of contamination. Gehsi knew, in his heart of hearts, they should never have come. It was wrong-headed.

Aye, and stupid to boot.

But he had no choice. A son should stand by his father. Always.

***

Warriors, chiefs and shaman filled the hall of the Ziggurat facing the central pit, swaying backward and forward like corn in a field, a malicious wind stroking their nodding heads.

Gehsi followed Tamber through the crush of bodies, aware of the dense, almost tropical heat, of raw, tired emotions fevered after a trying day.

Stern-faced he pushed through the crush of towering Malai, proud warrior of the Pugi, swallowing his fear, sucking it deep into his stomach, pressing it down in that chill place where doubts resided.

Upakahun sat on mound of rushes, surrounded by shaman and the greater chiefs.

Tamber pulled up in front of them his face drawn, pallid with radial lines of strain.

The shaman were dressed in furs, their hair spiked with oil mixed with blood and excrement. Over their shoulders hung the skulls of wolfs, bears, wild boar and scaly mouthed jah. A proud display, outward indication of the animals whose dreams they had conquered, the damp trails they prowled when they slept.

Power oozed from them; a dense, peppery smell that forced Gehsi's nostrils wide, his senses driven to heightened alertness.

Chiefs whose drinking bowls were the skulls of favored ancestors, dyed in cedar oil, displayed the skins of panther, of speckled Harna'jah. On their heads rested antlered helms or crimson albi headdresses. Many had mutilated their faces; the lines they carved the numbers of men they had fought, whose hearts they had devoured.

Upakahun rose. "Welcome, Nonei. The nation bids you speak your thoughts."

Tamber stepped forward and spat into the fire

then said a prayer of thanks to the first boar, Tenilukah . He kept his eyes on the ground, his head lowered, and spoke in a low voice so even Gehsi had to strain to hear what he said.

"The newcomers will blind you with wealth."

A murmur swept the crowd. "They will bind you in lies of their own making. They will geld you and rape your daughters." The murmur grew louder. "They will murder your sons and you will feel the lash of their whips on your backs."

Tabaduh swept to his feet.

He pointed at Tamber. "This bastard has no voice here and the words he brings us are a mockery of all we are."

Keklah Keli, hair done up a long spike, the bone necklace hanging from his shoulders clicking as he stepped forward pointing his finger at Tamber.

"Silence liar!"

Upakahun spoke. "He speaks in this hall by my will. He shall be granted an audience."

Tamber ignored the chief and his shaman and continued speaking, his tone measured, his voice quiet, the impact of the words all the more devastating for their lack of volume. "The men who have come here are but the first infection. A burgeoning pustule. The onset of nausea. " He slammed his fist into an open hand. " Destroy them now or a plague will sweep through these lands till we Malai live no more." He lifted his face to face the ravening crowd. "So speaks Raven. So speaks Garge. So speaks Kali."

Silence, punctuated by coughing, followed

the words.

Gehsi understood what Tamber had done by mentioning the names of the spirits who lived within him, for they had discussed it in the quiet of the previous night as they lay waiting for the morning light to break. His boast, his claim to be the vessel of three spirit gods of the Malai marked him as a shaman-priest more powerful than any other assembled in that room.

A claim that would be tested. Hard.

Keklah Keli, a pulse beating anger in his forehead, pulled a bone rattle from his jerkin, kissed it. He hopped on one leg building a concentric circle while closing in on Tamber. With every step he spat on the rushed and when he was close enough to reach out a hand and touch Tamber he bent over and sniffed Tamber from foot to head.

"I sense no spirits here. Nonei stands alone. As once before his words stink of betrayal. Of vanity and deception."

"Keklah Keli, it is you who lie. You served the elder Upakahun poorly. A lap dog sucking the marrow from the bone of its master. Now you would suck wealth from these newcomers. You think you can make fools of them but they will make a fool of you and drink their dinners from the gourd where your brains once resided."

"It is you who are the fool, Nonei. Ignorant and deluded as ever. An alliance with the Tribes of the Delta will make us rich. With the shells the foreigners provide we will buy tintuk in quantities unimaginable. We will sweep through the tribes of the interior like a winter storm. We will rule this land from coast to coast, Upakahun here leading us."

"The gods deride this path as folly. The longer we wait the greater the danger grows."

Keklah Keli moved a step closer to Tamber, hissing.

"You claim the power of three but I smell but weakness oozing from the pores of your rancid skin."

"I have power enough to smash a slug like you threefold."

Keklah Keli hopped closer, sniffed at Tamber again. "They have deserted you. They do not stand to defend." His smile was a thin slash of satisfaction. He pursed his lips, pulled them back so they were like two red slugs disappearing, pulled into the dark cave of his mouth.

His cheeks hollowed, his eyes lost their gleam, dulled and turned reddish amber as his skin coarsened.

His tongue licked out, lips reappearing as the face rearranged in a narrow feline cast. He gobbed a wad of spit at Tamber's face. Tamber ducked to one side, the spit landing on his shoulder. It scorched a dark hole ringed with flaming orange into Tamber's tunic.

From the flame grew dark shadows and from the shadows came mewling wraiths, fist sized, formed of the denigration of light.

One latched itself onto Tamber's hair. Mewling and hissing it perched on his head, long nail-like claws at the end of its hoofed feet digging into the forehead, drawing beads of blood. Five more flew around Tamber's face, lashing at his skin with tiny claws and hooked tails, scouring ridges in the flesh of his face.

The wraiths keened. A sound to fill a brave man's soul with liquid, to turn his legs to mush.

Sorcery to impress the weak of mind, Gehsi knew, with no real power behind it. Shadow without substance. A bluff of fear with no killer punch.

He waited for Tamber to counter it.

Tamber held out his arm, fingers bunched into a fist. He closed his eyes, muttered words of power in silence, but nothing happened. When he opened his eyes again his face was a mask of distress and Keklah Keli screamed in triumph.

"See!" Keklah Keli spun around to face the tribes as the shadow wraiths slashed at Tamber's face, soaking hair and tunic. "It is as I said. The gods have deserted him. He is less than Nonei. He is nothing."

Tabaduh roared and turned to the other chiefs. "Upakahun! See now! The bastard lied to worm his way in here. He is both a liar and betrayer of your trust. He must die."

Upakahun stared hard, first at Tamber, then at Tabaduh. He lowered his eyes and turned his head away. Tabaduh dashed forward, a skiri in one hand, a beating stick in the other. The wraiths had coalesced, a scattered fog thickening till they covered Tamber's face; sharp claws tore remorselessly at his face, stabbed at his eyes, sliced his nose to shreds. Tabaduh kicked at the

360

back of Tamber's knee and Tamber fell forward onto his knees, swaying awkwardly, hands at his sides as the chief raised his dagger over his head. Without thinking, Gehsi shot forward, spear raised and ready to strike.

He remembered Tamber's word as they trained bare-chested on the sand.

Strike from above with strength, like an ox with glistening horns, from below like a snake with hissing fangs.

Gehsi had taken Tabaduh's measure and found the chief wanting. Gehsi was more than equal to this match.

The leaf-shaped blade lashed out and took the chief above his ear, ran a funnel into his brain. Two-handed Gehsi pulled on the spear, the runnel dripping blood as it slipped free of the chief's head. Tabaduh tumbled to the ground; eyes wide open in livid shock as death stole his essence.

Gehsi turned to Keklah Keli. The shaman's mouth was open in a silent scream. Warriors bellowed in consternation, for those who could not see what had happened had the blood smell in their nostrils and could feel the tremors of coarse emotion radiating through the room. Gehsi swung the blade to the right. Using the spear as a sword he moved left aiming at a cross slash from his lowered position. Keklah Keli was an open target, his death all but certain. Gehsi sang his warcry as he swung.

Upakahun shot to his feet a tintuk blade in his hands. The blade shot out and parried Gehsi's strike.

Gehsi stepped to one side, pulling his blade back as he caught his breath, readying another strike, in a place now beyond thought.

Hands wrapped themselves around him, pulled him to the ground. Fists pummeled him, leather clad feet slammed into his abdomen, driving breath from his body, crashing into his head.

Black spots danced before his eyes as consciousness dimmed.

A boot heel slammed into his spread fingers and the pain was a red ball. He roared, flailed wildly about, but the crush of bodies forced him back down.

Before he fell for a last time he saw Tamber, on the ground curled like a fetus, the wraiths vanished. His face was a dark mask of blood, his nose a bloody wreck, black pits where his eyes should have been.

Gehsi held out his hand, reaching for Tamber even as he fell to the ground.

Father

I am sorry.

Forgive me.

I could not save you...

***

Tamber scrambled through dense fog, towards a distant light.

The fog was thick, yellow balls of damp cotton stealing the breath from his lungs, choking the life from him.

"Come, Tamber. Hurry! We await you."

That mocking voice. Kali waiting someplace ahead with his accursed brethren. They had manipulated him to going to the village then deserted him. Left him to face Keklah Keli alone, naked of power.

A bitter spleen of hatred coursed through him.

He opened his eyes, laid a hand on a smooth, cool rock and levered himself to his feet. He rubbed at his face, examined his hands.

He could see. How was that possible? Had not the wraiths had taken his eyes, plucking them out like oysters from a shell. He remembered: a flame as of hot pokers burning his face, claws flaying the skin and gouging the flesh from his head. Darkness had ruled absolute, a vassal only to the emperor of pain.

He remembered but his memories were trampled ice, broken mirrors, inchoate and appalling.

Which was just as well for his sanity.

He rubbed his face with blood-spattered hands, the blood dry and flaking. The skin of his face was smooth and soft. Too smooth. Like a child's skin, untouched by the cares of age.

He could see. His face was whole. Kali and the others had returned to him. Healed him

Relief curbed his anger and a hesitant smile cracked his new-born lips as he took in his surroundings.

Wind buffeted his face. He stood on a narrow pillar of black marble, the sun warm, carrion birds circling him.

The width of the pillar was less than a span, less than the distance from his elbow to the tips of his fingers.

Involuntarily, he took a step backward, the heel of one foot hanging for a heart-stopping second over the edge, the weight of impossible depths beneath tugging at him with the tiny mischievousness of evil sprites. He stepped forward sharply, vertigo almost pushing him over the forward edge as he balanced precariously on the lip of the spire. The sheer face of the pillar fell away and disappeared below into soft, downy clouds. The air was thin, weak in his lungs and bitter on his lips. He slumped, landing heavily on his rear, as his legs gave way, his stomach reaching for his mouth.

"He lives and breaths."

"Looks good, Kali."

"Good as new?"

"Still there is only so much even a god can hope to do."

A sympathetic tut. "When the raw material is this poor..."

"A silk purse from sow's ears I cannot recreate."

"Bastards!" Tamber struggled to his knees, his body still pulsing with shock. "You betrayed me. Let Keklah Keli win."

"Fair enough."

"A just summary."

"Hold on! Wait a moment. We only took back what we bestowed."

"True enough."

"Damned right."

"I take it back. Bloody humans! Ungrateful wretches. Hardly worth the bother."

Tamber steadied himself, feeling around to make sure his perch was secure, glad of the solid touch of stone beneath his fingers. The wind had risen and the sun had moved across the sky, a buttery light making a mirror of its polished surface.

"You betrayed me." A tremble in his voice betrayed the anger and fear that still possessed him.

"Loss focuses desire, hardens the heart."

"A necessary sacrifice."

"Perhaps now you will finally see, Tamber Whitehair."

"The final pieces are in place. Return now! Be the man you were born to be and do not lose sight of these lessons."

Their laughter wounded him, an arrow piercing the armor of his fragile defenses, but that only fueled his anger. In time even that mocking laughter faded and left him alone.

Alone on a lofty spire of stone to call his home.

The wheeling birds ran shadows along him as they rode the wind and the sun disappeared like a dream.

He stood finally, his legs shaky as a foal. The arank had claimed his life three times before.

What did one more death matter?

He threw himself over the edge, his heart

stopping- frozen in terror-long before the ground rose to meet him.

***

A door cracked open and light from without dazzled the darkened space within. Tamber stirred on the sodden ground, his shoulder stiff, throat dry, his head a dull ache. He blinked as the ferocious white speared his eyes.

Two men stood in the doorway, faint silhouettes against the daze, helms on their heads, tintuk swords in their hands.

"Sire, I fetched you soon as I saw. I did not know what else to do."

"You did well, Garna." He paused, moved two steps closer, into the room. "How, under the Great Soul, is this possible? His face-"

"This is a gift from the gods, Upakahun. He told us he had their ear, but we did not listen."

Upakahun let out a low moan. "I listened but not close enough."

He has been greatly wronged, Sire," Garna muttered.

"My keni fears the vengeance he will wreak."

Tamber groaned, forcing himself to sit up, his head dizzy and hollow, like something washed up pale on a beach.

"Upakahun?" He whispered through cracked lips. "Is that you?"

"I am so sorry, Nonei. You came here as my guest. I did not know Keklah Keli would go this far."

366

"Did the elders reach a decision?"

"Postponed for now. A great divide separates us. I no longer know how to bridge it."

"Leave that to me."

"You are in no condition." The chief's words were weighted with more sorrow than Tamber would have expected; pungent with grief and flavored with shame. Tamber struggled to ignore their import.

"We need to act now. Keklah Keli and his master have to be stopped."

Upakahun knelt, wrapped an arm around him, helped him to his feet. "Tabaduh is dead." He paused, as if debating whether or not to say more. "You need to come with me. Rest. Recover. Bide your time till you can face Keklah Keli."

Tamber's new eyes had stopped drizzling tears but the light still pained him but he could see well enough to know that they had thrown him into one of the little windowless huts where unruly slaves were educated, or where sacrificial victims were kept before being brought to the sacrificial stones, to meet the sharp edge of a tintuk blade.

Tamber shook his head. "We have wasted too much time already. We must finish this now!"

Still holding him tightly around the shoulders, Upakahun said: "So be it. But first come with me. I need to show you something."

Upakahun led him tenderly into the light. Albi squawked and the sound of the waves beating against the cliffs was the sound of his own heart beating. The sun warmed his skin and the world of color threatened to overwhelm his senses; the sky cerise and clear, the clouds gentle and tinged with poppy.

Fresh tears welled in Tamber's new eyes as they left the building.

His beating heart knew the answer to the question he had not dared voice. The gods had spoken of sacrifice, lightly, mocking him.

Not his sacrifice. Not this time. For all his fear in the shadow-world, on that tall dark pillar, he had known he would return and standing and falling had been, not easy, but certainly not final.

A terrible chore. Nothing more.

The gods had wanted a different sacrifice, more painful, and they got what they wanted.

He glanced at the idols, his head already shaking in denial.

Upakahun let go of his shoulders and he stumbled on, a pace or two, blinking as his eyes focused on the stone.

When he saw what they had done, what Keklah Keli had done, he fell to knees as the air went from his body.

Pain worse than anything physical, worse than when the arrack came.

Pain a scalding burn that emptied his soul.

"NOOOOO!

***

Tamber knelt on damp earth, pungent with salt and the promise of life, his arms wrapped around the sacrificial stone, his head leaning on the butchered thing that was Gehsi.

The warm skin of his cheeks on chill flesh.

They had killed slowly, peeling back the skin, probing beneath with the tips of their blades, cutting away chunks of flesh. Slowly building to a crescendo of pain, the power of the shaman ensuring Gehsi could never slip away into unconsciousness as they took him apart, piece by screaming piece.

Fingers, toes, nose, ears, eyes, tongue, hands, feet; taking him apart like a butcher would a hung deer or wild pig.

Except the pig or deer would be dead.

He could picture it- the beating drums, the stamping feet, the screaming women and children.

Shaman, smeared with mud, shit and ochre, howling as they danced around the central fire, the skiri in their hands slicing through the night, slicing skin, flesh; blood pouring in narrow rivulets, dark against the young man's smooth, amber skin.

In the end someone (Keklah Keli- who else but Keklah Keli?) had cut out Gehsi's heart, chewed on the muscle, sucking that precious blood into his stomach.

Sated Keklah Keli had cast Gehsi's heart over the cliff, discarded it like a child's broken toy, where it fell to the pounding sea below, or was chewed and eaten by diving albi.

Gehsi lived in Keklah Keli now, a beaten soul, slave to its master, nothing more than a factor of what he once was.

Somehow that hurt most. Not only was Gehsi

dead he was a soul slave, reduced to just another Pugi, subservient to a Malai master. To Keklah Keli of all men. That greedy, self-serving bastard!

"Why did you let this happen? Answer me Upakahun?

The young chief sat to his right him, his face a mask of shame. They were, for the moment alone, and Tamber still had not made up his mind how many, Upakahun included, he intended to kill before the next day dawned.

Blood would flow. That fact was more certain than sunrise. He owed it to Gehsi. He owed it to himself- the acrid taste of vengeance was like tidal pull in his soul.

"Gehsi slew Tabaduh." Upakahun said in a low voice.

"What?"

"After Keklah Keli set the wraiths on you, Tabaduh stepped forward to finish the job. Gehsi took him down. He saved your life."

Tamber nodded, pursed his lips, the pain flaring again.

Gehsi! You stupid fool! The gods would never have let me die. I am their pet, their source of boundless amusement.

"And, with Tabaduh dead, Keklah Keli had all the excuse he needed. I take it he took Gehsi here?"

"Tabudah's chosen men wanted Gehsi butchered on the spot but Keklah Keli wanted more. He desired to drink his power. To wallow in his victory. So he suggested this. A night and a day of slaughter. An offering to the gods, to Great

370

Blue Soul, to lend us guidance in the resolution of our differences. Gehsi was the starter. You are the main course."

"When am I to be served?"

"Today. At sunset. When you are dead the vote will be finally held. Keklah Keli is certain of his victory."

"I asked you why you let this happen!"

"Gehsi was Pugi. To the rest of these men an aberration. An animal who speaks our language like one of us, who does not lower his eyes in our presence."

"Gehsi was a better man than you or me. A man, damn you-"

"A man who killed a chief. Tabudah's tribe had a right to vengeance." Upakahun laid his hand on Tamber's shoulder. "I argued against it but the council of shaman chose to ignore my advice. I could do nothing." Upakahun's voice faltered, faded away.

Tamber wanted to strike out, to rend the chief's head from his shoulders. Wanted to but would not. Upakahun was a young man, a good man, finding his way through the jungle of power. He had no power of life and death in situations like this. Gehsi had spilt Malai blood. For a Pugi the only penalty possible was death, no matter the circumstances.

"I will be here when they return. The bastards who did this thing will pay."

Upakahun stared at the sky, adam's apple swallowing, his eyes dull reflections of the sky.

"Keklah Keli yes. Not the others. I beg you,

Nonei."

"All who partook deserve to die."

"I cannot allow that."

Tamber closed his eyes lowered his head. Pounding blood had given him a throbbing headache and the void of his soul was a dark empty pit, its song a siren.

A pit alive and malicious, wanting to swallow him whole.

Tamber turned to the younger man, could see clouds of doubt in the younger man´s eyes. "What you ask of me is hard, Upakahun? My soul sings for blood."

"If we wish to unite our people there must be no more blood shed than is necessary. I will be at your side. We must see this thing through together."

Tamber lowered his head. Nodded.

It was the will of the gods. They would have their sacrifice and the Malai would earn a final chance.

***

Keklah Keli appeared at the head of an entourage of chiefs and shaman, dressed in full finery.

Spiked hair, hung with a dozen rings of shells, each shell a deep and glimmering turquoise, the spikes topped with crimson feathers lending him height and an aggressive confidence, his whole presence screaming- I am the chosen one. It is I who have the ear of the gods.

His cape of scaly Jah skin glimmered as he strode forward, his face was white alabaster, circles of jade paint streaking from the eyes.

In one hand was a skiri of black obsidian, in his right hand the femur of a child. Tamber could feel the power, the tormented souls trapped and bound in the hollows of the yellow bone. A powerful thing, yet brittle in its way for the nature of porous stone was not unlike the nature of the souls trapped within. Hard and ungiving till put under pressure.

It would cause Tamber no problem.

They had not spotted him yet for the stones of sacrifice blocked their view. When he tops the hill, turns and sees the open door of the pen where he hoped to keep me, then his heart will beat faster, his will shall begin to fail, and he will feel the relentless call of fate.

And the weakness of his hollow soul will become evident.

Upakahun sat beside Tamber, a long spear of tintuk wood in his hand. The spear had been fire-hardened and then molded with prayer and its tip gleamed like the living tongue of a Jah.

Tamer glanced at him and Upakahun nodded. He stood and together they strode forward into view. Keklah Keli was the first to spot them, before the chiefs and other shaman, and his eyes betrayed his fear.

He stopped in his tracks and the others stopped with him. He stepped back, pushing into a shaman behind him, as if hoping to flee but the tide of people streaming up behind forced him to hold his ground.

Upakahun handed the spear to Tamber and Tamber strode forward to meet the shaman. He stopped beside the last of the sacrificial stones, the stone staring into eternity from wide, empty eyes.

The gaze of the first ancestor, his body entombed within, forever judging. Keklah Keli wilted beneath that stony gaze. He held the child's femur in front of him like a ward. The crowd, silent now with dim intent pushed him forward.

"You killed my son, Keklah Keli."

"He killed a chieftain of the Malai." Keklah Keli turned around, grasping at one final hope. "Men of the Three Lagan Marsh Clans, together we slaughtered the Pugi beast. Will you rest with that? This one." He pointed at Tamber, the bone in his hand faintly shaking. "Is he not also responsible for your chief's death?"

Tamber laughed and the scorn in the sound seemed to wilt Keklah Keli's defiance.

"Turn and face me shaman. No one will help you now. Look at my face. My eyes. The gods have chosen. You are not worth the spit beneath our feet."

Keklah Keli turned in a crouch, snarling and sprang at Tamber, the bone held before him like short sword.

The power reached out towards Tamber like a sharp, enervating scream, a dark bolt of inky pain. Tamber shut it from his mind and met Keklah Keli with the spear. Keklah Keli tried to duck out of the way, roaring at Tamber, spit flecking from his lips. He was too slow. The spear pierced his abdomen and Tamber rammed it home, two-handed with all the strength he possessed as his father had taught him when he was still a young man. The spear sheared through the shaman's thin body, exited from his back. Tamber used his momentum to run forward, Keklah Keli like an insect staked on a twig, as Tamber held him over his head. He ran with him to the wall of an outhouse and slammed the spear into its side, with a jarring twist of his wrists.

Keklah Keli screamed, face crumpled with agony, tears rolling from his eyes. He had wet himself and the stain was evident through the fine Jah cloak. Two crimson feathers fell to the ground as he banged his head on the wooden wall.

Tamber wasn't finished, not by a long way. He laid his hands on Keklah Keli, closed his eyes and said a prayer to his trinity of gods.

Demanding their presence, granting him power to work through him.

In an instant the power of the gods was in his fingers, like a fierce, bitter tingling. He placed a splayed palm on Keklah Keli's weakly bucking form.

The shaman had bitten through his lower lip, the death throes already upon him, his face pale, his eyes almost emptied.

"You do not escape so easily, you bastard." Tamber barked loudly. He wanted them to hear, this tribe of people who had cast him out. He wanted them to know and fear.

He was Nonei but he had the power of three. He had returned and he was stronger than any of them.

Let them witness. Let them tremble.

The power crackled through Keklah Keli and his head jumped back, as if slapped hard by an invisible hand. The shaman opened his eyes and glanced palely around, the pain ravaging his face, creating deep ravines where none had previously existed.

"Keklah Keli hear this," Tamber bellowed. "You live now and you will live again, tied to this spear for eternity. Suffer its pain for if you remove it you will die." He slapped Keklah Keli hard on the chest and the shaman screamed with the pain. "Hear me you bastard. Withdraw the spear and free your soul, free yourself from your torment, then your essence becomes mine. I will feed your soul to the harlik."

Audible gasps rose from amongst the crowd and Keklah Keli stared in horror at Tamber, for he, of all of them, best understood the choice being offered; a living torment or oblivion and torment in death.

A choice that was no choice.

Tamber turned his back on the man, casting him from his mind. Kai had butchered Gehsi, had fed on his soul.

Tamber could not undo that but his vengeance ensured Keklah Keli would never, in this life or the next, find peace.

It would not bring back Gehsi but as vengeance it would suffice.

He walked towards the Ziggurat, the eyes of the crowd on him, and as he passed they fell in behind him till Keklah Keli's frightened cries faded away.

***

"We are agreed?"

Upakahun glanced around at the chiefs and one by one they lowered their heads. They had been in the Ziggurat less than an hour.

"It is settled. We move tomorrow. Nonei, what say you?"

"My father is buried east of the shaman's cave. I want his body returned here and buried with full ceremony."

Upakahun nodded.

"I want my slut of a sister, her children cast out. There names are never to be spoken amongst us again."

Upakahun eyes blinked a grudging agreement.

"I have no other terms."

The aroma of burning tintuk was both sweet and acrid, the smoke itself like a drug casting light into forms it would not otherwise inhabit. Tamber felt like he was swimming under water in a darkening pool, the sun above dimming as he swam. The chiefs and the shaman had voted. They were agreed. The newcomers were a threat and they would be exterminated. The work of the Elder Council was done.

"Do you wish your old name back?"

Tamber shook his head. "My name is Nonei. I have no other name. Whoever I was is no more."

Upakahun shook his head sadly. "As you say,

377

Lord Shaman."

Tamber rose to his feet, back stiff, head swimming. The chiefs remained seated, a gesture of respect. He brushed himself down and was readying his exit when a commotion at the door drew his attention.

A messenger ran past the guards at the wide doors of the ziguarrat. A young child, clothes torn and grimy, face matted with dirt and sweat, eyes sunken with tiredness- he swayed with exhaustion as he pulled up before them.

With difficulty he prostrated himself before Upakahun. "Chief of the Lower Tribes, I have traveled far." His voice caught in his throat, deep emotion barely contained. "I bring you greetings from my tribe."

A strange formulation. Messengers usually recited the names of the chief or shaman who had sent them. Greetings from a tribe? The words held an awful, hollow ring.

"What tribe are you boy?"

He rose to his feet. "The Asdas, sire. What is left of them."

Tamber could hardly breathe. He felt like someone had kicked him hard in the stomach, again and yet again.

Sweat broke out on his brow.

"Spit it out, boy."

Tears welled in the messenger's eyes, his face crumpled, as if trying to formulate with words a memory he preferred neither to recreate nor share.

"Tingan is dead. Ambakan is held hostage. A third of my tribe is dead." He choked on the words. "Men, women and children. As many again were sick when I left--"

"Sick." Tamber sat back down hard. He had felt it, this plague. Had smelt it on the winds, sweet and foul like the rot in a week-old corpse but had not known what the smell signified.

"When I left. Bleeding from their eyes. Sores on their bodies."

Tamber turned to Upakahun, grabbed his arm.

"Before it is too late, Brother, ready your host. If we delay we are lost."

One of the chief's of the Lower Delta tribes raised his voice in protest. "We cannot walk into plague, Nonei. We must avoid the contamination of foul spirits."

Tamber brushed at his long hair, wiping the words away. "I can contain the infection." He stared hard at each man in turn. "The worm turns. This plague is the work of the newcomers but it is not a problem. Think. These newcomers will know that what they have unleashed will unite us sooner or later. They will make preparations to leave and if they escape to their country they will return here, next summer or the summer after, and in all the years following, and they will be numerous as locusts. When that happens the days of the Malai will end."

Silence followed this pronouncement. Upakahun's face was naked in its bewilderment, his face betraying his youth.

Still the steely strength Tamber had sensed in him shone through.

He was first to move, first to his feet.

"Nonei warned us once before and we did not listen. That shall not happen again. Ready the warriors. We leave at dawn."

The spell broke, and the chief's scrambled to their feet, rushing for the door.

So much to do. Food and provisions to be gathered. Weapons to be cleaned and polished.

Goodbyes to be said.

The brief remainder of a day and one night to do so. Tamber watched as they left, at a loose end now that his words had finally had their impact.

He sank back to the rugs on the floor, breathing deeply to imbibe the tintuk smoke, letting its tart power rush through him.

Trying to focus, to achieve a semblance of peace in his thoughts.

But peace evaded him for he could not help feel that he had failed, that the birds had already flown their coop and the hunters had arrived too late.

***

They set off early, away from the coast east towards the forests, the women keening as they left, children hiding beneath the long cloth of their mother's dresses or scampering after them waving training swords of blunt obsidian.

Six hundred warriors of the yangmpabat, twelve shaman and four dozen wardogs. They made their way in stern silence through the undergrowth, light bathing the crowns of the trees a harsh contrast to the dimness of the forest floor.

They cut through the thin corridor of forest to the north, onto the wild plains of waving long grass where long-horned graak lived in massive, thundering herds hunted by skulking hal'jah and thick-pelted jaguar. They paused for food, sitting in the long-grass near a stony stream whose banks were thick with reddish mud. When they finished eating Tamber handed each man a hard-shelled kekan nut. They broke them using flint and obsidian from the hide bags tied to their belts, then chewed slowly. When they were done Tamber gave the order. They rose to their feet, spirits beginning the slow drift from their bodies as the drug took hold. They set off through the grass at a gentle lope. The sun slowly climbed across the wide plain, across waving grass stretching to a green infinity; a land locked sea of sage-green. As the timid light of evening day gave way to a spreading darkness they took a short break for water. Tamber wiped sweat from his eyes, the pain of stiff limbs still a distant threat, as the drug worked its plodding way through his body.

The sun was a candescent semicircle of purple and orange when they set off again into a gathering darkness. As the last of the sunlight faded, stars spangled the sky like ice on a dark blanket, and the night was ripped by the harsh roar of hunting hal'jah and the clicks of the half-men, hidden Tamber knew in the long grass at the edge of the great herds.

Each in their own way waiting to pounce.

The route Tamber had chosen barely edged the fringes of the great plain and Tamber did not think they would be bothered by the predators, but it was better to be careful than sorry. He ordered the outliers closer to the main host and had his men light their pitch torches and stick together.

Trouble enough waited ahead. They did not need to lose men here.

They reached the rolling foothills of the Northern Spine at midday the next day, and the long grass gave way to a steadily rising hump of rotten limestone and purple heather. Still they had not rested, had not eaten, had not slept.

Towards nightfall, beneath the ominous shadow of a worn shoulder of rock, they rested for an hour, ate and drank. The effect of the kehan was still strong for the nuts, freshly plucked from their host trees, had been juicy with sap.

That was for the best. The nuts were rare enough, and Tamber had a supply good for less than a week. The longer the effects lasted the better.

Wary of injury they moved at a measured pace through the treacherous limestone of the foothills, a long winding torch-lit column. Stars bred above, a wild profusion that humbled them all. In the depths of that long night Upakahun started to sing; a haunting song of violence and regret, a song of the ancestors and their fight for a place in the world, a song most of all of pride.

> With sword and blade we laid them waste,
> beneath the forests, the Allahlio

382

With blood and bone we paid the price
the slaughter at the Pass of Chan
When my brother comes again
tell him I died and when
tell him I died and why
tell him to sing a song of death
as his soul passes by.

Tamber, numbed by the drug found himself joining in, tears rolling from his eyes, down his cheeks into his cotton jerkin. If they failed to stamp out the infestation that had set foot on their lands, memories such as these would be lost.

A culture, a people destroyed.

He had seen that in his dreams of worlds. Kali and the Raven had taken him by the arm and shown him. He had seen it happen again and again.

Such racial memories as lived in such songs were fragile as raw eggs but they were the very thing that made them Malai.

He would fight and die to protect the beauty of what had been and what might still be.

As he ran he sang, and his voice blasted from his throat into the high hills where mountain cats screeched and owls swooped and the umber eagles soared from their perches onto unsuspecting deer perched high on wind-blown crevices.

***

The first of the northern settlements lay

383

across a hump of marsh, in the lee of a bend of the gently winding Otau. Two Flamingo, the settlement's name, was built on marsh reclaimed from the gods of earth and was a spiritual home for the people in the north.

The water was choppy, gray reflecting the dense sky. Rain driven by a howling wind pelted down, forced its way beneath Tamber's cape of jah leather, soaking his tunic and chilling his flesh.

Tamber strode forward alone. Through the haze of falling water, above the choppy water of the Otau, he could make out stone buildings and the huge majesty of the Ziggurat. The temple stood taller than a mature yantze fir, wide as a small cliff.

He sniffed the air.

The smell of plague, of rotting bodies filled his nostrils, the wind doing little to dispel the greasy stink.

Exhausted, his wracked body filled with aches, his eyes dense with grit, now that the drug had all but faded, he lowered himself to his knees. He swayed like that a moment then laid himself on the soaking mud, crushing reeds as he lay prostrate on the soaking mud.

He closed his eyes and sang a prayer of power, quietly, vehemently.

Fear it not. The voice was Kali's, as chill and ironic as ever. *We gods will see your people safe through this.*

Why let it happen in the first place? Tamber demanded, struggling against the anger raging in

384

his blood.

The newcomers have power. We could do nothing for those who lived here. Had your people listened---

Yes! Tamber knew. Had they but listened, in the dawn of his youth so long ago. None of this would have happened.

Or would it?

He did not, could not, know and dim remonstrations were pointless now.

As pointless as love or grief.

They had a war to win. That was it and that was all.

Can we cross in safety?

The plague will not touch you. Already it has burnt through the weak. It has no more power. Rise Tamber and meet your enemy. Your nightmares have been realized.

Tamber gagged, had to force warmly, acidic bile down his throat as they entered Two Flamingo for the stink of death was a dense wall.

All round him warriors, and not just the green and inexperienced, spewed their guts. They fell to their knees, moaning, wringing their hands, calling to the gods for justice. Swollen, blood-encrusted bodies lay on wooden pallets in great piles near the entrance, surrounded by clouds of buzzing flies, seeding death with their maggot children.

Survivors stared at them from bruised eyes; like ghosts doubting their own existence. Upakahun ordered the men to spread out and search the village. They did their best for the survivors, sharing food with them, urging the few remaining warriors to take their place in the battle line.

It made little difference. The village was a hollow entity, the life ripped from its soul.. The few remaining elders met with Upakahun and Tamber under the shadow of the Ziggurat, in front of a hewn wooden idol coated with the dried blood of thousands of years of sacrificial offerings. Their leader, a shaman of renown known as Bebat the Goat, spoke for them, his voice a broken wheeze.

"We sent a host of three hundred warriors to fight with the other Delta Men. Just over one hundred returned from the fort of the newcomers, and they were already fouled with the sickness. We did what we could. He shook his head, his pale face a thin line of grief. "None of our powers sufficed. None of us knew how to heal the abomination."

Tamber's voice cracked, "How many?"

"A thousand three hundred souls has become less than three hundred. Most of the children were taken. They plague saved only old women. Old men." He cackled, his voice that of a half-lunatic. "In fear, I prayed not to be taken. Now when I wake each morning I wish I had been." He closed his eyes as if willing himself not to see, to feel. "We are finished."

Tamber grabbed the old man hard, pulling his beard till he cried in pain.

"Live old man. Fight with us and have your vengeance. If you do not I will cut your tongue out and feed it to the dogs. Do you understand me?"

Bebat snarled, like a wounded dog spitting his anger. He beat at Tamber with his thin fists, Tamber taking the blows, for they were ineffectual and wild.

The shaman subsided, anger spent, and leaned on a wooden pillar.

"Why would I fight beside you, Tamber Whitehair."

Tamber started, hearing his real name said aloud for the first time in more years than he could remember.

Bebat cackled, his eyes gleaming with malice. "Some of us remember, still. A proud young man full of hope and vanity who thought the world was his. Some remember how he was brought low. Lower than a pig. Lower than a Pugi. Even here in Two Flamingo we know your story."

Tamber hissed and held one hand palm out, index finger raised in warning.

"They call me Nonei now, you bastard. Breathe that name again and I will tear your heart from its pitiful cage." He half-turned away and then spun back on his heels, arm extended. The blow caught Bebat hard on the side of the head and sent him sprawling. "You and your kind refused to listen to me once. Smug you were. And stupid. You helped bring us to this."

Bebat crawled away, casting terrified glances over his shoulder at Tamber.

Tamber sucked air, calming his anger, willing

387

it away.

Bebat was old, broken and distraught. He needed no further humiliation. The tirade served nothing but to alienate him and his people.

Tamber closed on the old man, leaned over him and pulled him by his shoulder to his feet.

"Brother, the past is sealed. The future is uncertain. Lance the boil of anger in your heart as I lance mine. We two have a common enemy. Do you agree?"

Bebat rubbed his cheek, the side of his mouth pearled with blood, and spat sideways away from Tamber.

"You are Nonei, now? So be it."

"Will you fight?"

Anger blazed in Bebat's eyes, a pure clean anger, scorched of fear.

"I will fight and I will lead those of my people who come with me. The bastards who set loose the foul spirits of this plague do not deserve to live."

***

The outriders hooted, the sound of a gilded owl.

Upakahun crouched and led the way forward, sure on his feet as a mountain goat, silent as a panther.

In contrast Tamber felt like a blundering oaf as he stepped on needles and cones and tripped over fallen branches.

The moon was up, the stars myriad and bright

but their light could not penetrate the darkness and Tamber followed Upakahun as best he could, for the younger man's eyes were stronger and better suited to this work.

They crawled along the side of a mossy dike, above a snaking stream, and eased their heads over the edge.

The vantage point was at the edge of the tree line, the outline of the fort visible below.

"See there." Upakahun pointed. The two large ships bobbed on the dark water of the bay, light from their portholes casting a streak of yellow over the water.

Faint across the distance came the sound of fevered hammering, the bell of angry voices.

"They are readying their ships."

"We have to strike fast."

"What do you read, Warleader?"

Upakahun eyed the fort. It guarded the lip of a grassy promontory. Beyond, the grass seceded to sand as the bar ploughed deep into the raging water. The lee of the causeway gave the ships cover from the anger of the spirit of the sea.

"If they bring their ships in close they can withdraw or bring in reinforcements. Our first priority is to isolate the fort. We attack before daybreak. With the canoes Bebet gave us we will attack at the same time from the sea, land on the headland and ensure none escape. I will lead the bulk of our forces from here."

"What of the ships?"

"We will take hostages. Make the crews come ashore in exchange for their comrades."

389

Tamber shook his head. "Not good enough."

"Why?"

"If the ships sail..."

Upakahun lowered his eyes. If the ships left, brought word back to their homeland, then the world of the Malai would end.

That was Tamber's prophecy, all those years ago, and nothing that had come to pass had given them no reason to believe anything had changed.

"You heard Bebet's warning. About what happened to the canoes that attacked the ships?" Upakahun said.

"We attack at dawn. Use fishing canoes, navigate through fog."

"Fog? Unlikely at this time of year?"

"I will conjure it up." He sketched with his hand. "A dozen smaller canoes approach from the far side of the bay while your forces keep the fort and the ship's crew focused on what's happening onshore."

Upakahun looked unhappy. "What if something happens to you, Nonei?"

Tamber smiled sadly. "Failing to destroy these vermin dooms us all. We must succeed Warleader. Know this in your heart and may it lend your arm strength."

Without replying, Upakahun eased himself down the lip of the slope and strode away towards his men who were waiting in silence amongst the trees.

His shoulders looked bowed by the weight of his responsibility and Tamber felt for the man.

In a few short hours their fate would be

decided. No! They dared not fail.

***

That night the Malai host spent in preparation. Babet and his shaman slaughtered a handful of Tang hostages - Tamber had forbidden the traditional use of slave Pugi- ate their hearts for the power still beating within, and bathed in their still warm blood. From the spread of bloodied innards they predicted victory, their eyes glazed and eerie in the light of the campfire.

Warriors drank kai-wine and chewed kekan nuts, painted their bodies with ochre stripes, praying to Yangwas in Great Blue Heaven to gird their keni, to give them the power to make a name for themselves, a name others would remember and call to before future battles.

A name of power.

They cleaned their blades, donned helmets- the skulls of panthers, of jah, bear and wolf- and thick cotton armor then gathered in the center of the camp, the light of campfires shadowing their hidden faces as they danced and chanted, moving slowly at first and ever faster in a rhythmic beat like running, yet never moving from their place in the larger circle.

They sang to Yangti, praying for the strength of tintuk in their arms and soul.

-armor to harden their hearts.

Tamber led his band of men away from the larger host with the canoes Bebet had given them. Each canoe needed a party of eight men to carry it

391

and the strain, even then, was appalling.

They struggled through the trees, sweating and panting, reached the shoreline, water lapping against sand, bone-white in the moon's chill rays. Tamber screamed at them to hurry and the power of the kekan girded their limbs. Sweat pouring from their running bodies they covered the leagues along the flat, wet sand reached the spit of land jutting into the bay in the early hours of the morning.

Dawn had not yet bleached the horizon; they had made it with time to spare and Tamber ordered pickets set and the men to rest out of sight of the ocean.

Alone he wandered towards lapping waters, his sandaled feet crunching crab shells, lights from the fort casting diffuse yellow light. He could see the bobbing ships about three hundred fathoms offshore, less than a league away.

He sat cross-legged on the beach and called for his gods. "Show me, Raven."

Raven appeared, an impenetrable shadow with glowing orange points for eyes, and gestured for him to come closer. Tamber climbed onto the god's feathered back and they rose into the sky on flapping wings, for Raven had become a sparrow and Tamber an invisible insect on its back. They dipped across the water making for the fort. Most of the defenders slept in the long central hall, lumpen snoring figures. A dozen armored guards patrolled the walls. The fort, Tamber judged, had been scoured clean of provisions. They had arrived just in time, the vermin were planning an escape and that escape was imminent.

Kali banked and rose, his small wings beating wildly.

They spotted the host about a league from the shore- Upakahun leading his men from the front, beating their way through dense trees, cutting through tangles of dead wood and undergrowth, leaping over sluggish streams, muddy banks. Each fifth man carried either a ladder hewn of freshly cut wood, or a rope of knotted bark topped with a bone-hook. When they reached the edge of the tree line east of the fort they gathered in one pulsing mass as they said final prayers to their ancestors begging them for help.

Upakahun hefted his sword. Called for silence then waved them forward.

They ran, a large mass of screaming men, whose combined voices sent a thrill, fear mixed with wonder, through Tamber's soul. The naked ferocity of their guileless attack made him proud of who and what he was.

A renewal of love he had not expected in those long, barren days of his isolation.

His only regret was that Gehsi could not be here to witness this; the great, unified strength of his people.

"Enough," he said to Raven. "Bring me back."

He opened his eyes, dawn a vague promise in the sky. Across the bay the host melted into a amorphous, barely visible mass; voices thin across the water as they charged towards the fort.

From the parapet walk of the fort rose the

shouts of sentries raising the alarm, of horns blowing.

Amna screamed in a flash of unreal violence as flame broke amongst the host of Malai. Distant screams carried across the narrow bay. Tamber sought out his warcaptains and ordered the beginning of their attack. They ran from behind the hump-backed dunes where they had sought shelter, canoes like tortoise shells over their heads, down the soft sand of the beach.

Reaching the water they launched their flat-bottomed vessels, clambered swiftly aboard. Ten to a canoe, a dozen canoes in all. Their approach would lead them first out past the promontory then back to shore to the rear of the ships. The beetlemen would never expect an attack from beyond the shores.

Tamber sat at the prow of the first boat and called to the three gods in his mind. They came to him in a shimmer of gray light; Kali, Raven and the dark shadows and crevices that was Garge. Tamber held his hands out over the prow, over lapping, moonlit water, as his mind sank into the dim morass of the Other Place- the place of dream, where strange beasts wandered, the source of shamanic Power. The three gods gathered around him, clasped him in their arms, like foul parents proud of the achievements of their spoiled offspring.

He shuddered, as a light like a wave of light and wind shot through him. Words poured from his mouth in languages he did not recognize, carrying a freight of pain from worlds distant as the memories of a living moon.

A fog sprang up halfway across the bay, the curling white tendrils slowly thickening like a soup.

The journey past the ships and back would not take long; the sea was tranquil and quiet, the day already ripe with the promise of heat. The canoes started forward, men kneeling over the wales, water sliding from oars as the canoes powered effortlessly forward.

***

The hornblower blew the alarm. Heeb's shrill voice cut through the camp like a thrown spear.

"The bastards are attacking."

Edo blinked awake, threads of sleep unraveling to pitch him into a nightmare that had breached the carapace between dream and reality.

He was on his feet in an instant, struggling into his armor. He reached for his sword, knocked over the bowl of drinking water near on the wooden dresser.

"Poxed Malyn's Blood."

Sounds of alarm rose from the eastern wall. He ran through the sleeping hall, kicking and cursing still sleeping men. Many had been drunk the night before and they staggered blearily to their feet. Pugi, Malai and Tang whores rose, wrapping thin cotton slips around their shoulders, wide-eyed as understanding filtered into their brains.

However unlikely it seemed, a Malai host

was attacking.

He shoved his way past the bottleneck at the double doors and ran across the courtyard for the palisade. Two at a time he climbed the wooden rungs leading to the walkway. A vast host of Malai had appeared out of the tree line and were swarming towards the fort, yipping like locusts.

The gunners were in place arming the scorpion.

"Get up here, you bastards" he bellowed at no one in particular, pacing the walls, shoving men into line.

"We are ready to fire, Domin."

The Entargió of the gunners had appeared on his right shoulder.

"Do it man! Beat the bastards back."

He could not believe this was happening. The nightmare he had averted, the massed attack he had feared for months, here, now. How in all that was good had this happened?

The scorpion fired and amna screamed as it punched its deadly cargo into the night. The barrel of mil-fire slammed into the ground and exploded. Flames swallowed Malai warriors, the blue fire turning them into living torches.

The second scorpion fired, its aim to the left and wide of the mass of men, the fire setting alight grass, flames spreading west with the gentle wind.

"Correct your fucking aim," Edo railed helplessly.

The crossbowmen were on the palisade, bows at their feet twisting the coiled rope that armed their weapons.

They raised their bolts and fired. Bolts slammed into flesh, pierced cotton armor and flesh.

The two scorpion fired again, balls of fire exploding over the heads of the attackers, flame devouring as it touched flesh, the cried of the wounded mixing with the fierce, animal yells of the still charging warriors.

"Edo, we won't hold them."

Heeb's face was grimy with dirt and sweat. Late into the night he had been supervising the packing of provisions, most of which had been brought to the ships on supply boats. He stank of alcohol and must have joined the festivities, festivities Edo had for once allowed; a decision he now regretted.

He had been blindsided, too confident of invincibility.

The screaming Malai host was less than six hundred spans away. The crossbows fired again and a short hail of metal punched holes in their rows, warriors toppling with blood pouring from vicious wounds.

"We can't stop them," Heeb shouted, close enough to Edo's ear for it to hurt.

"Are the sailors are aboard as ordered?"

"Since least night."

"Shit!" He scratched his head. "Heeb take half the men and supply boats. Go now! We'll follow. Keep the ships at anchor till I get there." Heeb hesitated a bare second. "Damn it now! Before the bastards get to the wall." He turned searching for the familiar face. "Ferie, get the horses saddled and mounted. You'll bulwark our withdrawal."

Heeb and Ferie rushed off bellowing orders. Edo dashed for the gun platform, grabbed a crossbow from the hand of one of the departing soldiers.

"Bolts." The man swung his sheaf from his back handed them to Edo.

Edo placed the bow at his feet, wound the windless hard, jammed the bolt in place and leaned over the parapet taking aim.

A shaman was leading the charge; hair spiked and matted a drape of human skin around his shoulder. Edo fired. The bolt shot from the crossbow, the recoil dipping the front of the weapon. The bolt flew low and took the shaman in the groin. The bastard doubled over, and the line of men behind him pulled up.

The sight of a fallen shaman putting the fear of the gods in them. The shaman straightened, pulled the bolt from his bloodied groin, a grimace on his face as he stumbled forward, the bloodied femur his hand pointing forward, at Edo.

Edo throat constricted. He could not breathe. An iron band, invisible but real for all that, had constricted round his neck. He struggled for air, scraping at the flesh of his neck, but to no avail.

The shaman's eyes were locked on his as blood pounded in his head and waves of sick black threatened to overwhelm him. Those eyes; like the twin suns of an ancient, terrible place; a place of shame and fear where terror ruled a world of filth and spilt blood.

Demensidos the warlock spotted Edo's distress and ran towards him, fingers splayed. He laid his fingers around Edo's neck and said something in a quiet voice, words like buzzing flies whose tenor Edo could not comprehend.

It worked. The invisible vice loosened. Edo sobbed, sucking breath into burning lungs. A wave of dizzy blackness forced him to hold tight to the warlock.

The Malai warriors had taken note of the power of their shaman, the power to maim and kill at a distance and had taken heart. They surged forward with renewed vigor, their cry a terrible, shrill keening.

The first of them were at the walls, hoisting ladders, casting barbed ropes onto the walkway. Edo picked up his fallen crossbow and pulled the metal clasp beneath the stock. The bolt flew into the face of a climbing Malai warrior, a fierce looking man with eyes as black as coal. At this distance the bolt punched a hole out of the warrior's head and slammed into the cotton armor of the man climbing behind. Both warriors fell from the ladder, knocking into those climbing behind. Edo cast away the crossbow and drew his sword. A Malai warrior swung over the parapet. Edo stabbed him in the neck, twisted with his wrist, then pulled to withdraw the blade. The man fell to his knees, eyes wide, a gurgling sound issuing from his open mouth. He held his fingers to his neck to stem the blood as life faded from his eyes.

All along the wall the Malai had breached their defenses, isolating pockets of defenders.

"Fall back in order!" Edo ordered in a raspy voice. "To me! Quick as you can. Back to the boats."

He leapt down the ladder to the ground and ran away half-way across the courtyard then turned. He bellowed orders, pushing and shoving his remaining men into a defensive line. One man, a Scian mercenary, pushed past him and Edo rammed him in the neck with the pommel of his sword.

"Stand the line, damn you. Stand the line or we are all dead."

When he had forced what remained of his forces into double line- crossbows to the rear, armed swords and pikes to the front -they backed slowly towards the rear of the fort

A scatter of Malai, no more than three dozen had made it inside the walls but the harsh screams of victory from the other side of the walls sent fingers of ice down his spine.

He imagined them like a mass of serpents sliding up the wall, poison in their tongues and death in their bite.

A Malai, some minor chieftain judging by the Jah-jaw topped with crimson feathers in his helm, reached the top of the wall, saw Edo's line and bellowed at the mill of leaderless men hesitating before the row of pikes. He leapt from the wall and was quickly followed by others as he dashed forward. Strong. Agile. So different to the broken Malai in the villages and towns in the weeks since the plague died out. Large, screaming men whose bodies emitted an alien stink.

Edo had to check himself not to flee, for if he gave way his men would follow and the Malai would wreck their terrible vengeance.

"Crossbows. Volley now."

A dozen bolts spat forward. Half a dozen Malai fell but their headlong charge did not falter. The first to reach the Aonian line were impaled on thrusting pikes but still they came on, their numbers a swelling tide. Edo ducked beneath a swinging wooden sword that hissed as it swung through the air. The sword took the man nearest him in the chest and sheared right through his body. Edo stepped forward out of line and stabbed the exposed warrior in the groin.

The crossbows catunked and a second volley of bolts flew into the milling warriors at point-blank range.

Edo swing at the chief and stabbed him in the chest. When he fell backward the Malai broke finally, withdrawing in haste, leaving a scatter of wounded behind, as they scrambled for safety from flying, slashing steel.

Already the walls were filling with more of their number, screaming and wild.

As Edo guided his thinning line of warriors ever backward the warlock strode out of his quarters, a grim look on his pale face.

"Domin, take your men now and run. I can hold them for a few minutes. No more.

The warlock did not wait for a reply but strode past them in the direction of the Malai, hands held before him, a dark cloud dense and sulfurous building around him.

Edo surveyed his small host. Seventeen men left, at least six wounded that he could see. "You heard the man. Now might be a good time to run."

Leading his men Edo sprinted towards the small sally gate on the far wall through which Heeb would have already left. They had to hope that the Malai had not already flanked the fort. Once out the gate they had less than three hundred spans to the beach itself and then another two hundred or so to the sheltered bay west of the spit of sand where they had built the pier. If the Malai got between them and the water, they were doomed. He paused at the sally gate, ushering his men through. He risked a quick glance behind. The warlock was spinning in a wild circle, bolts like sparks of white lightening pouring from him. The Malai were all around him, swarming like mad ants. Many fell back, skin sizzling and burning, but for each one who fell another appeared, sword hacking.

The wizard's wild spin slowed, and the gouts of white fire died to a trickle as a shaman appeared and held out a splayed hand in the warlock's direction. The shaman-Edo recognized him as the same man he had struck with a crossbow bolt- raised his arm and from a distance of ten spans lifted the warlock off the ground. With a contemptuous wave of his hand the Shaman cast the warlock against the wall of the communal hall where he crumpled to the ground and lay still. Edo raised his hand in farewell and muttered a quick and silent prayer for the man's soul before he thrust through the gate. Outside a mounted Ferie was waiting with four other mounted warriors, horses snorting and pawing the ground in front of the small gate.

The Malai were still scared shitless of the horses. They were the last chance to buy the last few seconds we need to see us safe.

Ferie had angled his horse close to him.

"Get going, Domin. We'll give you time enough."

Ferie leaned down and held out his hand. Edo clasped it at the elbow in the traditional Caedian style. He grinned as he realized what he had done, at the look of shocked amusement in Ferie's eyes. Fuck it, the man deserved a bit of respect. Caedian or not, he had proved himself over and over again. In the face of this new enemy, old enmities seemed rather pointless?

Edo unclasped his had, saluted and stamped at double time after his men; across gray sand and tufted sea grass, making for the pier. The action was less than a tactical withdrawal and not quite panicked flight.

It would do.

Halfway to the shore he stopped and turned.

The first scattered bands of Malai had circumnavigated the fort and Malai from the fort were swarming out the gate.

Ferie and the other horses were a pitifully thin line of protection.

"Five minutes, Ferie. Then get to the boats. We'll wait as long as we can." Edo bellowed.

Ferie waved his hand in acknowledgement, pulled his full-helm shut, lowered his cavalry lance and spurred his mount forward in line with the other riders.

Edo watched as they slammed into a panicking mass of Malai warriors. Men fell crushed beneath stamping forelegs swords slashed into heads and shoulders, blood whipped from gashed wounds in great arcs in the dawn light.

Ferie and all his men made it through unhurt, past the mill of confused Malai, to a stand of wind-blown trees to the west of the fort where they wheeled about, formed a fresh line and cantered back to the beach.

The Malai warriors, held back; uncertain in the face of this unaccustomed threat though Edo saw a chieftain bellowing orders at a man in a jaguar helm.

It would not be long before they found a strategy to isolate the horsemen and cut them down one by one.

"Get out of there, Ferie," Edo bellowed. His raspy voice did not carry far and Ferie did not acknowledge his shout, but spurred the line forward into the gathering band of Malai pouring from the rear of the fort. Edo sprinted towards the pier. The dories were in the water, the men aboard, oars to hand, waiting for him.

He leaped from the wooden pillar, landed awkwardly one foot in the water, scraping his knee on the strake.

He waved at the other boat. "To the ships. To the ships!' He turned to a sergeant, the ranker in his boat.

"Take us out a little then stop. We'll give the Caedian and his men a little longer."

The sergeant made an unhappy face but nodded his agreement and steered the boat offshore, out of bow range.

A riderless horse appeared on a mound of damp sand near the pier, blood pouring from wounds on its back, the chill cries of stamping Malai following from behind as it whinnied and stamped about in ever more desperate circles.

Edo had almost given up when Ferie appeared with another rider, west of where the boat drifted, cut off from the pier by the growing mass of warriors.

The Caedian pointed further west and spurred his horse.

"Get after them," Edo said quietly and his men dipped their oars in the water and paddled hard on the gentle surf for all they were worth.

They rounded the spit. Ferie and the other rider had discarded their armor and were wading in the water, surf boiling around their waists. Rocks cruel and sharp looking tattooed the shore and rose from the swirling water like blades.

"Can't rightly get any closer, Domin. Not without risking the boat." The sergeant muttered, pointing at a row of low-lying reefs barely visible above the swirling water.

"Swim, Ferie, For fuck's sake get a move on." Edo bellowed but his words were swallowed by the wind. Howling Malai had reached the shore and were wading into the water after Ferie. Ferie did not hesitate but dove headlong into a swelling wave and swam for the boat, long confident strokes cutting the water. The other man delayed too long. A spear knocked from his feet, long enough for three Malai warriors to reach him. Screaming and hollering they prodded him back into the shallows at sword point where they hacked him apart on the foreshore. Like slaughtering a goat, Edo thought disgustedly. But they would show a goat more respect. Bastards. At least it bought Ferie a little time and the Caedian made it to the ship ten spans ahead of his nearest Malai pursuers. Edo and the sergeant reached out and pulled him dripping water onto the low-slung boat.

"Row us the crap out of here." the Sergeant yelled, face red and veins prominent on his neck. The first of the swimming Malai were barely five spans from the boat as the oars dipped in the water. Edo lifted the punting pole high and as the first Malai warrior, a short stone blade in his mouth, his wooden sword scabbarded on his back, reached the area below the gunwale. Edo brought the pole straight down on the man's head, Blood like smoke rose to the surface as he disappeared into the murky, frothy water. A second Malai got his hand on the wale. The sergeant holding the tiller with his off hand sliced at the Malai with his short sword. The Malai screamed, let go, as the top two digits of three of his fingers fell into the spoil water in the belly of the small boat.

Edo bent his back to his rowing and they easily made distance on the pursuing Malai.

When they were safe, perhaps three hundred spans from shore, he turned to a still gasping Ferie. "You did well. For a Caedian."

Ferie shivering in his soggy clothes smiled grimly.

"Just get us home, Domin. I am heartily sick of fleeing this land."

Edo smiled weakly though he would rather have cried. It had all happened so quickly.

Despite everything they had achieved they were fleeing. Fleeing Tallamun, the land of his dreams. Fleeing the new kingdom.

He turned back for a last look at the tree-lined shore. Still it was not a total disaster. Thanks to their foresight the ships were as seaworthy as they would ever get. Their cargo of amna was aboard, stowed safely below decks with enough water and food to see them home. Granted, they had been lucky. If the attack had come even a day earlier they would not have been fully ready. As it was, despite the inevitable sadness, he felt no loss. They had not been defeated. They would return.

***

Thick fog swallowed them, dampening sound. Tamber, senses heightened by the arms of the gods wrapped tight around him, led in the first canoe; the fog was thick as a raincloud and the others paddled blind. They rowed beyond the southern headland and turned north, deepwater waves heaving and pushing their light canoes like driftwood. A soft wind fanned through the fog and with the waves cross-currenting they had to paddle hard.

From ahead and to their right came the scream of roaring amna and a flash like lightning roared through the fog; the ships firing at the men attacking the fort, blindly Tamber hoped for the fog must hamper their vision.

Tamber ordered the rudder man to turn back towards land and the canoes aided by the current washing in behind picked up speed again.

How long had it been since they set off? It seemed an eternity and the strain of holding the fog tolled hard on Tamber but he knew it could not have been more than a half an hour.

The massive bulk of the first ship appeared, looming out of the fog like a sculpted mountain. The rowers dropped their paddles, reached for their swords and small shields as the rudder men guided them on the gentle current of the sheltered bay.

The sounds of battle, men screaming in pain, the clash of weapons, the ululation of Malai warcries, were louder now and Tamber sighed in relief; the initial attack had not failed and the Malai were pressing the fort. Now it was up to him to destroy the ships.

Tamber gestured at the rudder man to steer athwart the ship and pointed at the five boats nearest him.

Tamber would lead them against the second ship, the one anchored closer to shore. The remaining six canoes drifted close to the lowering ships. Voices called from starboard, the gunners, the ships captain, the whole crew it seemed, were concentrated on what was happening on shore.

The warriors in the first boat shimmied up a guide rope. Noiselessly they pulled themselves over the side. Tamber pointed at the rudder man of his canoe. Speed was of the essence now; they had to trust that the boarders he had assigned would do their job. Tamber and his remaining men needed to get to the second ship before the alarm was raised..

Tamber grabbed a loose paddle and stroked through lead-gray water, in time with the men on his boat as they moved off north-east.

The sun had climbed halfway over the horizon and was spraying bars of bright yellow and orange across a cloud-dappled sky.

They were over one hundred spans from the first ship and could still see it for the fog, though still thick, was breaking up and nothing the gods did would stop that. In the end nature could only be cheated, not defied.

Tamber sent his enhanced senses ahead where he remembered the second ship was.

Nothing!

He blinked, fear grabbing his groin and squeezing hard.

It could not be!

He let the paddle fall from his hands and closed his eyes, focusing his senses.

The damned thing had disappeared.

Traceless in the fog.

He refocused his mind's search, cutting vast arcs through the ocean as the fog evaporated.

From behind came the sound of battle as the crewmen on the first ship fell to his boarders.

Still nothing

The ship had disappeared.

***

Tamber fought hard to swallow the sick dread that infected him.

The second ship was gone and with it their hopes.

"Return to Garna and the first ship." he ordered, trying not to let his disappointment show.

A lot of men had died. Was their sacrifice in vain?

They steered the rocking boat around and they set off against the waves. The fog was lifting and they caught sight of the ship a quarter of a league away, looming through the wispy remains of fog.

"Go quietly. We do not yet know who rules the ship."

They approached from the stern, tense and nervous for the silent ship was like a leviathan from the Northern Wastes, the long tongues of its weapons deadly as a harlik's tongue.

A cry rang out, a shrilling keen of Malai victory and Tamber joined in the shouts that broke in relief from his men.

Garna and his boarders had secured the ship and subdued the crew. That much had succeeded at least.

Tamber ordered the tillermen to head for the

guy ropes. Faces beamed down at him as leapt for the damp ropes. Garna held out a hand and hoisted him on board, wrapped him in a bear hug. The ship swayed gently to the sound of lapping water, and wood creaked as they swayed.

"You did well, brother."

Garna smiled at the honorific. "We locked any survivors in a room beneath the deck. Vessels for the Shaman to call their shadows."

"Good."

Garna stepped closer, a worried look on his face. "What of the other ship?"

"Gone."

Garna's face crumpled.

Tamber slapped the warrior on his shoulder. "We did all we could. Upakahun has reason to be proud of you." To his own ears the words rang hollow but Garna seemed buoyed by them.

"This ship. I can hardly believe it is the work of men," The warrior said with awe and fear.

Tamber understand the younger man's feelings; the sheer craft that had gone into producing this thing. Skills his people desperately lacked.

"In my dreams I have seen ships five times this size." Tam shuddered. "Many died today and though we have won, we have also failed."

Garna lowered his eyes. "What can we do?"

"Wait. They will be back. In the meantime we must make ready."

A shout rang out from a Malai warrior watching near the stern.

"A boat approaches."

411

<u>The blood magic of your shaman is powerless</u> <u>against these people. There is but one solution.</u> <u>You know what to do</u>, Kali's voice's hissed in Tamber's head and the god's face flashed before his eyes.

<u>This will change us and I fear not for the</u> <u>better.</u>

Now the alternative to change is extinction. There is no choice. You know this. Show your people the path to the future.

Tamber blinked as Kali left him. Garna was looking at him in alarm and Tamber smiled reassuringly "Take me to the prisoners you culled for us. The shaman will have to wait for their blood. It is time, I think for us to be humble and learn."

***

Tamber climbed down the rickety ladder to the hold.

Crates and wooden barrels stacked high, filled most of the space. The wall behind him was full to the rafters with sacks.

The smell of smoked meat and food soaked in vinegar, of corn and bread and alcohol, was overpowering in its strange familiarity.

"Where are t hey?"

"One level below. Where the water laps amongst stone."

"Ballast. A bilge." He tasted the unfamiliar words gleaned from his dream travels. "Get their leader up here and at least one more who speaks

412

our language. Quick for we have little time."

Garna pulled up a hatch and lowered himself within, three armed warriors following close behind.

Tamber stared in the darkness below, caught glimpses of huddled figures, some whimpering in terror, others staring at Garna and his men with sullen, angry faces.

Garna returned, his warriors pushing two men ahead of them.

Garna forced the two men to their knees and they stared at the ground, apparently submissive. Tamber took a moment to examine them for this was the nearest -despite visions and forewarnings- he had ever been to one of these outsiders.

Small, unprepossessing, their stink bitter and harsh. The races of men came in all shapes and sizes, the stocky Tang, the small lithe Pugi, the mindless half-men but these two were singularly unprepossessing; they looked soft and smelled rotten but Tamber understood that they were vermin; he had thought them beetles but that was not so. They were little different to rats, spreading germs and gnawing at the foundations of those societies they visited, till those foundations crumbled and they arose from the rubble as conquerors.

They were the plague.

"Who speaks our language?"

"I know some words." The speaker had a harsh, unpleasant voice. A fresh scar cut across his forehead at right angles to an old wound, long healed. He did not look at Tamber but the throbbing muscle in his cheek hinted at the volcano of anger in his heart.

Tamber lowered his face, closer to the man, and spoke quietly. "Your name is?"

"Alix Jar Din Desponazzia."

"Stand up, rat."

The man named Alix shook his head. Either his comprehension of the Malai language was dim or he simply refused. Tamber shrugged. It made no difference to him. He signaled Garna who swung the flat of his blade at the man's skull, hard enough to send him flying to the ground.

Not hard enough to disable or kill. A mere warning for now.

"Take them up," Tamber said to Garna.

Garna signaled at his guards and they hustled the men up the ladder, blood dripping on the rat-man's singlet.

On deck Tamber sucked the fresh sea air into his lungs and closed his eyes, kneading his forehead where his head ached.

He pointed at a scorpion and addressed a bowed and bloody Jar. "Show me how to fire that thing."

"Fuck off, pigman."

Tamber smiled. This one at least owned a warrior's heart. He had an inkling then, a germ of an idea which chilled him to the bone; these rat men were small, ill-formed, their sallow skin gleamed like unhealthy corn, they had the gibbous eyes of children caught by the wasting sickness and their stink was unbearable.

But amongst them were warriors and they

414

were clever- the ship was proof of that- plus they had the advantage of numbers.

One ship had escaped. The rat men would return. A multitude. Unstoppable. Unless...

The thought, sparked Tamber's rage.

He turned to the second man who had not stopped whimpering since they had culled him from below and now, as Tamber approached, backed away screaming. Tamber snarled in disgust when the man soiled himself. One of Garna's guards prodded him back, at the end of a sword and Tamber grabbed the man by the throat, lifting him in the air.

Kali be with me now.

He spoke the words the gods had taught him and breathed out, his mouth near the man's nose.

Tamber let the man fall and pointed at Alix Jar.

"This happens when you do not help."

The sailor screamed and coughed blood. Blood flowed from him like a gushing river and his tongue purple and swollen flopped from his mouth like a stranded fish.

His body convulsed, eyes filled with red, a stream flowing from his ears and nose as he scrambled blindly on the deck, beating at it weakly with his hands.

He shuddered one last time, his last gasp followed by fraught silence.

Tamber glanced at Jar. The little man was staring at his dead comrade, dispassionately. That will soon change, Tamber thought.

The dead man's back moved. Jolted once,

forward and back and a long, inhuman scream issued from him. His back arched, to the point where the spine ruptured, gouting blood and flesh and splintered bone.

An alkj' jah emerged from the wreckage of the body, cooing slightly. A baby, purblind, still unable to fly, its leather wings weak and soaked in blood.

It opened its beak wide, sharp teeth showing. Garna growled and stepped forward, sword raised.

Tamber hissed a warning and shook his head.

He stepped forward, bent over and gently lifted the beast in his hands, stroking it. He plucked a scrap of the dead man's liver and fed it to the jah. It clucked and moaned happily. He stroked it and it let out in a happy sigh like a hiss.

Tamber looked back at the man named Jar and saw terror in his eyes.

Jar opened his mouth as if to speak but no words emerged. He gasped for air.

"Show me," Tamber said with a smile. "Or I'll use you to create a sibling for this child of mine."

Jar blinked rapidly in stunned affirmation.

"Anything," he mumbled, lips trembling. "Anything."

Tamber smiled and stroked the jah.

"My pretty. My baby. The corpses of the future will feed you well. That is my promise to you."

***

416

"Where the hell did this blasted fog spring from?"

The sergeant, a burly Aonian, shook his head in disgust and tilted his head back and to the right, chin jutting forward as if willing the fog to part. They had come five or six hundred spans offshore when the fog appeared. Suddenly, as if from nowhere. Dense, thick air, slightly fey as if tinged with foul magic.

"The Abril should be north of here."

"All respect, sir. I were with the marines in Caedia and on the Northern Wastes. You are pure infantry. So, if you'd be so good as to shut up and let me concentrate, I'd much appreciate the kindness."

Edo smiled grimly and let the Sergeant continue his search. This was no time to stand on the finesse of rank.

Adrift in the fog they should have found the ship already and Edo was beginning to worry. What if Heeb and the men who had set out earlier panicked and sailed without them?

The thought was unthinkable and thus, in the army, inevitable. In Edo's absence Heeb commanded the ships. Would he wait, risk his neck for Edo? Would he set sail east simply to spite Edo? They had functioned well enough together but neither fully trusted the other.

"Hold on for us, you bastards," he muttered.

"By Tyran's breath, I hope they hear you sir."

Gaps started to appear in the fog, the sea a choppy wash of gray water lit by the weak light of early morning, and still they could not find the

417

ship. Other than the lapping of water against the wale and the sound of oars in water they were wrapped in a cocoon of silence.

"Gods damn it. They're gone. Bear north now. Maybe we can intercept them."

"As you wish sir," the sergeant answered, his voice deflated.

They trawled the water of the bay for half an hour, cutting east to west, the fog easing, until isolated shreds remained, ghostlike and meandering over the water. The day was heating up as the run rose. Smoke wafted over the distant shoreline. Malai depredations in the fort. Edo prayed none of his men had been caught alive; for surely they would then wish themselves dead.

"I see it, sir."

The sergeant thrust a hand and two splayed fingers to the west. Edo stared at the distant blue horizon, seeing nothing at first. Like a prayer answered the ship appeared, its dim bulk a distant shadow in the hazy light.

They hove closer, the men straining on the paddles as relief spread through them.

"That's not the Abril, sir."

"What?"

"It's the Vorco."

Edo turned to look at the man. "They were supposed to sail before us. Are you sure?"

"Look at the mainmast, sir. That eye on the stem head. Ain't no doubt."

Edo felt a vague, uneasiness settle over him, a ragged edge of frustration. Nothing yet had gone right today but he could conceive no reason why

418

the Vorco had not sailed. It was fully loaded, fully equipped and as seaworthy as it was ever going to be. What was Jar waiting for? And the ship's captain? Edo had a bad feeling.

"Go easy now, Sergeant. Approach but quietly. Keep a sharp look out."

"Looks okay to me, Sir."

Edo snarled.

"Do as I fucking say, Sergeant."

They came close enough to see the distant figures of men on board, though they could not make out faces. The scorpion were largely unmanned, which was to be expected, but one of them swiveled in their direction.

"I think we'd better do something sir. Hail them before they begin to shoot."

Edo stood, took of his crested helm, placed it on the punting pole and waved.

"Domin preparing to aboard," he bellowed despite the dryness of his throat, keeping up the cry till someone on the ship someone waved a hand, though whether in warning or welcome Edo could not tell.

The twisted mouth of the scorpion swiveled on its rack, still tracking their approach. Bellowed shouts from the ship carried far over the water.

"Something stinks." Trickles of sweat had sprung up on the Sergeant's face. He rubbed his sleeve across his forehead.

"Those voices."

"Not ours? Not Aonian"

"No..."

A puff of light spat from the scorpion

followed by the delayed screech of Amna.

"Out! Get out!"

The wooden cask exploded over their heads. Edo, standing already, tossed himself forward, over the wale of the small boat into freezing water. He caught a brief glimpse of blinding blue light, flame that scorched and burnt his back and flamed the left side of his face.

Pain sang a discordant symphony and his lungs started to fill with water, as the blue-fire burnt his face, and cindered the clothes on his back. He beat at it with his sleeve, pulling the sticky, tar-like substance onto his hands where the flames sprang alive again. He wiped it off on his trousers, the flames transferring to the cloth. He closed his eyes; let himself be sucked deep into the water by his armor as the flames gathered renewed strength.

He struggled at the ties at his side, fingers, numbed and cold, fumbling as darkness filled his brain, the pain as skin and flesh sizzled unbearable.

The armor came away. He kicked off his boots, pulled off his scorching shirt and trousers and kicked for the surface. The light of the boat, the shades of the blue flames were still visible, and he swam away from the boat to avoid the tar, drifting now under water as well as above, jets of cold blue flame still shooting from it.

Beautiful really, the way the blue fire shone through the murky salt water, like the deadly drifting jellyfish that washed up on the beaches of Deira in winter.

He almost didn't make it. The pain gnawed his strength and he had been under water for over two minutes when he broke the surface, sucking air into rasping lungs.

He swallowed water, spluttered and coughed, almost sinking again, tears and seawater spoiling his eyes. He blinked his vision clear. The rowing boat was aflame, bobbing aimlessly about three hundred paces away. He could see charred remains, among them the blackened husk of the sergeant leaning over the tiller at the stern.

The waves rose and fell, like a bully in a market, pushing him towards shore. He scanned the water desperately, looking for any others who may have escaped. Twice he saw what he thought were bobbing heads, drifting hundreds of spans away from him, all following the tides. Helpless human buoys.

Like flotsam, he thought bitterly.

Flotsam from the wreckage of his beautiful dream.

***

The smoldering tar had eaten the flesh of his right cheek to the bone. His back felt like it had been keelhauled for days on the barnacles of the Vorco. The cold numbed the rest of his body and what little strength he had left ebbed to a thin white line of heat in a vast eternal darkness.

He was well past halfway to shore but the pain had grow too large, too monumental. A ploughshare cutting running deep rills through

421

him.

Unconsciousness took him.

The darkness akin to death.

***

The scorpion spat fire. Ferie rose to his feet and pushed himself over the wale as the missile exploded. He dived, making for the chill darkness of deep water.

Water protect me. Keep me safe.

Oh, Mother Laurel. Grant me your blessing.

He avoided the fire completely and rose to the surface between the rowing boat and land. He looked around for other survivors. One or two had made it and were swimming for shore. The others all gone. They he spotted the Domin. Saw him rise to the surface fifty spans or so away flame rising from his back, his face a mess of scorched flesh.

Ferie was a sailor but unlike most sailors he could swim and well. Had learnt it from his father; him and his brothers; they would swim a mile across the deep, blue waters of the corrie lake in the deep valley near their home, another mile back again before breakfast, his father yelling all the time, demanding that they be warriors, men of honor, forcing them onward. Always forcing them.

True half-bloods. The proud nobility of once proud Caedia.

Ferie set off in pursuit of Edo. The waves caused him to lose sight of the Domin once or twice but somehow he always found the man again, a lonely head bobbing over gray water. Ferie caught up fast. The Domin was swimming ever more slowly as the sap of the tar that fed the flames ate him alive.

Ferie was less than fifty spans when the bobbing head disappeared under water. He sucked air into his lungs, dived. Close to the surface visibility was good enough for him to spot the sinking body. Edo looked unconscious, was possibly dead, by the time Ferie managed to grab hold of his shoulder.

Careful not to let the smoldering tar touch his flesh, he grabbed the unresisting officer by the hair and pulled him to the surface.

Land was a bare five hundred spans away but to swim straight to shore now would be suicidal. The Malai owned Tallamun and they would be spreading the length of the bay searching for survivors, reestablishing their writ. Reckoning the odds he decided to swim parallel to the shore away from the Malai host. He had strength enough for now, even with Edo weighing him down. When he could go no further he would swim towards land and pray he had put enough distance between himself and the marauders.

Lying on his back, he kicked through the water, his memories of his childhood vivid in his mind.

A world, a time, wiped out; destroyed by the nation of the man he was saving from death.

A grim irony that.

In this place, his best friend was also his old

enemy.

Mind you; this far from home, screaming savages, baying for their blood, the past and the old country, seemed hardly to matter.

What _did_ matter was survival. Honor and friendship, too, he supposed. Nothing more.

***

Ferie pulled Edo ashore on a stretch of stony beach, littered with the lurid empty shells of a dozen different types of sea-creature; large lobster-like beasts with purple shells, even larger cylindrical shells of blue-green, arrow shaped shells of a golden hue glittered like precious bars of gold.

He pulled the Domin higher onto the beach, and when he had regathered his strength shouldered, grunting. The Domin was a big man. He stumbled forward until they were hidden from sight in a dense thicket of yangtze fir. The laid the Domin on the ground gently. The Aonian was still alive but only just; flesh on the right side of his face burnt back to the bone in places; the nose was ruined and one eye lost, scorched flesh oozed puss and blood. His shoulders and back were cooked meat. Ferie shook his head, in amazement that the Domin was still alive.

Driven, he thought. That it what it is. He will not easily surrender. His kind never do. Still; Ferie had more reason to be grateful to the man than not and was determined do his best for him. A question of honor, his father would have said.

But what could they do? They were stranded. There would be no help from the Vorco and if they were caught by the Malai they would wish themselves dead long before darkness took them.

He lay back against the gray bole of a tree, shivering in the cold, dimly aware of a pair of cruel-voiced jah in the forests bellowing as they hunted age-worn tracks.

He must have slept for sun and shadows had moved further along the sky when he started awake, a germ of an idea formed in his mind.

The Tang were their best and only hope. Edo had treated them well enough and they shared a common loathing of the Malai.

There was a small encampment less than ten leagues away, roughly northeast. A slave camp, run by a handful of Malai overseers, but if he could establish contact with the slaves he might find someone there to help him.

What choice did they have?

He hoisted Edo onto his back and set off stumbling into the vast and empty wilderness, cursing silently.

Why did he always end up back in Tallamun no matter how far he ran? What curse blighted his soul to bring back here again and again?

***

Tamber watched as the boat sank and turned to face deep water. The sound of the sea lapping against the wooden ship, the tang of saltwater and burned flesh filled his senses. He closed his eyes and opened his inner eye.

The rats would come again, in great waves, bringing pestilence, their hearts filled with vengeance. Tamber would be ready. His people would learn, unite, adapt and be stronger. They would seek out the deathwalkers and bind the dead to their cause. They would visit the center of this world that was theirs and befried other races, conquer them if need be. Gehsi had shown him the value of other men. They would make warriors of the Pugi, the Tang and others. They would build alliances and in growing numbers, grow stronger.

His people would survive the plague brought by these human rats. They must for the sake of the children and the old gods. For the sake of both the past and the future. They were People, fully human, like none other but to survive they would have to reach out and gather their brothers to their fold.

THE END